DEVIL'S HIGHWAY

BENJAMIN PERCY
WRITER

BRENT SCHOONOVER
ARTIST, COVER ARTIST

NICK FILARDI
COLORIST, COVER COLORIST

SAL CIPRIANO
LETTERER

  AWA_studios AWAstudiosofficial UPSHOT_studios UPSHOTstudiosofficial

Axel Alonso Chief Creative Officer
Ben Buckley EVP, Revenue and Operations
Chris Burns Production Editor
Stan Chou Art Director & Logo Designer
Michael Coast Senior Editor
Jaime Coyne Associate Editor
Meryl Federman Accounting & Finance Associate
Frank Fochetta Senior Consultant, Sales & Distribution

William Graves Managing Editor
Bill Jemas CEO & Publisher
Amy Kim Events & Sales Associate
Bosung Kim Production & Design Assistant
Allison Mase Executive Assistant
Dulce Montoya Associate Editor
Kevin Park Associate General Counsel
Lisa Y. Wu Marketing Manager

DEVIL'S HIGHWAY, VOLUME 1. February 2021. Published by Artists Writers & Artisans, Inc. Office of publication: 150 West 28th Street, 4th Floor, Suite 404. New York, NY 10010. © 2021 Artists Writers & Artisans, Inc. or their respective owners. All Rights Reserved. No similarity between any of the names, characters, persons, and/or institutions in this magazine with those of any living or dead person or institution is intended, and any such similarity which may

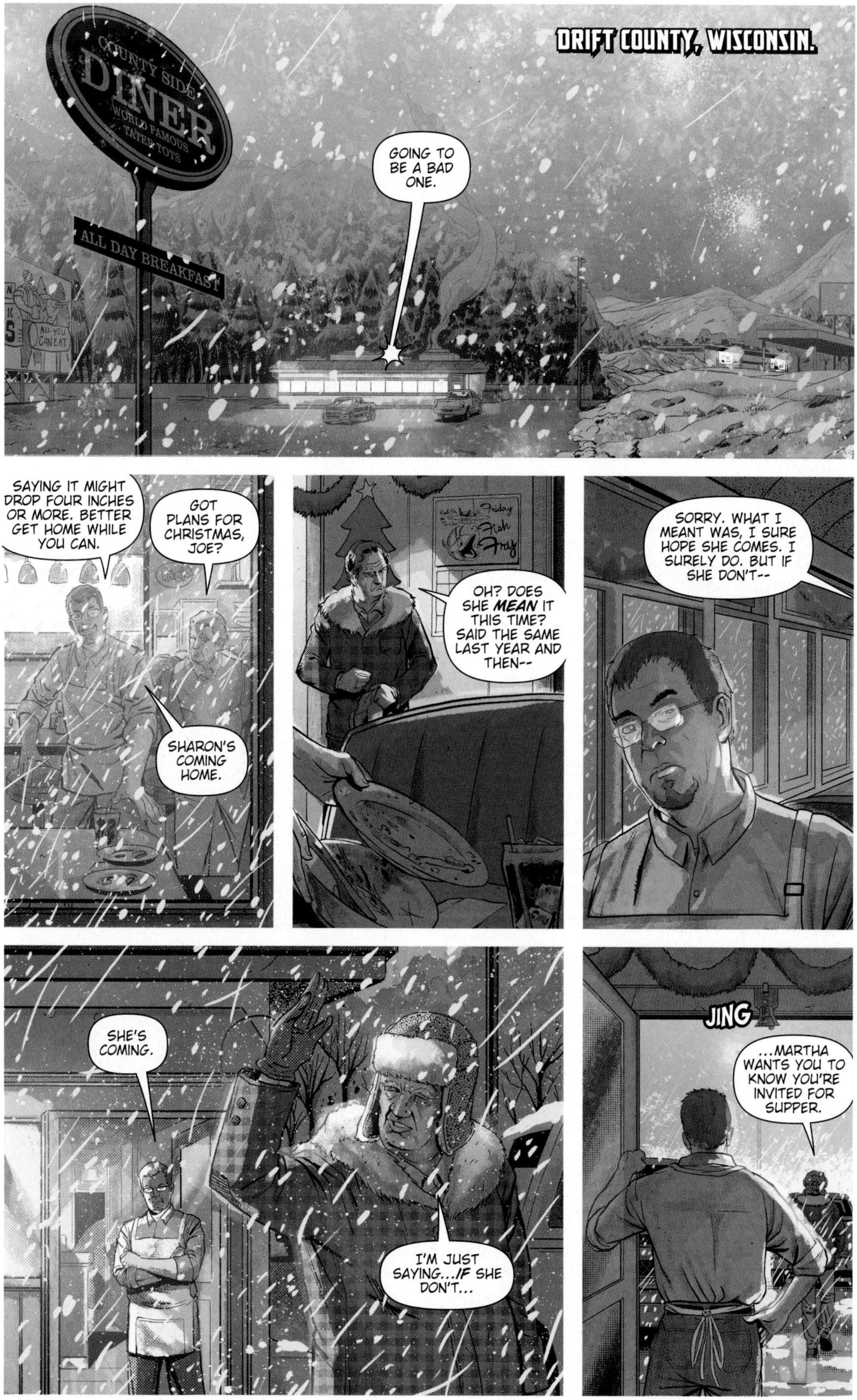
DRIFT COUNTY, WISCONSIN.
COUNTY SIDE DINER WORLD FAMOUS TATER TOTS
ALL DAY BREAKFAST
ALL YOU CAN EAT
GOING TO BE A BAD ONE.
SAYING IT MIGHT DROP FOUR INCHES OR MORE. BETTER GET HOME WHILE YOU CAN.
GOT PLANS FOR CHRISTMAS, JOE?
SHARON'S COMING HOME.
OH? DOES SHE *MEAN* IT THIS TIME? SAID THE SAME LAST YEAR AND THEN--
SORRY. WHAT I MEANT WAS, I SURE HOPE SHE COMES. I SURELY DO. BUT IF SHE DON'T--
SHE'S COMING.
I'M JUST SAYING...*IF* SHE DON'T...
JING
...MARTHA WANTS YOU TO KNOW YOU'RE INVITED FOR SUPPER.

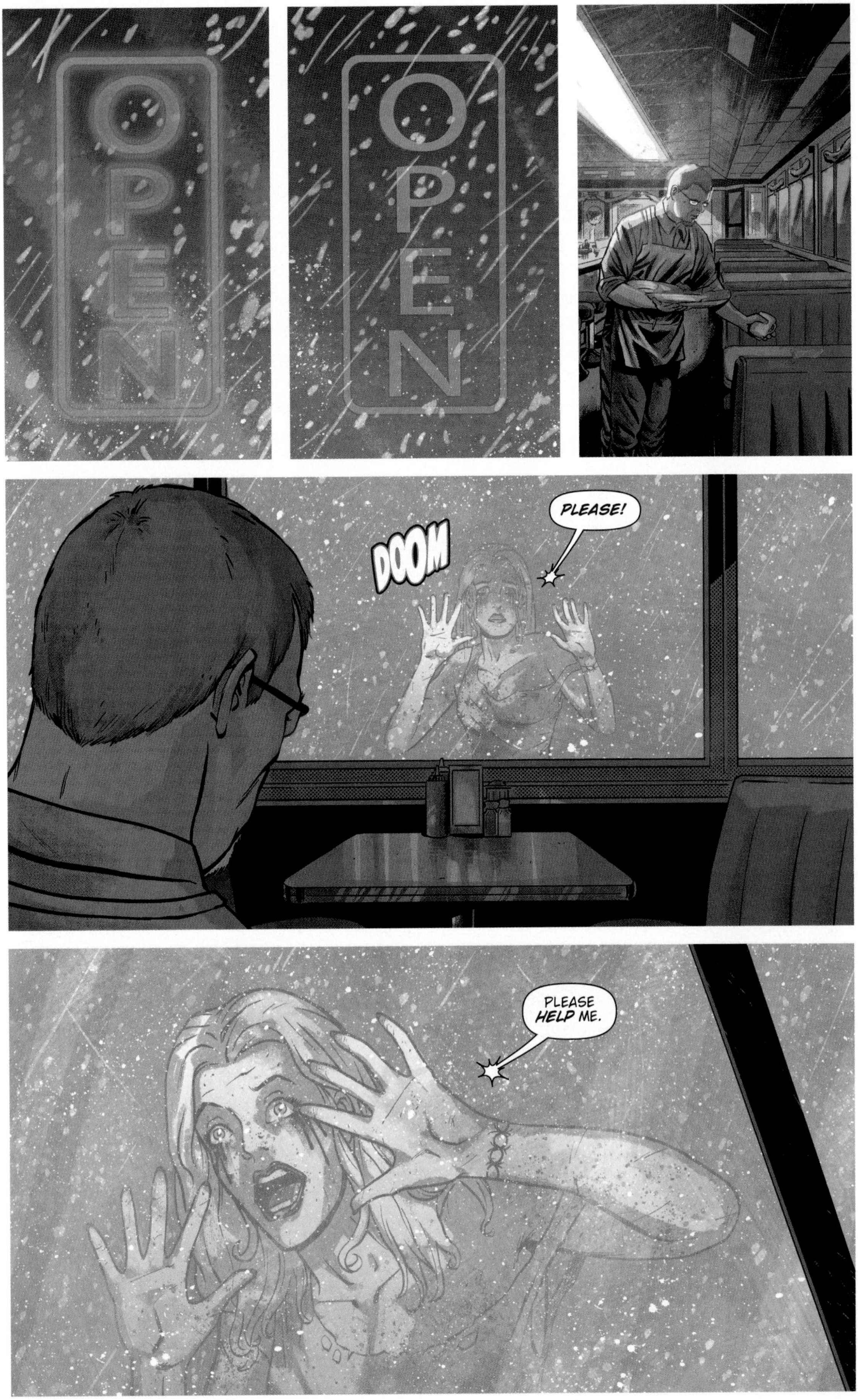
OPEN
OPEN
DOOM
PLEASE!
PLEASE HELP ME.

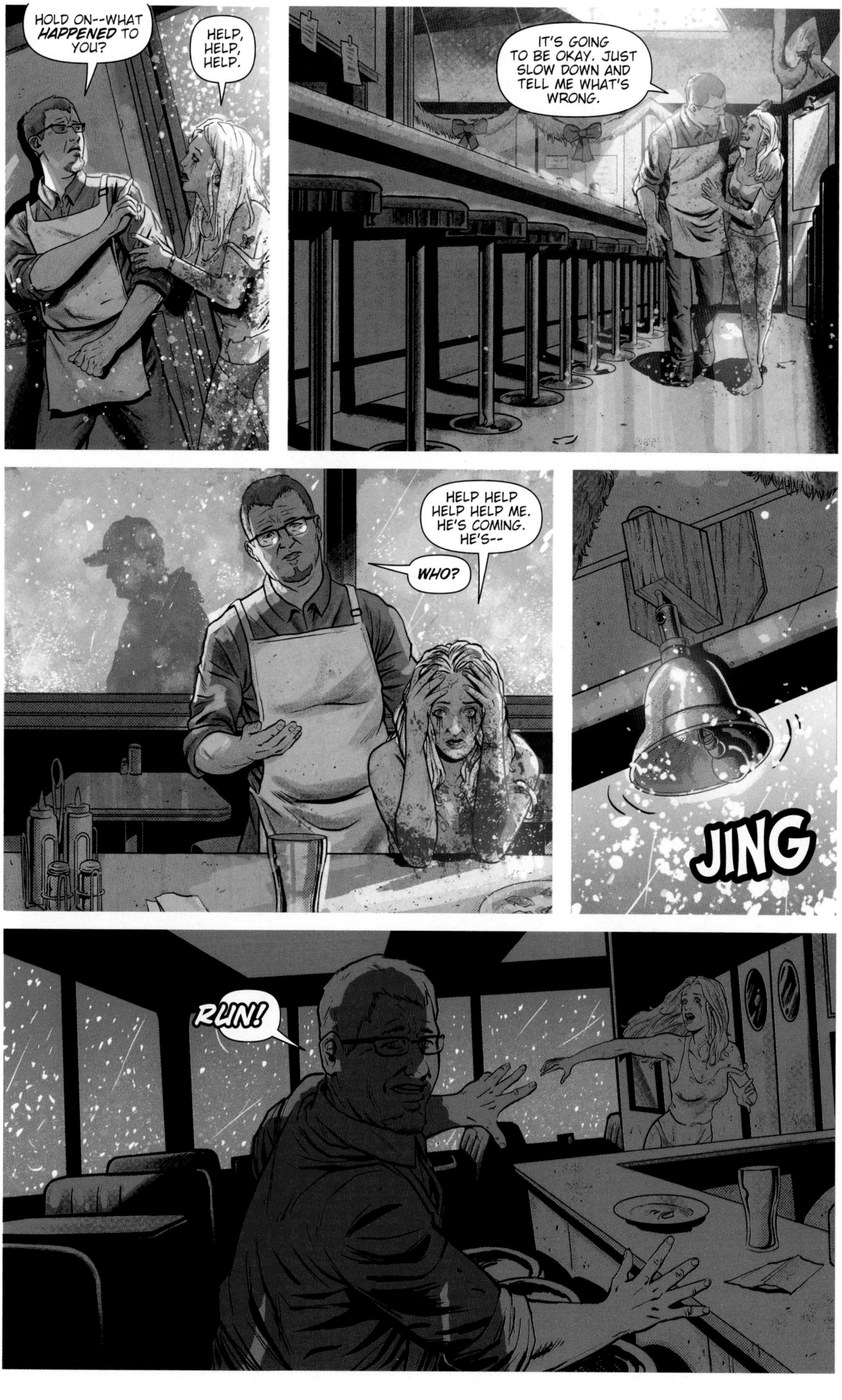
HOLD ON--WHAT *HAPPENED* TO YOU?
HELP, HELP, HELP.
IT'S GOING TO BE OKAY. JUST SLOW DOWN AND TELL ME WHAT'S WRONG.
HELP HELP HELP HELP ME. HE'S COMING. HE'S--
WHO?
JING
RUN!

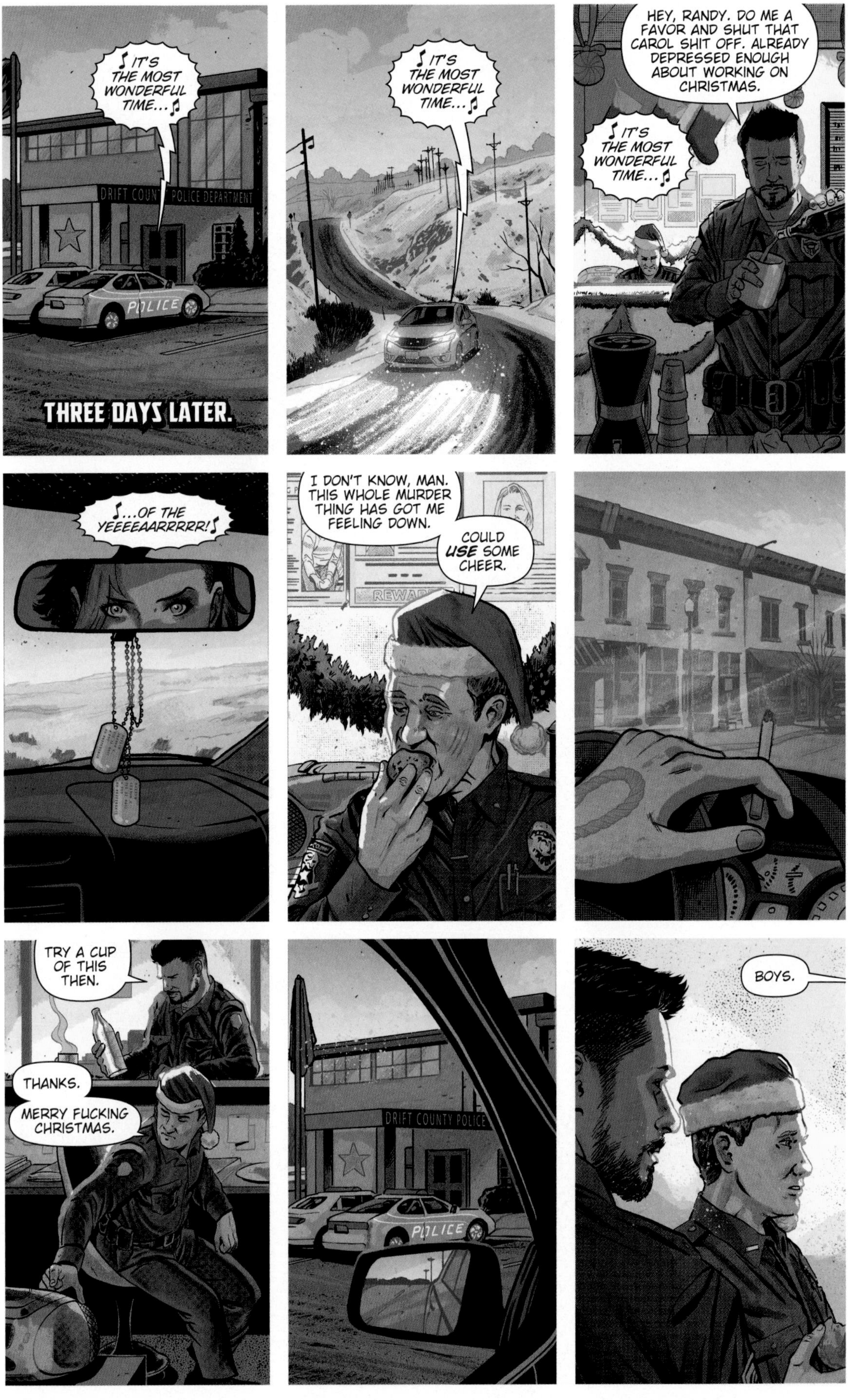
♪ IT'S THE MOST WONDERFUL TIME... ♫
DRIFT COUNTY POLICE DEPARTMENT
POLICE
THREE DAYS LATER.
♪ IT'S THE MOST WONDERFUL TIME... ♫
HEY, RANDY. DO ME A FAVOR AND SHUT THAT CAROL SHIT OFF. ALREADY DEPRESSED ENOUGH ABOUT WORKING ON CHRISTMAS.
♪ IT'S THE MOST WONDERFUL TIME... ♫
♪...OF THE YEEEEAARRRRR! ♪
I DON'T KNOW, MAN. THIS WHOLE MURDER THING HAS GOT ME FEELING DOWN.
COULD USE SOME CHEER.
TRY A CUP OF THIS THEN.
THANKS.
MERRY FUCKING CHRISTMAS.
DRIFT COUNTY POLICE
POLICE
BOYS.

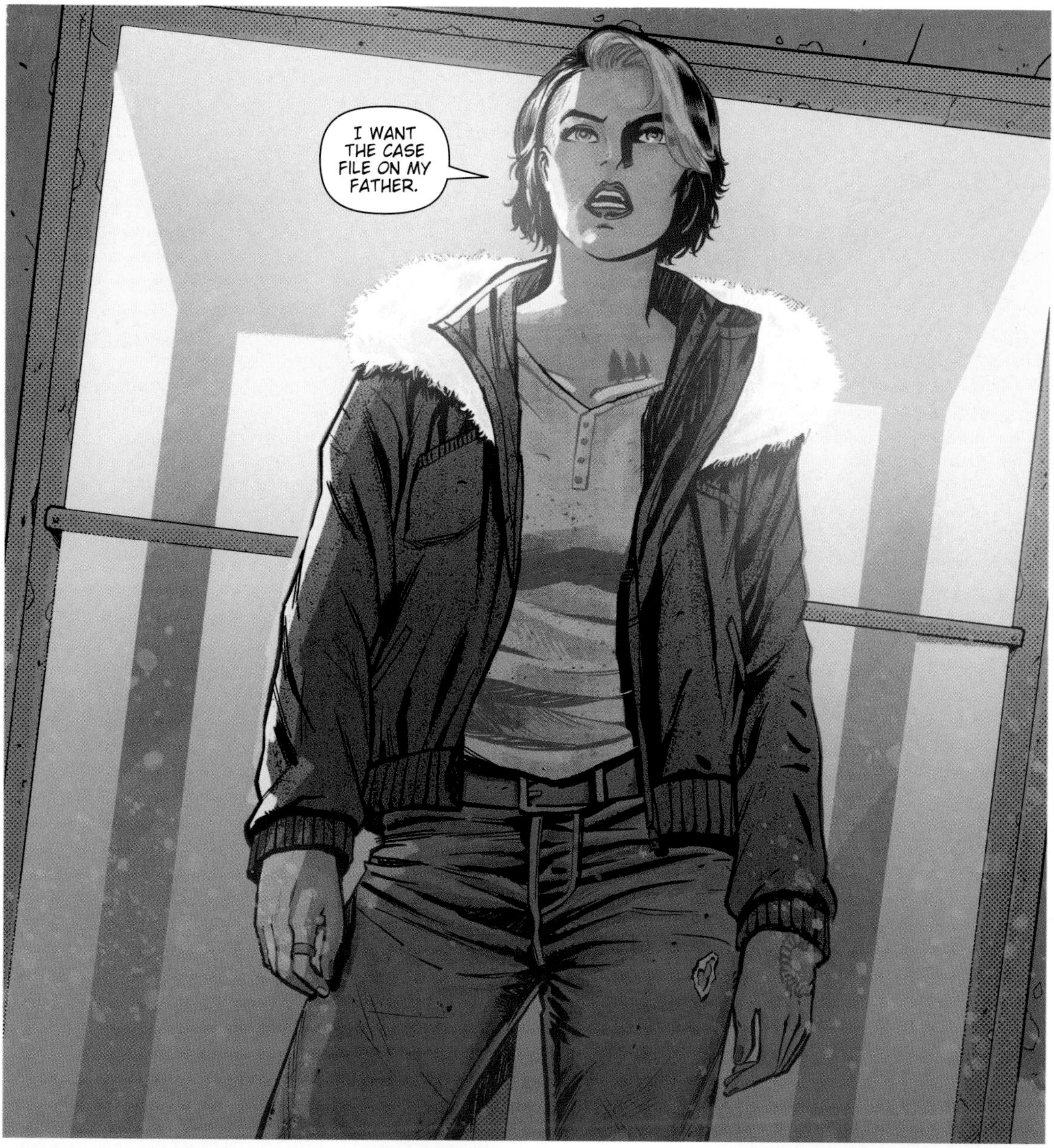
I WANT THE CASE FILE ON MY FATHER.

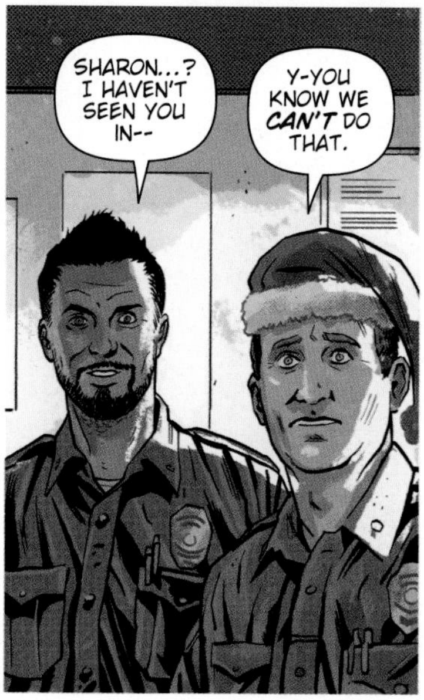
SHARON...? I HAVEN'T SEEN YOU IN--
Y-YOU KNOW WE *CAN'T* DO THAT.

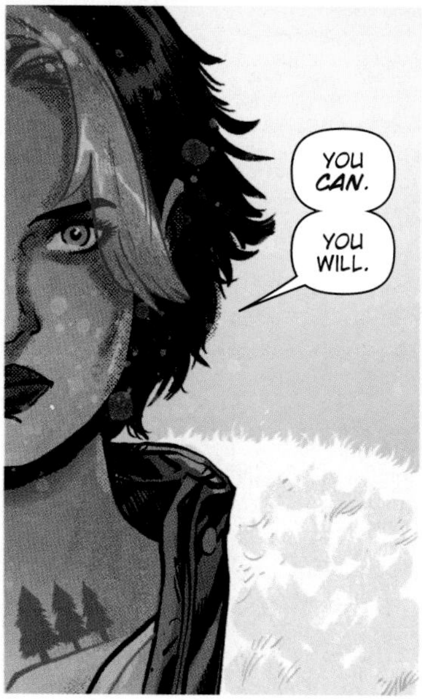
YOU *CAN*.
YOU WILL.

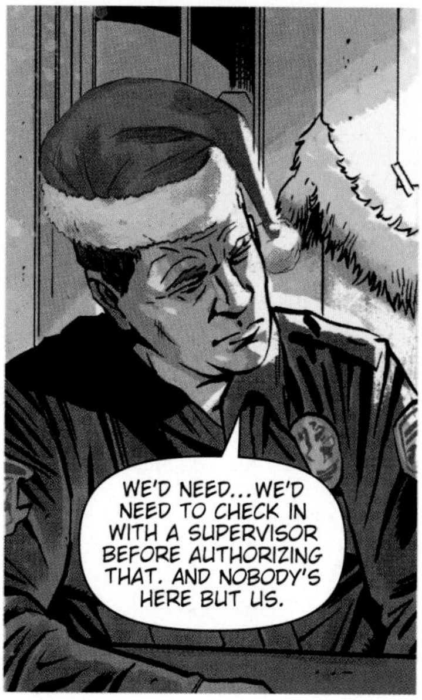
WE'D NEED...WE'D NEED TO CHECK IN WITH A SUPERVISOR BEFORE AUTHORIZING THAT. AND NOBODY'S HERE BUT US.

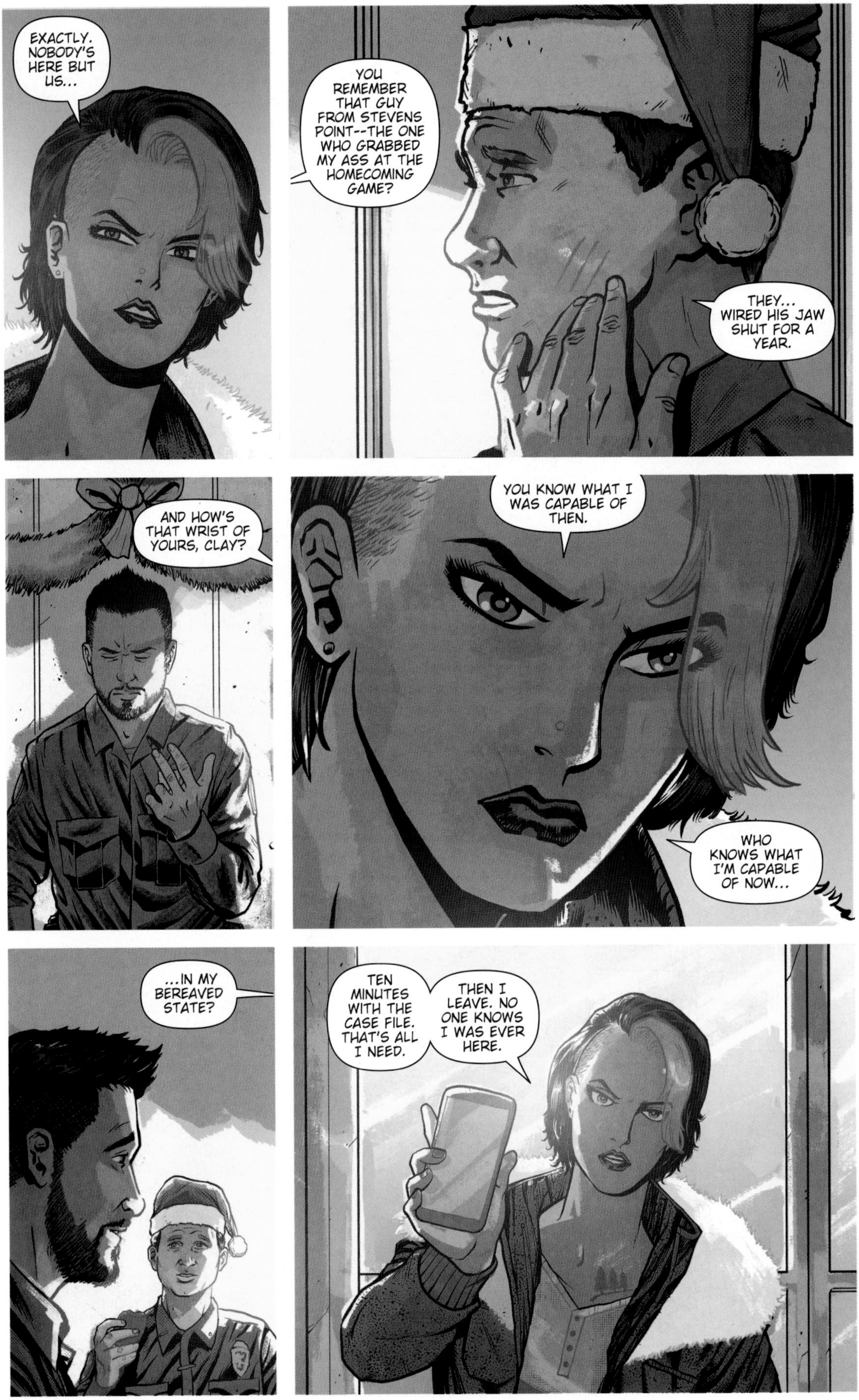
EXACTLY. NOBODY'S HERE BUT US...
YOU REMEMBER THAT GUY FROM STEVENS POINT--THE ONE WHO GRABBED MY ASS AT THE HOMECOMING GAME?
THEY... WIRED HIS JAW SHUT FOR A YEAR.
AND HOW'S THAT WRIST OF YOURS, CLAY?
YOU KNOW WHAT I WAS CAPABLE OF THEN.
WHO KNOWS WHAT I'M CAPABLE OF NOW...
...IN MY BEREAVED STATE?
TEN MINUTES WITH THE CASE FILE. THAT'S ALL I NEED.
THEN I LEAVE. NO ONE KNOWS I WAS EVER HERE.

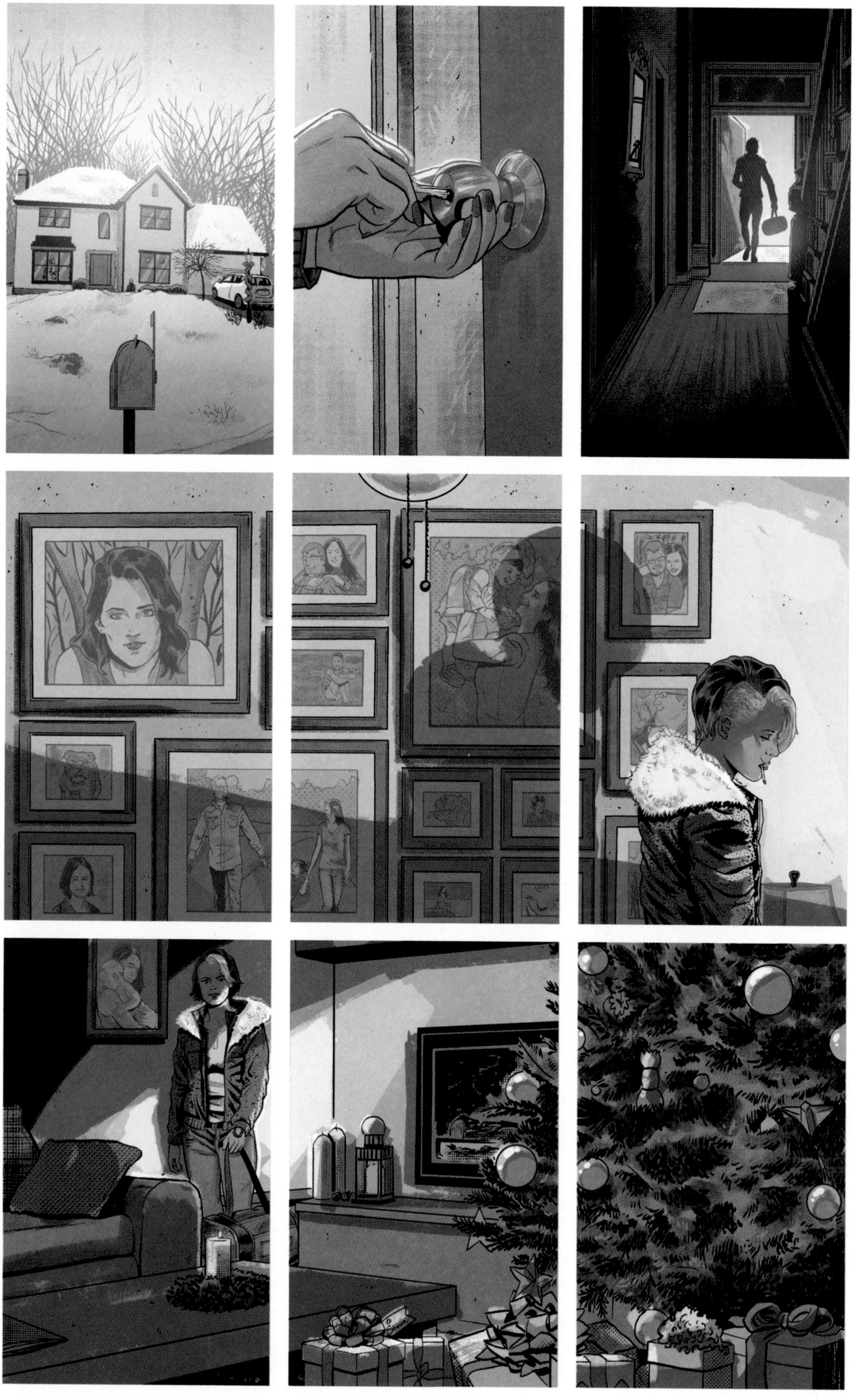

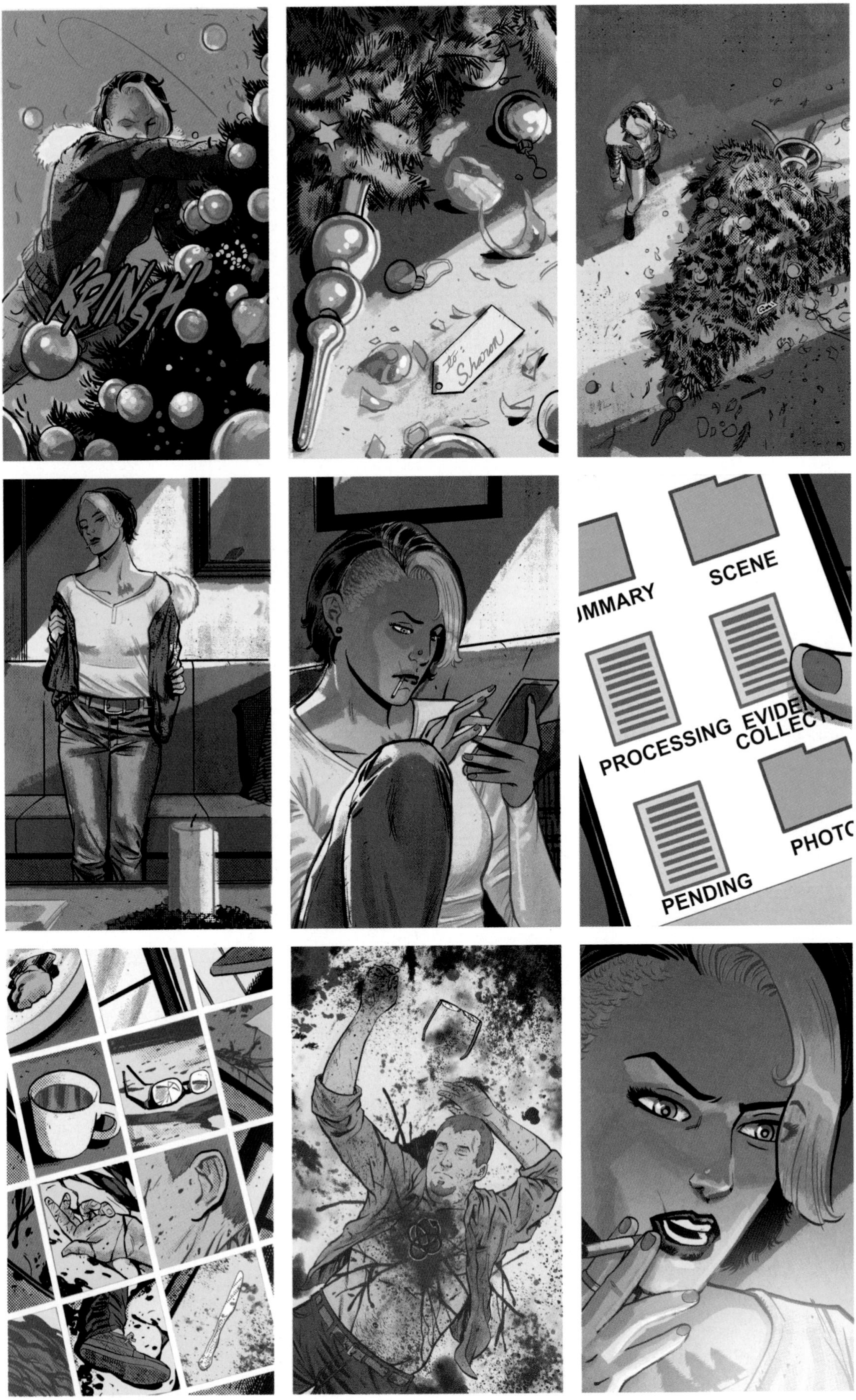
KRINSH
to: Sharon
UMMARY
SCENE
PROCESSING
EVIDE
COLLECT
PENDING
PHOTO

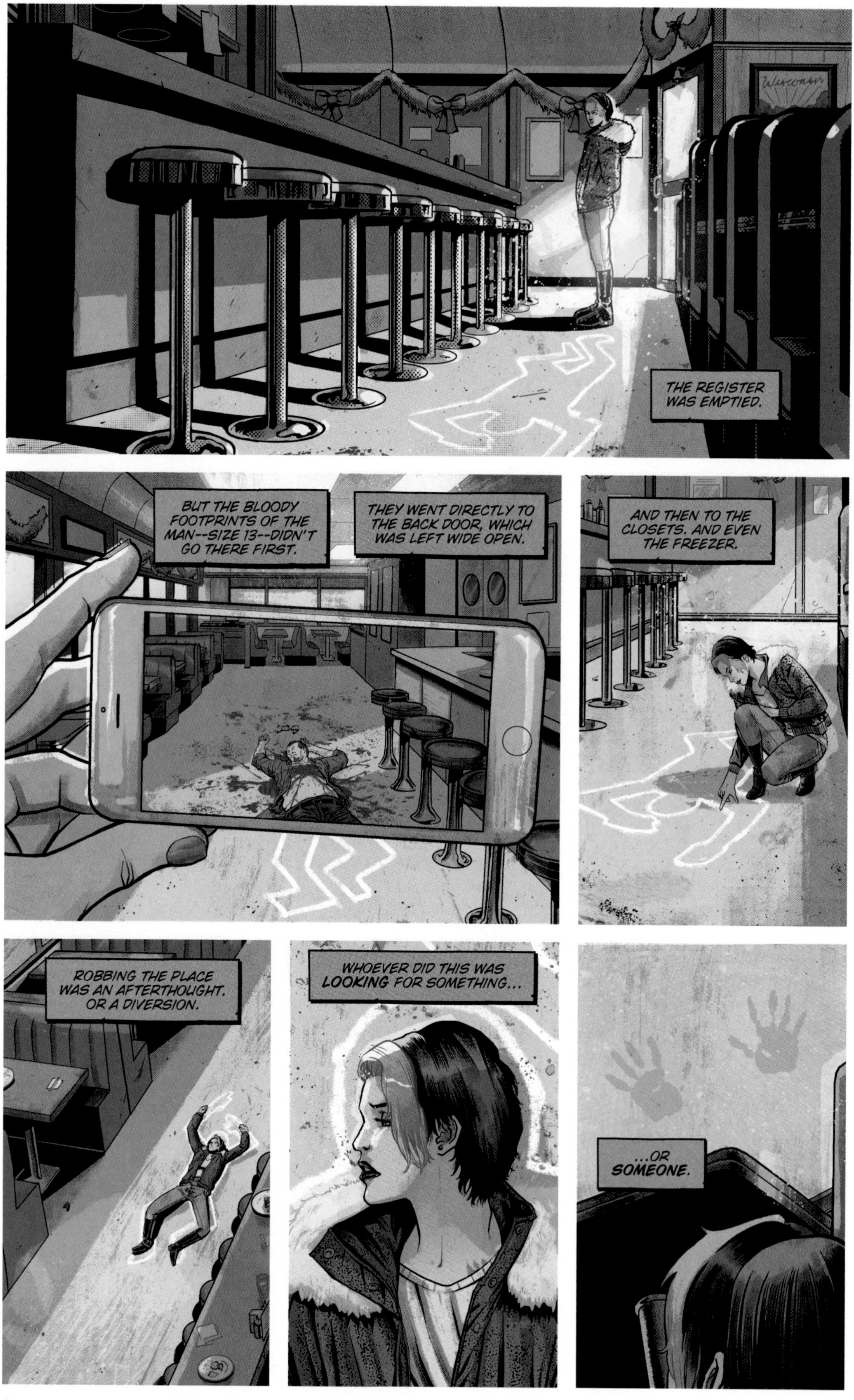
THE REGISTER WAS EMPTIED.
BUT THE BLOODY FOOTPRINTS OF THE MAN--SIZE 13--DIDN'T GO THERE FIRST.
THEY WENT DIRECTLY TO THE BACK DOOR, WHICH WAS LEFT WIDE OPEN.
AND THEN TO THE CLOSETS. AND EVEN THE FREEZER.
ROBBING THE PLACE WAS AN AFTERTHOUGHT. OR A DIVERSION.
WHOEVER DID THIS WAS LOOKING FOR SOMETHING...
...OR SOMEONE.

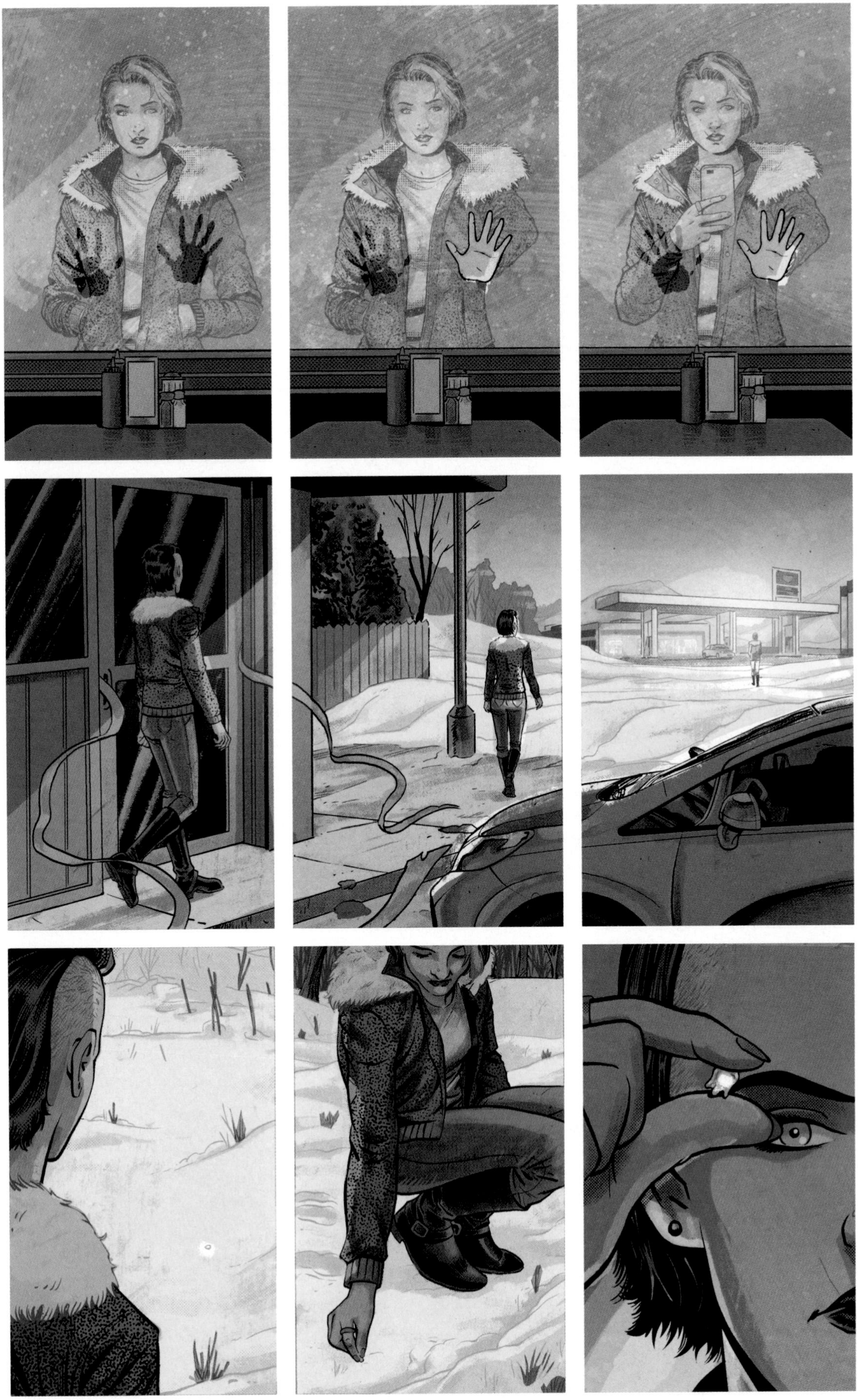

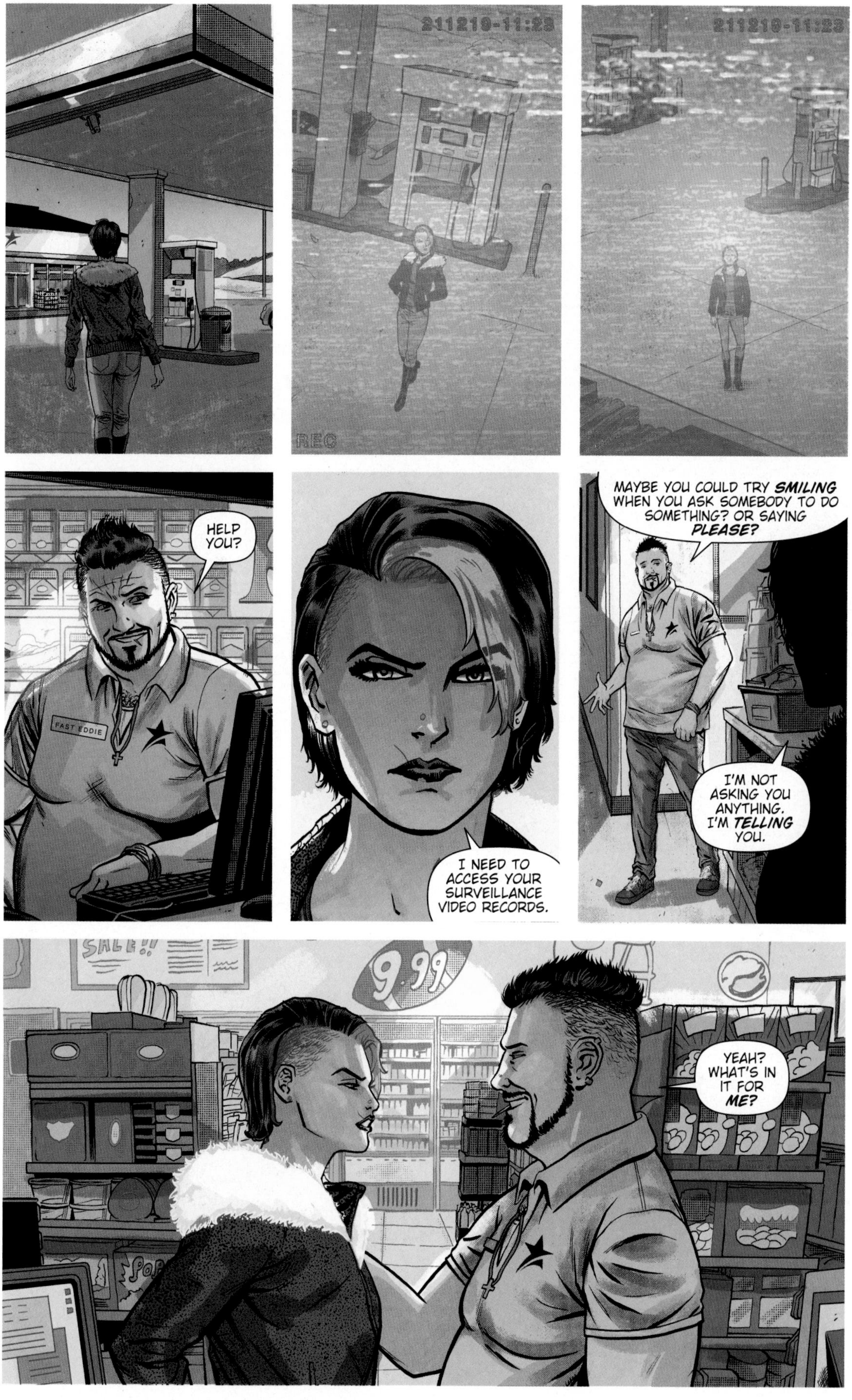
211219-11:23
REC
211219-11:23
HELP YOU?
FAST EDDIE
I NEED TO ACCESS YOUR SURVEILLANCE VIDEO RECORDS.
MAYBE YOU COULD TRY SMILING WHEN YOU ASK SOMEBODY TO DO SOMETHING? OR SAYING PLEASE?
I'M NOT ASKING YOU ANYTHING. I'M TELLING YOU.
SALE!!
9.99
YEAH? WHAT'S IN IT FOR ME?

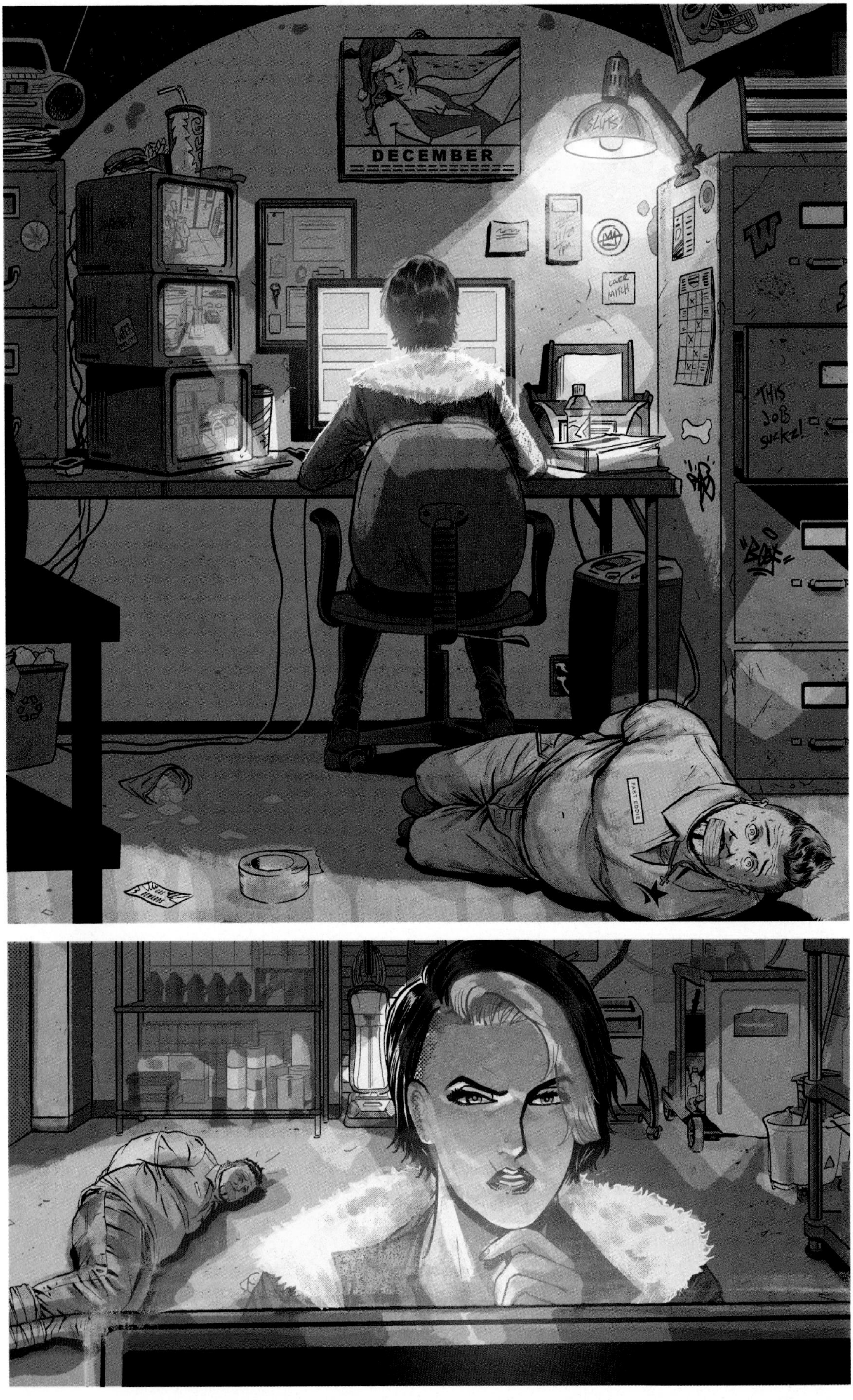
DECEMBER
COVER MITCH
THIS JOB SUCKZ!
FAST EDDIE

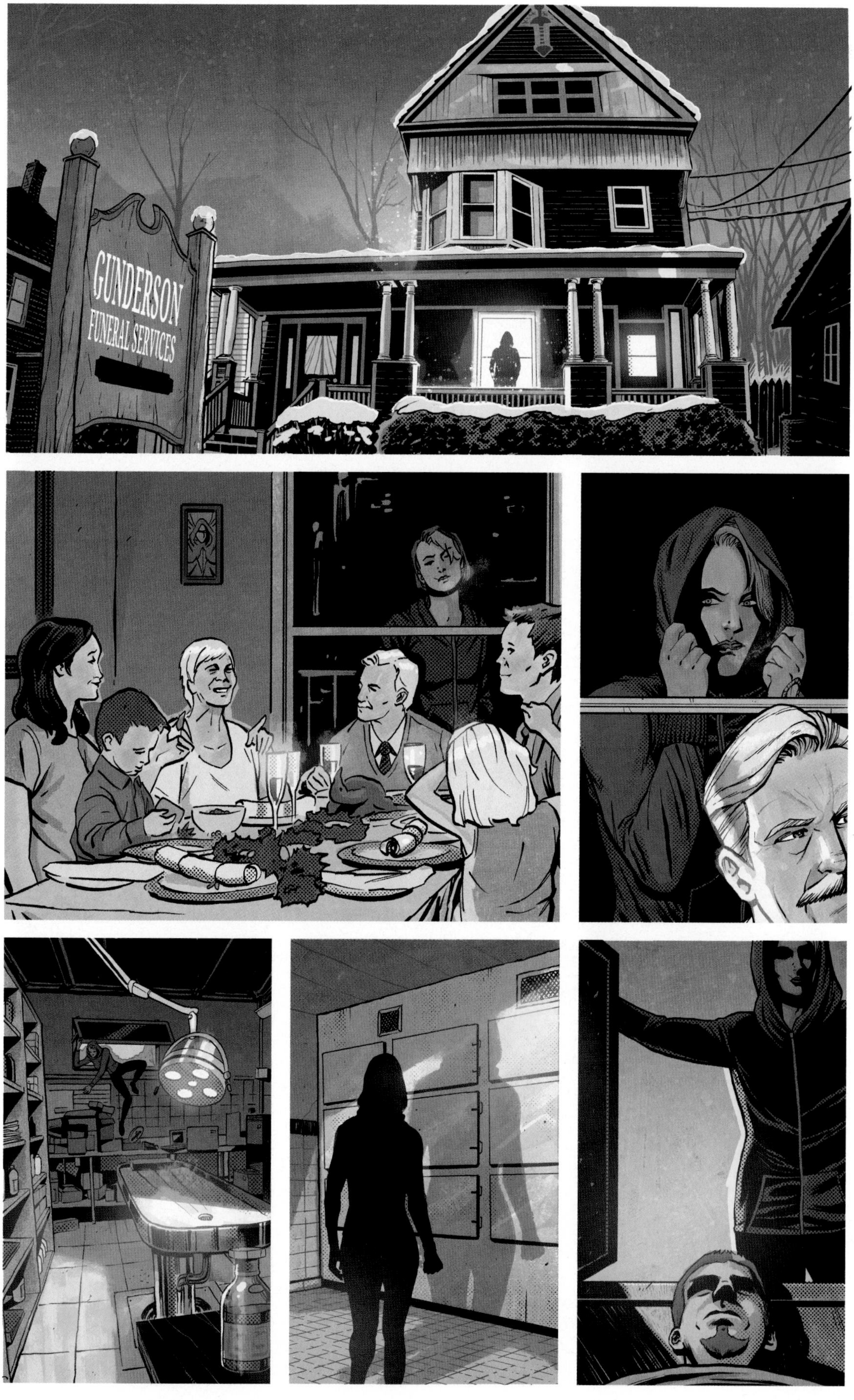
GUNDERSON
FUNERAL SERVICES

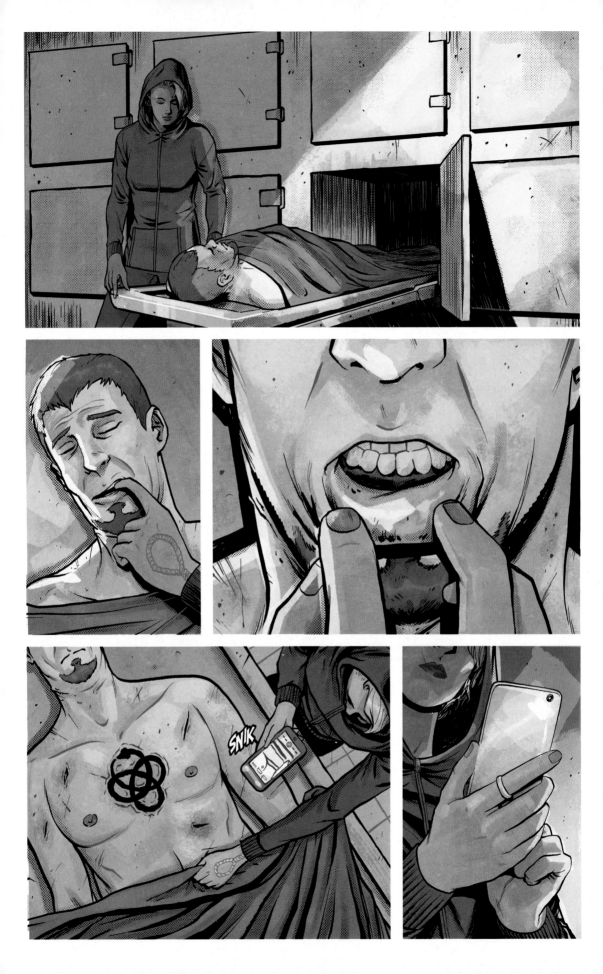

SNIK

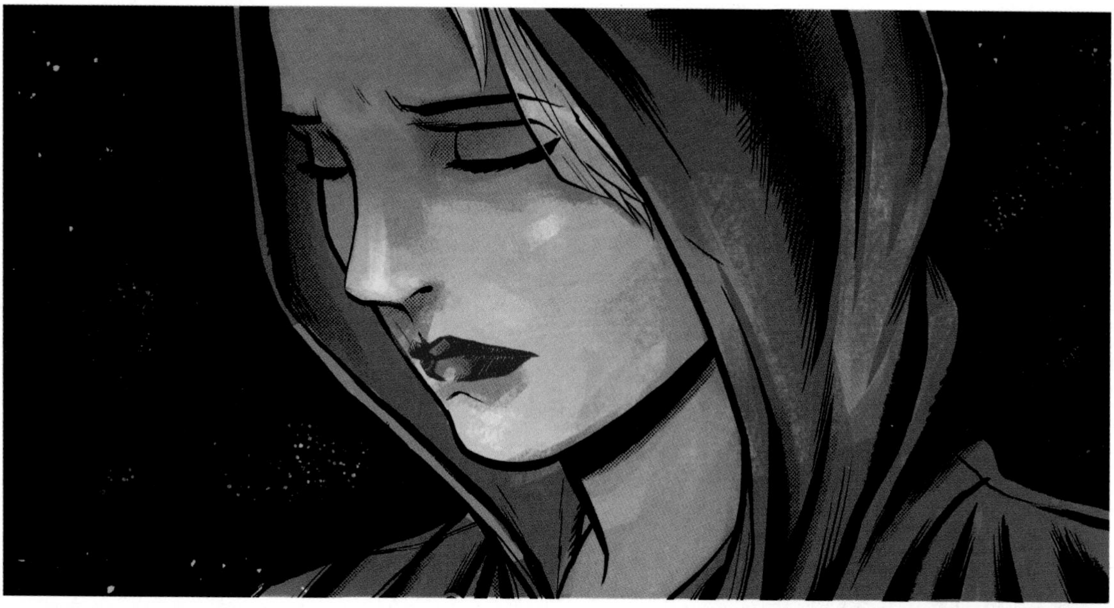

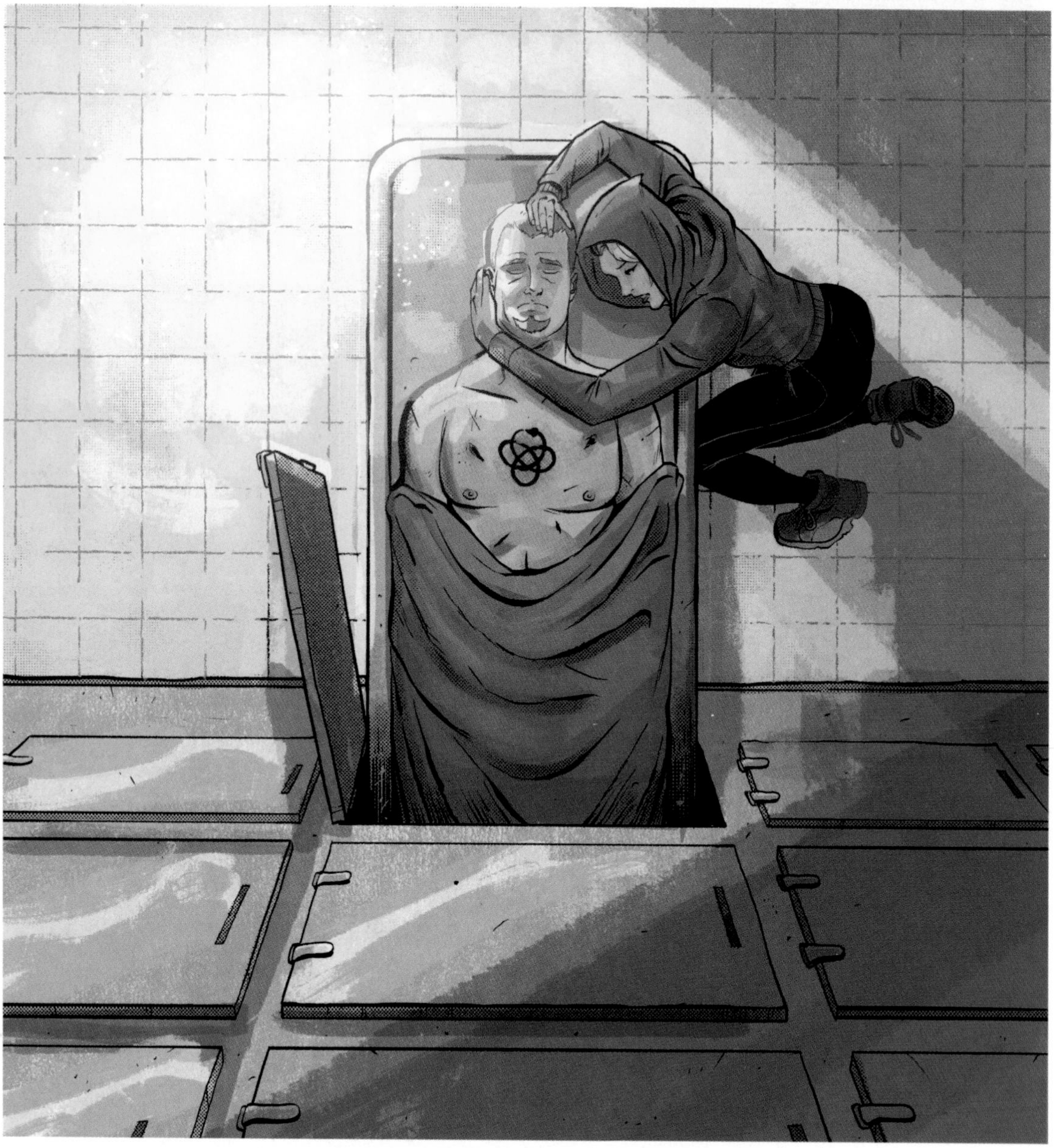

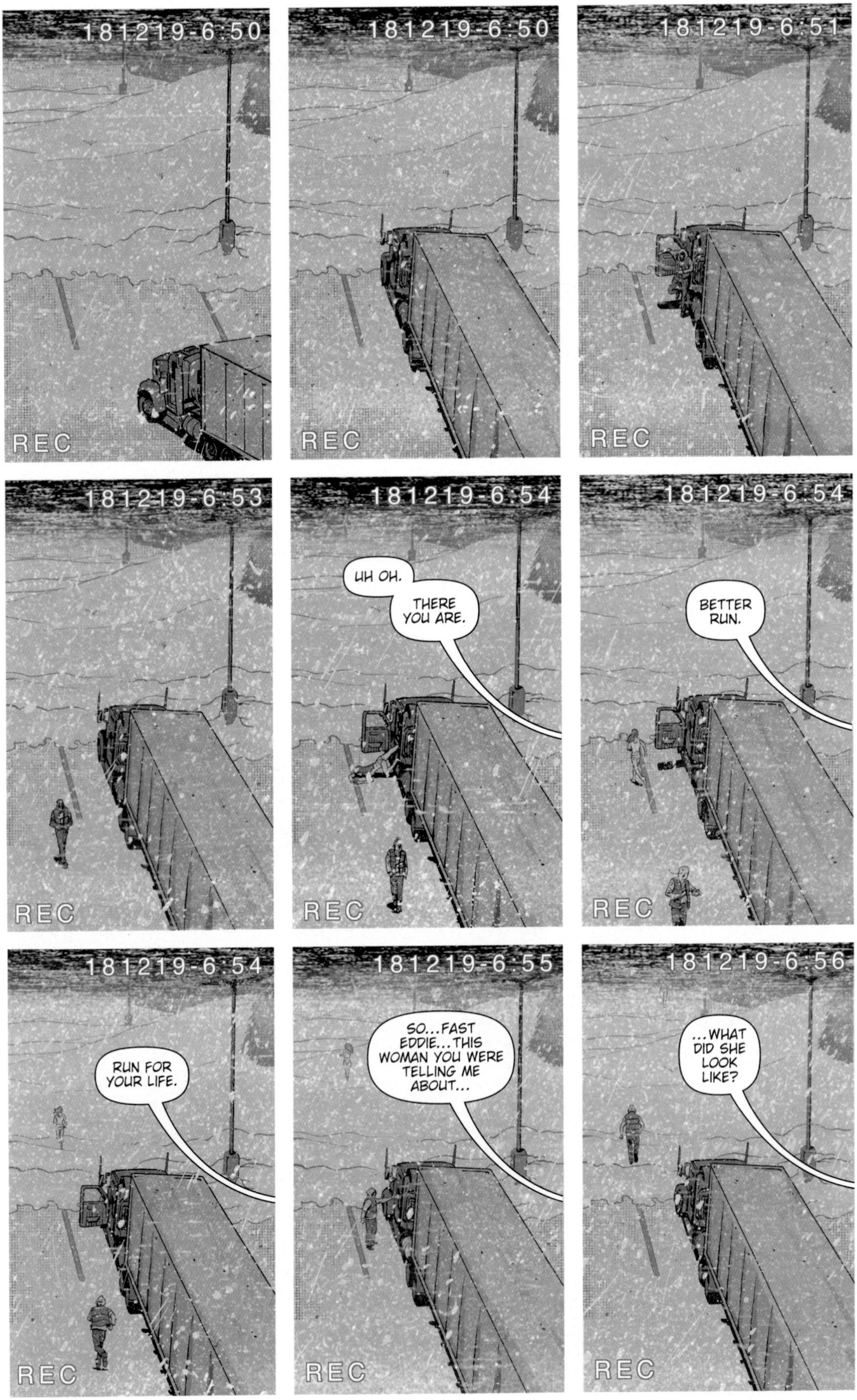
181219-6:50
REC
181219-6:50
REC
181219-6:51
REC
181219-6:53
REC
181219-6:54
UH OH.
THERE YOU ARE.
REC
181219-6:54
BETTER RUN.
REC
181219-6:54
RUN FOR YOUR LIFE.
REC
181219-6:55
SO...FAST EDDIE...THIS WOMAN YOU WERE TELLING ME ABOUT...
REC
181219-6:56
...WHAT DID SHE LOOK LIKE?
REC

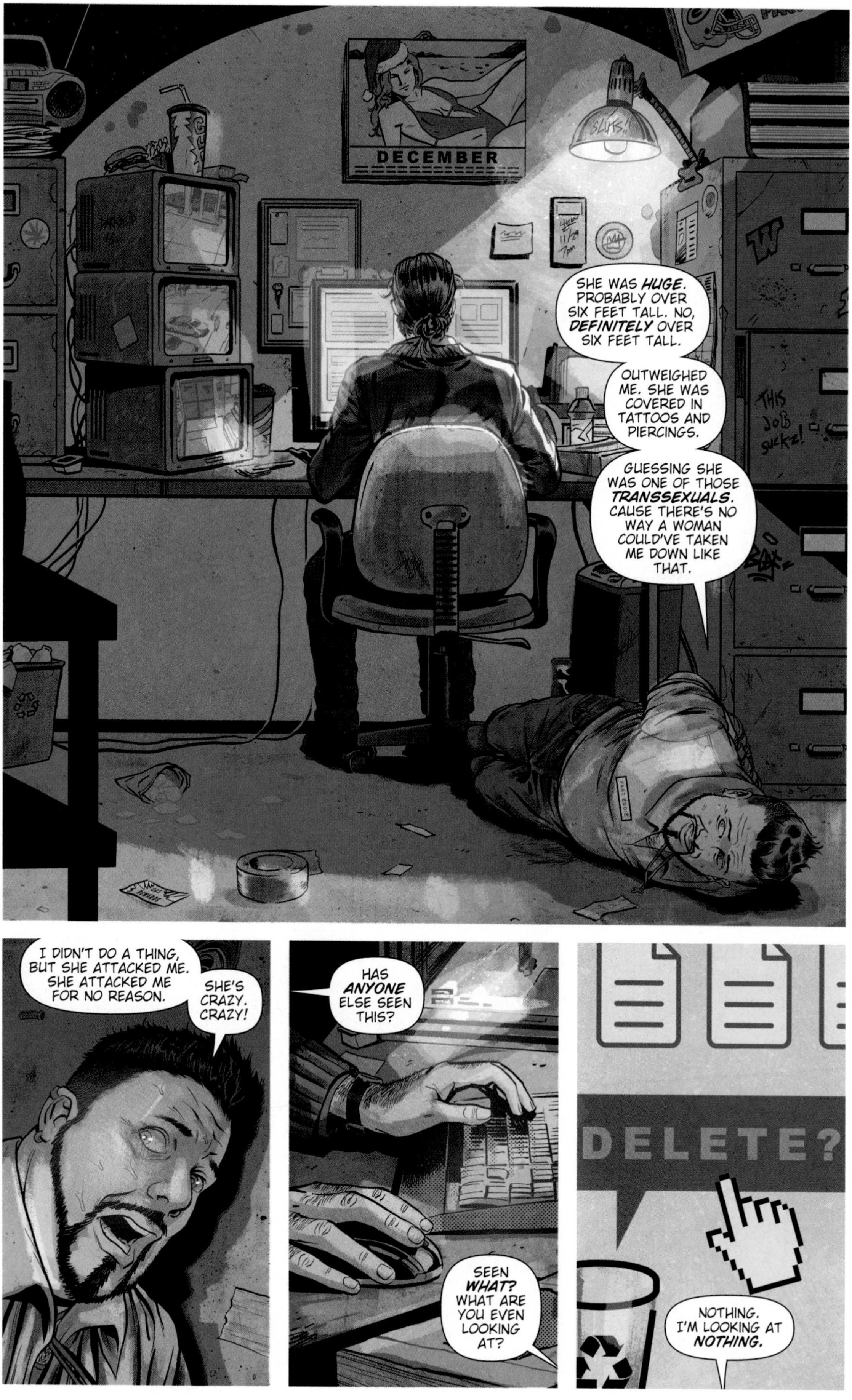
DECEMBER
SLUTS!
THIS JOB SUCKZ!
SHE WAS *HUGE*. PROBABLY OVER SIX FEET TALL. NO, *DEFINITELY* OVER SIX FEET TALL.
OUTWEIGHED ME. SHE WAS COVERED IN TATTOOS AND PIERCINGS.
GUESSING SHE WAS ONE OF THOSE *TRANSSEXUALS*. CAUSE THERE'S NO WAY A WOMAN COULD'VE TAKEN ME DOWN LIKE THAT.
I DIDN'T DO A THING, BUT SHE ATTACKED ME. SHE ATTACKED ME FOR NO REASON.
SHE'S CRAZY. CRAZY!
HAS *ANYONE* ELSE SEEN THIS?
SEEN *WHAT?* WHAT ARE YOU EVEN LOOKING AT?
DELETE?
NOTHING. I'M LOOKING AT *NOTHING.*

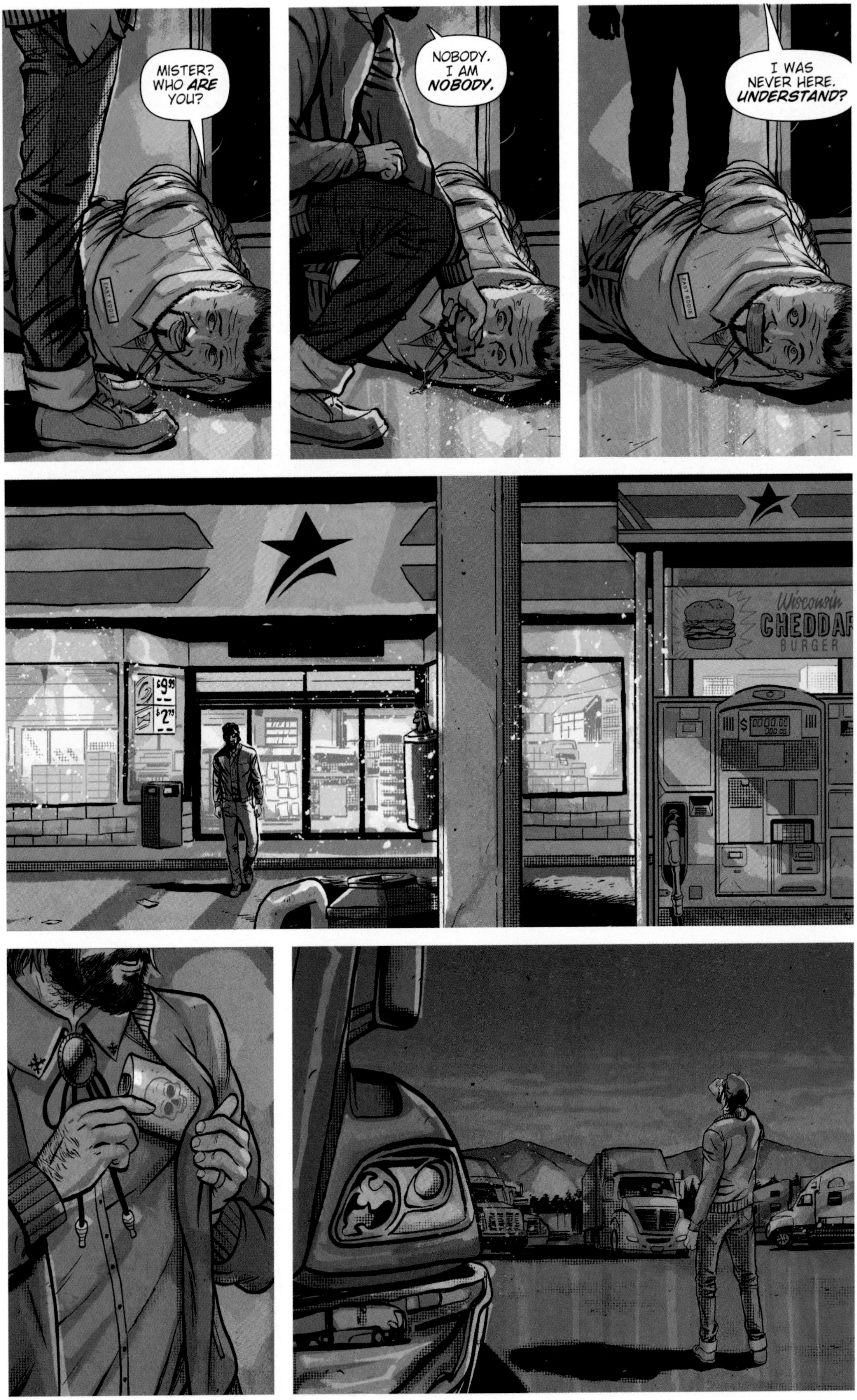
MISTER? WHO ARE YOU?
FAST EDDIE
NOBODY. I AM NOBODY.
I WAS NEVER HERE. UNDERSTAND?
FAST EDDIE
Wisconsin CHEDDAR BURGER
$9.99
$2.79

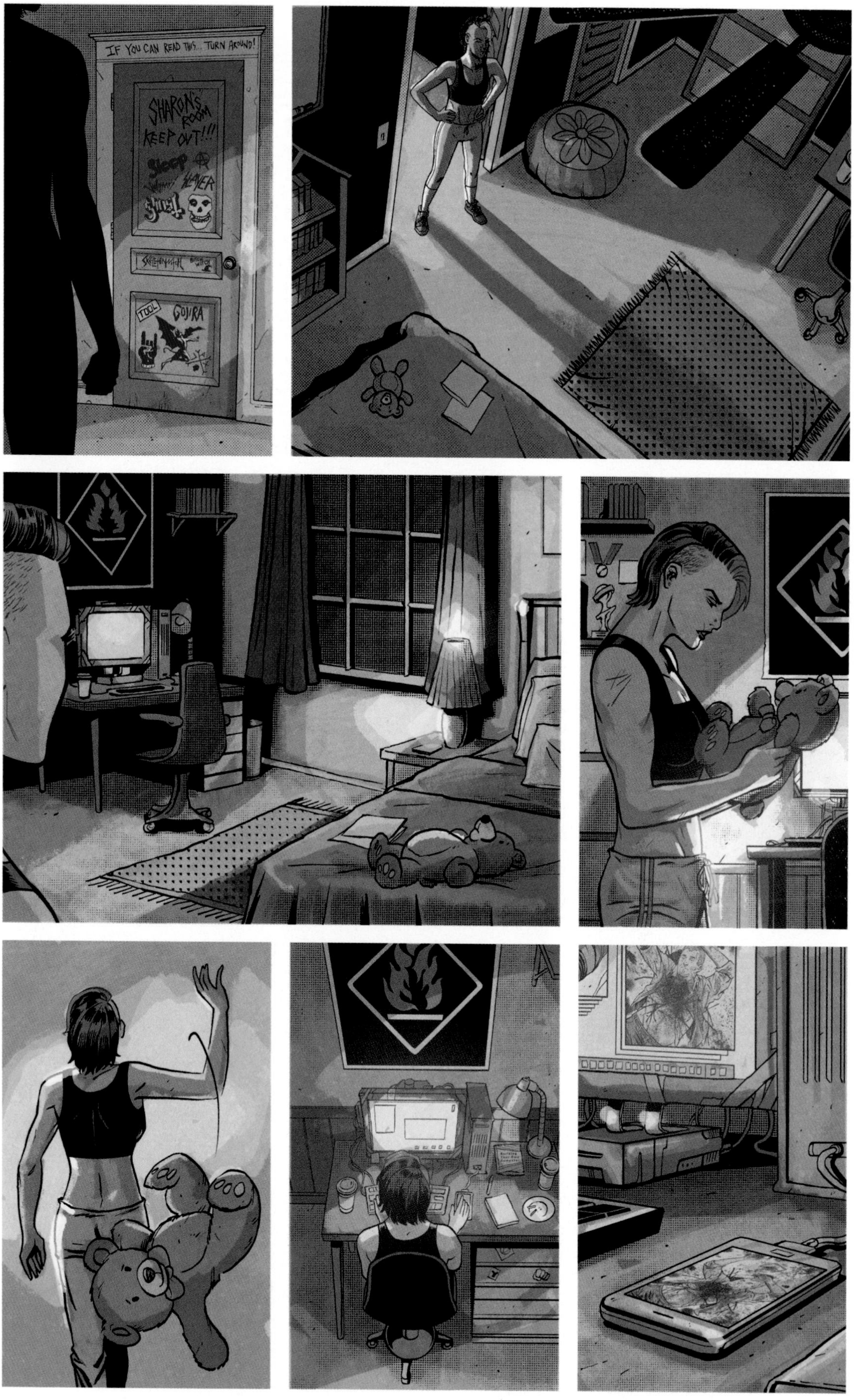
IF YOU CAN READ THIS... TURN AROUND!
SHARON'S ROOM KEEP OUT!!!
Sleep
SLAYER
Ghost
TOOL
GOJIRA

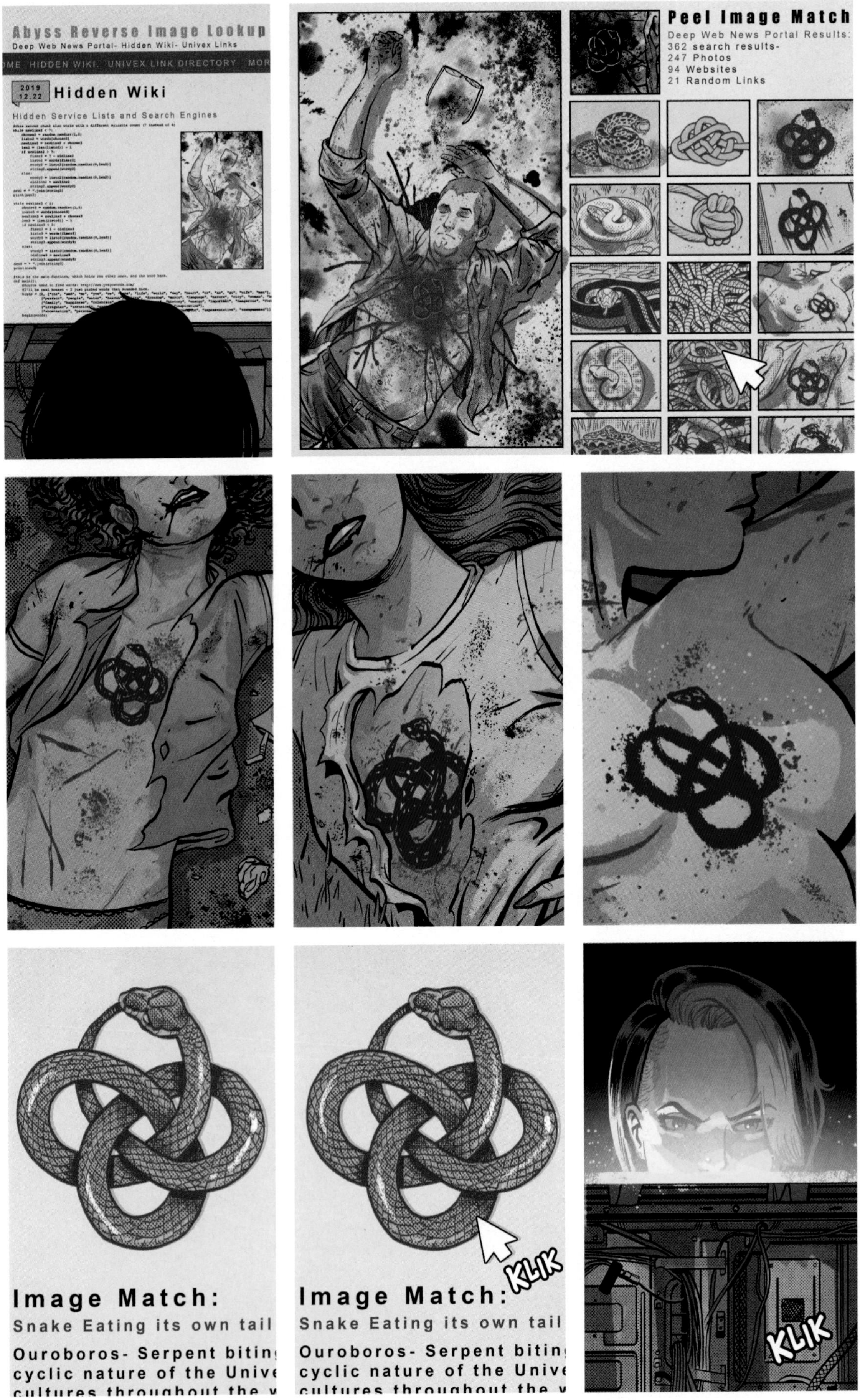
Abyss Reverse Image Lookup
Deep Web News Portal- Hidden Wiki- Univex Links
OME HIDDEN WIKI. UNIVEX LINK DIRECTORY MOR
2019 12.22
Hidden Wiki
Hidden Service Lists and Search Engines
Peel Image Match
Deep Web News Portal Results:
362 search results-
247 Photos
94 Websites
21 Random Links
Image Match:
Snake Eating its own tail
Ouroboros- Serpent biting
cyclic nature of the Unive
KLIK
Image Match:
Snake Eating its own tail
Ouroboros- Serpent biting
cyclic nature of the Unive
KLIK

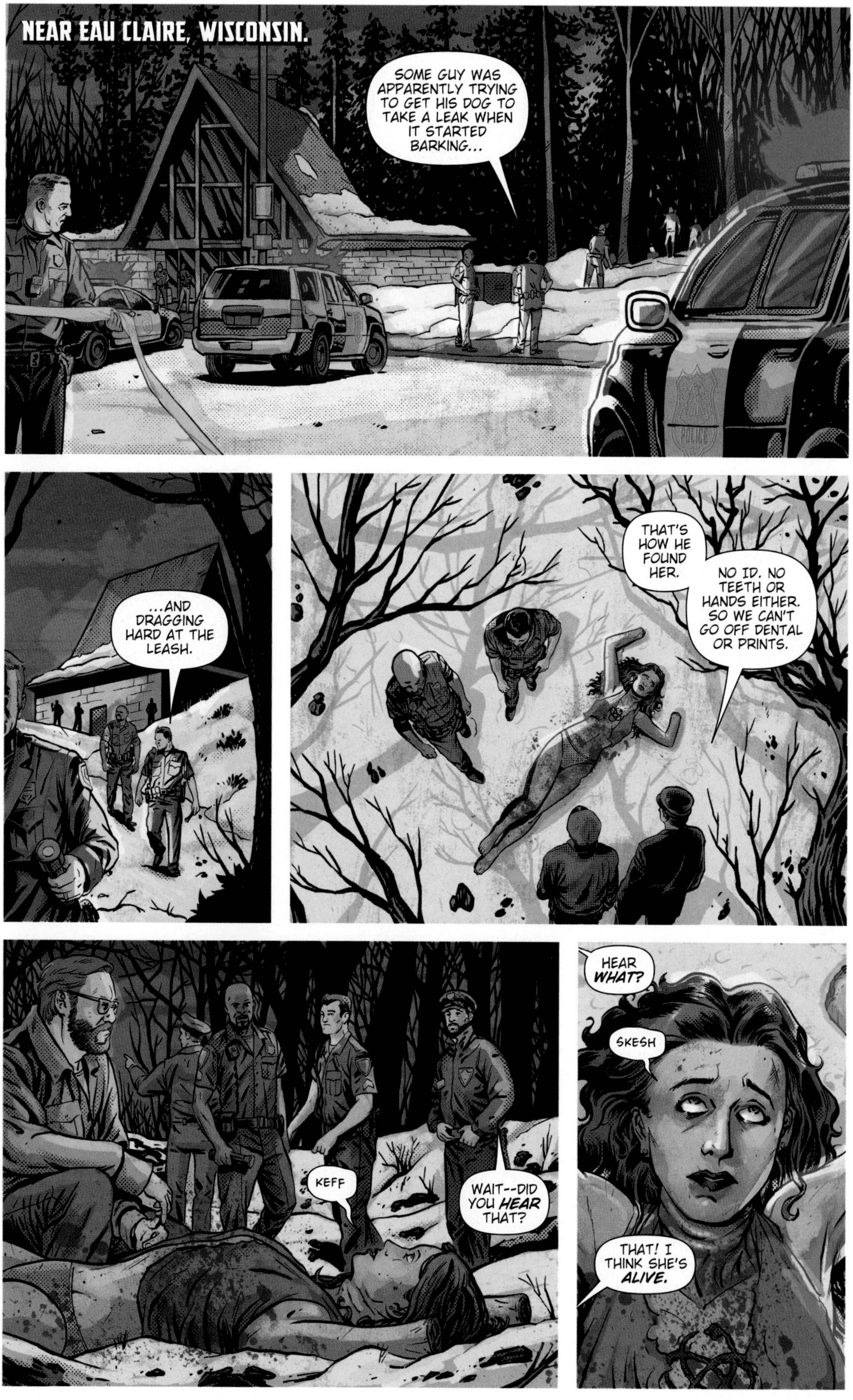
NEAR EAU CLAIRE, WISCONSIN.
SOME GUY WAS APPARENTLY TRYING TO GET HIS DOG TO TAKE A LEAK WHEN IT STARTED BARKING...
...AND DRAGGING HARD AT THE LEASH.
THAT'S HOW HE FOUND HER.
NO ID. NO TEETH OR HANDS EITHER. SO WE CAN'T GO OFF DENTAL OR PRINTS.
KEFF
WAIT--DID YOU HEAR THAT?
HEAR WHAT?
SKESH
THAT! I THINK SHE'S ALIVE.
POLICE

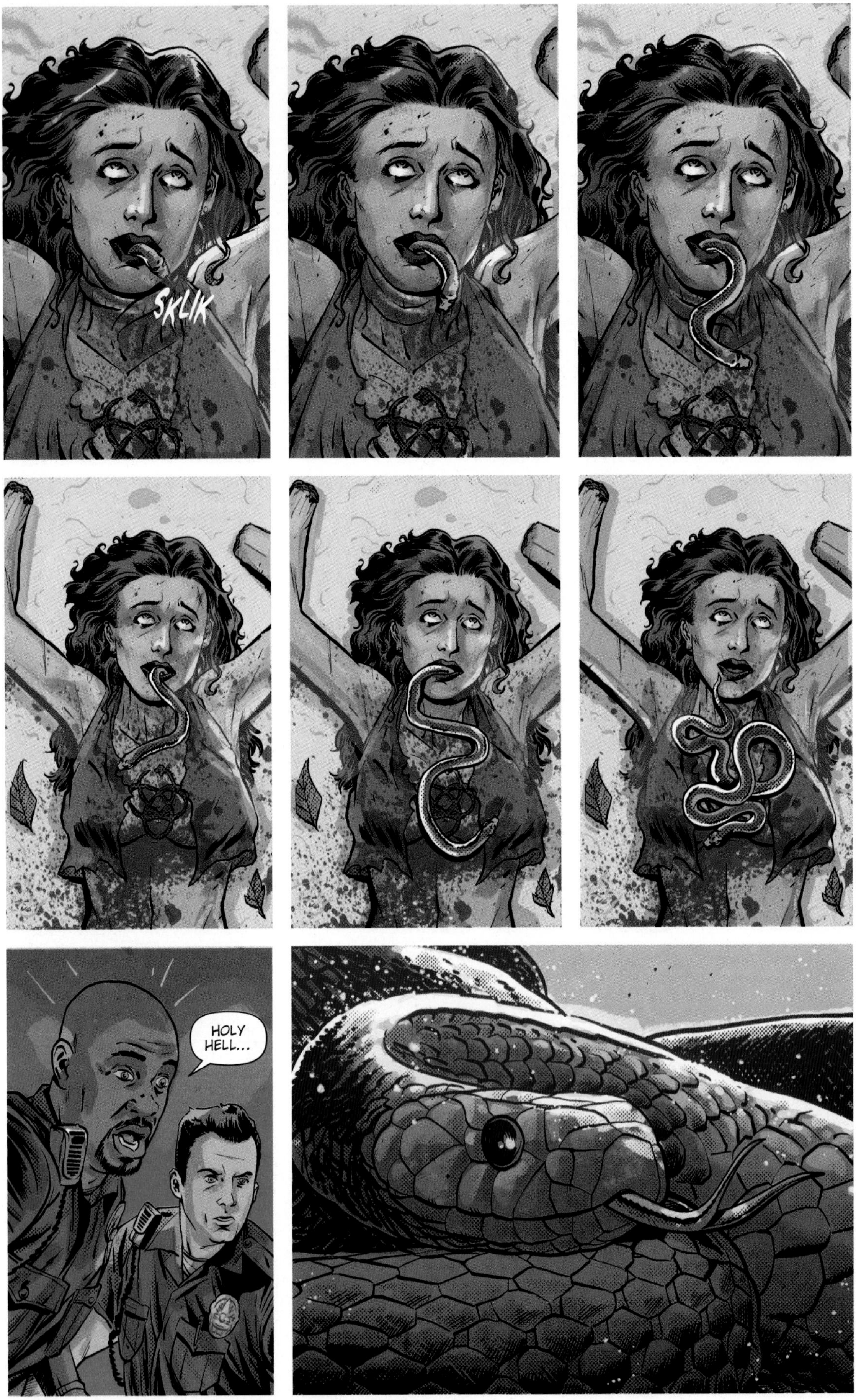
SKLIK
HOLY HELL...

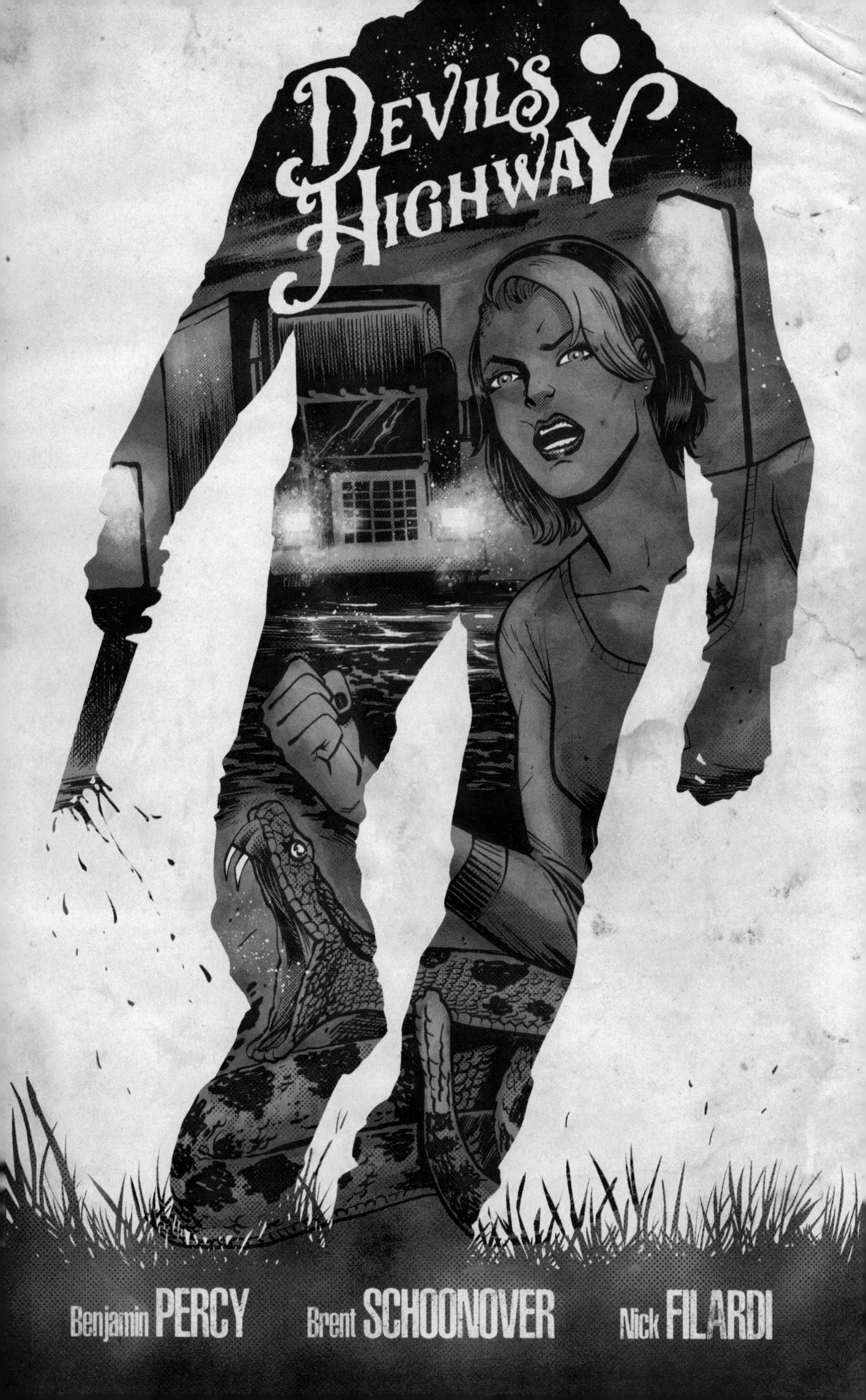

DEVIL'S HIGHWAY
Benjamin PERCY
Brent SCHOONOVER
Nick FILARDI

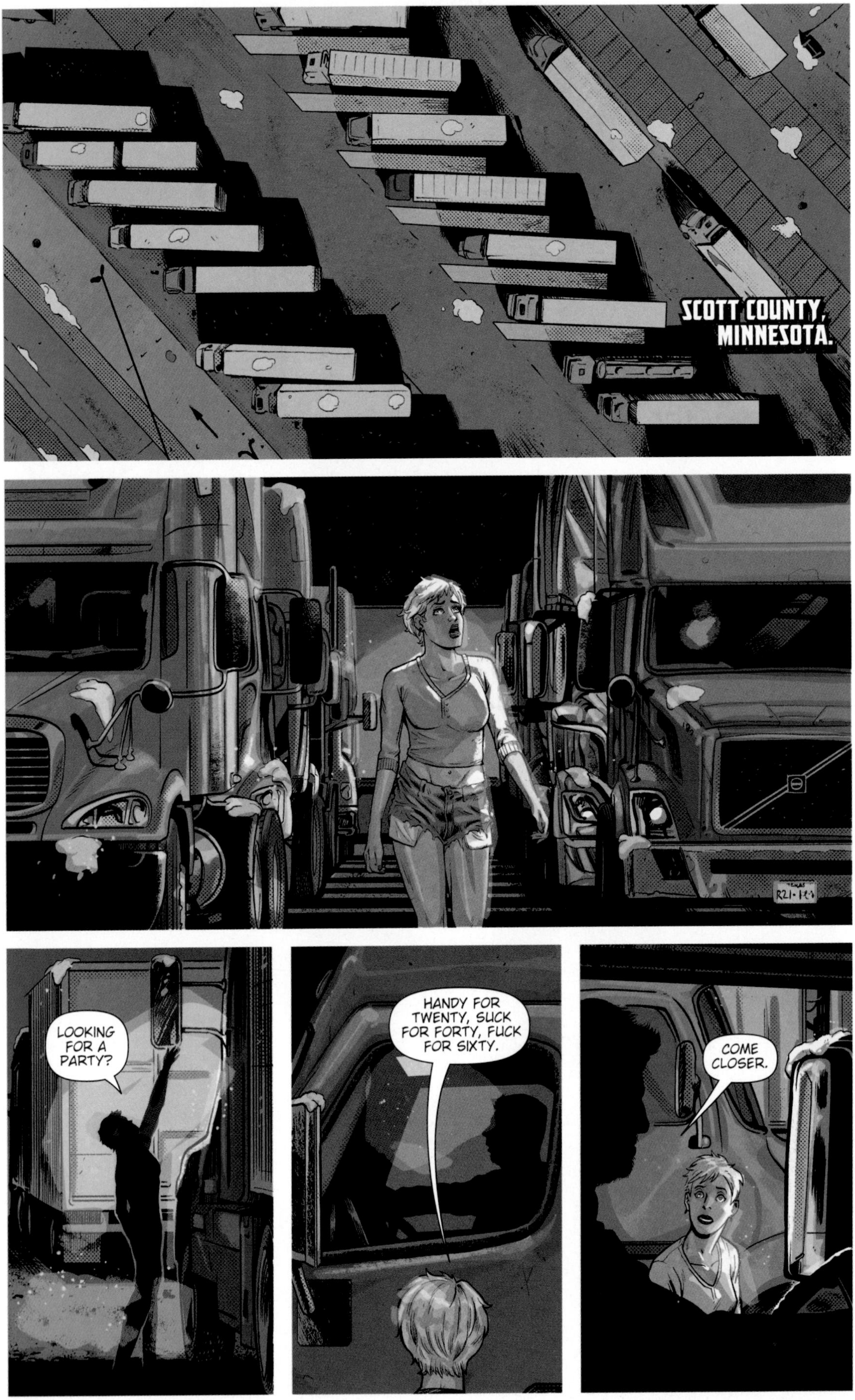
SCOTT COUNTY, MINNESOTA.
LOOKING FOR A PARTY?
HANDY FOR TWENTY, SUCK FOR FORTY, FUCK FOR SIXTY.
COME CLOSER.

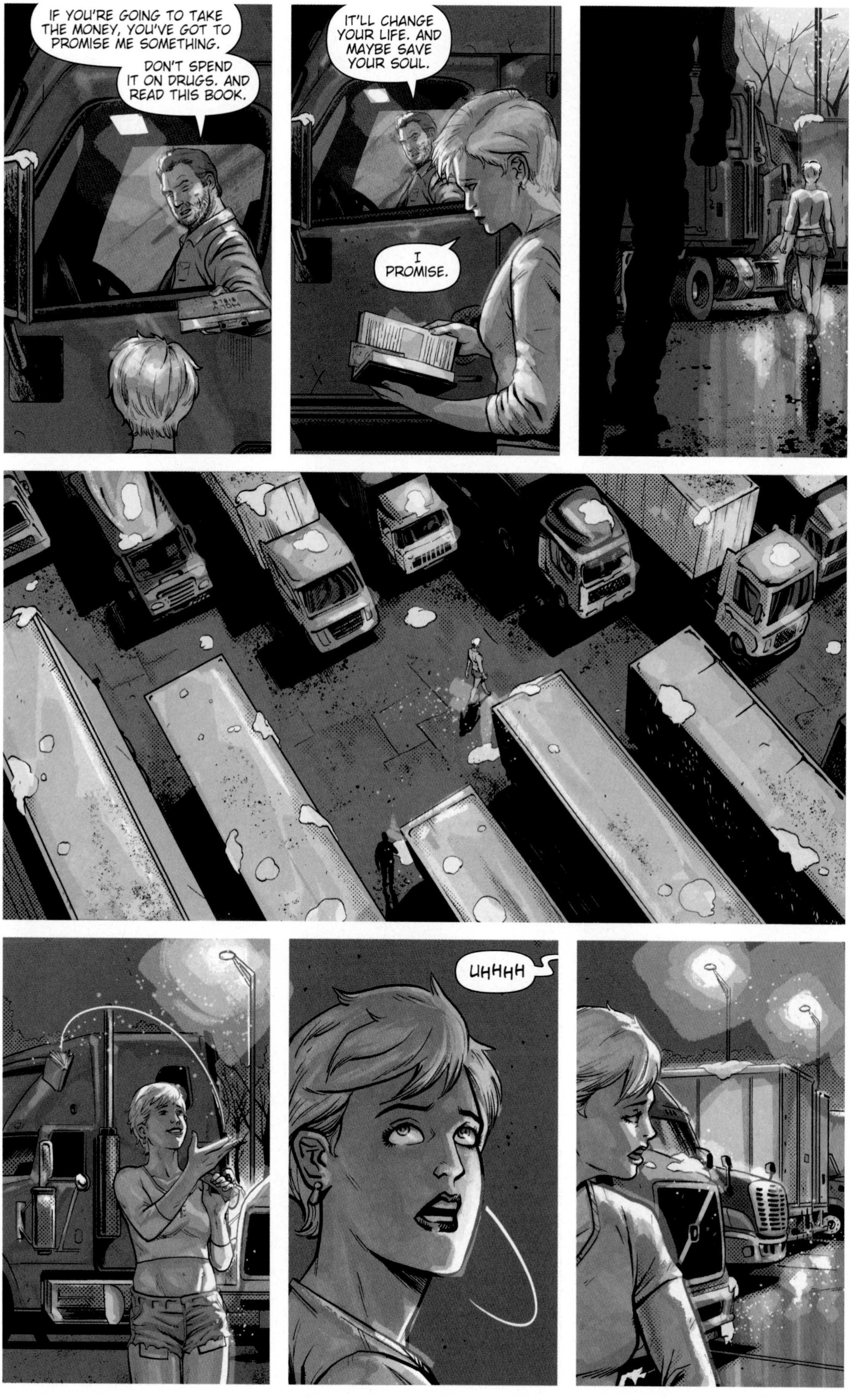
IF YOU'RE GOING TO TAKE THE MONEY, YOU'VE GOT TO PROMISE ME SOMETHING.
DON'T SPEND IT ON DRUGS. AND READ THIS BOOK.
IT'LL CHANGE YOUR LIFE. AND MAYBE SAVE YOUR SOUL.
I PROMISE.
UHHHH

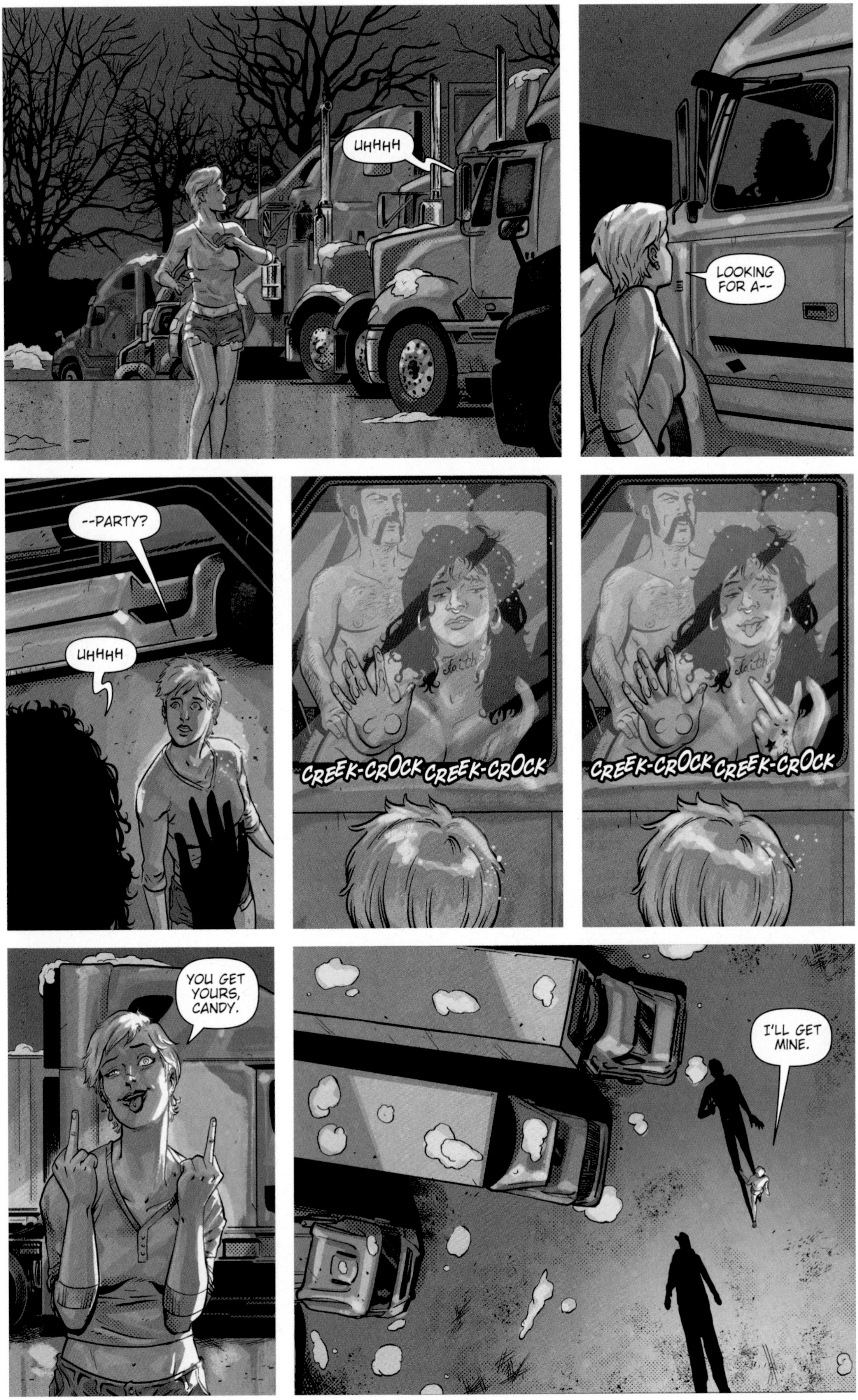
UHHHH
LOOKING FOR A--
--PARTY?
UHHHH
CREEK-CROCK CREEK-CROCK
Faith
CREEK-CROCK CREEK-CROCK
YOU GET YOURS, CANDY.
I'LL GET MINE.

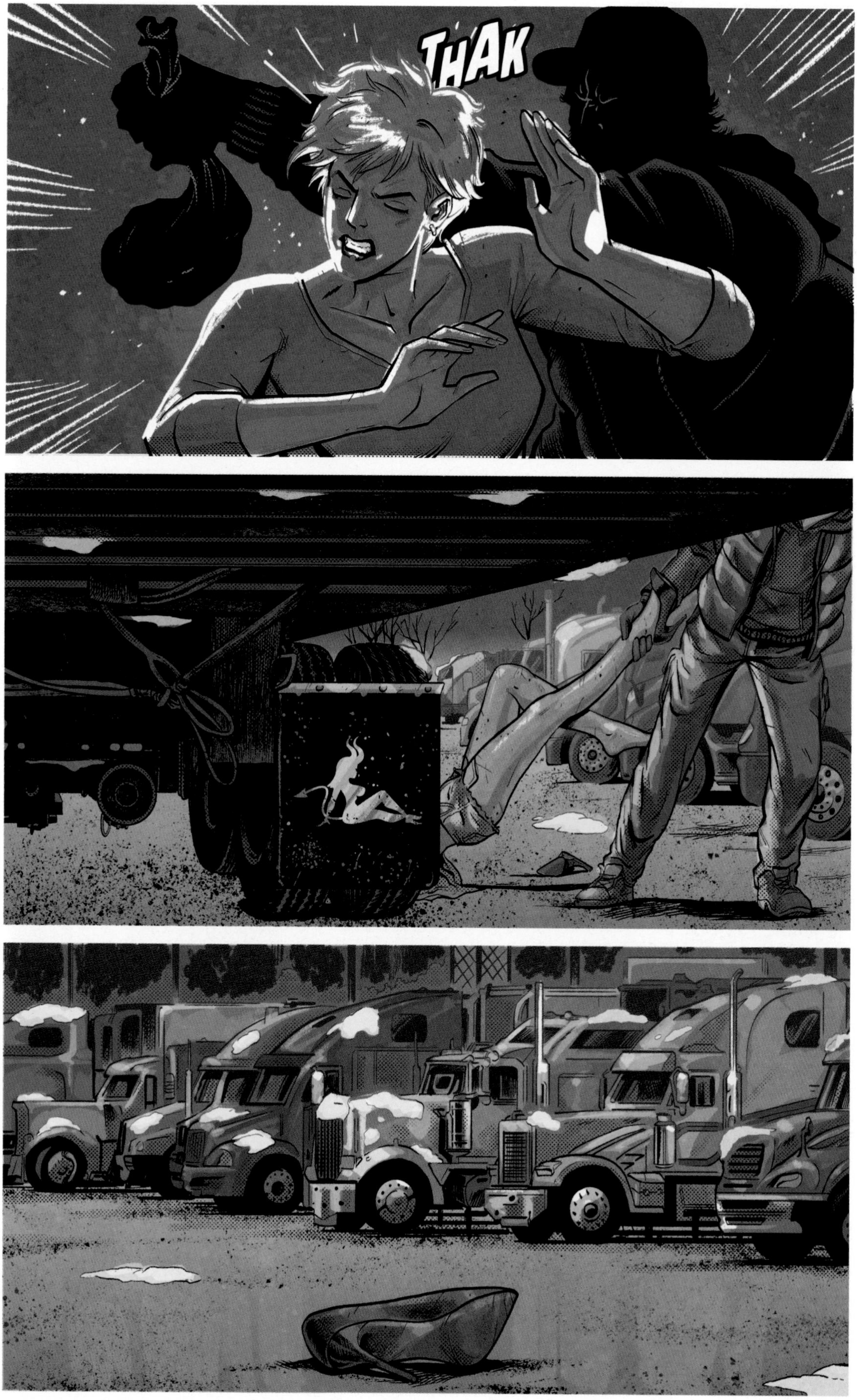
THAK

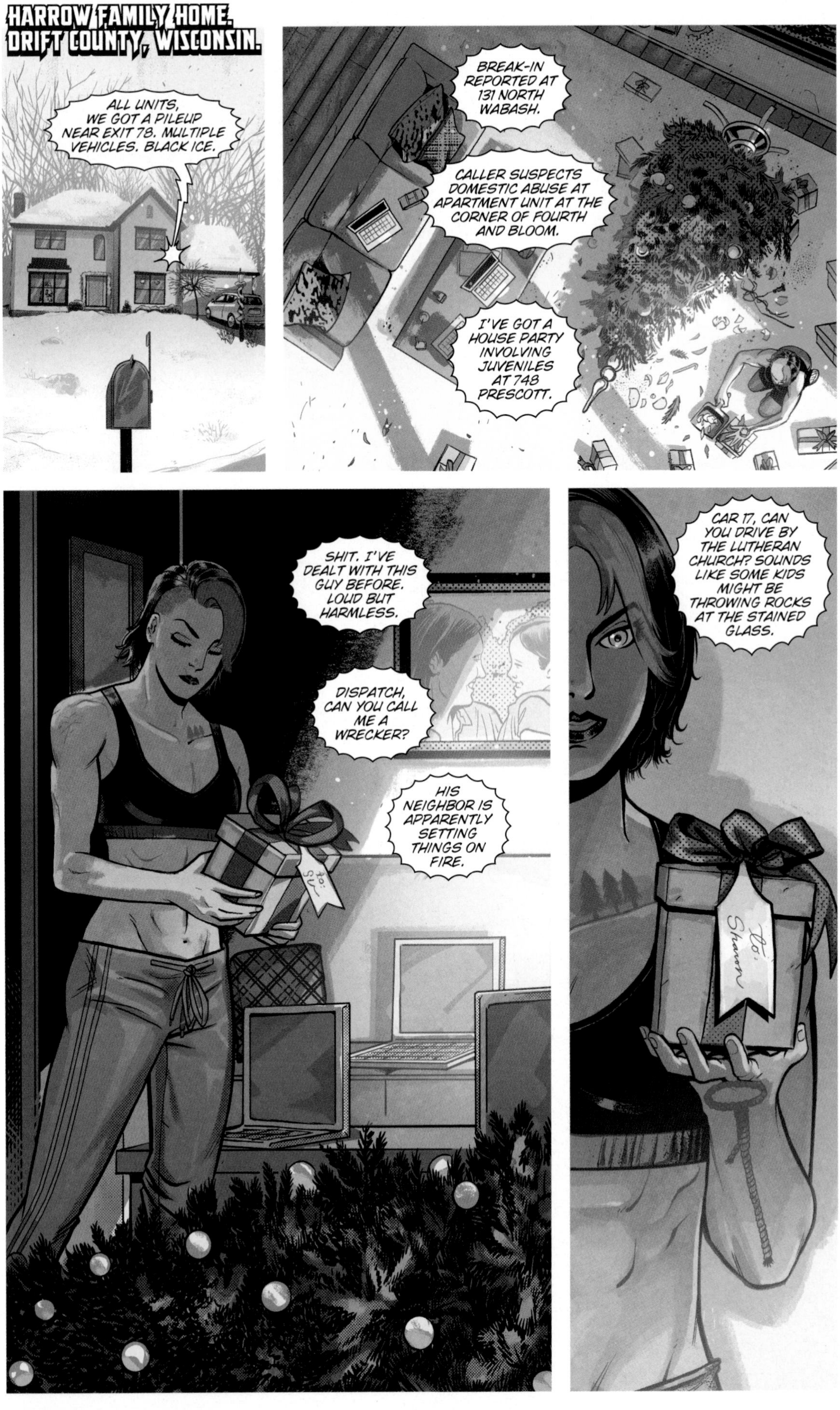
HARROW FAMILY HOME. DRIFT COUNTY, WISCONSIN.
ALL UNITS, WE GOT A PILEUP NEAR EXIT 78. MULTIPLE VEHICLES. BLACK ICE.
BREAK-IN REPORTED AT 131 NORTH WABASH.
CALLER SUSPECTS DOMESTIC ABUSE AT APARTMENT UNIT AT THE CORNER OF FOURTH AND BLOOM.
I'VE GOT A HOUSE PARTY INVOLVING JUVENILES AT 748 PRESCOTT.
SHIT. I'VE DEALT WITH THIS GUY BEFORE. LOUD BUT HARMLESS.
DISPATCH, CAN YOU CALL ME A WRECKER?
HIS NEIGHBOR IS APPARENTLY SETTING THINGS ON FIRE.
CAR 17, CAN YOU DRIVE BY THE LUTHERAN CHURCH? SOUNDS LIKE SOME KIDS MIGHT BE THROWING ROCKS AT THE STAINED GLASS.
To: Sharon

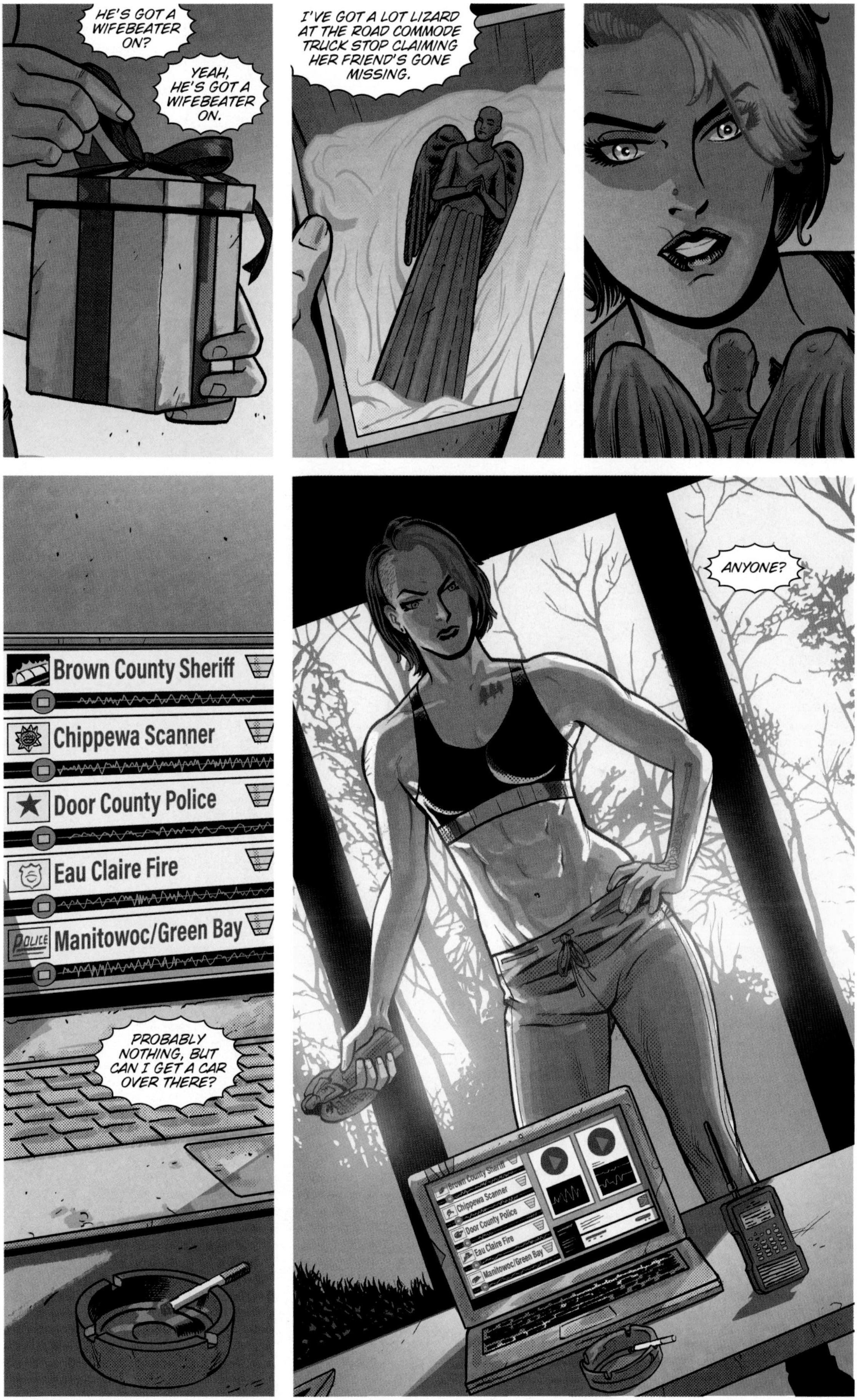
HE'S GOT A WIFEBEATER ON?
YEAH, HE'S GOT A WIFEBEATER ON.
I'VE GOT A LOT LIZARD AT THE ROAD COMMODE TRUCK STOP CLAIMING HER FRIEND'S GONE MISSING.
Brown County Sheriff
Chippewa Scanner
Door County Police
Eau Claire Fire
Manitowoc/Green Bay
PROBABLY NOTHING, BUT CAN I GET A CAR OVER THERE?
ANYONE?

LATE TWENTIES. TRACES OF COCAINE, HEROIN, AND MDMA IN HER BLOOD.

SHE TESTS POSITIVE FOR HEP C, CHLAMYDIA, AND GONORRHEA.

EAU CLAIRE, WISCONSIN.

I CULLED FIVE DIFFERENT SEMEN SAMPLES FROM HER MOUTH AND VAGINAL CAVITY.

ANOTHER DEAD PROSTITUTE. EASY PICKINGS, I GUESS.

IT'S NOT THAT IT DON'T MATTER. BUT IT DON'T COUNT.

YOU SAY THAT LIKE HER DEATH DOESN'T MATTER.

NO ID. NO PRINTS. NO DENTAL. MEANS YOU'RE NOBODY.

DEPARTMENT'S GOT A LONG LIST OF PRIORITIES. NOBODIES DROP TO THE BOTTOM OF IT.

EVEN *NOBODIES* WITH SNAKES SHOVED DOWN THEIR THROATS?

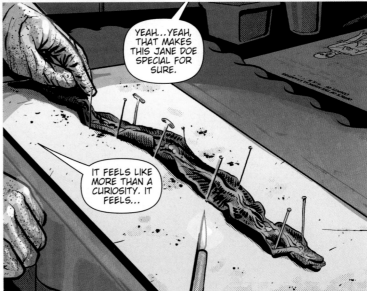

YEAH...YEAH, THAT MAKES THIS JANE DOE SPECIAL FOR SURE.

IT FEELS LIKE MORE THAN A CURIOSITY. IT FEELS...

...RITUALISTIC.

SHOULDN'T YOU BE CHECKING TO SEE IF THIS HAS HAPPENED ELSEWHERE?

TROUBLE IS, I DON'T GOT ACCESS TO ANY ADJACENT DATABASES. MEANS I HAVE TO MAKE INDIVIDUAL QUERIES.

THAT TAKES TIME I DON'T GOT.

I NEED A BREAK. I'LL BUY YOU A SANDWICH IF YOU MAKE SOME CALLS.

YEAH, YEAH--FINE.

I JUST DON'T UNDERSTAND WHY THERE ISN'T A CENTRALIZED DATABASE.

WELL, THERE'S ALWAYS THE FEDS.

BUT THE SHERIFF WOULD RATHER CUT OFF HIS LEFT NUT THAN DEAL WITH THEM.

HOPEFULLY IT'S JUST SOME FREAK THING.

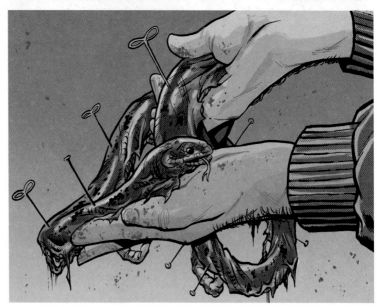

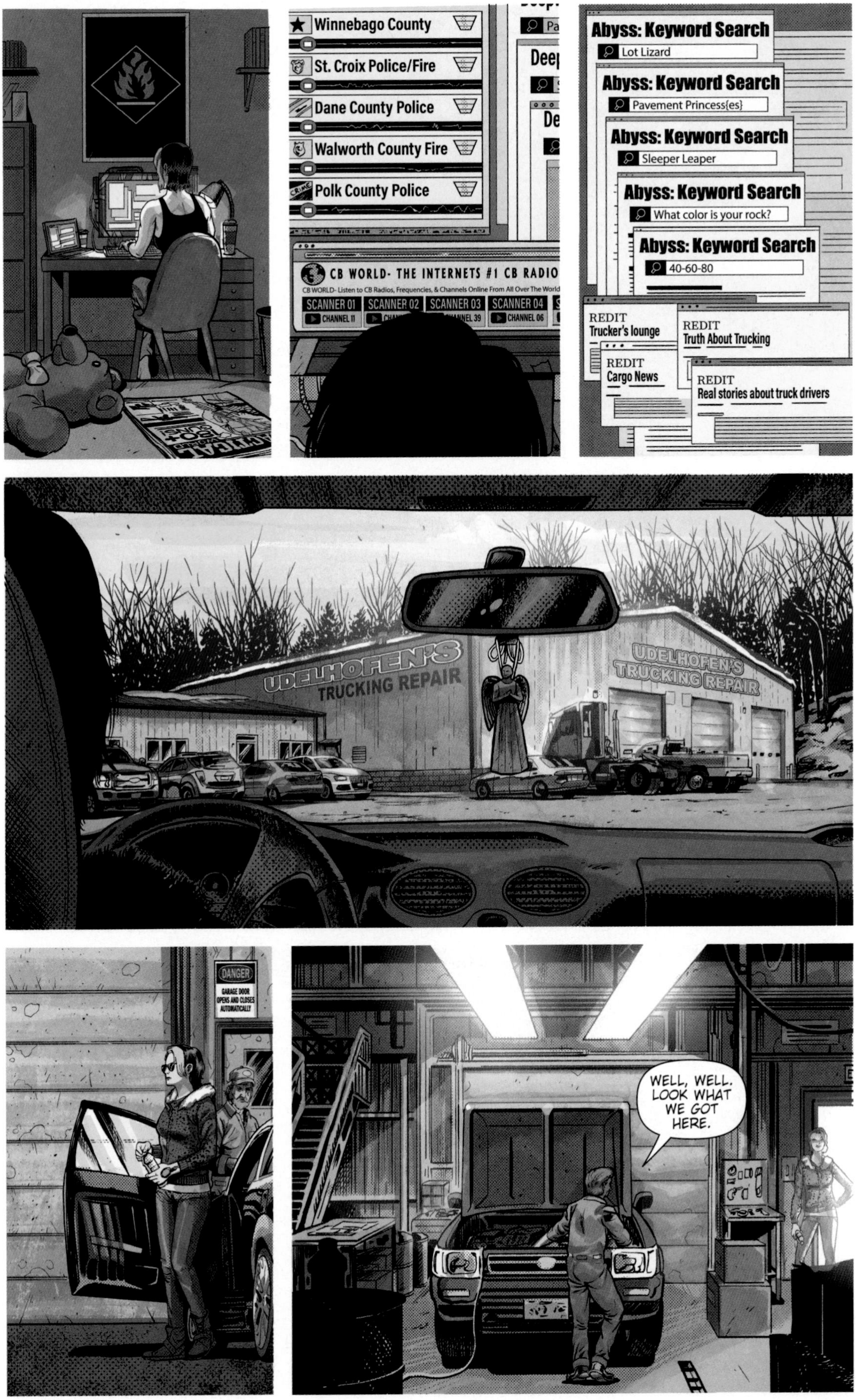
Winnebago County
St. Croix Police/Fire
Dane County Police
Walworth County Fire
Polk County Police
CB WORLD- THE INTERNETS #1 CB RADIO
CB WORLD- Listen to CB Radios, Frequencies, & Channels Online From All Over The World
SCANNER 01 CHANNEL 11
SCANNER 02
SCANNER 03 CHANNEL 39
SCANNER 04 CHANNEL 06
Abyss: Keyword Search
Lot Lizard
Abyss: Keyword Search
Pavement Princess{es}
Abyss: Keyword Search
Sleeper Leaper
Abyss: Keyword Search
What color is your rock?
Abyss: Keyword Search
40-60-80
REDIT
Trucker's lounge
REDIT
Truth About Trucking
REDIT
Cargo News
REDIT
Real stories about truck drivers
UDELHOFEN'S
TRUCKING REPAIR
UDELHOFEN'S
TRUCKING REPAIR
DANGER
GARAGE DOOR OPENS AND CLOSES AUTOMATICALLY
WELL, WELL. LOOK WHAT WE GOT HERE.

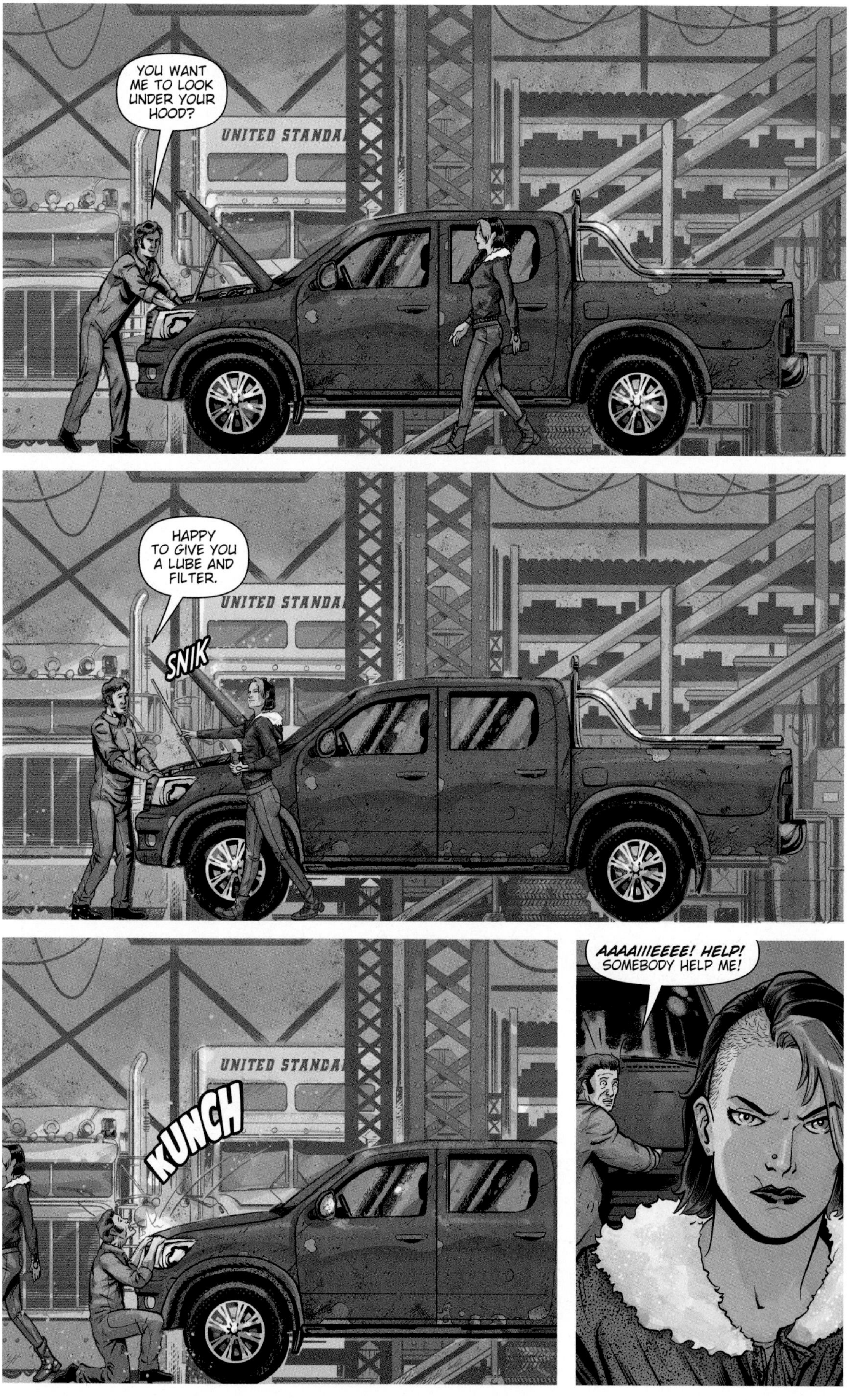
YOU WANT ME TO LOOK UNDER YOUR HOOD?
HAPPY TO GIVE YOU A LUBE AND FILTER.
SNIK
KUNCH
AAAAIIIEEEE! HELP! SOMEBODY HELP ME!

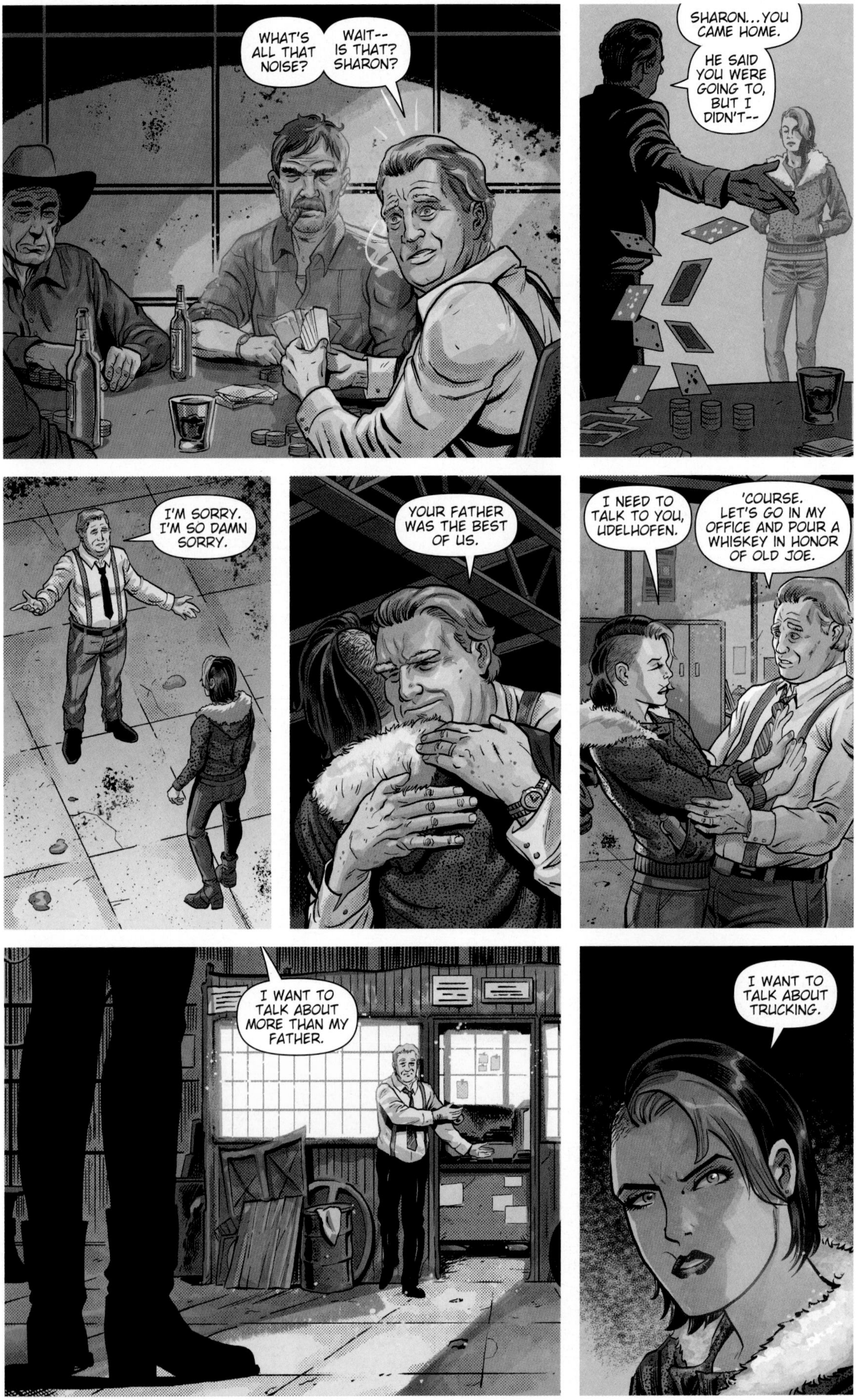
WHAT'S ALL THAT NOISE?
WAIT-- IS THAT? SHARON?
SHARON...YOU CAME HOME.
HE SAID YOU WERE GOING TO, BUT I DIDN'T--
I'M SORRY. I'M SO DAMN SORRY.
YOUR FATHER WAS THE BEST OF US.
I NEED TO TALK TO YOU, UDELHOFEN.
'COURSE. LET'S GO IN MY OFFICE AND POUR A WHISKEY IN HONOR OF OLD JOE.
I WANT TO TALK ABOUT MORE THAN MY FATHER.
I WANT TO TALK ABOUT TRUCKING.

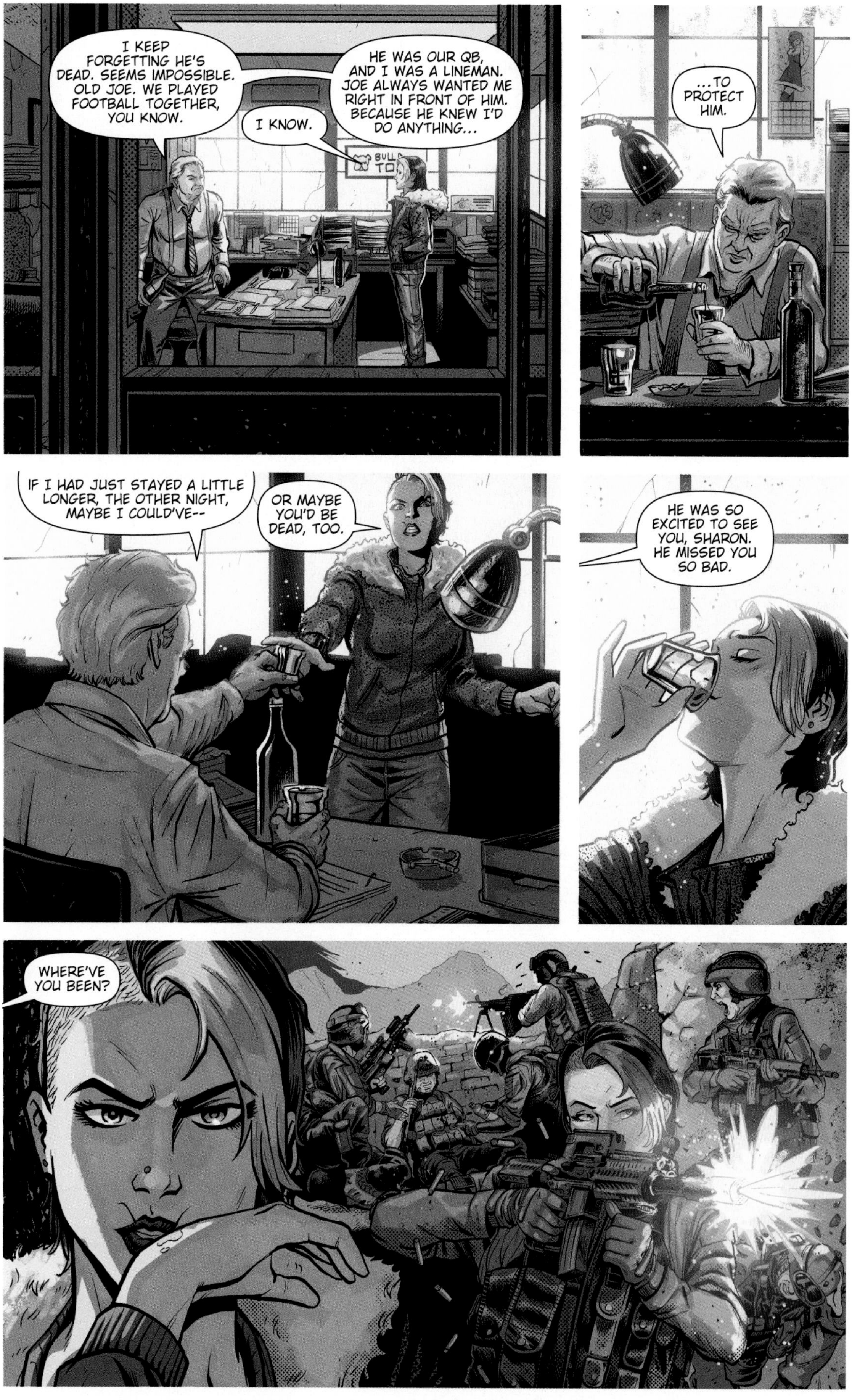
I KEEP FORGETTING HE'S DEAD. SEEMS IMPOSSIBLE. OLD JOE. WE PLAYED FOOTBALL TOGETHER, YOU KNOW.
I KNOW.
HE WAS OUR QB, AND I WAS A LINEMAN. JOE ALWAYS WANTED ME RIGHT IN FRONT OF HIM. BECAUSE HE KNEW I'D DO ANYTHING...
...TO PROTECT HIM.
IF I HAD JUST STAYED A LITTLE LONGER, THE OTHER NIGHT, MAYBE I COULD'VE--
OR MAYBE YOU'D BE DEAD, TOO.
HE WAS SO EXCITED TO SEE YOU, SHARON. HE MISSED YOU SO BAD.
WHERE'VE YOU BEEN?

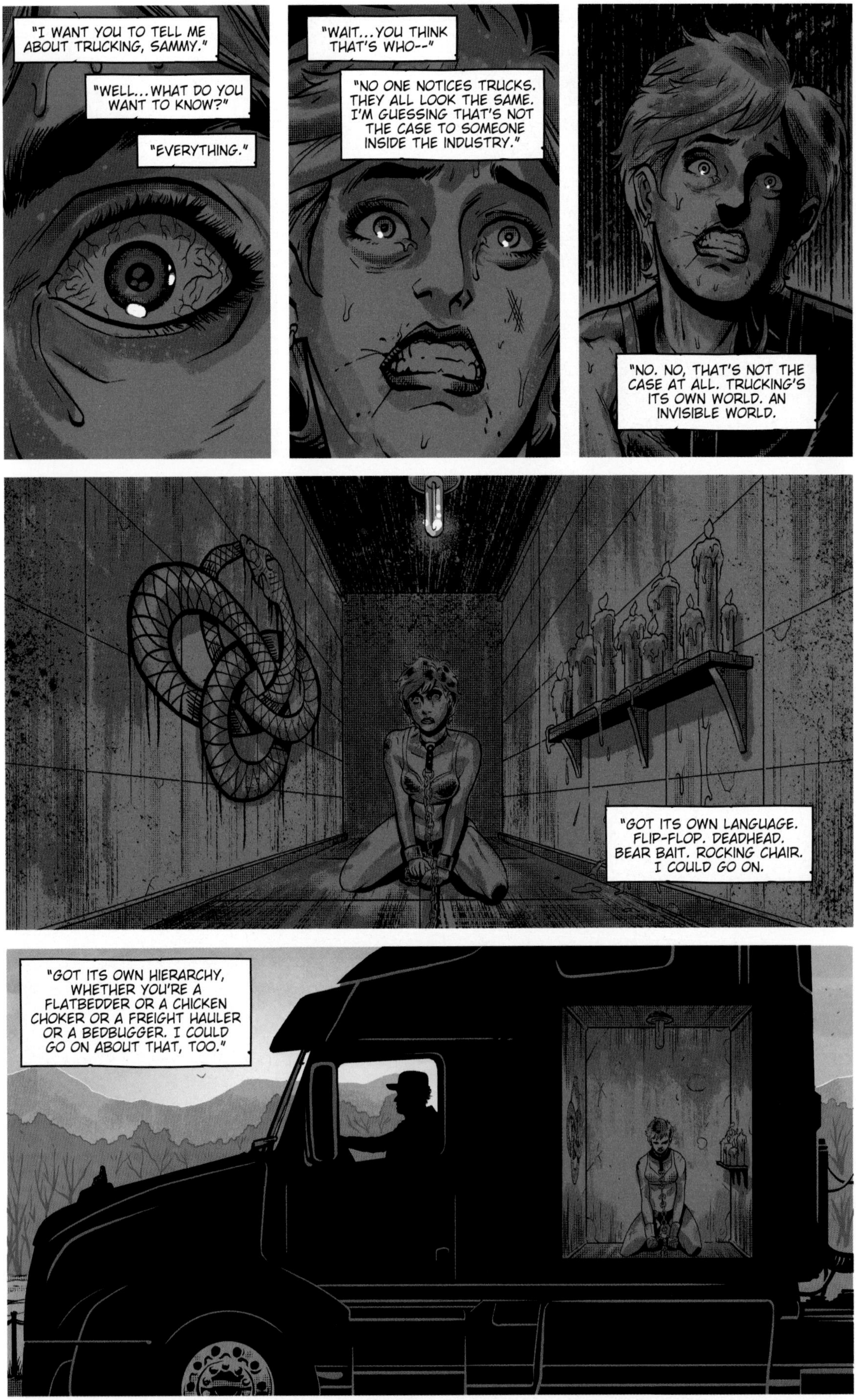
"I WANT YOU TO TELL ME ABOUT TRUCKING, SAMMY."
"WELL...WHAT DO YOU WANT TO KNOW?"
"EVERYTHING."
"WAIT...YOU THINK THAT'S WHO--"
"NO ONE NOTICES TRUCKS. THEY ALL LOOK THE SAME. I'M GUESSING THAT'S NOT THE CASE TO SOMEONE INSIDE THE INDUSTRY."
"NO. NO, THAT'S NOT THE CASE AT ALL. TRUCKING'S ITS OWN WORLD. AN INVISIBLE WORLD.
"GOT ITS OWN LANGUAGE. FLIP-FLOP. DEADHEAD. BEAR BAIT. ROCKING CHAIR. I COULD GO ON.
"GOT ITS OWN HIERARCHY, WHETHER YOU'RE A FLATBEDDER OR A CHICKEN CHOKER OR A FREIGHT HAULER OR A BEDBUGGER. I COULD GO ON ABOUT THAT, TOO."

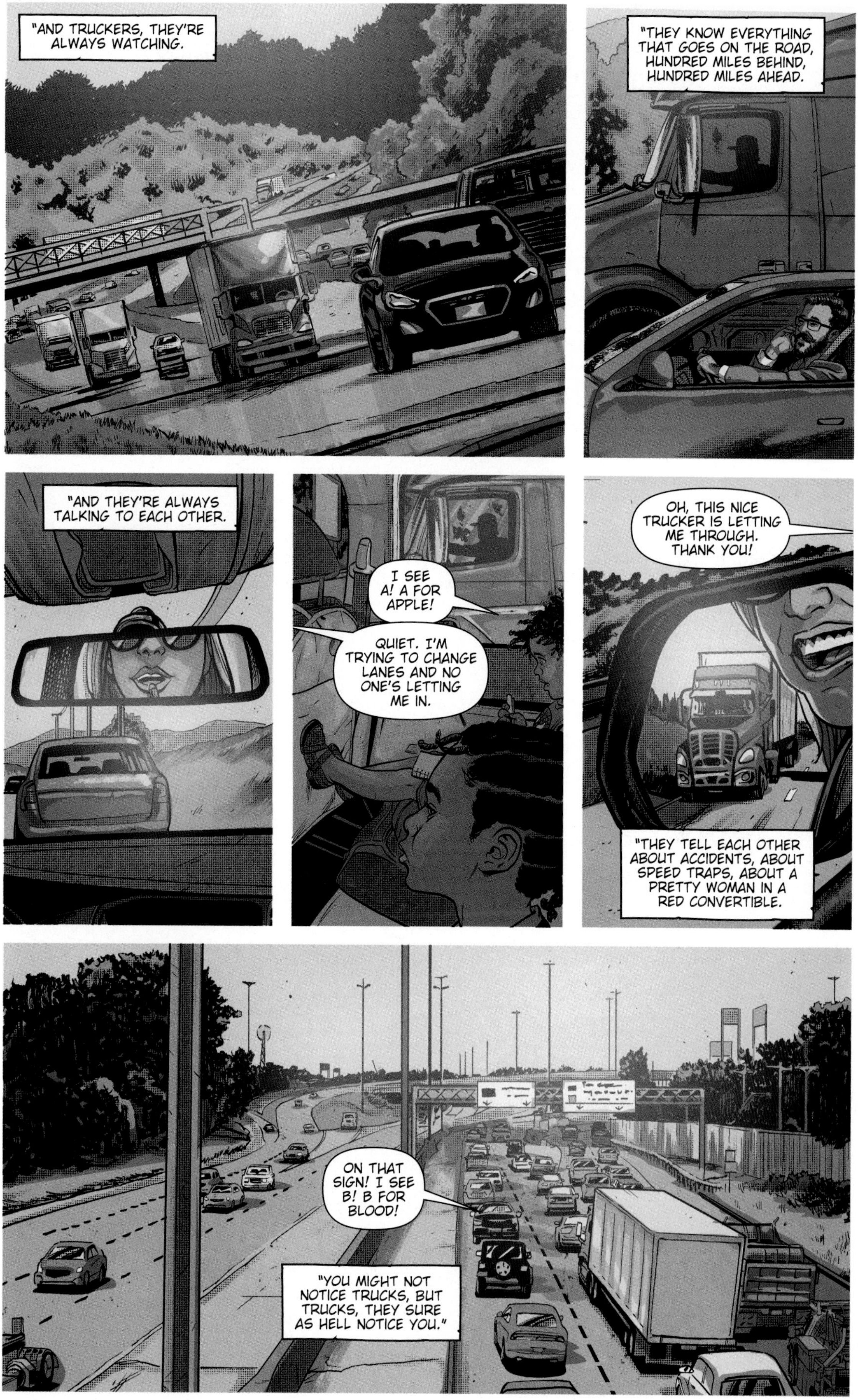
"AND TRUCKERS, THEY'RE ALWAYS WATCHING.
"THEY KNOW EVERYTHING THAT GOES ON THE ROAD, HUNDRED MILES BEHIND, HUNDRED MILES AHEAD.
"AND THEY'RE ALWAYS TALKING TO EACH OTHER.
I SEE A! A FOR APPLE!
QUIET. I'M TRYING TO CHANGE LANES AND NO ONE'S LETTING ME IN.
OH, THIS NICE TRUCKER IS LETTING ME THROUGH. THANK YOU!
"THEY TELL EACH OTHER ABOUT ACCIDENTS, ABOUT SPEED TRAPS, ABOUT A PRETTY WOMAN IN A RED CONVERTIBLE.
ON THAT SIGN! I SEE B! B FOR BLOOD!
"YOU MIGHT NOT NOTICE TRUCKS, BUT TRUCKS, THEY SURE AS HELL NOTICE YOU."

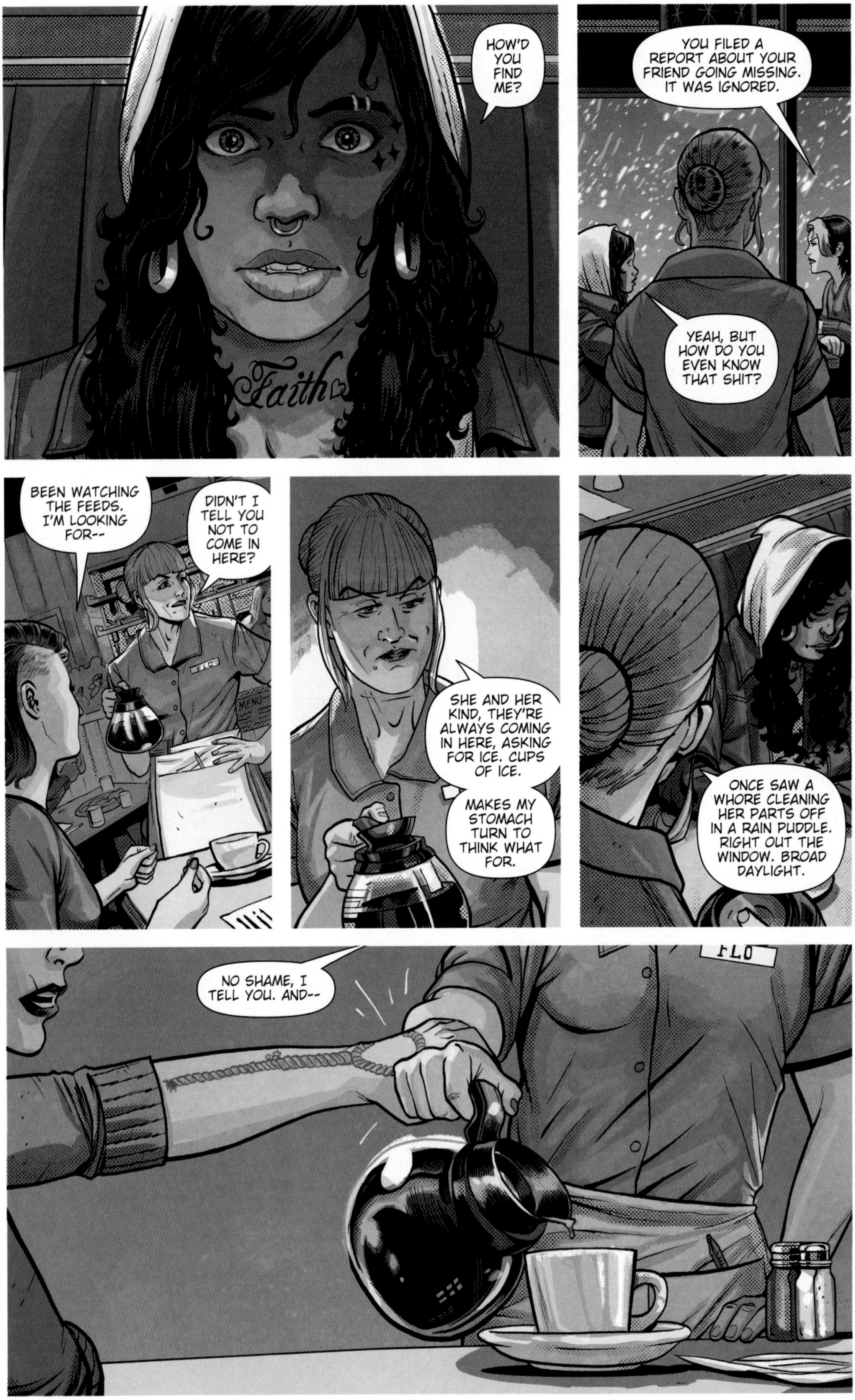
HOW'D YOU FIND ME?
YOU FILED A REPORT ABOUT YOUR FRIEND GOING MISSING. IT WAS IGNORED.
YEAH, BUT HOW DO YOU EVEN KNOW THAT SHIT?
BEEN WATCHING THE FEEDS. I'M LOOKING FOR--
DIDN'T I TELL YOU NOT TO COME IN HERE?
FLO
MENU
SHE AND HER KIND, THEY'RE ALWAYS COMING IN HERE, ASKING FOR ICE. CUPS OF ICE.
MAKES MY STOMACH TURN TO THINK WHAT FOR.
ONCE SAW A WHORE CLEANING HER PARTS OFF IN A RAIN PUDDLE. RIGHT OUT THE WINDOW. BROAD DAYLIGHT.
NO SHAME, I TELL YOU. AND--
FLO

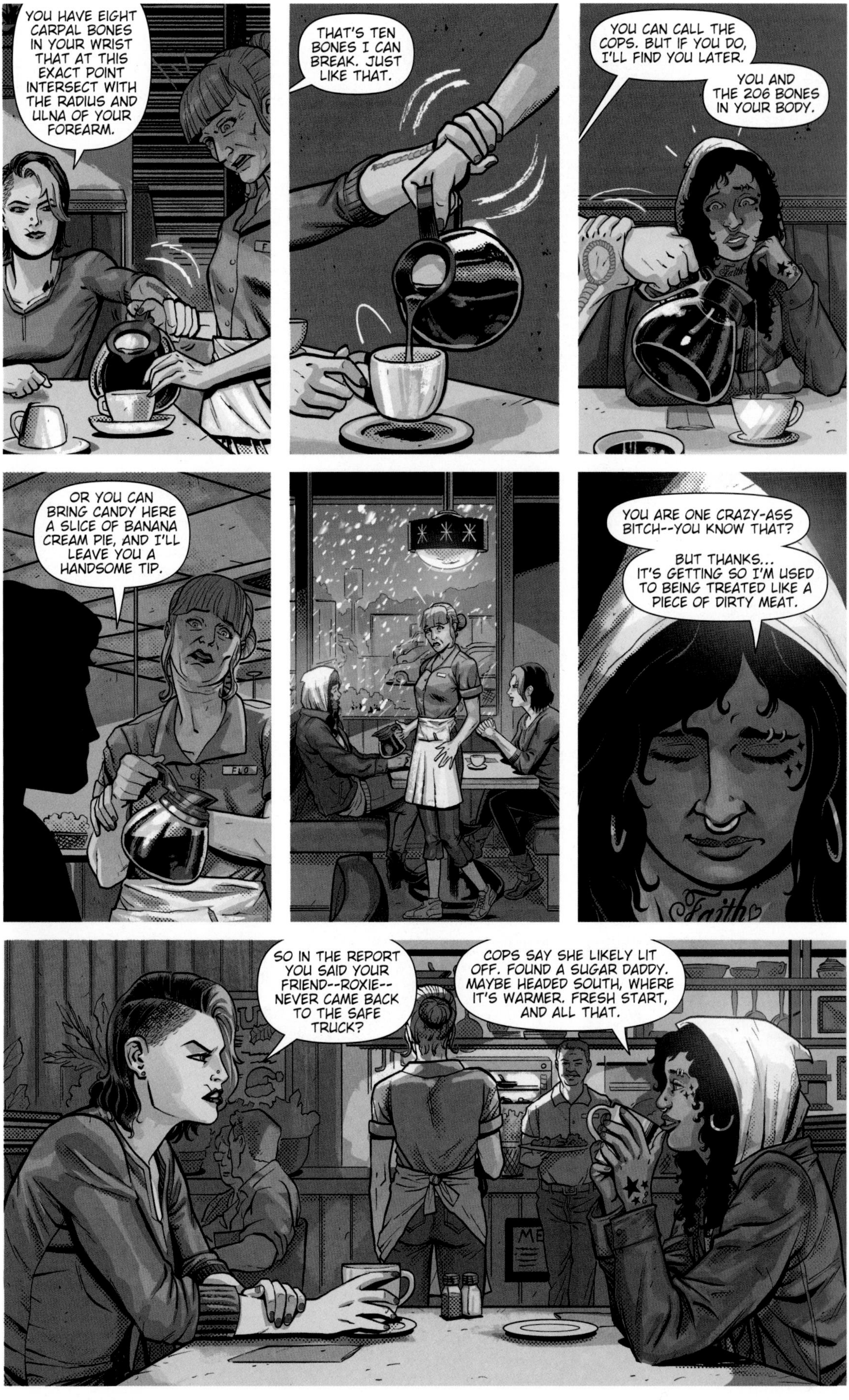
YOU HAVE EIGHT CARPAL BONES IN YOUR WRIST THAT AT THIS EXACT POINT INTERSECT WITH THE RADIUS AND ULNA OF YOUR FOREARM.
THAT'S TEN BONES I CAN BREAK. JUST LIKE THAT.
YOU CAN CALL THE COPS. BUT IF YOU DO, I'LL FIND YOU LATER.
YOU AND THE 206 BONES IN YOUR BODY.
OR YOU CAN BRING CANDY HERE A SLICE OF BANANA CREAM PIE, AND I'LL LEAVE YOU A HANDSOME TIP.
FLO
YOU ARE ONE CRAZY-ASS BITCH--YOU KNOW THAT?
BUT THANKS... IT'S GETTING SO I'M USED TO BEING TREATED LIKE A PIECE OF DIRTY MEAT.
Faith
SO IN THE REPORT YOU SAID YOUR FRIEND--ROXIE--NEVER CAME BACK TO THE SAFE TRUCK?
COPS SAY SHE LIKELY LIT OFF. FOUND A SUGAR DADDY. MAYBE HEADED SOUTH, WHERE IT'S WARMER. FRESH START, AND ALL THAT.

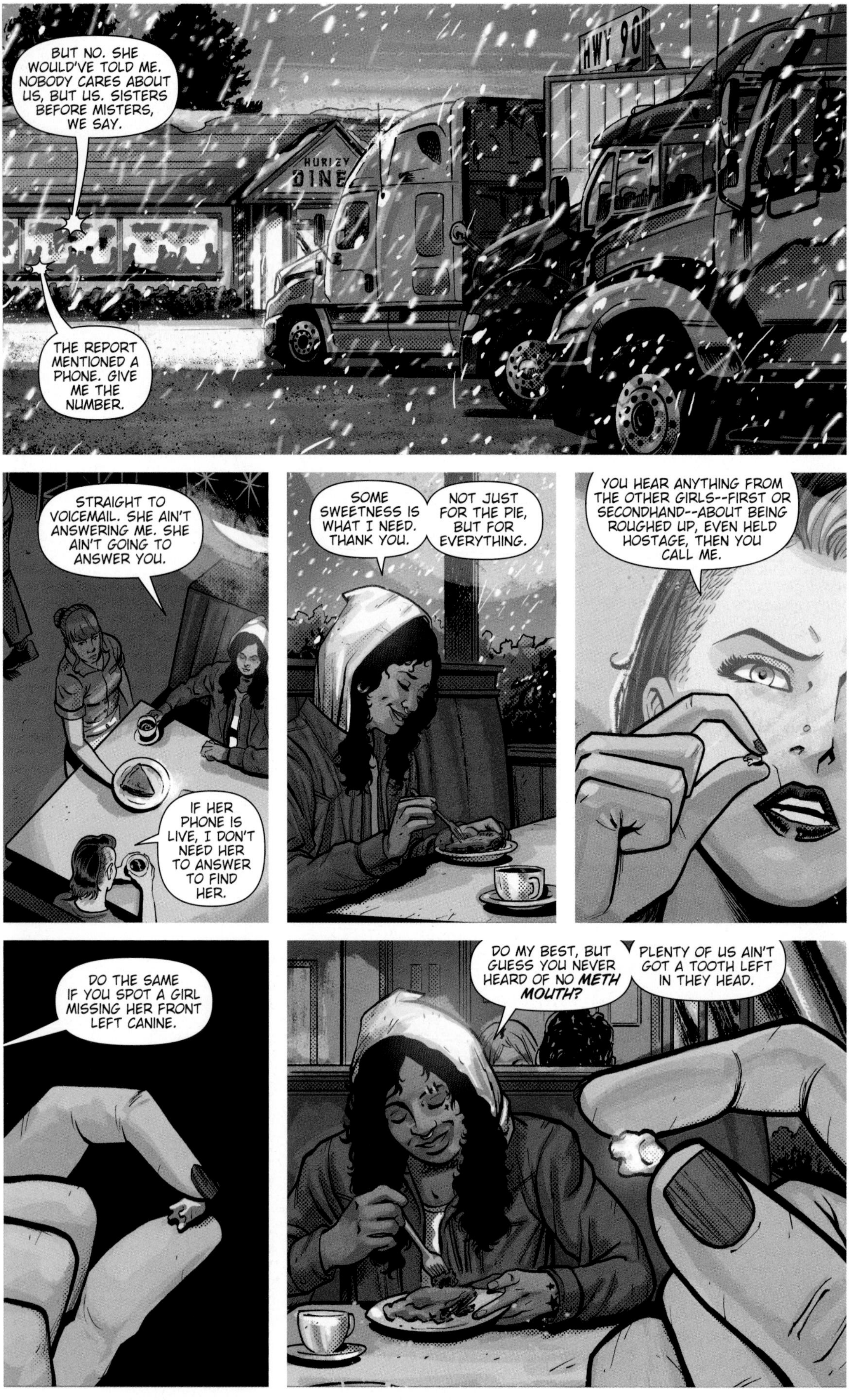

BUT NO. SHE WOULD'VE TOLD ME. NOBODY CARES ABOUT US, BUT US. SISTERS BEFORE MISTERS, WE SAY.
THE REPORT MENTIONED A PHONE. GIVE ME THE NUMBER.
HWY 90
DINE
STRAIGHT TO VOICEMAIL. SHE AIN'T ANSWERING ME. SHE AIN'T GOING TO ANSWER YOU.
IF HER PHONE IS LIVE, I DON'T NEED HER TO ANSWER TO FIND HER.
SOME SWEETNESS IS WHAT I NEED. THANK YOU.
NOT JUST FOR THE PIE, BUT FOR EVERYTHING.
YOU HEAR ANYTHING FROM THE OTHER GIRLS--FIRST OR SECONDHAND--ABOUT BEING ROUGHED UP, EVEN HELD HOSTAGE, THEN YOU CALL ME.
DO THE SAME IF YOU SPOT A GIRL MISSING HER FRONT LEFT CANINE.
DO MY BEST, BUT GUESS YOU NEVER HEARD OF NO METH MOUTH?
PLENTY OF US AIN'T GOT A TOOTH LEFT IN THEY HEAD.

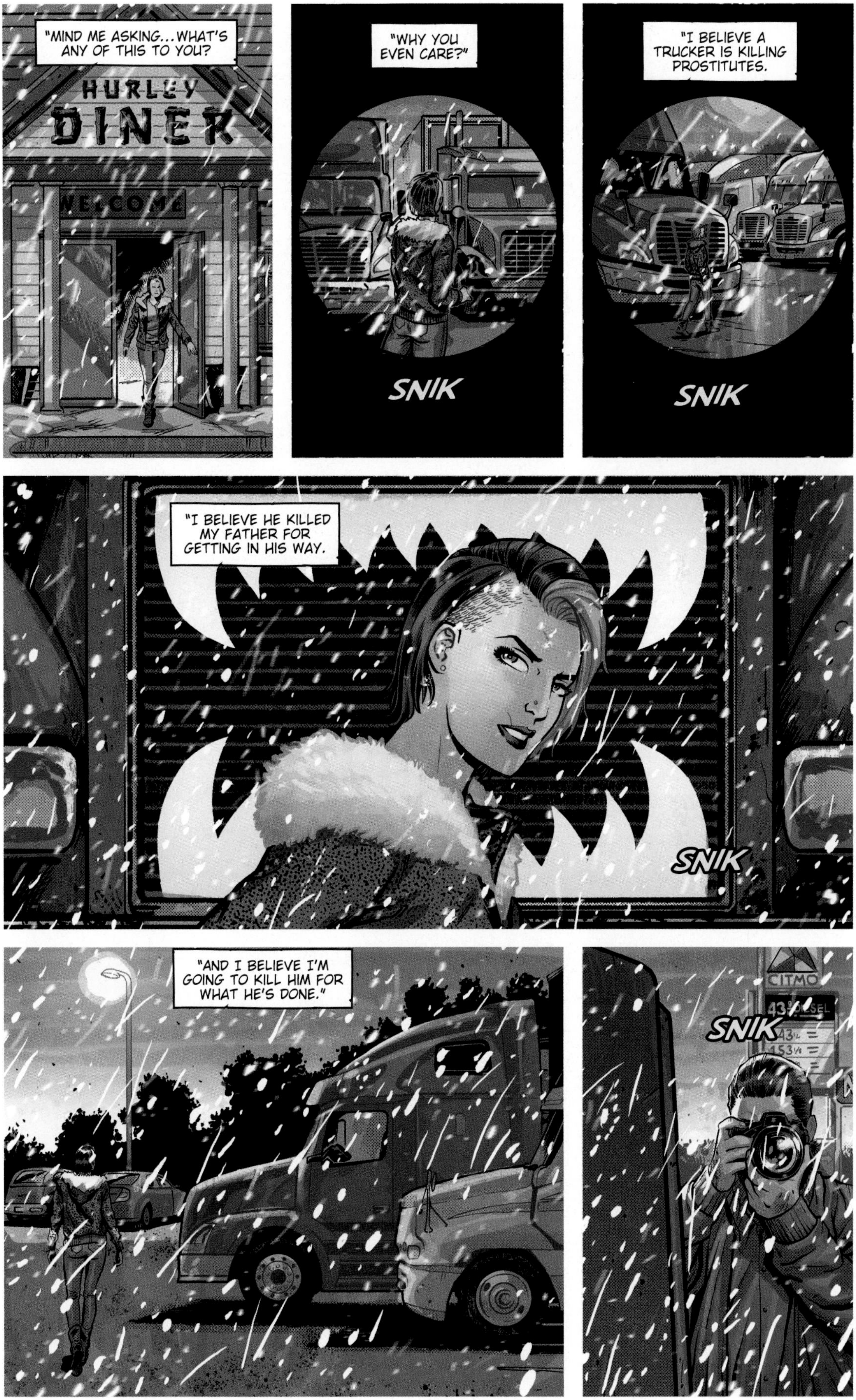
"MIND ME ASKING...WHAT'S ANY OF THIS TO YOU?
HURLEY
DINER
WELCOME
"WHY YOU EVEN CARE?"
SNIK
"I BELIEVE A TRUCKER IS KILLING PROSTITUTES.
SNIK
"I BELIEVE HE KILLED MY FATHER FOR GETTING IN HIS WAY.
SNIK
"AND I BELIEVE I'M GOING TO KILL HIM FOR WHAT HE'S DONE."
CITMO
SNIK

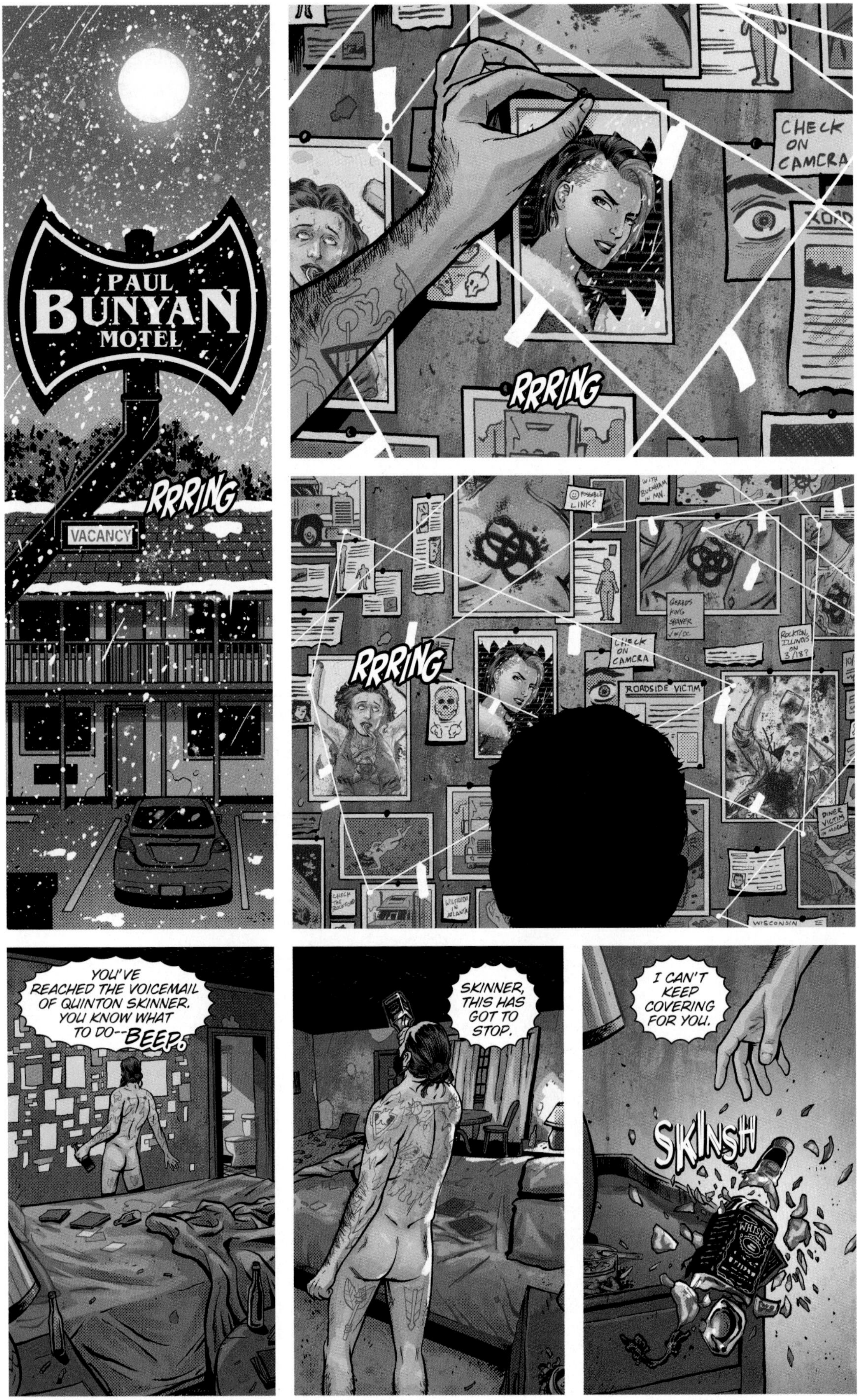
PAUL BUNYAN MOTEL
VACANCY
RRRING
RRRING
CHECK ON CAMERA
RRRING
POSSIBLE LINK?
CHECK ON CAMERA
ROADSIDE VICTIM
ROCKTON, ILLINOIS ON 3/18?
WISCONSIN
YOU'VE REACHED THE VOICEMAIL OF QUINTON SKINNER. YOU KNOW WHAT TO DO--BEEP.
SKINNER, THIS HAS GOT TO STOP.
I CAN'T KEEP COVERING FOR YOU.
SKINSH
WHISKEY

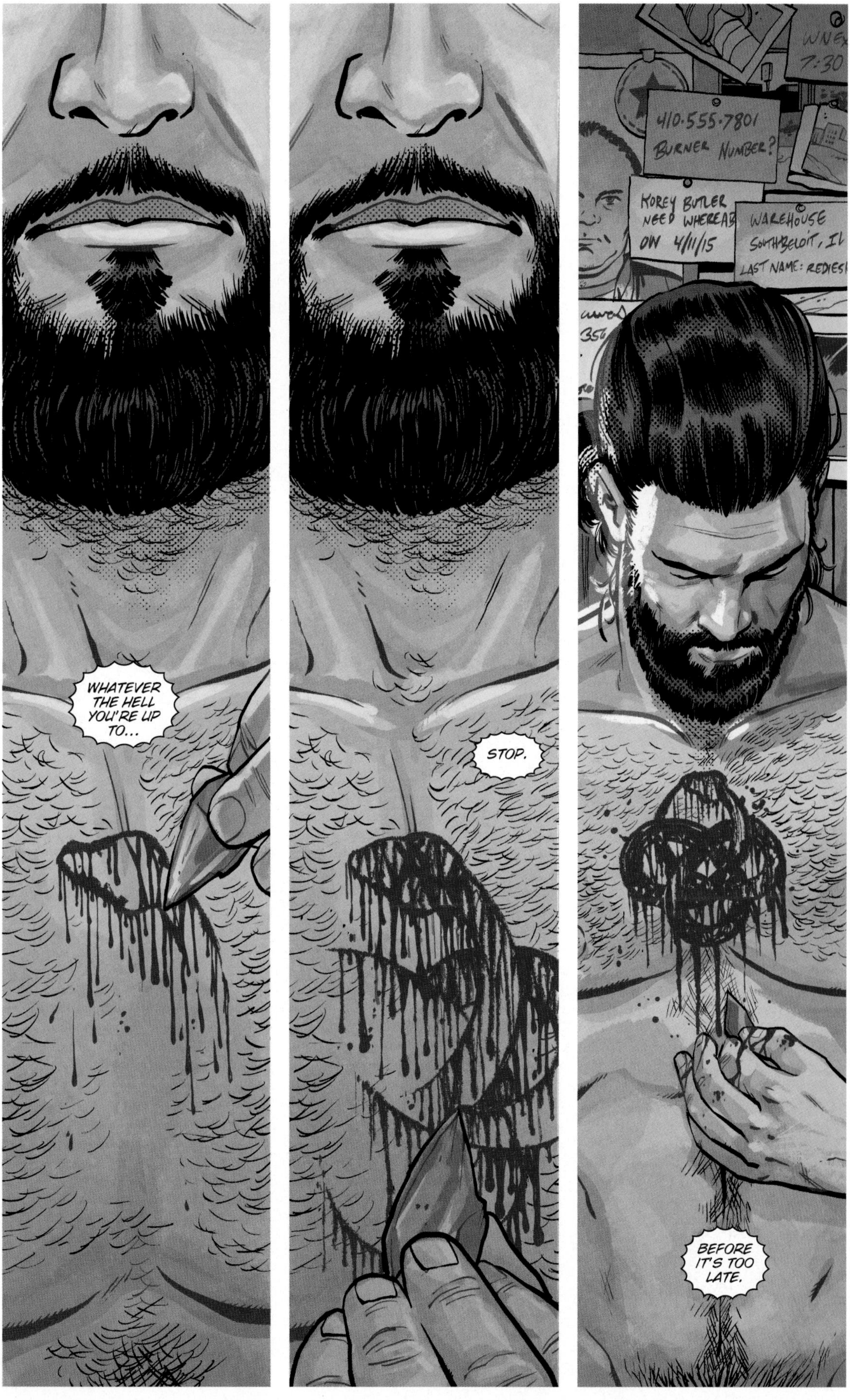
WHATEVER THE HELL YOU'RE UP TO...
STOP.
WNEX 7:30
410-555-7801
BURNER NUMBER?
KOREY BUTLER
ON 4/11/15
WAREHOUSE
SOUTH BELOIT, IL
BEFORE IT'S TOO LATE.

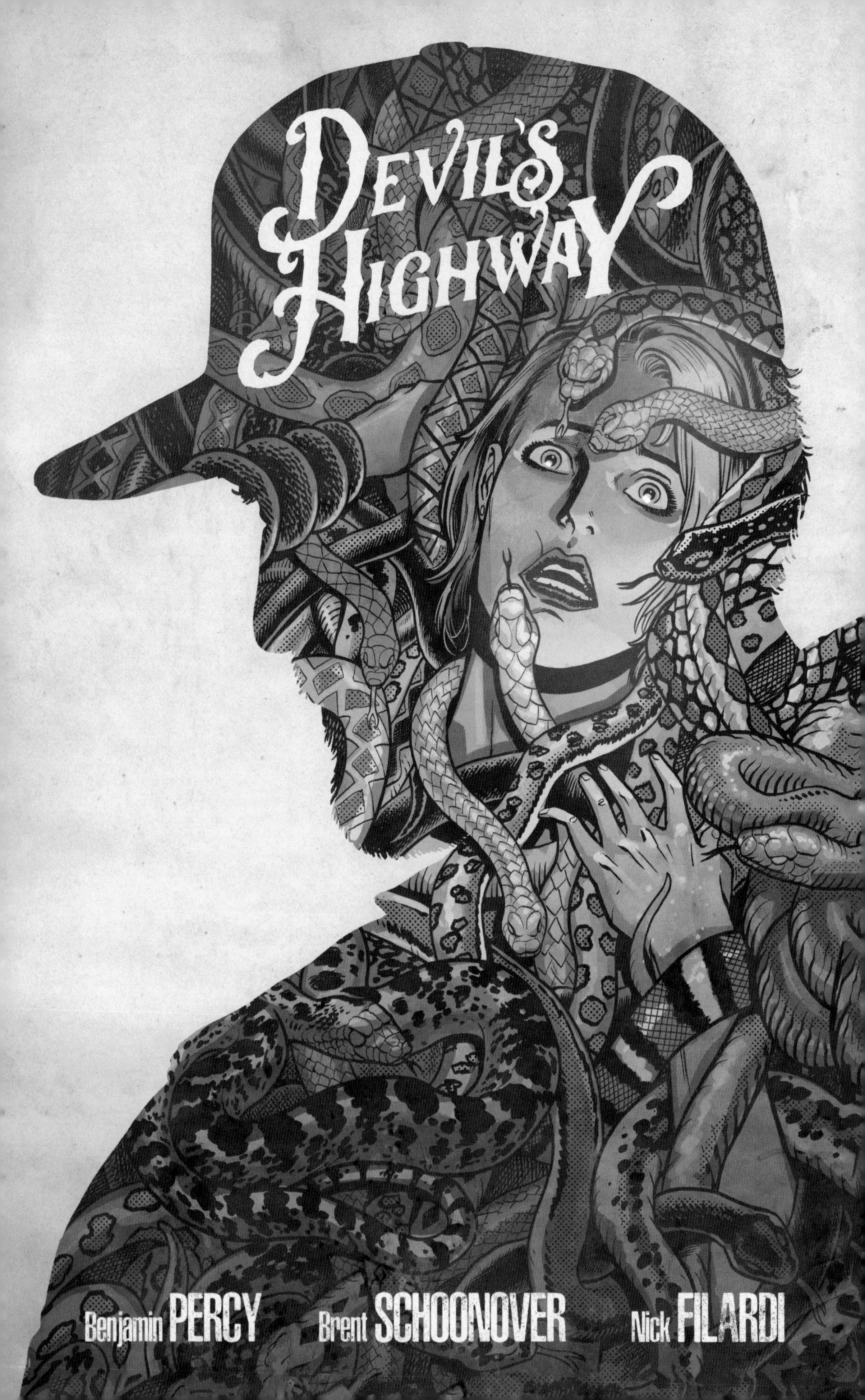
DEVIL'S HIGHWAY
Benjamin PERCY
Brent SCHOONOVER
Nick FILARDI

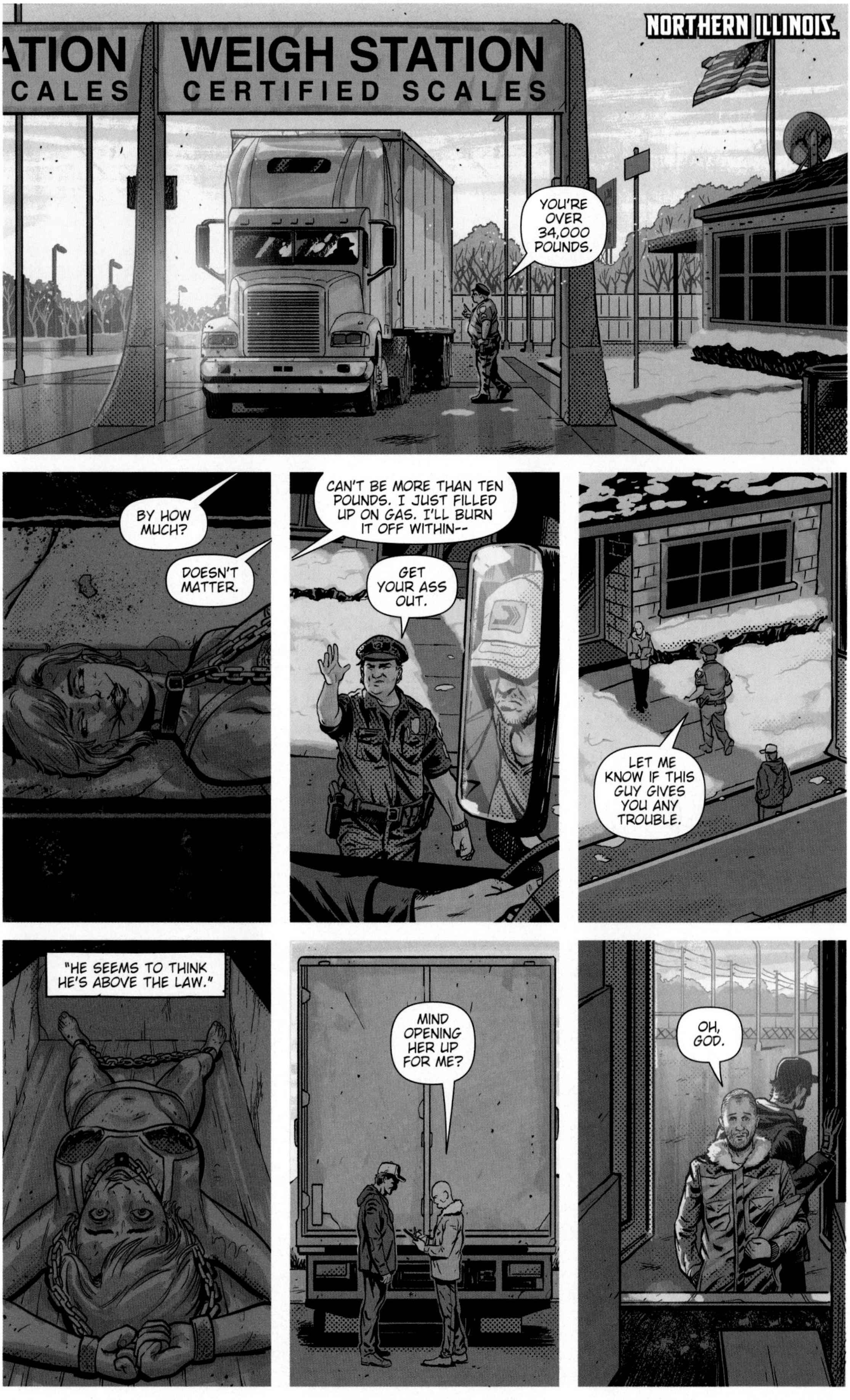
NORTHERN ILLINOIS.
WEIGH STATION
CERTIFIED SCALES
ATION
CALES
YOU'RE OVER 34,000 POUNDS.
BY HOW MUCH?
DOESN'T MATTER.
CAN'T BE MORE THAN TEN POUNDS. I JUST FILLED UP ON GAS. I'LL BURN IT OFF WITHIN--
GET YOUR ASS OUT.
LET ME KNOW IF THIS GUY GIVES YOU ANY TROUBLE.
"HE SEEMS TO THINK HE'S ABOVE THE LAW."
MIND OPENING HER UP FOR ME?
OH, GOD.

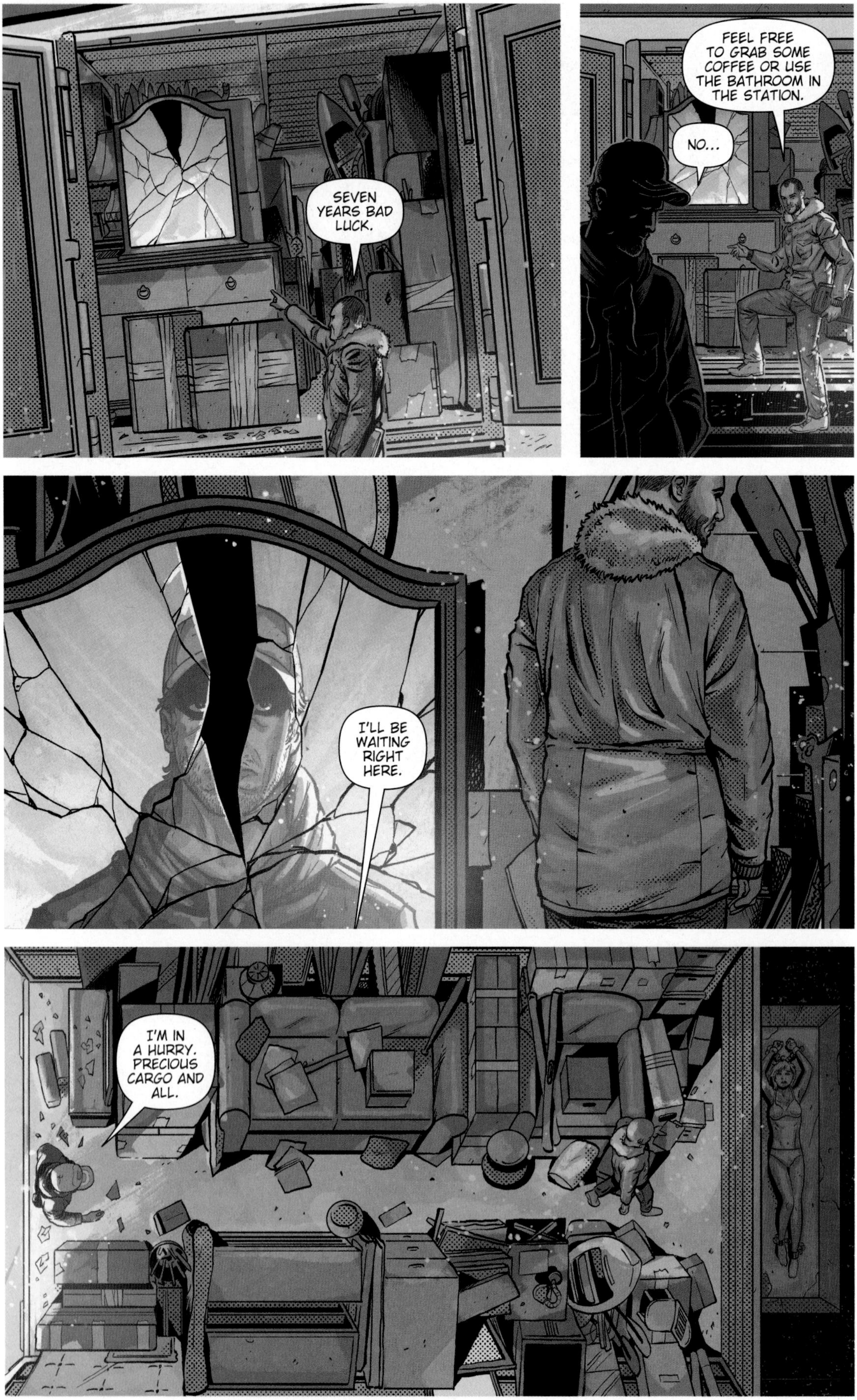
SEVEN YEARS BAD LUCK.
FEEL FREE TO GRAB SOME COFFEE OR USE THE BATHROOM IN THE STATION.
NO...
I'LL BE WAITING RIGHT HERE.
I'M IN A HURRY. PRECIOUS CARGO AND ALL.

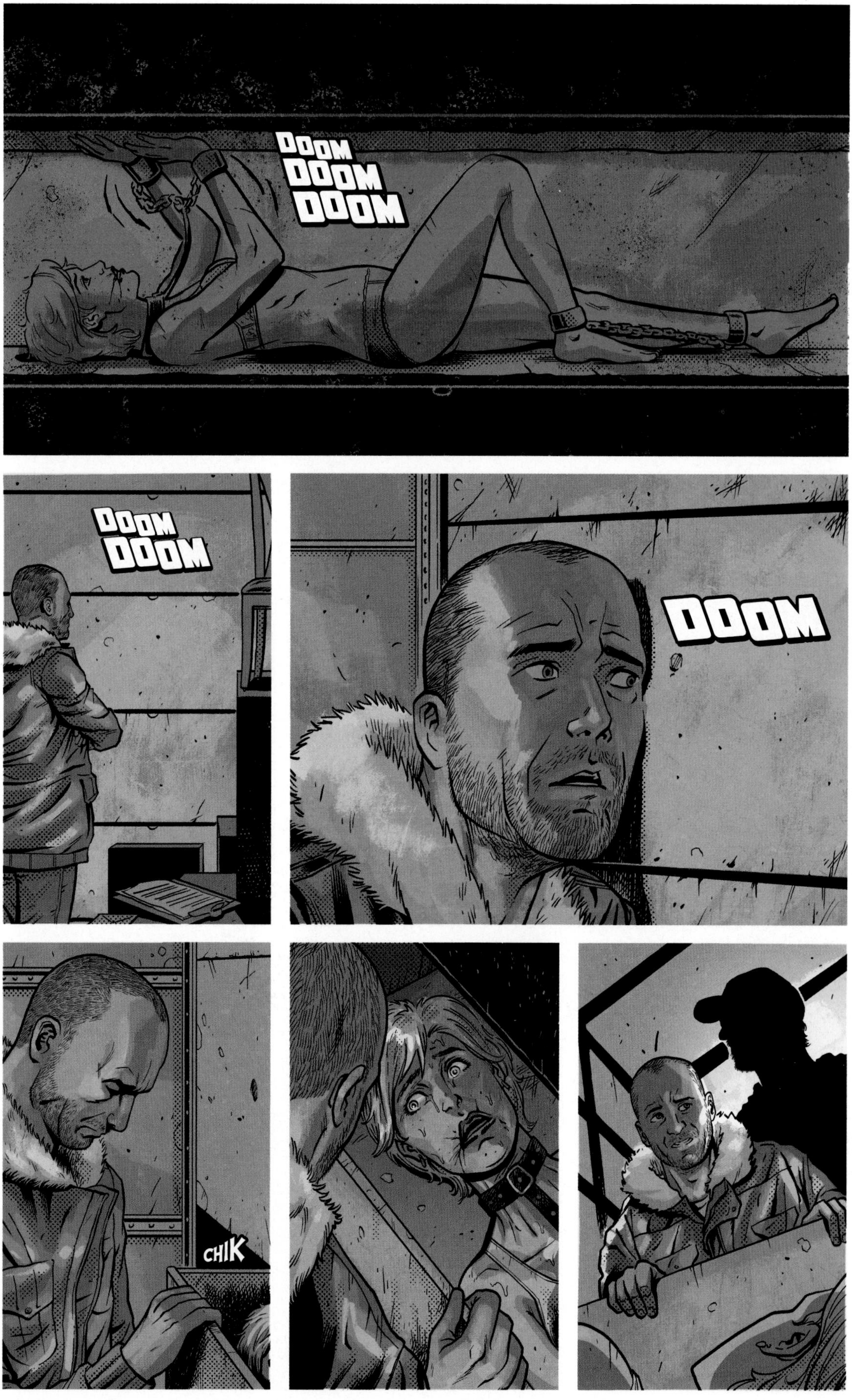
DOOM
DOOM
DOOM
DOOM
DOOM
DOOM
CHIK

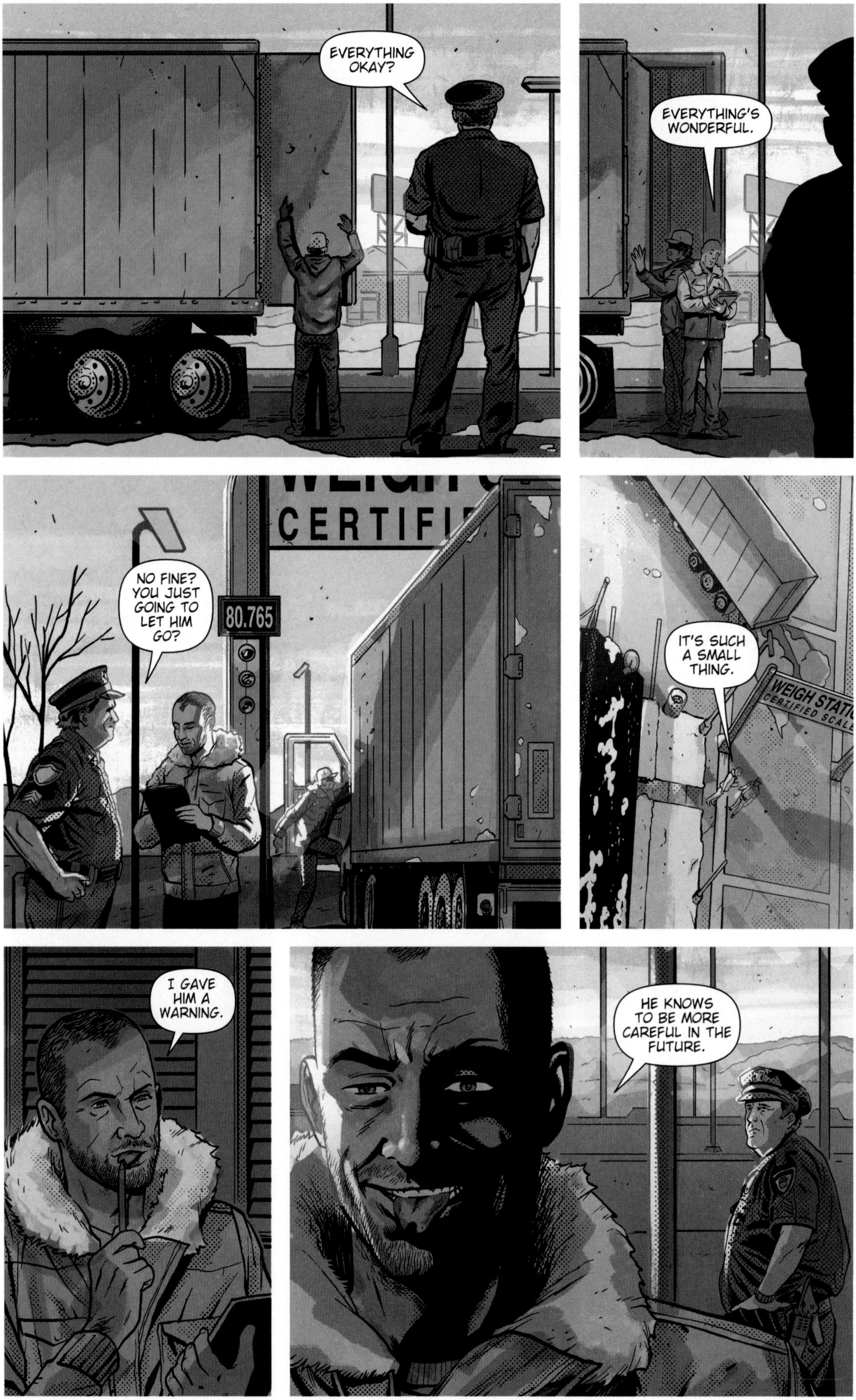
EVERYTHING OKAY?
EVERYTHING'S WONDERFUL.
WEIGH
CERTIFI
NO FINE? YOU JUST GOING TO LET HIM GO?
80.765
IT'S SUCH A SMALL THING.
WEIGH STATI
CERTIFIED SCALE
I GAVE HIM A WARNING.
HE KNOWS TO BE MORE CAREFUL IN THE FUTURE.

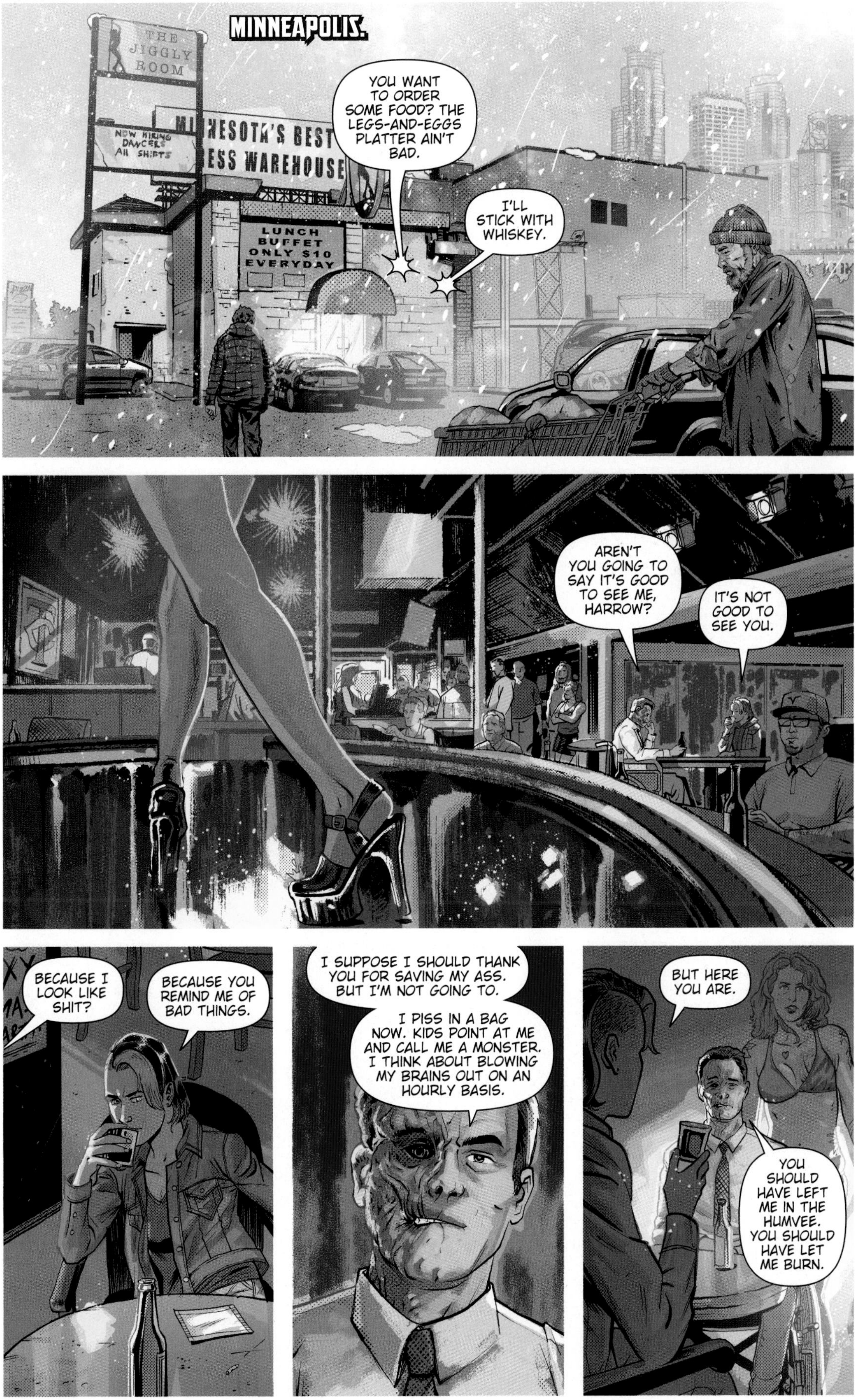
MINNEAPOLIS.
THE JIGGLY ROOM
NOW HIRING DANCERS ALL SHIFTS
LUNCH BUFFET ONLY $10 EVERYDAY
YOU WANT TO ORDER SOME FOOD? THE LEGS-AND-EGGS PLATTER AIN'T BAD.
I'LL STICK WITH WHISKEY.
AREN'T YOU GOING TO SAY IT'S GOOD TO SEE ME, HARROW?
IT'S NOT GOOD TO SEE YOU.
BECAUSE I LOOK LIKE SHIT?
BECAUSE YOU REMIND ME OF BAD THINGS.
I SUPPOSE I SHOULD THANK YOU FOR SAVING MY ASS. BUT I'M NOT GOING TO.
I PISS IN A BAG NOW. KIDS POINT AT ME AND CALL ME A MONSTER. I THINK ABOUT BLOWING MY BRAINS OUT ON AN HOURLY BASIS.
BUT HERE YOU ARE.
YOU SHOULD HAVE LEFT ME IN THE HUMVEE. YOU SHOULD HAVE LET ME BURN.

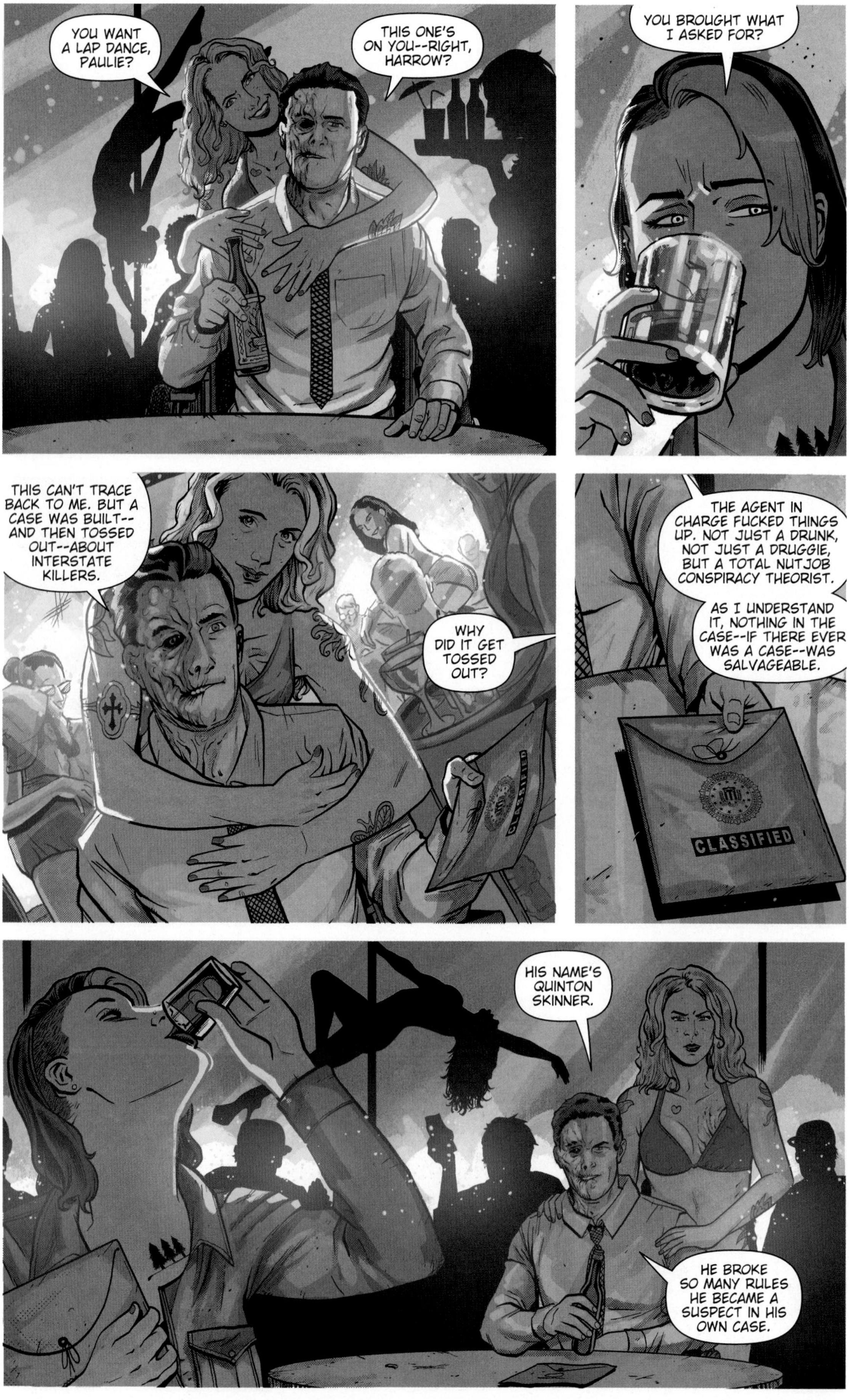
YOU WANT A LAP DANCE, PAULIE?
THIS ONE'S ON YOU--RIGHT, HARROW?
YOU BROUGHT WHAT I ASKED FOR?
THIS CAN'T TRACE BACK TO ME. BUT A CASE WAS BUILT-- AND THEN TOSSED OUT--ABOUT INTERSTATE KILLERS.
WHY DID IT GET TOSSED OUT?
CLASSIFIED
THE AGENT IN CHARGE FUCKED THINGS UP. NOT JUST A DRUNK, NOT JUST A DRUGGIE, BUT A TOTAL NUTJOB CONSPIRACY THEORIST.
AS I UNDERSTAND IT, NOTHING IN THE CASE--IF THERE EVER WAS A CASE--WAS SALVAGEABLE.
CLASSIFIED
HIS NAME'S QUINTON SKINNER.
HE BROKE SO MANY RULES HE BECAME A SUSPECT IN HIS OWN CASE.

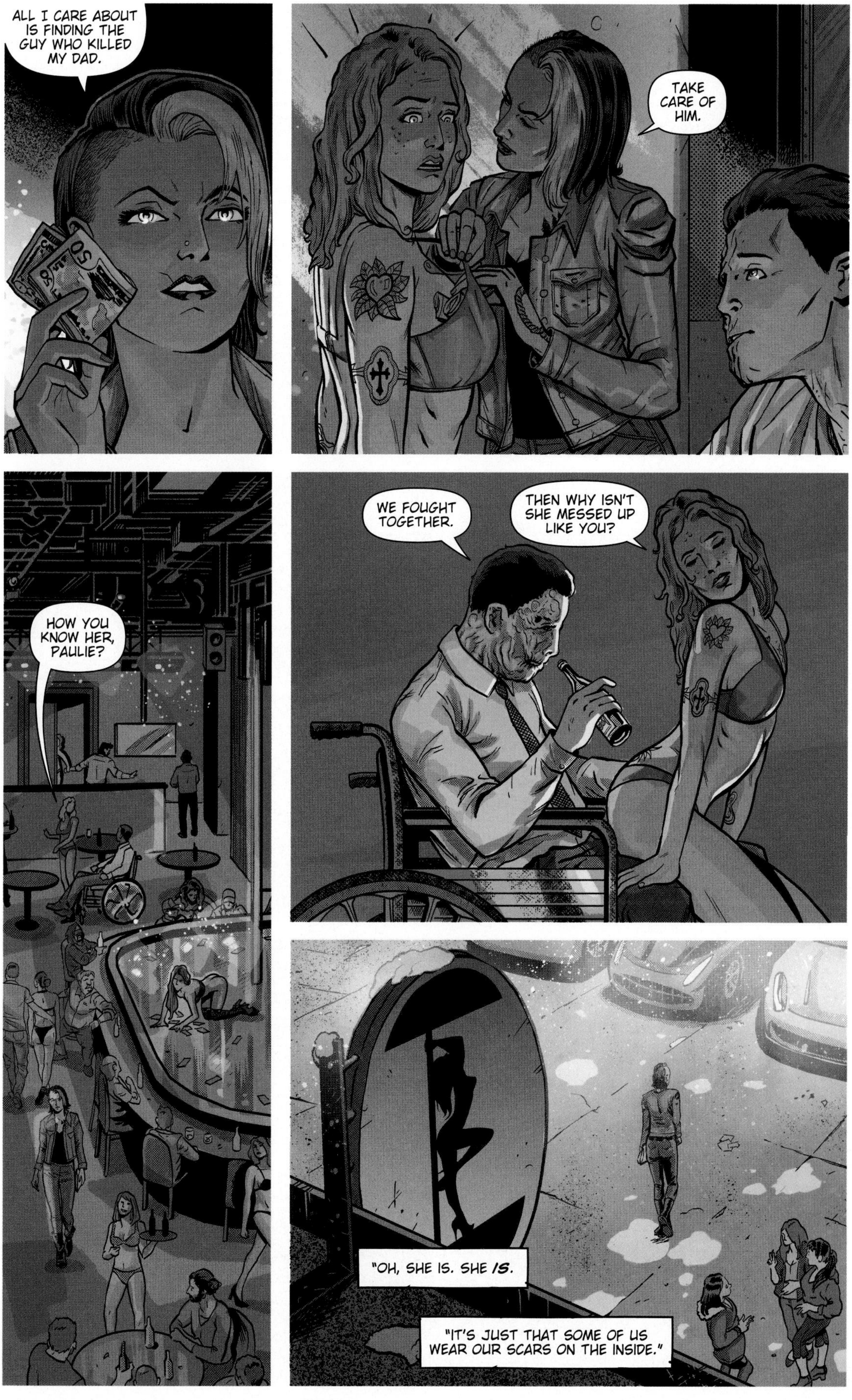
ALL I CARE ABOUT IS FINDING THE GUY WHO KILLED MY DAD.
TAKE CARE OF HIM.
HOW YOU KNOW HER, PAULIE?
WE FOUGHT TOGETHER.
THEN WHY ISN'T SHE MESSED UP LIKE YOU?
"OH, SHE IS. SHE *IS*.
"IT'S JUST THAT SOME OF US WEAR OUR SCARS ON THE INSIDE."

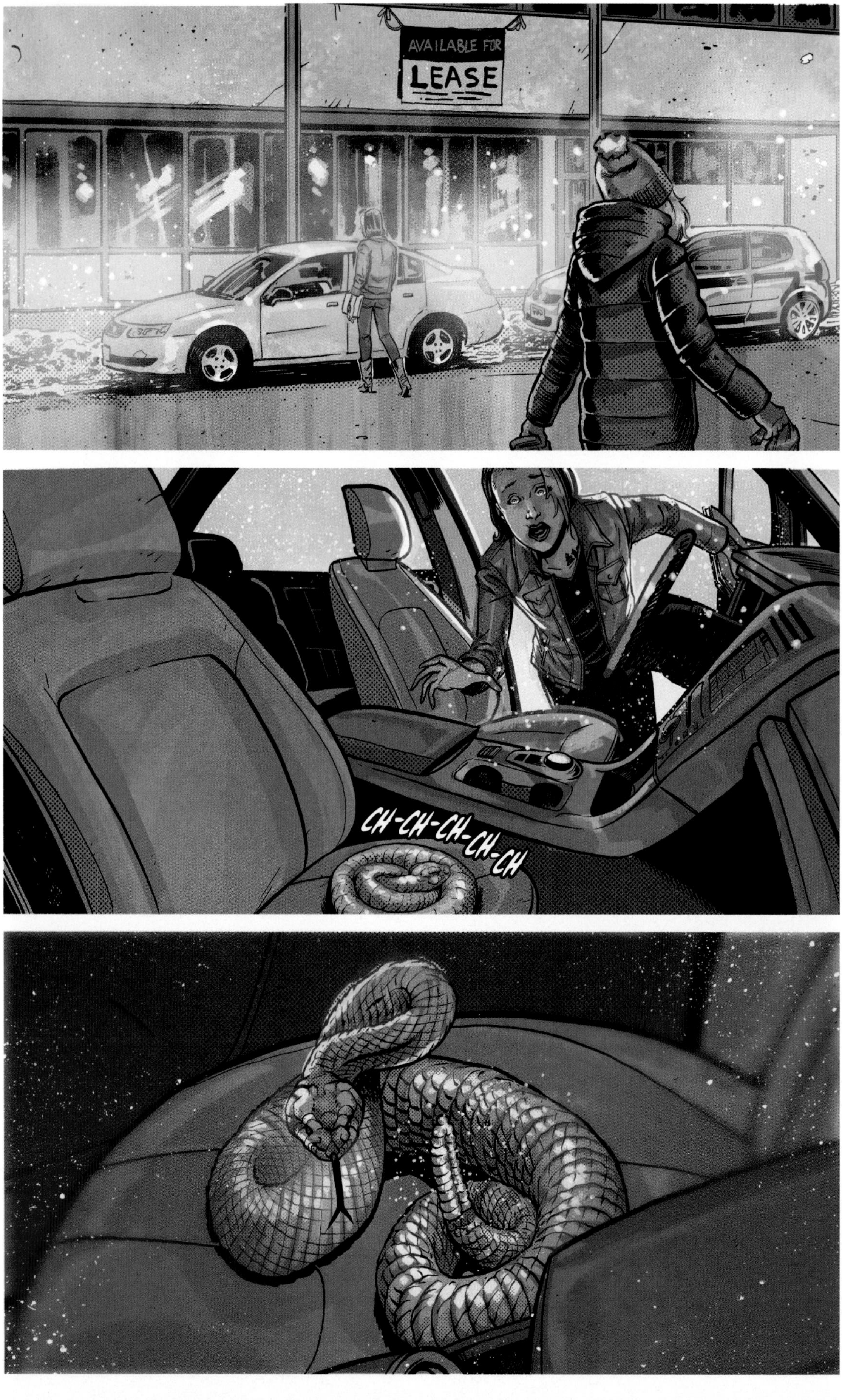
AVAILABLE FOR
LEASE
CH-CH-CH-CH-CH

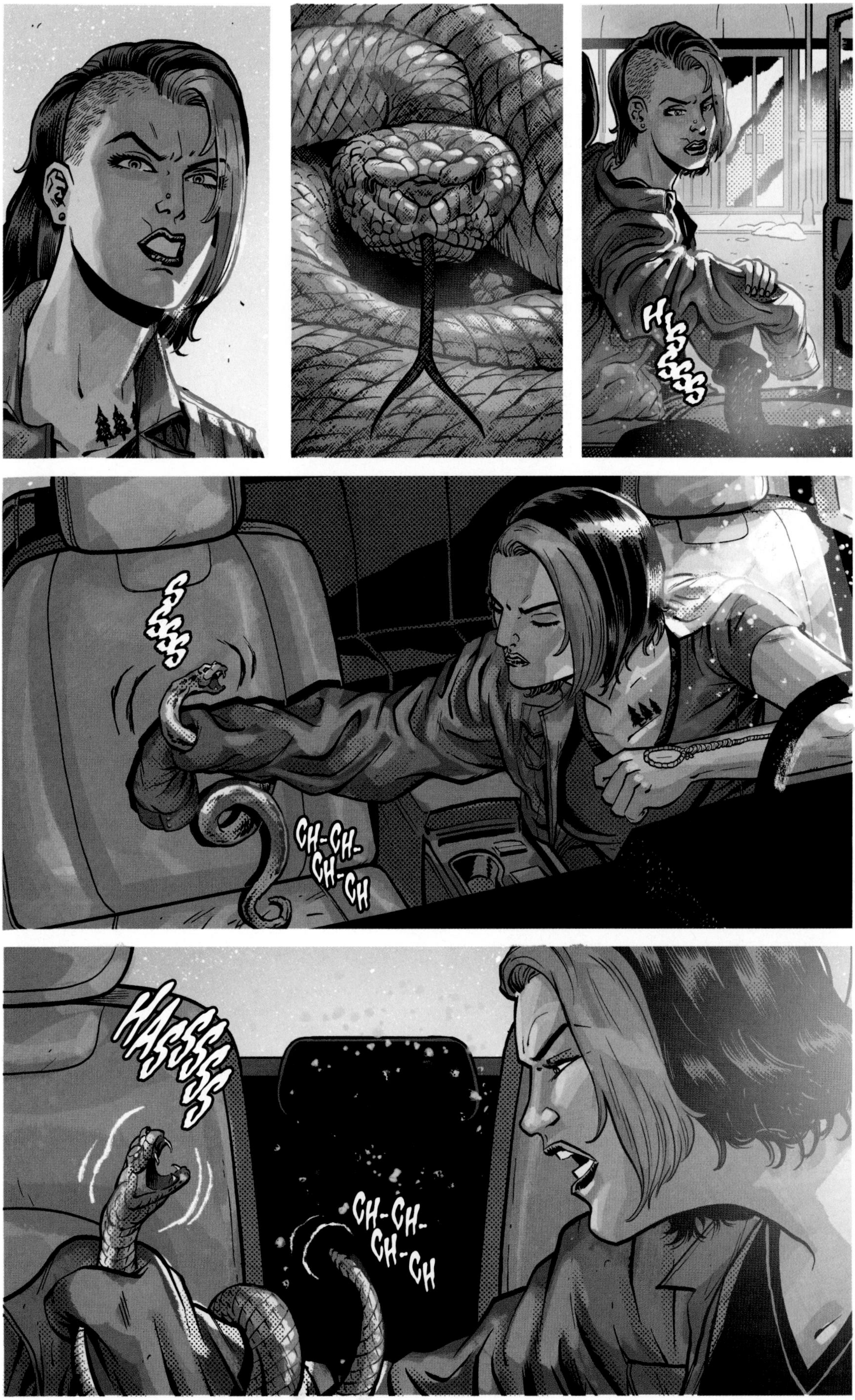
HISSSS
SSSS
CH-CH-CH-CH
HASSSSS
CH-CH-CH-CH

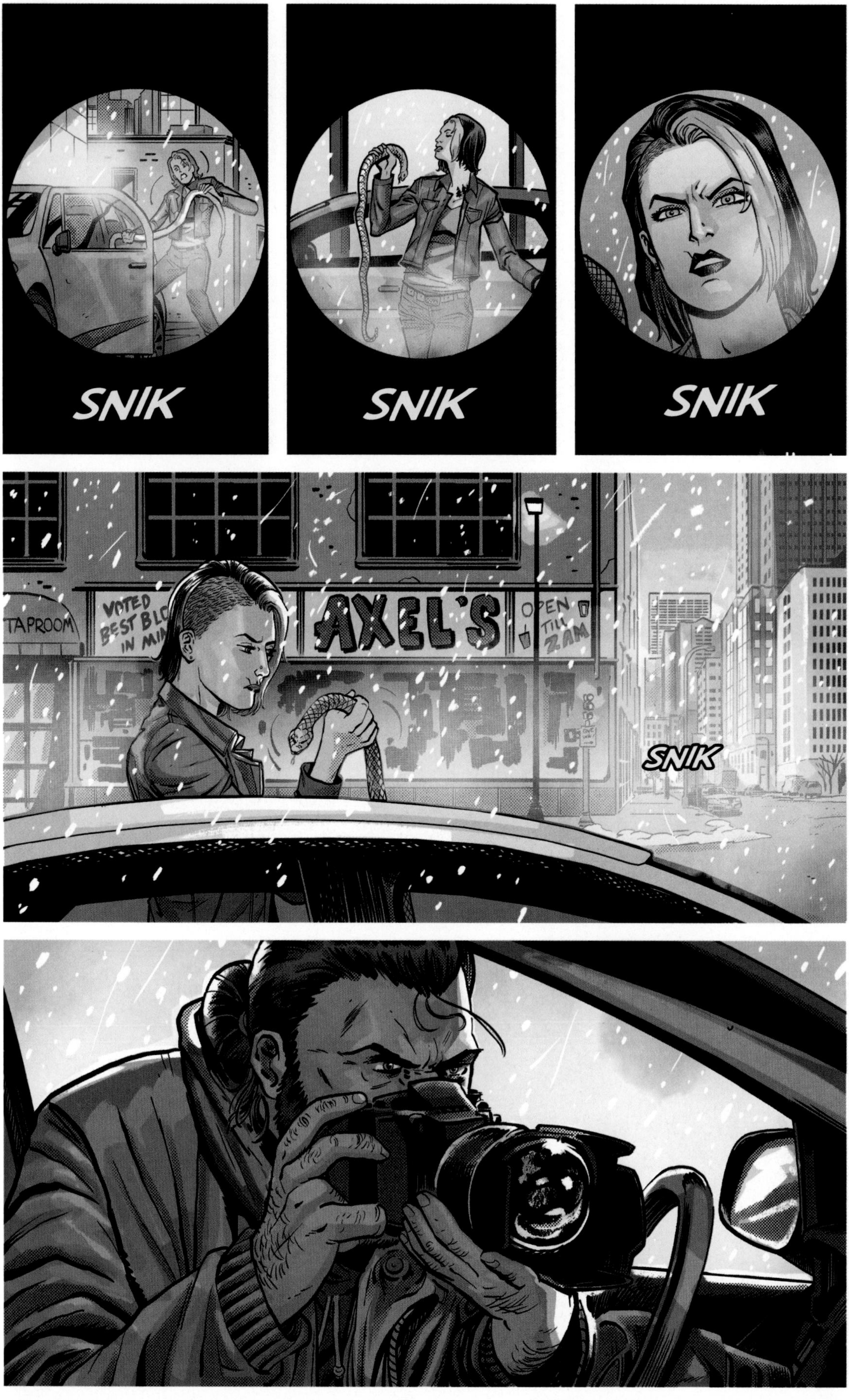
SNIK
SNIK
SNIK
TAPROOM
VOTED
BEST
AXEL'S
OPEN
TILL
2AM
SNIK

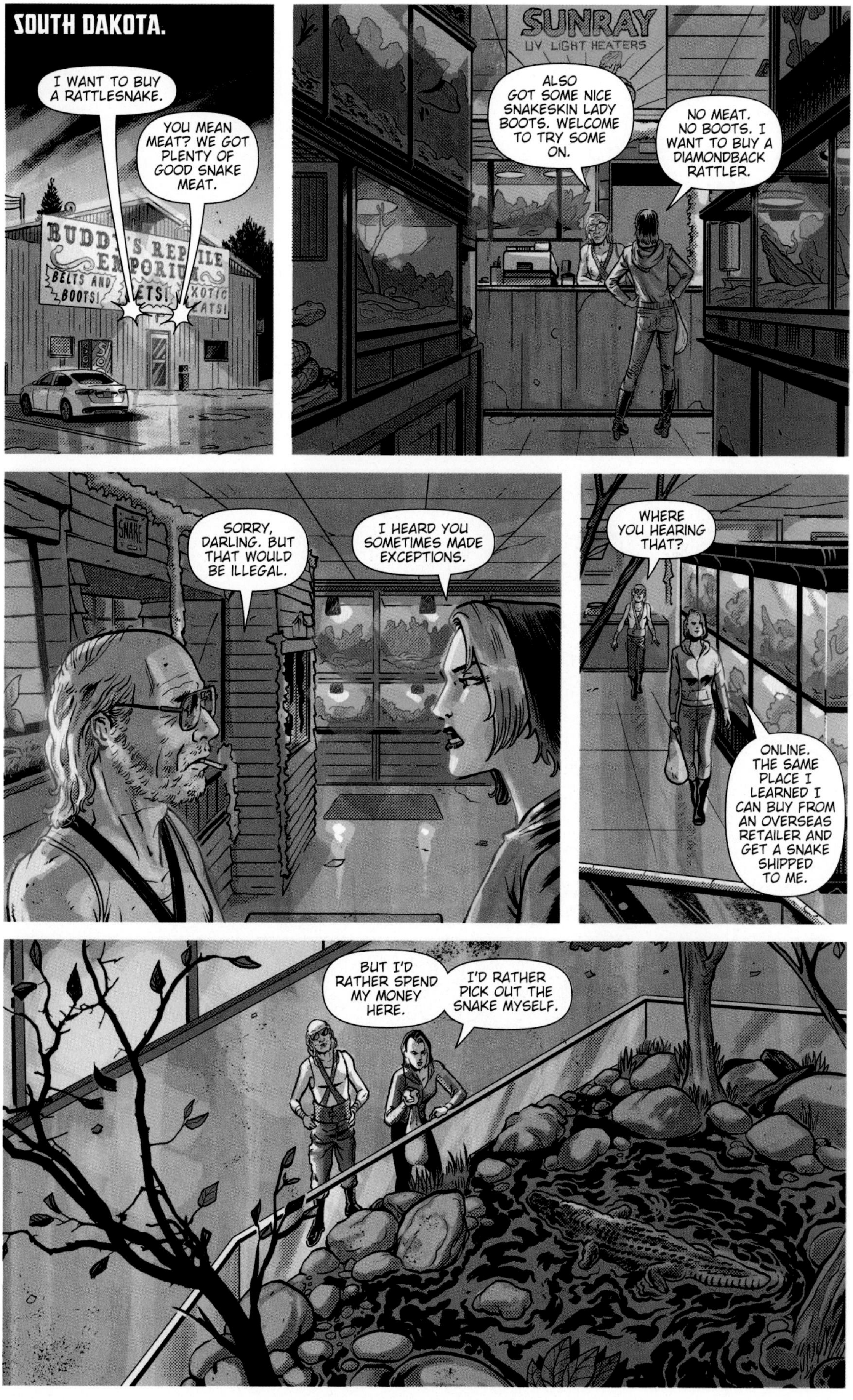
SOUTH DAKOTA.
I WANT TO BUY A RATTLESNAKE.
YOU MEAN MEAT? WE GOT PLENTY OF GOOD SNAKE MEAT.
BELTS AND BOOTS!
SUNRAY
UV LIGHT HEATERS
ALSO GOT SOME NICE SNAKESKIN LADY BOOTS. WELCOME TO TRY SOME ON.
NO MEAT. NO BOOTS. I WANT TO BUY A DIAMONDBACK RATTLER.
SNAKE
SORRY, DARLING. BUT THAT WOULD BE ILLEGAL.
I HEARD YOU SOMETIMES MADE EXCEPTIONS.
WHERE YOU HEARING THAT?
ONLINE. THE SAME PLACE I LEARNED I CAN BUY FROM AN OVERSEAS RETAILER AND GET A SNAKE SHIPPED TO ME.
BUT I'D RATHER SPEND MY MONEY HERE.
I'D RATHER PICK OUT THE SNAKE MYSELF.

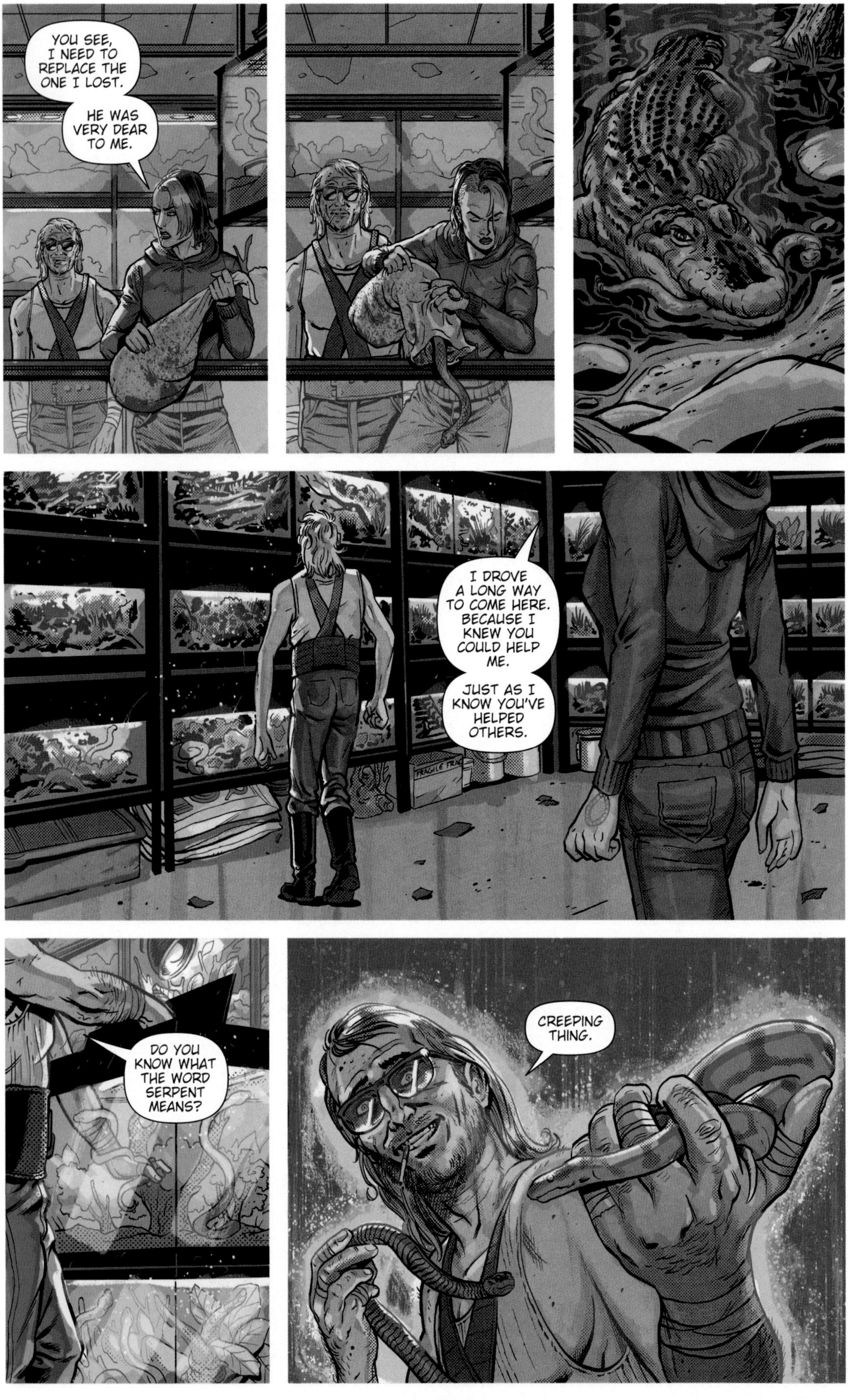
YOU SEE, I NEED TO REPLACE THE ONE I LOST.
HE WAS VERY DEAR TO ME.
I DROVE A LONG WAY TO COME HERE. BECAUSE I KNEW YOU COULD HELP ME.
JUST AS I KNOW YOU'VE HELPED OTHERS.
FRAGILE
DO YOU KNOW WHAT THE WORD SERPENT MEANS?
CREEPING THING.

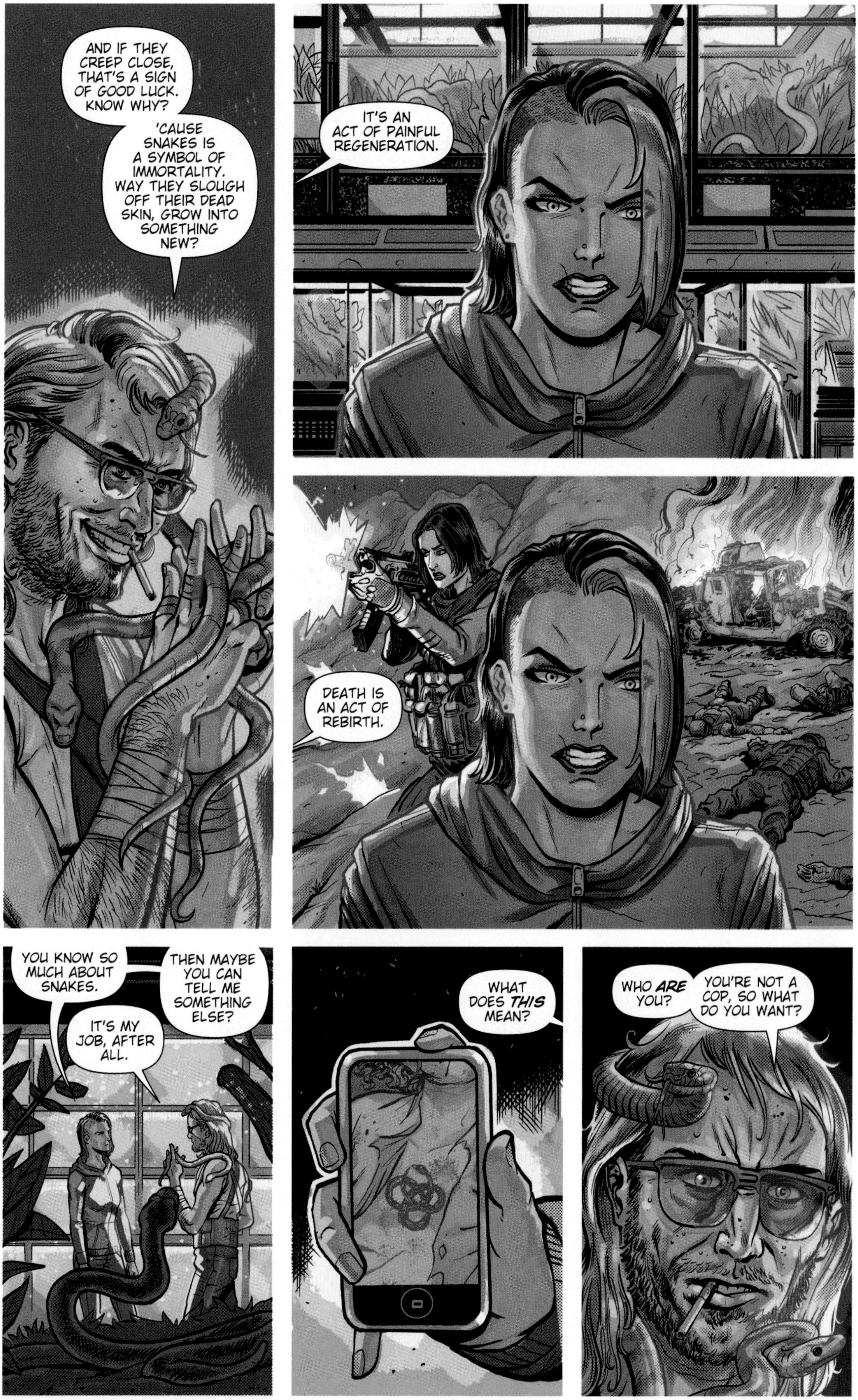
AND IF THEY CREEP CLOSE, THAT'S A SIGN OF GOOD LUCK. KNOW WHY?
'CAUSE SNAKES IS A SYMBOL OF IMMORTALITY. WAY THEY SLOUGH OFF THEIR DEAD SKIN, GROW INTO SOMETHING NEW?
IT'S AN ACT OF PAINFUL REGENERATION.
DEATH IS AN ACT OF REBIRTH.
YOU KNOW SO MUCH ABOUT SNAKES.
IT'S MY JOB, AFTER ALL.
THEN MAYBE YOU CAN TELL ME SOMETHING ELSE?
WHAT DOES THIS MEAN?
WHO ARE YOU?
YOU'RE NOT A COP, SO WHAT DO YOU WANT?

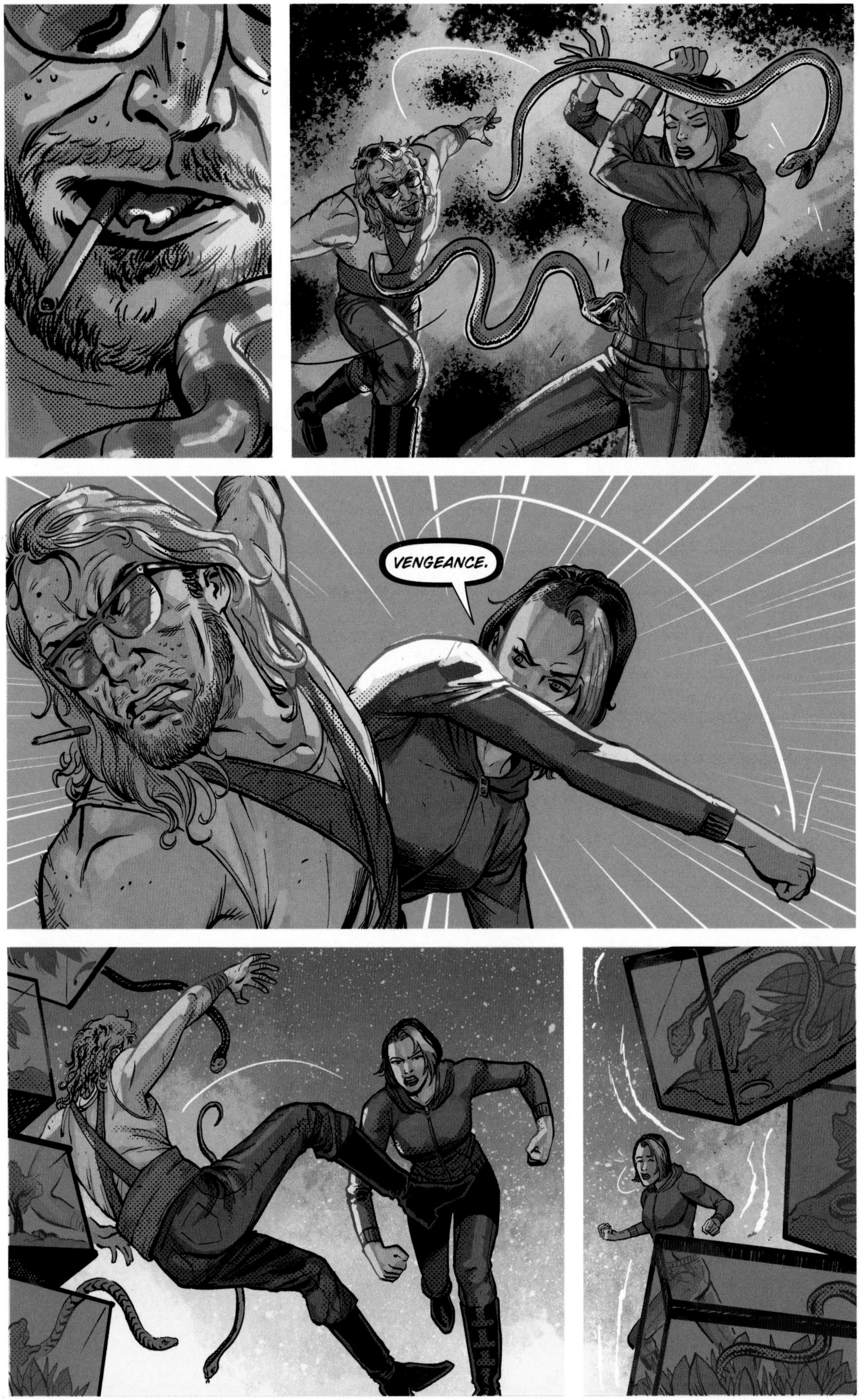
VENGEANCE.

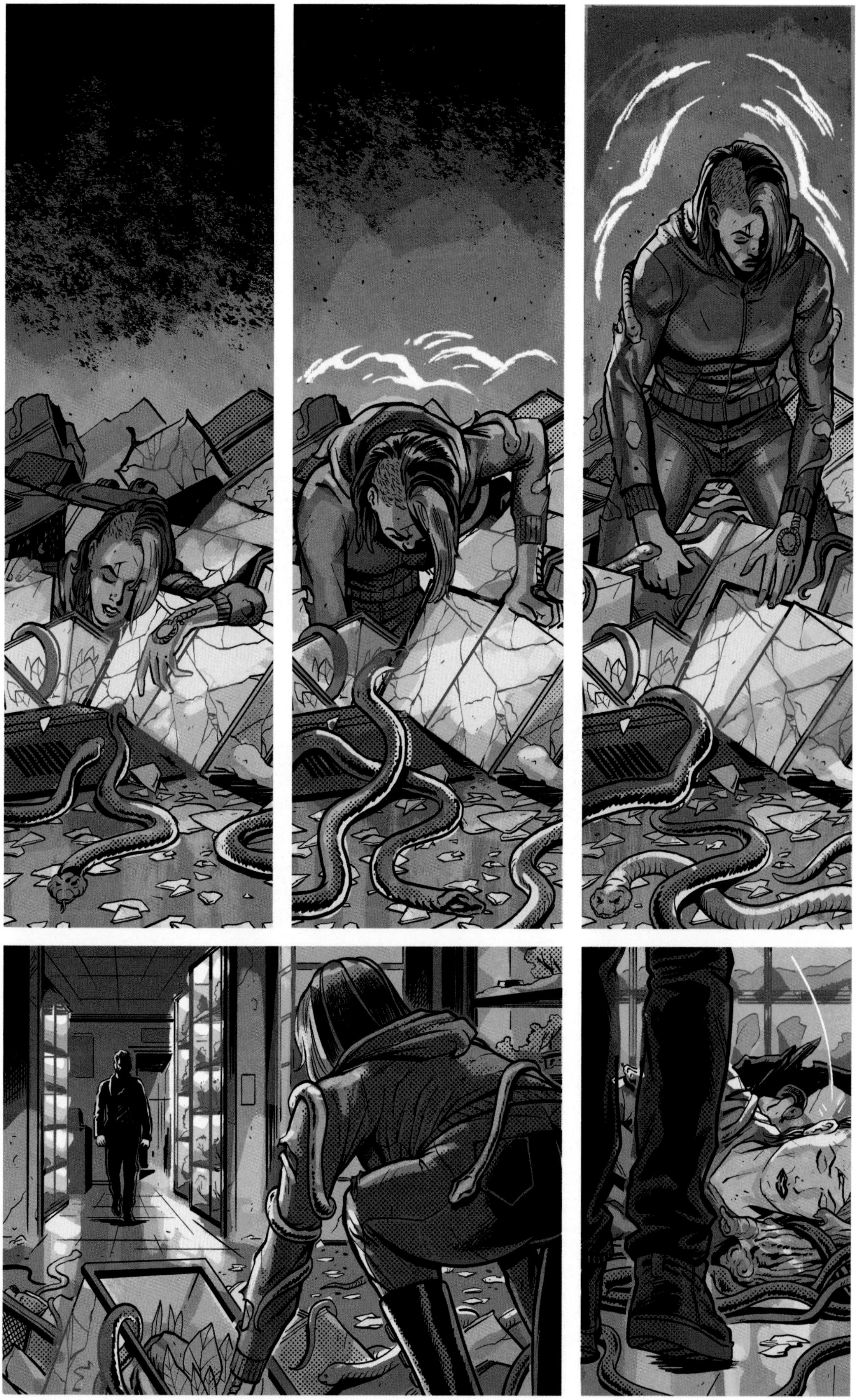

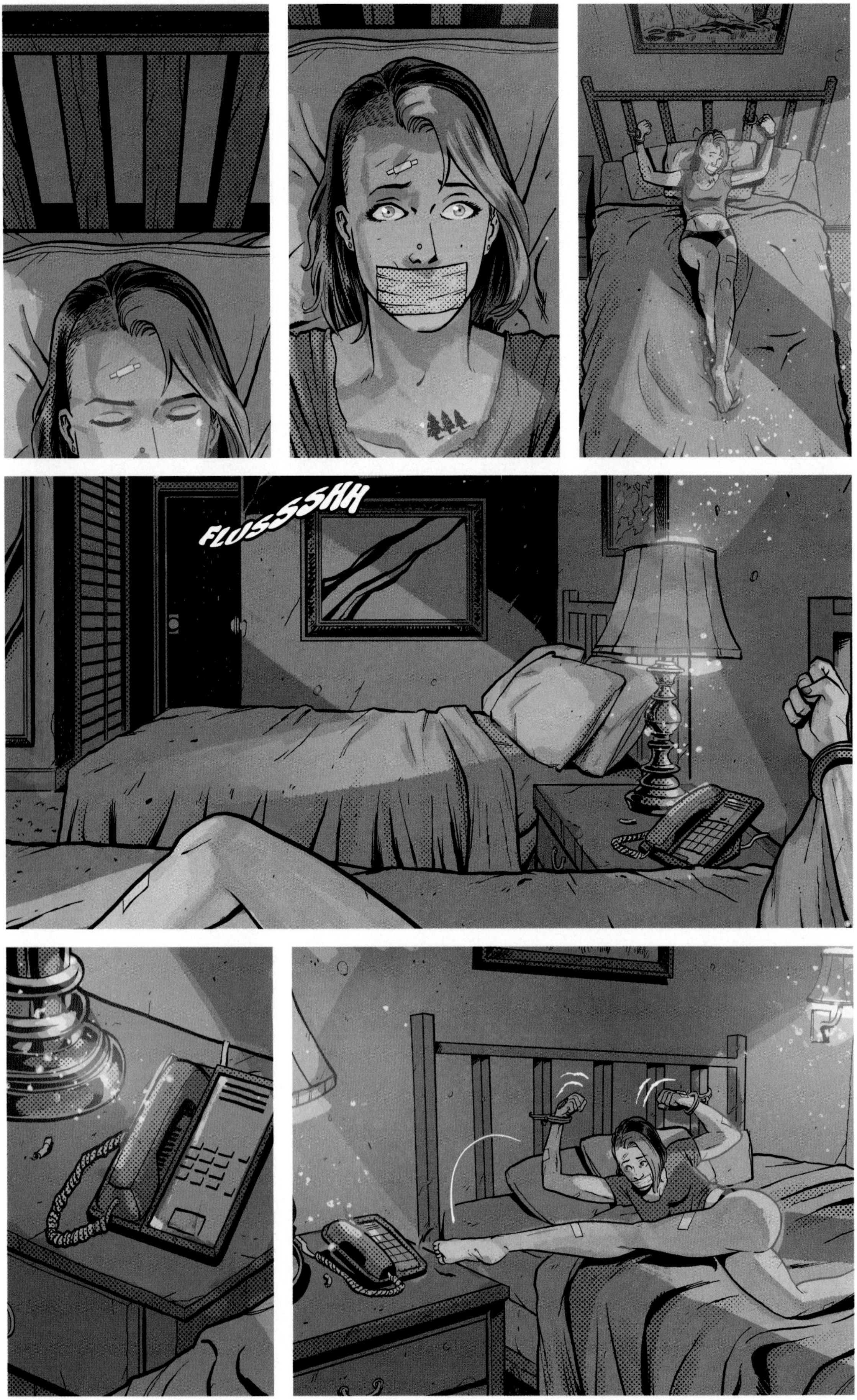
FLUSSSHH

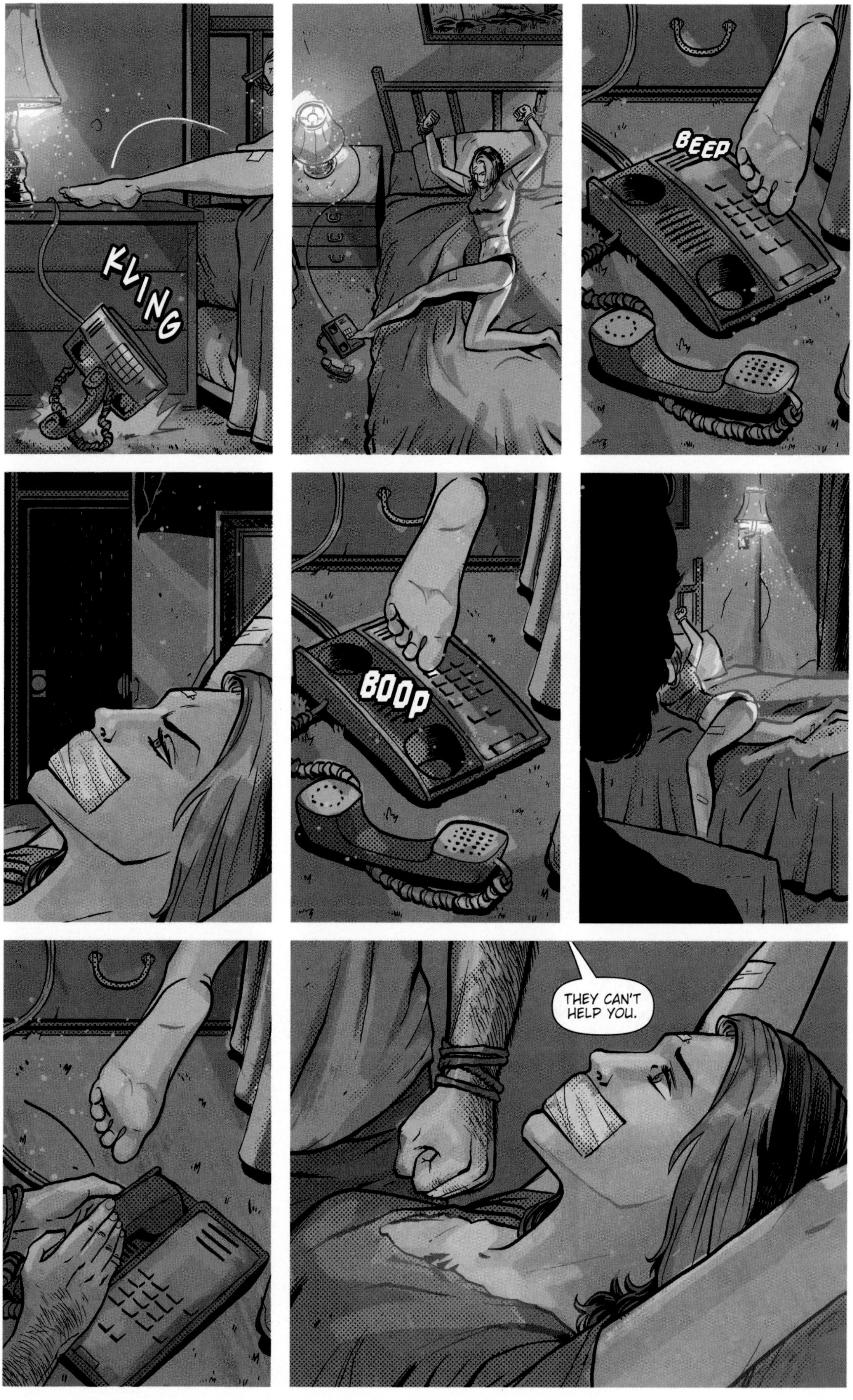
KVING
BEEP
BOOP
THEY CAN'T HELP YOU.

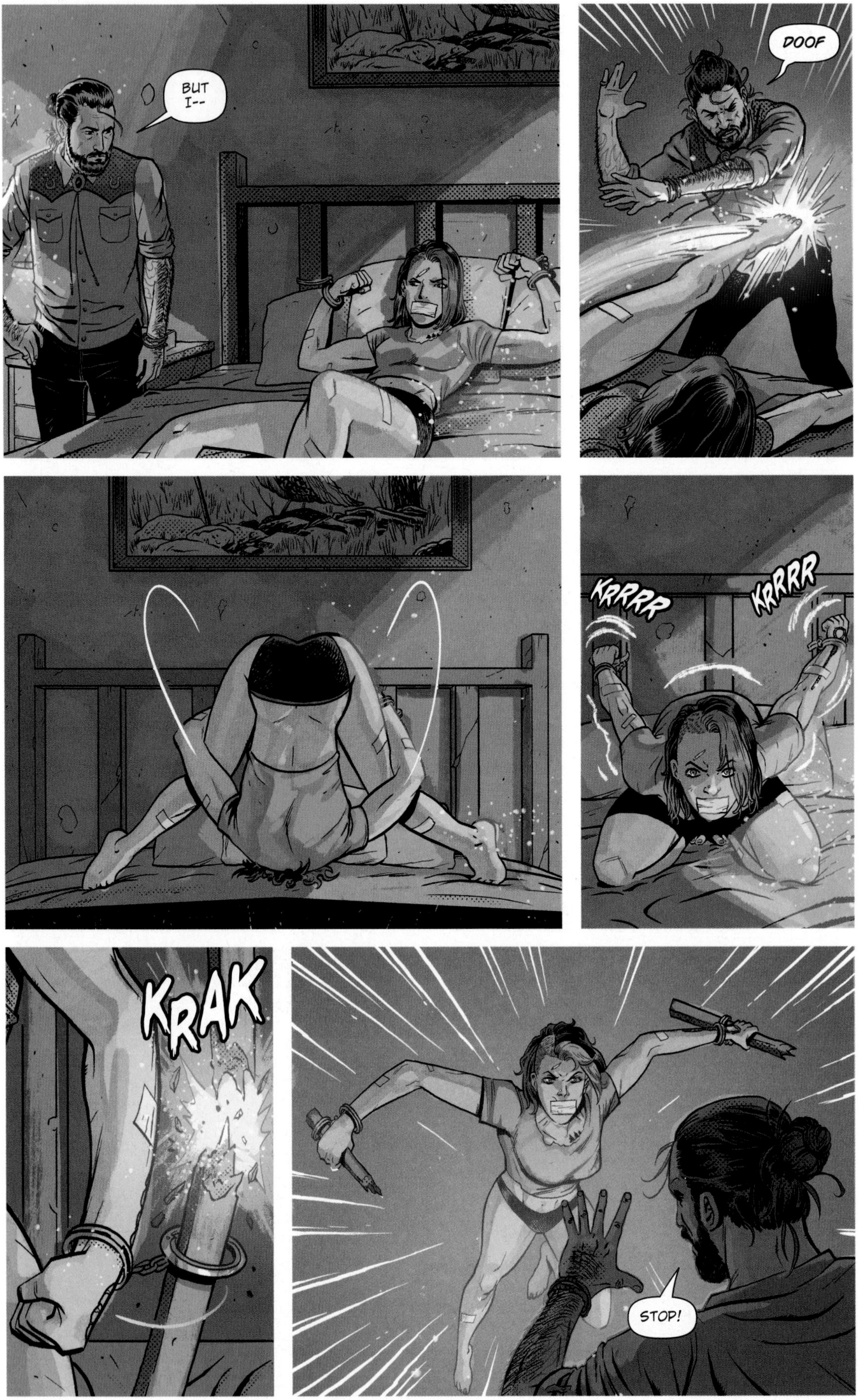
BUT I--
DOOF
KRRRR
KRRRR
KRAK
STOP!

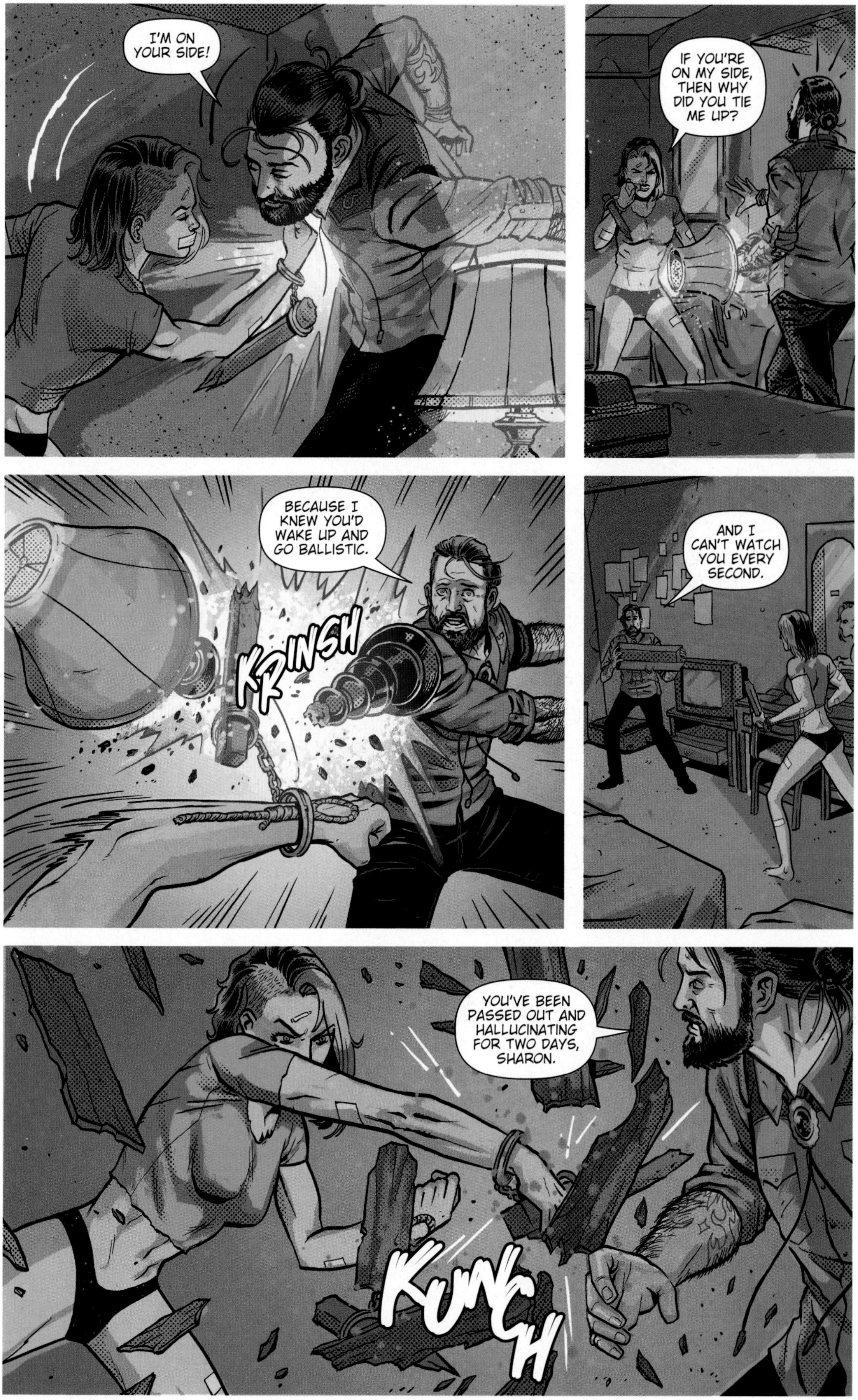
I'M ON YOUR SIDE!
IF YOU'RE ON MY SIDE, THEN WHY DID YOU TIE ME UP?
BECAUSE I KNEW YOU'D WAKE UP AND GO BALLISTIC.
KRINSH
AND I CAN'T WATCH YOU EVERY SECOND.
YOU'VE BEEN PASSED OUT AND HALLUCINATING FOR TWO DAYS, SHARON.
KUNCH

TWO DAYS...

I'M THE ONE WHO BANDAGED YOU UP. I'M THE ONE WHO GAVE YOU THE ANTI-VENOM. I'M THE ONE WHO'S BEEN KEEPING YOUR FEVER DOWN WITH ICE PACKS.

WHY DIDN'T YOU TAKE ME TO THE HOSPITAL?

BECAUSE THEN THEY'D KNOW WHERE TO FIND YOU.

"THEY"?

YES. THEY. THEY ARE MANY.

UNSOLVED ROADSIDE MURDERS ALONG MIDWESTERN HIGHWAYS

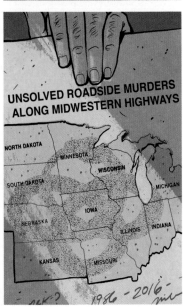

UNSOLVED ROADSIDE MURDERS ALONG MIDWESTERN HIGHWAYS

NORTH DAKOTA

MINNESOTA

SOUTH DAKOTA

WISCONSIN

MICHIGAN

NEBRASKA

IOWA

ILLINOIS

INDIANA

KANSAS

MISSOURI

1986 - 2016

DEVIL'S HIGHWAY
Benjamin PERCY
Brent SCHOONOVER
Nick FILARDI

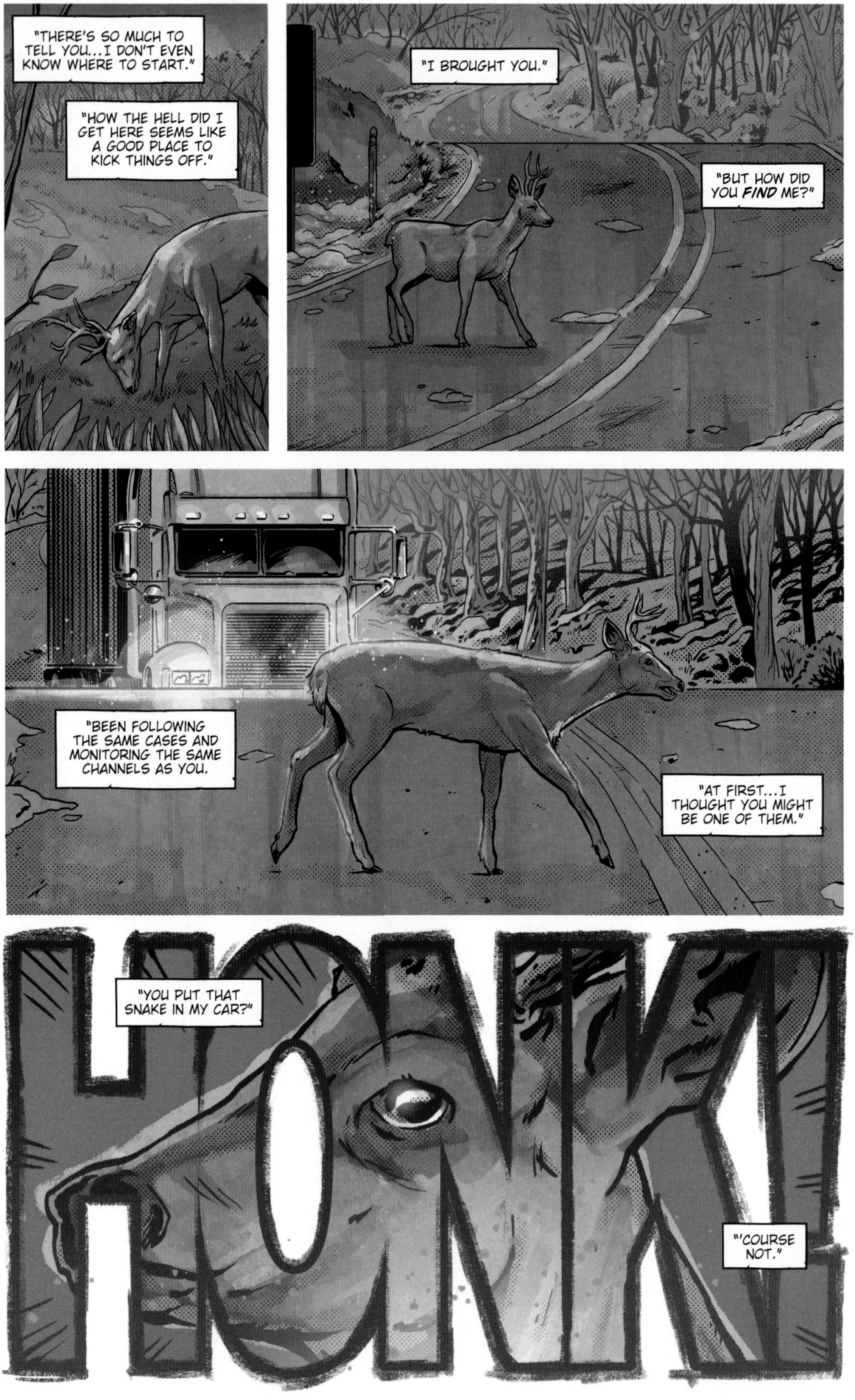
"THERE'S SO MUCH TO TELL YOU...I DON'T EVEN KNOW WHERE TO START."
"HOW THE HELL DID I GET HERE SEEMS LIKE A GOOD PLACE TO KICK THINGS OFF."
"I BROUGHT YOU."
"BUT HOW DID YOU *FIND* ME?"
"BEEN FOLLOWING THE SAME CASES AND MONITORING THE SAME CHANNELS AS YOU.
"AT FIRST...I THOUGHT YOU MIGHT BE ONE OF THEM."
HONK!
"YOU PUT THAT SNAKE IN MY CAR?"
"'COURSE NOT."

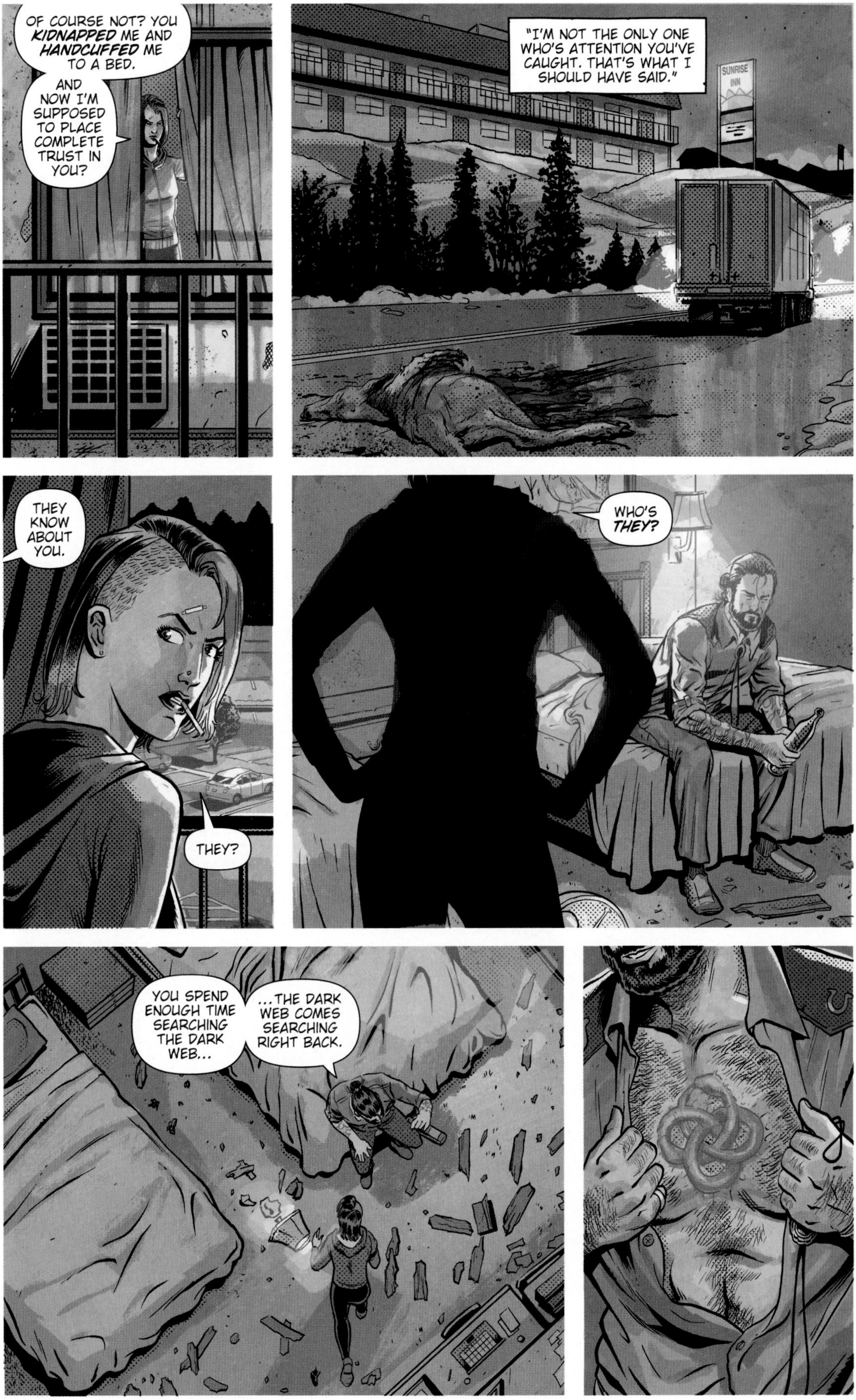
OF COURSE NOT? YOU KIDNAPPED ME AND HANDCUFFED ME TO A BED.
AND NOW I'M SUPPOSED TO PLACE COMPLETE TRUST IN YOU?
"I'M NOT THE ONLY ONE WHO'S ATTENTION YOU'VE CAUGHT. THAT'S WHAT I SHOULD HAVE SAID."
SUNRISE INN
THEY KNOW ABOUT YOU.
THEY?
WHO'S THEY?
YOU SPEND ENOUGH TIME SEARCHING THE DARK WEB...
...THE DARK WEB COMES SEARCHING RIGHT BACK.

YOU DID THAT TO YOURSELF?

I WAS... I HAD A LITTLE TOO MUCH AND I...

MY OLD BOSS, HE SAID I LET MYSELF GET TOO WRAPPED UP IN MY CASES.

HE SAID I HAD TOO MUCH EMPATHY. A DANGEROUS AMOUNT OF EMPATHY. YOU KNOW WHAT I MEAN?

NO.

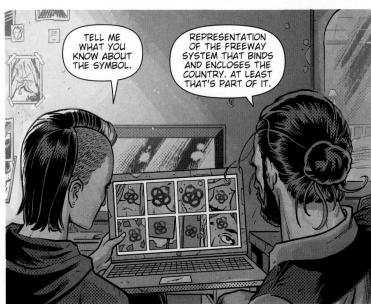

TELL ME WHAT YOU KNOW ABOUT THE SYMBOL.

REPRESENTATION OF THE FREEWAY SYSTEM THAT BINDS AND ENCLOSES THE COUNTRY. AT LEAST THAT'S PART OF IT.

WHAT'S THE OTHER PART?

OCCULTIST STUFF I DON'T QUITE UNDERSTAND.

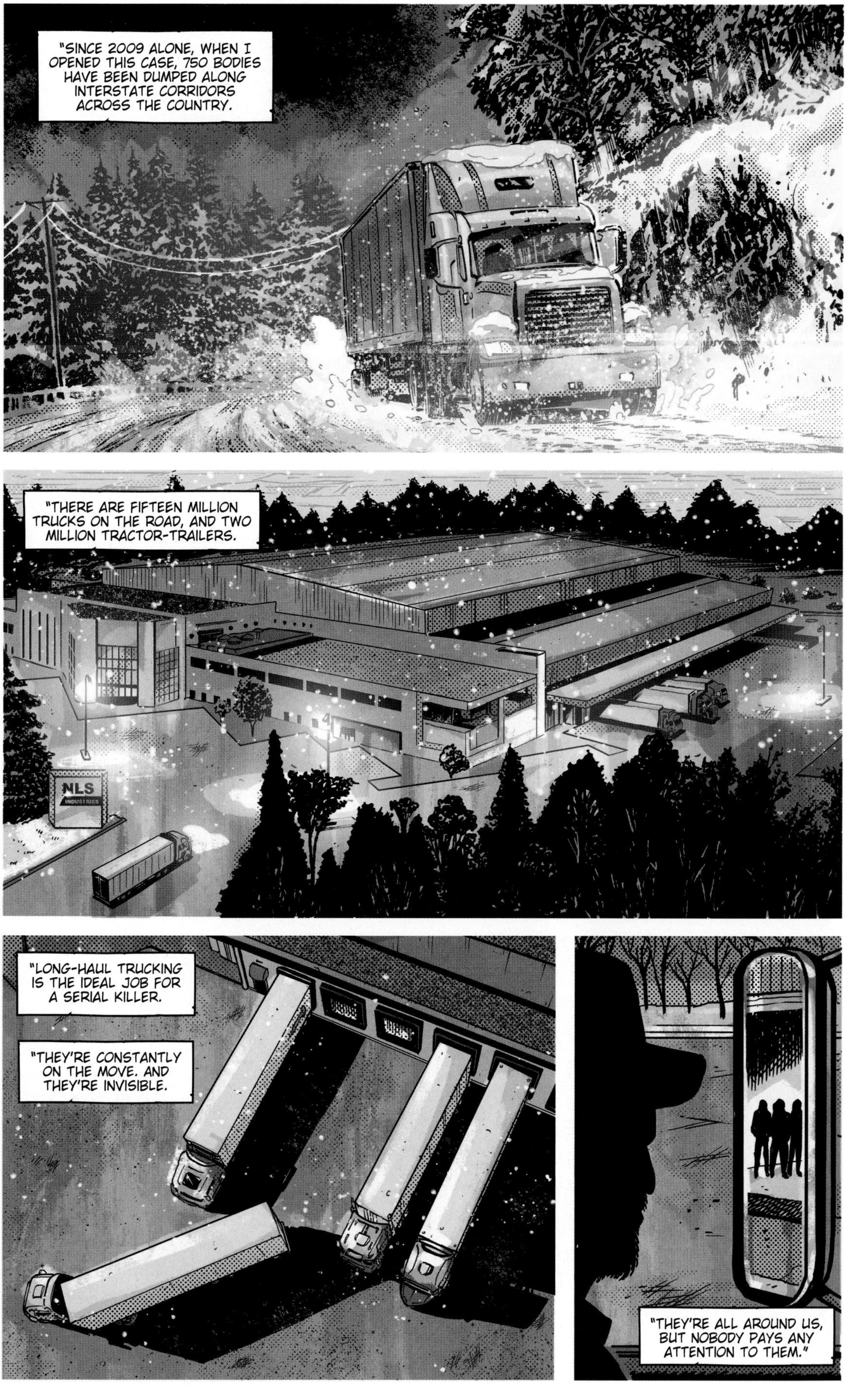
"SINCE 2009 ALONE, WHEN I OPENED THIS CASE, 750 BODIES HAVE BEEN DUMPED ALONG INTERSTATE CORRIDORS ACROSS THE COUNTRY.
"THERE ARE FIFTEEN MILLION TRUCKS ON THE ROAD, AND TWO MILLION TRACTOR-TRAILERS.
NLS
INDUSTRIES
"LONG-HAUL TRUCKING IS THE IDEAL JOB FOR A SERIAL KILLER.
"THEY'RE CONSTANTLY ON THE MOVE. AND THEY'RE INVISIBLE.
"THEY'RE ALL AROUND US, BUT NOBODY PAYS ANY ATTENTION TO THEM."

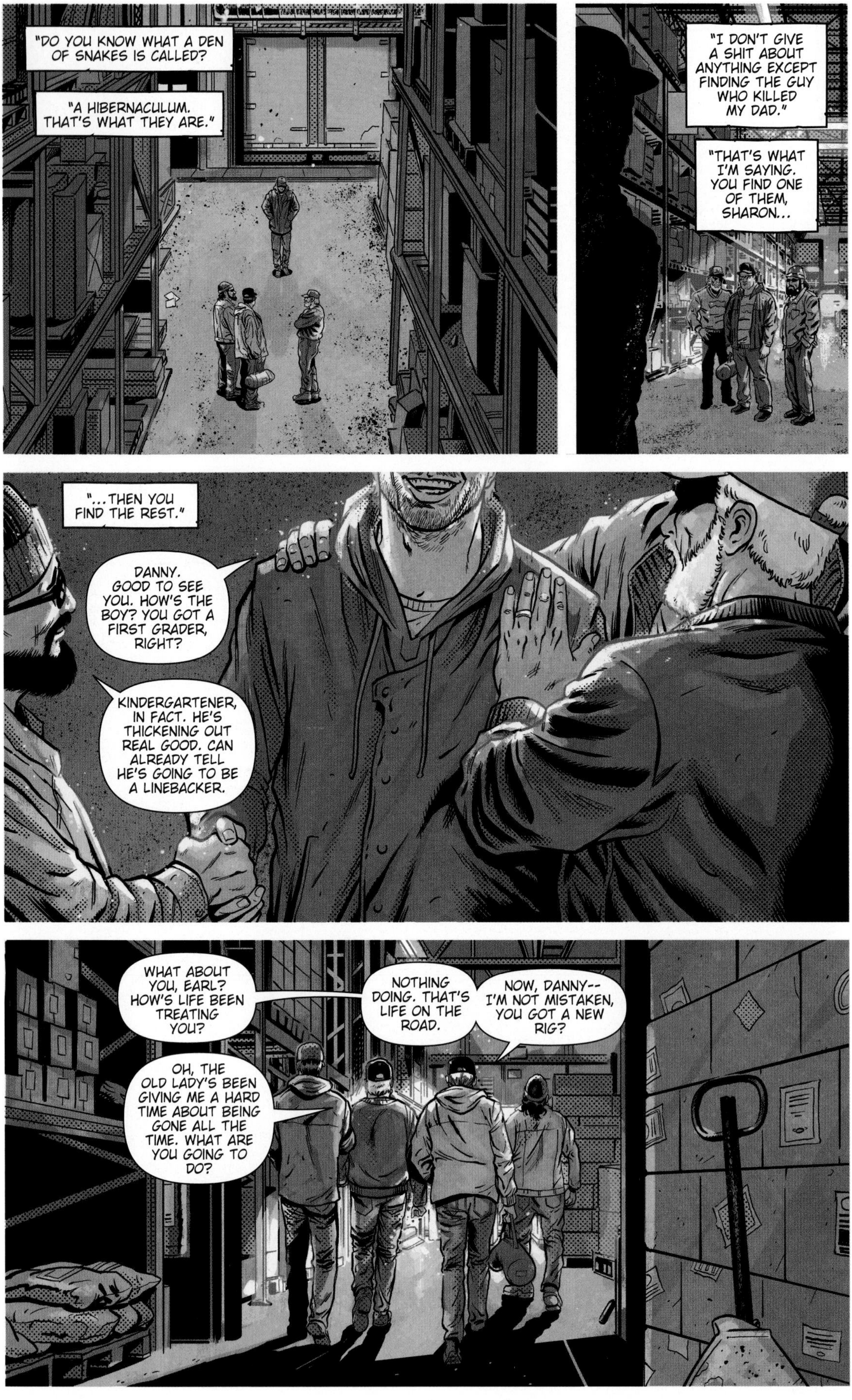
"DO YOU KNOW WHAT A DEN OF SNAKES IS CALLED?
"A HIBERNACULUM. THAT'S WHAT THEY ARE."
"I DON'T GIVE A SHIT ABOUT ANYTHING EXCEPT FINDING THE GUY WHO KILLED MY DAD."
"THAT'S WHAT I'M SAYING. YOU FIND ONE OF THEM, SHARON...
"...THEN YOU FIND THE REST."
DANNY. GOOD TO SEE YOU. HOW'S THE BOY? YOU GOT A FIRST GRADER, RIGHT?
KINDERGARTENER, IN FACT. HE'S THICKENING OUT REAL GOOD. CAN ALREADY TELL HE'S GOING TO BE A LINEBACKER.
WHAT ABOUT YOU, EARL? HOW'S LIFE BEEN TREATING YOU?
OH, THE OLD LADY'S BEEN GIVING ME A HARD TIME ABOUT BEING GONE ALL THE TIME. WHAT ARE YOU GOING TO DO?
NOTHING DOING. THAT'S LIFE ON THE ROAD.
NOW, DANNY-- I'M NOT MISTAKEN, YOU GOT A NEW RIG?

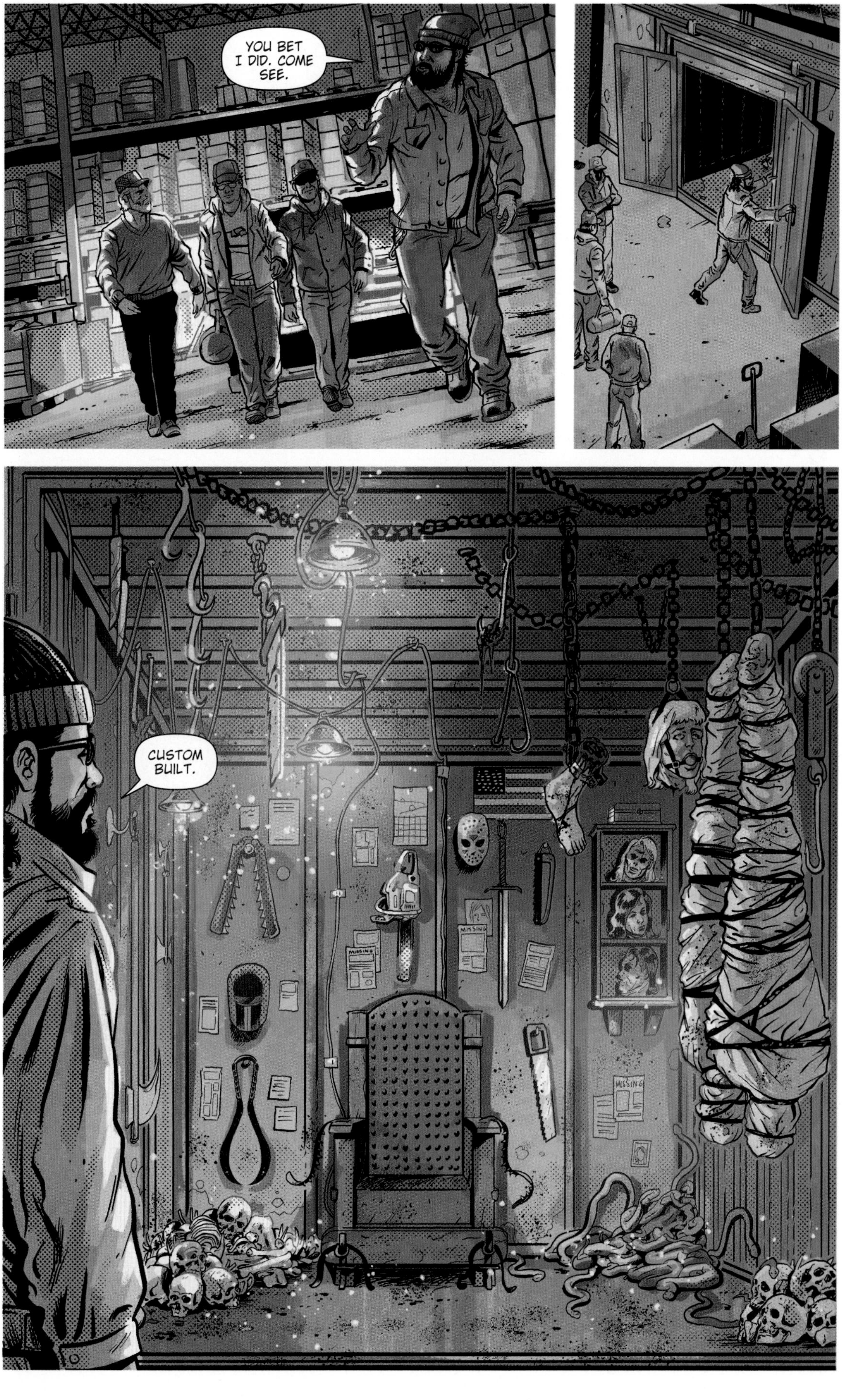
YOU BET I DID. COME SEE.
CUSTOM BUILT.

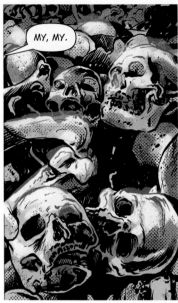

MY, MY.

WHAT SAY WE GIVE THE NEW TRAILER A TEST RIDE?

WE WERE UNDER THE IMPRESSION YOU MIGHT HAVE BROUGHT ALONG A PACKAGE?

I'M A TRUCK DRIVER, AREN'T I?

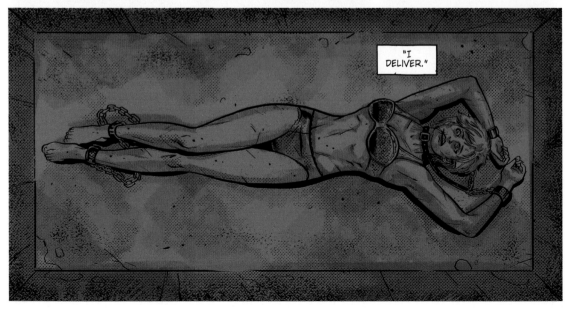

"I DELIVER."

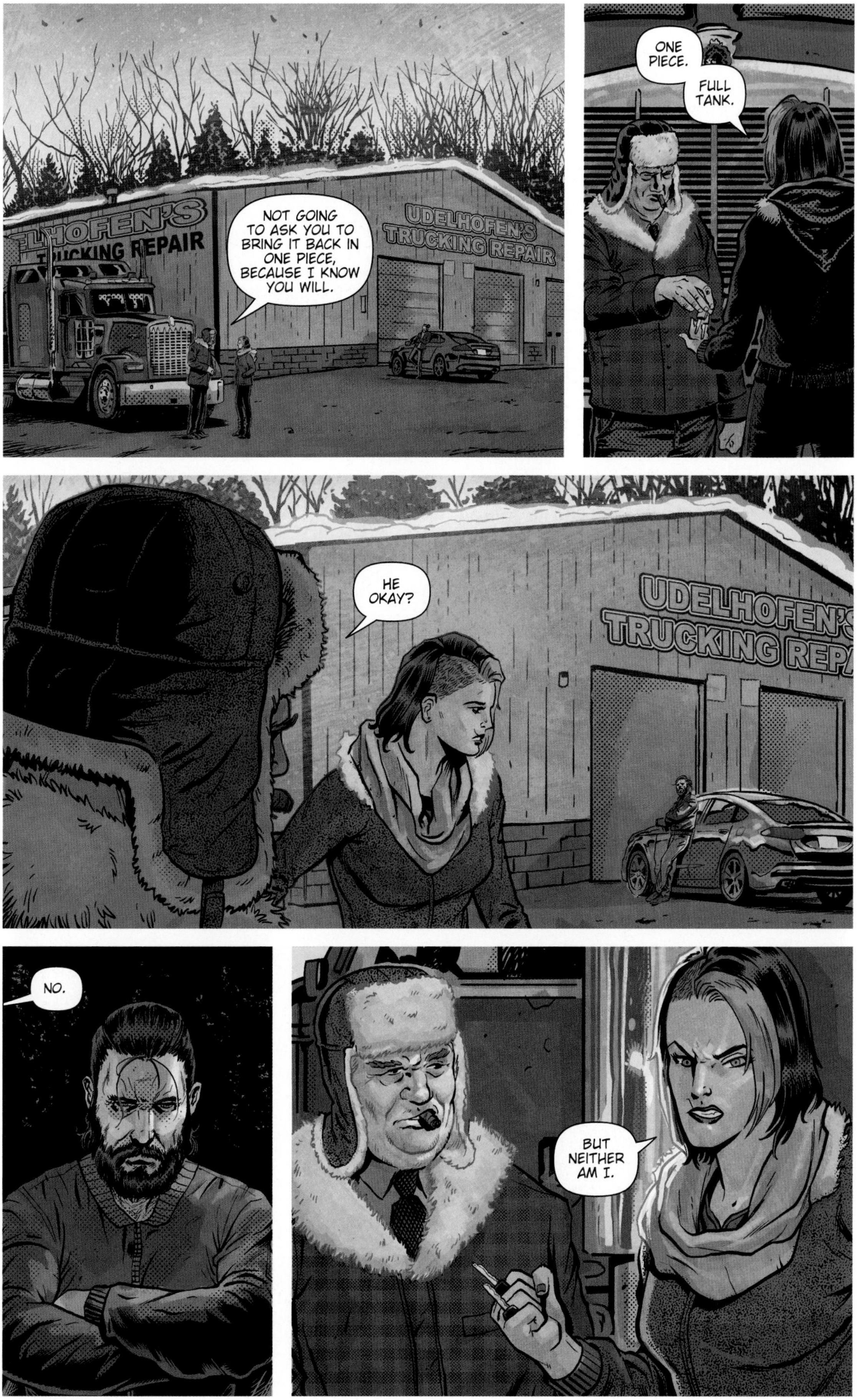
UDELHOFEN'S TRUCKING REPAIR
NOT GOING TO ASK YOU TO BRING IT BACK IN ONE PIECE, BECAUSE I KNOW YOU WILL.
ONE PIECE.
FULL TANK.
HE OKAY?
NO.
BUT NEITHER AM I.

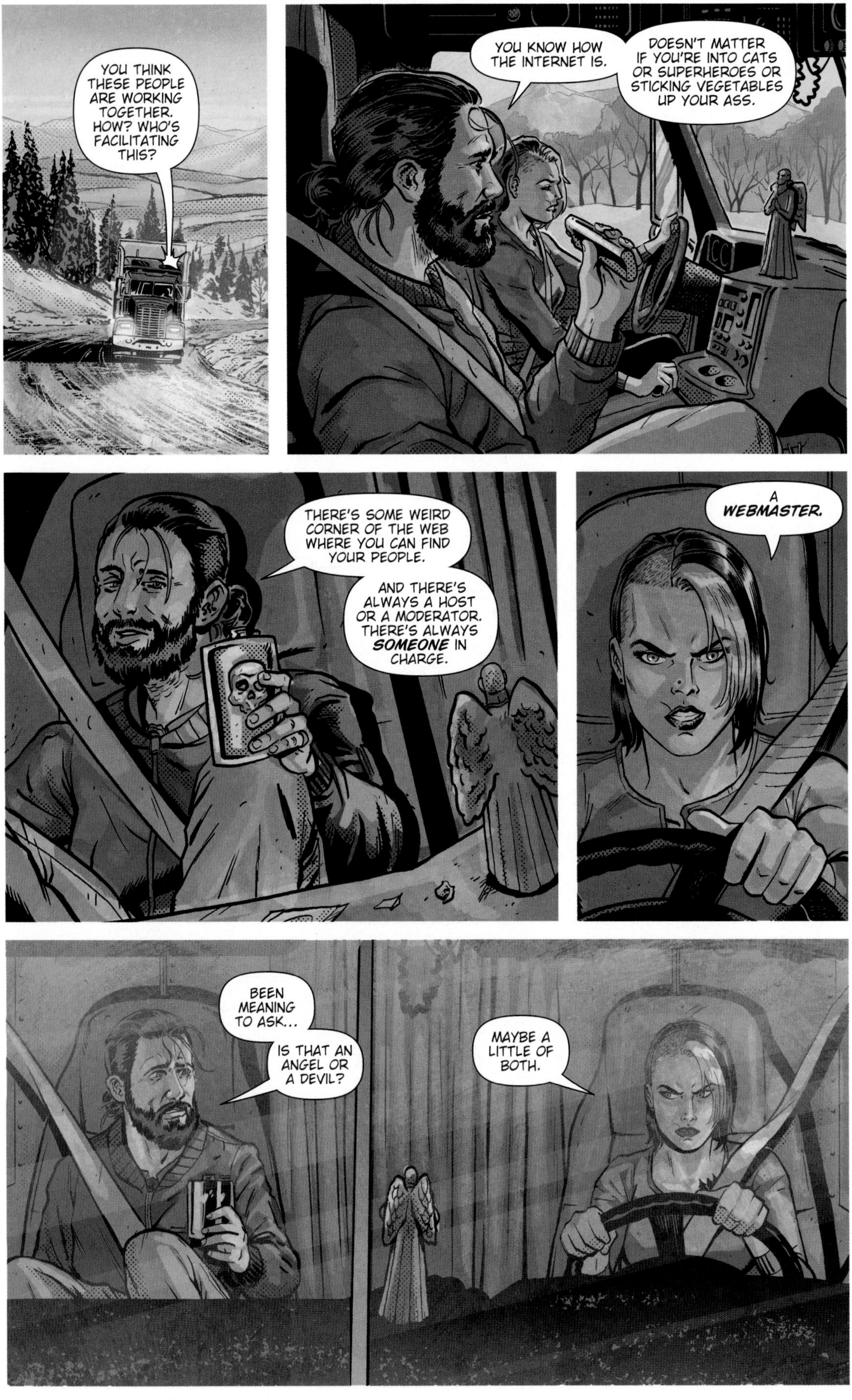
YOU THINK THESE PEOPLE ARE WORKING TOGETHER. HOW? WHO'S FACILITATING THIS?
YOU KNOW HOW THE INTERNET IS.
DOESN'T MATTER IF YOU'RE INTO CATS OR SUPERHEROES OR STICKING VEGETABLES UP YOUR ASS.
THERE'S SOME WEIRD CORNER OF THE WEB WHERE YOU CAN FIND YOUR PEOPLE.
AND THERE'S ALWAYS A HOST OR A MODERATOR. THERE'S ALWAYS *SOMEONE* IN CHARGE.
A ***WEBMASTER.***
BEEN MEANING TO ASK...
IS THAT AN ANGEL OR A DEVIL?
MAYBE A LITTLE OF BOTH.

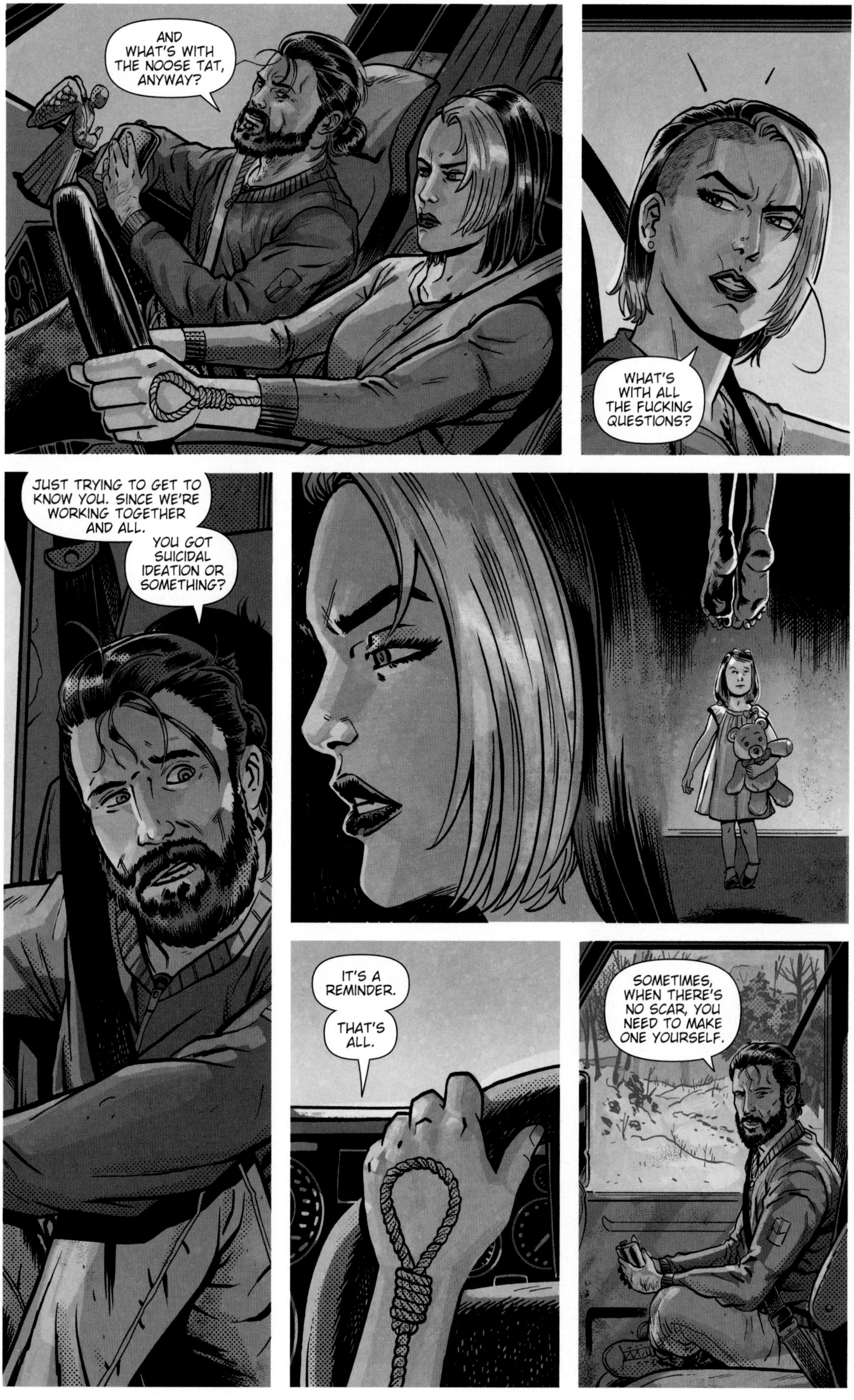
AND WHAT'S WITH THE NOOSE TAT, ANYWAY?
WHAT'S WITH ALL THE FUCKING QUESTIONS?
JUST TRYING TO GET TO KNOW YOU. SINCE WE'RE WORKING TOGETHER AND ALL.
YOU GOT SUICIDAL IDEATION OR SOMETHING?
IT'S A REMINDER.
THAT'S ALL.
SOMETIMES, WHEN THERE'S NO SCAR, YOU NEED TO MAKE ONE YOURSELF.

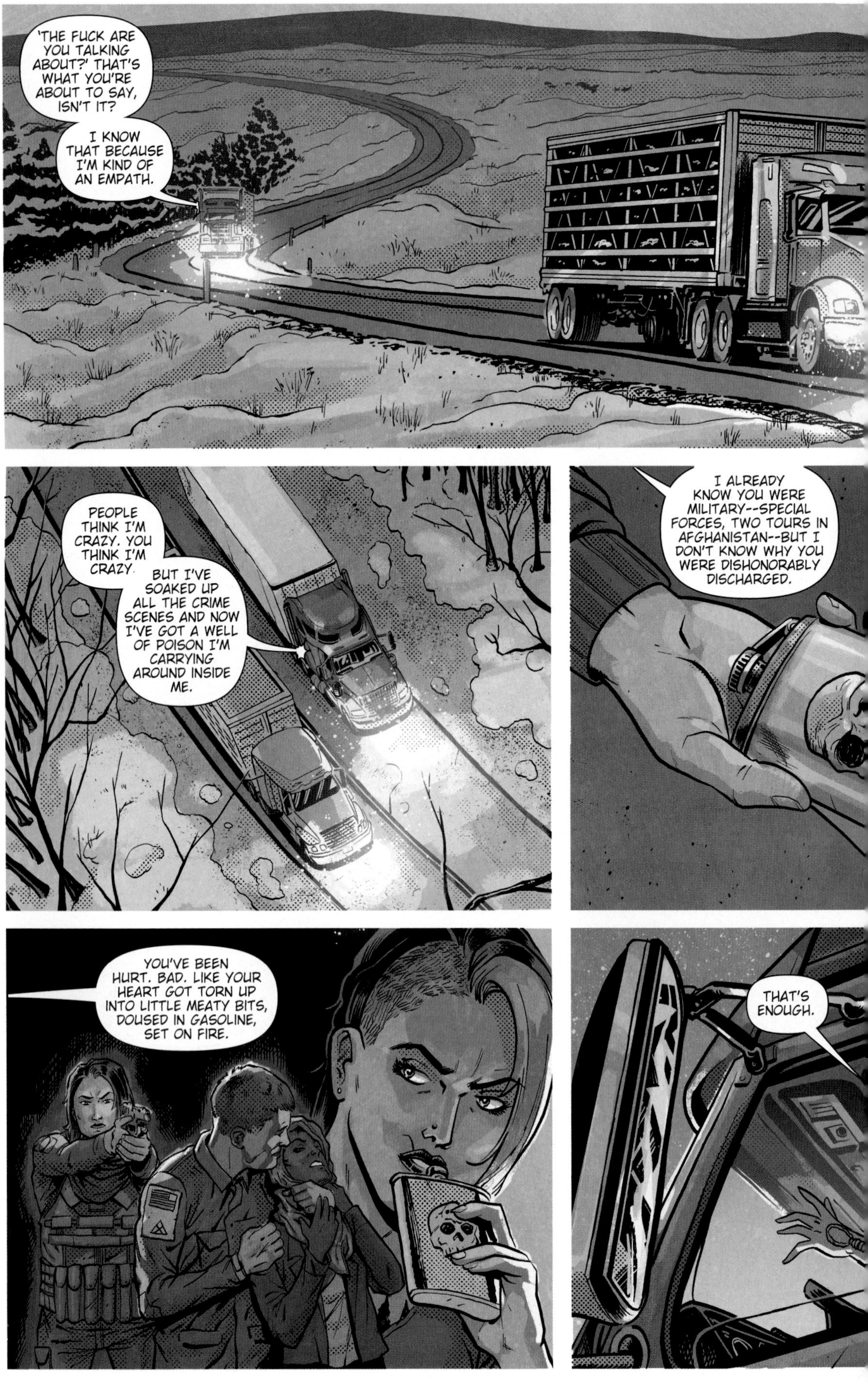
'THE FUCK ARE YOU TALKING ABOUT?' THAT'S WHAT YOU'RE ABOUT TO SAY, ISN'T IT?
I KNOW THAT BECAUSE I'M KIND OF AN EMPATH.
PEOPLE THINK I'M CRAZY. YOU THINK I'M CRAZY.
BUT I'VE SOAKED UP ALL THE CRIME SCENES AND NOW I'VE GOT A WELL OF POISON I'M CARRYING AROUND INSIDE ME.
I ALREADY KNOW YOU WERE MILITARY--SPECIAL FORCES, TWO TOURS IN AFGHANISTAN--BUT I DON'T KNOW WHY YOU WERE DISHONORABLY DISCHARGED.
YOU'VE BEEN HURT. BAD. LIKE YOUR HEART GOT TORN UP INTO LITTLE MEATY BITS, DOUSED IN GASOLINE, SET ON FIRE.
THAT'S ENOUGH.

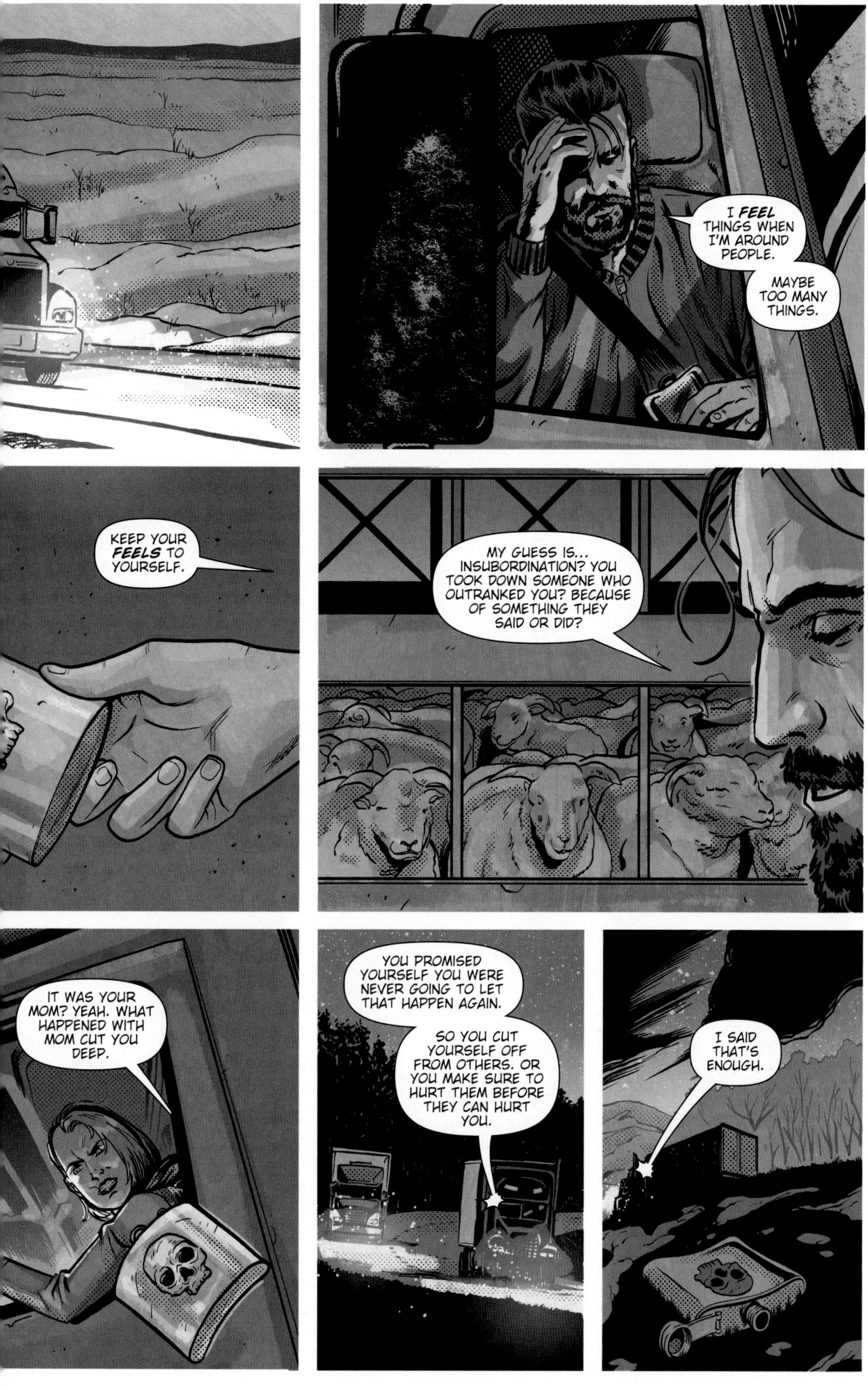
I FEEL THINGS WHEN I'M AROUND PEOPLE.
MAYBE TOO MANY THINGS.
KEEP YOUR FEELS TO YOURSELF.
MY GUESS IS... INSUBORDINATION? YOU TOOK DOWN SOMEONE WHO OUTRANKED YOU? BECAUSE OF SOMETHING THEY SAID OR DID?
IT WAS YOUR MOM? YEAH. WHAT HAPPENED WITH MOM CUT YOU DEEP.
YOU PROMISED YOURSELF YOU WERE NEVER GOING TO LET THAT HAPPEN AGAIN.
SO YOU CUT YOURSELF OFF FROM OTHERS. OR YOU MAKE SURE TO HURT THEM BEFORE THEY CAN HURT YOU.
I SAID THAT'S ENOUGH.

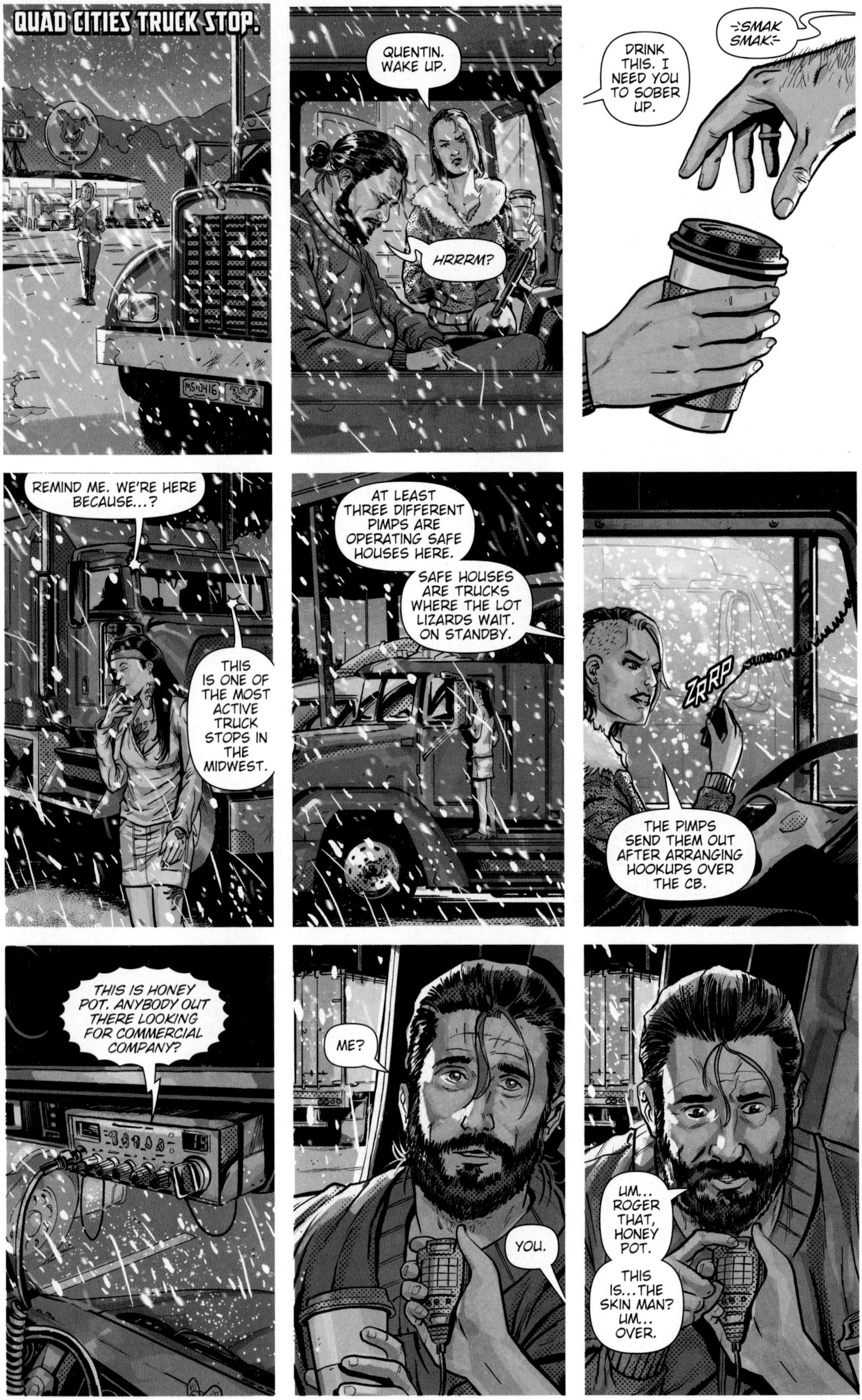
QUAD CITIES TRUCK STOP.
MS-U416
QUENTIN. WAKE UP.
HRRRM?
SMAK SMAK
DRINK THIS. I NEED YOU TO SOBER UP.
REMIND ME. WE'RE HERE BECAUSE...?
THIS IS ONE OF THE MOST ACTIVE TRUCK STOPS IN THE MIDWEST.
AT LEAST THREE DIFFERENT PIMPS ARE OPERATING SAFE HOUSES HERE.
SAFE HOUSES ARE TRUCKS WHERE THE LOT LIZARDS WAIT. ON STANDBY.
ZRRP
THE PIMPS SEND THEM OUT AFTER ARRANGING HOOKUPS OVER THE CB.
THIS IS HONEY POT. ANYBODY OUT THERE LOOKING FOR COMMERCIAL COMPANY?
ME?
YOU.
UM... ROGER THAT, HONEY POT.
THIS IS...THE SKIN MAN? UM... OVER.

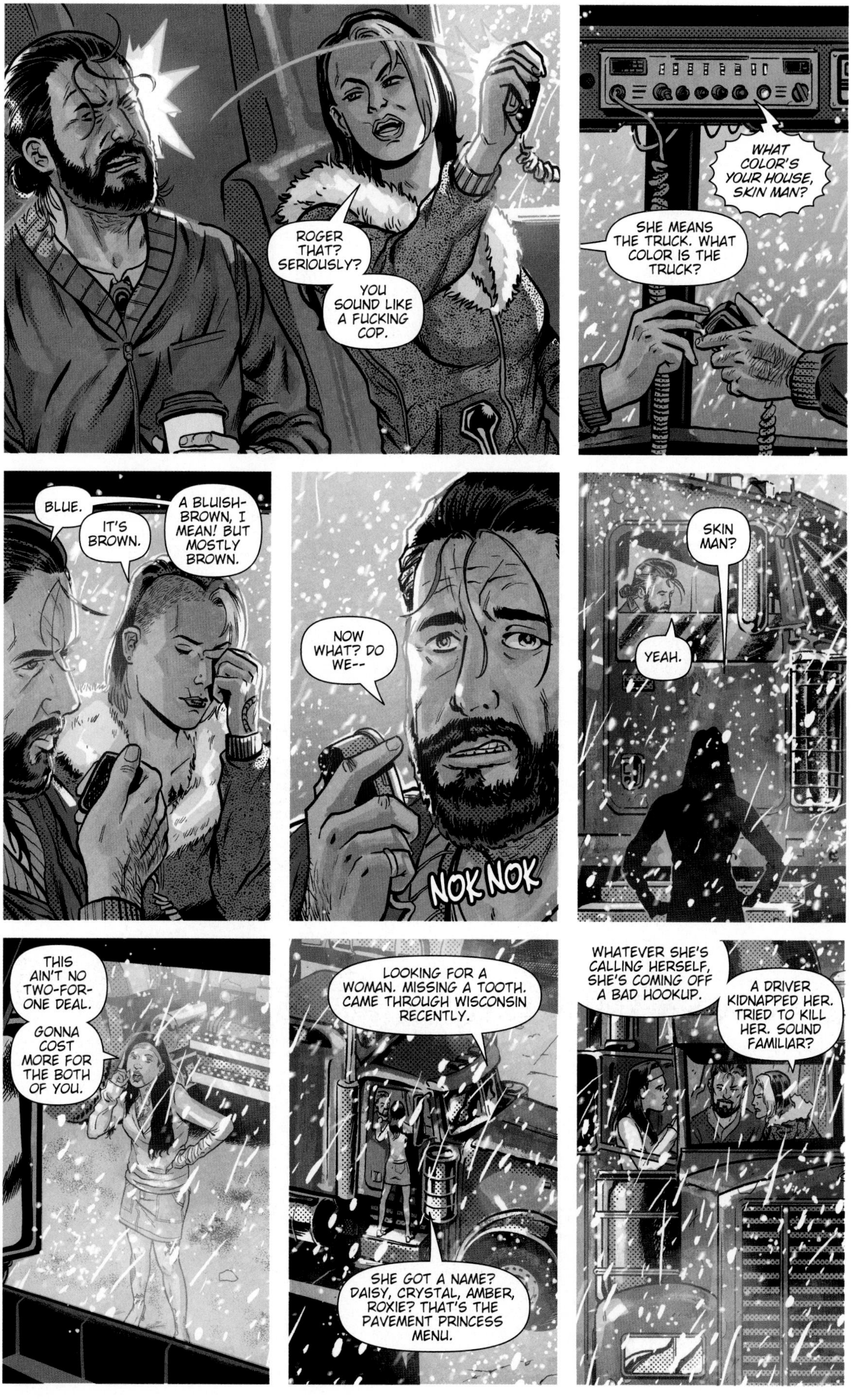

ROGER THAT? SERIOUSLY?
YOU SOUND LIKE A FUCKING COP.
WHAT COLOR'S YOUR HOUSE, SKIN MAN?
SHE MEANS THE TRUCK. WHAT COLOR IS THE TRUCK?
BLUE.
IT'S BROWN.
A BLUISH-BROWN, I MEAN! BUT MOSTLY BROWN.
NOW WHAT? DO WE--
NOK NOK
SKIN MAN?
YEAH.
THIS AIN'T NO TWO-FOR-ONE DEAL.
GONNA COST MORE FOR THE BOTH OF YOU.
LOOKING FOR A WOMAN. MISSING A TOOTH. CAME THROUGH WISCONSIN RECENTLY.
SHE GOT A NAME? DAISY, CRYSTAL, AMBER, ROXIE? THAT'S THE PAVEMENT PRINCESS MENU.
WHATEVER SHE'S CALLING HERSELF, SHE'S COMING OFF A BAD HOOKUP.
A DRIVER KIDNAPPED HER. TRIED TO KILL HER. SOUND FAMILIAR?

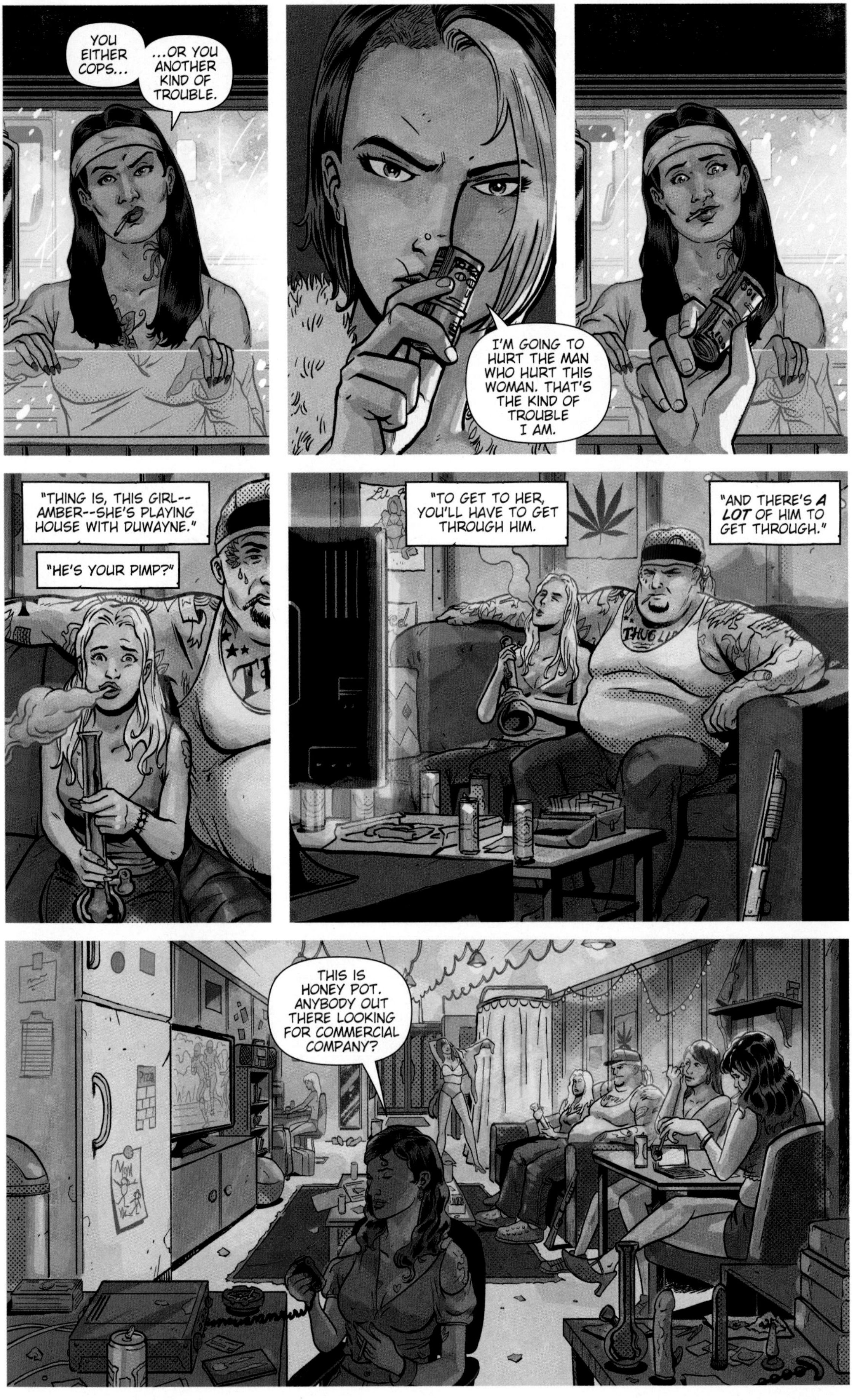
YOU EITHER COPS...
...OR YOU ANOTHER KIND OF TROUBLE.
I'M GOING TO HURT THE MAN WHO HURT THIS WOMAN. THAT'S THE KIND OF TROUBLE I AM.
"THING IS, THIS GIRL--AMBER--SHE'S PLAYING HOUSE WITH DUWAYNE."
"HE'S YOUR PIMP?"
"TO GET TO HER, YOU'LL HAVE TO GET THROUGH HIM.
"AND THERE'S *A LOT* OF HIM TO GET THROUGH."
THIS IS HONEY POT. ANYBODY OUT THERE LOOKING FOR COMMERCIAL COMPANY?

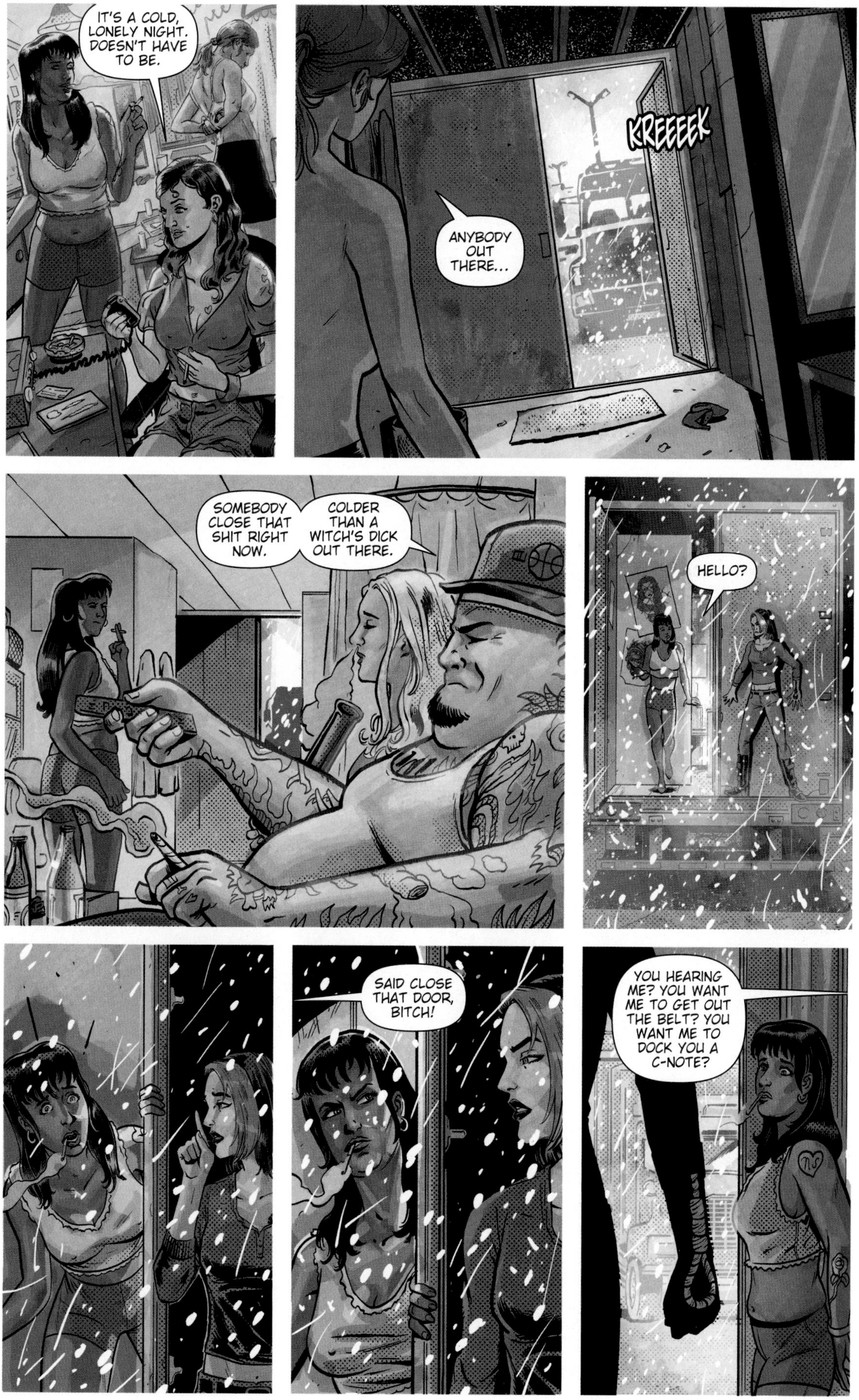
IT'S A COLD, LONELY NIGHT. DOESN'T HAVE TO BE.
KREEEEK
ANYBODY OUT THERE...
SOMEBODY CLOSE THAT SHIT RIGHT NOW.
COLDER THAN A WITCH'S DICK OUT THERE.
HELLO?
SAID CLOSE THAT DOOR, BITCH!
YOU HEARING ME? YOU WANT ME TO GET OUT THE BELT? YOU WANT ME TO DOCK YOU A C-NOTE?

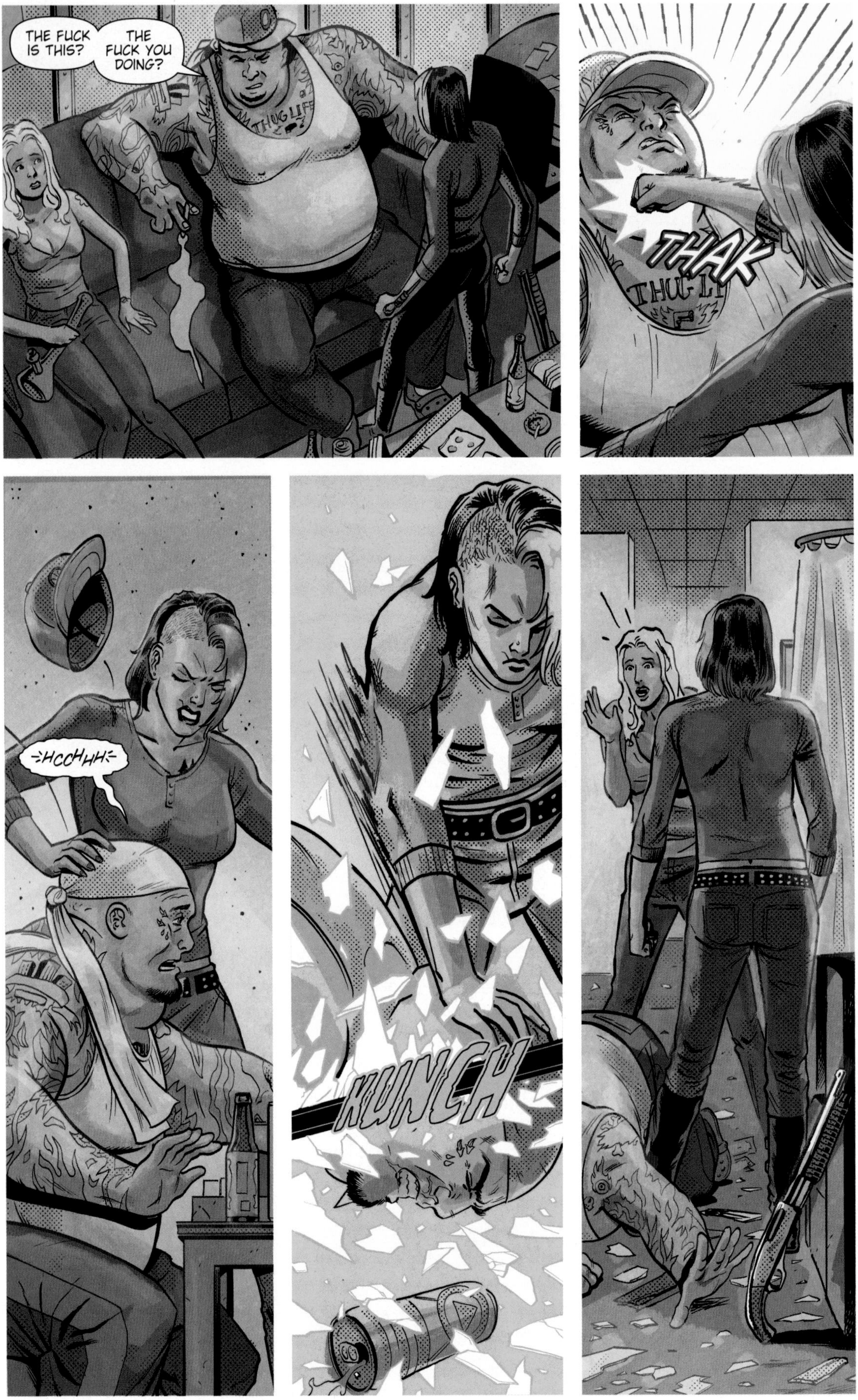
THE FUCK IS THIS?
THE FUCK YOU DOING?
THUG LIF
THAK
THUG-LI
HCCHHH
KUNCH

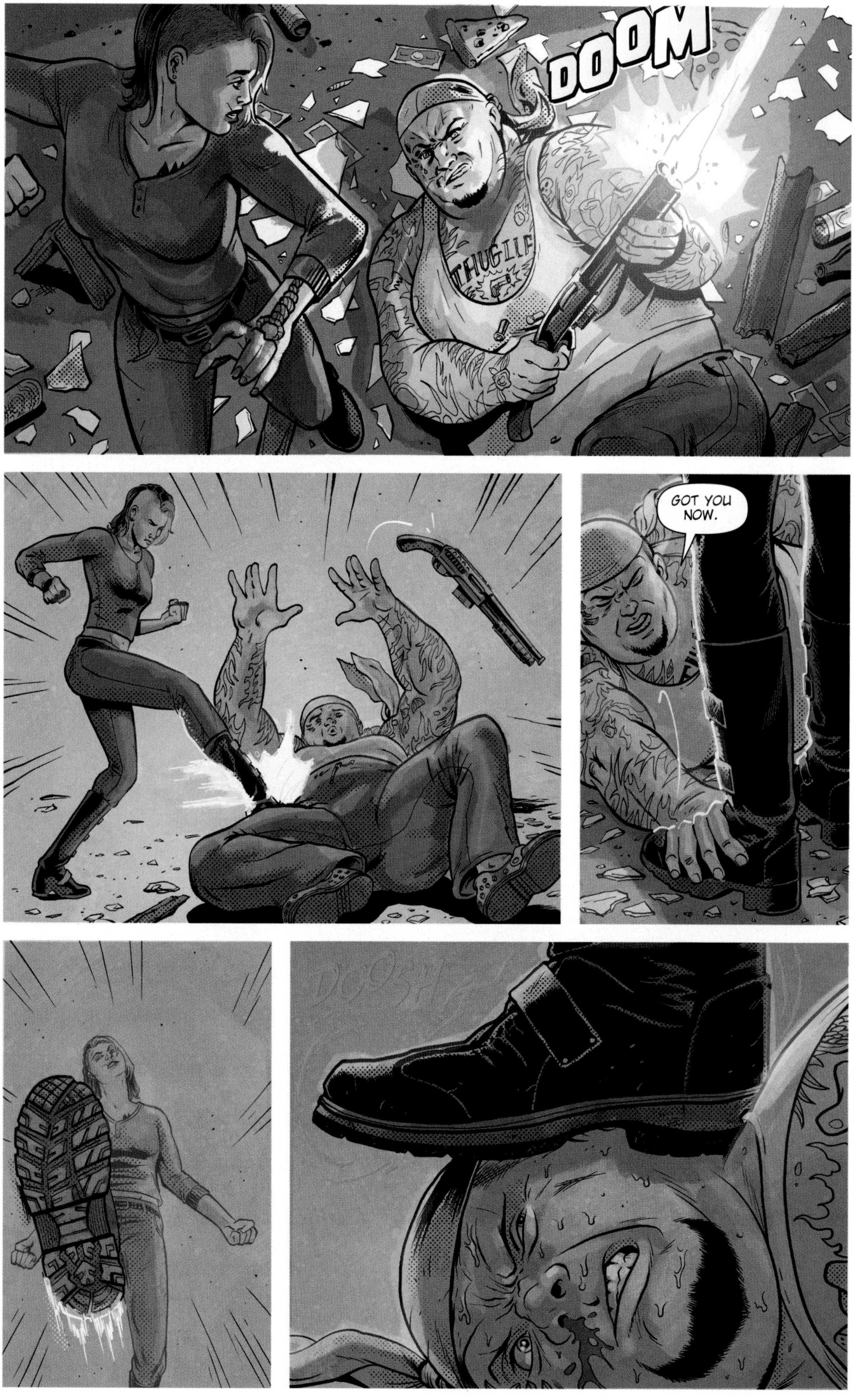
DOOM
GOT YOU NOW.

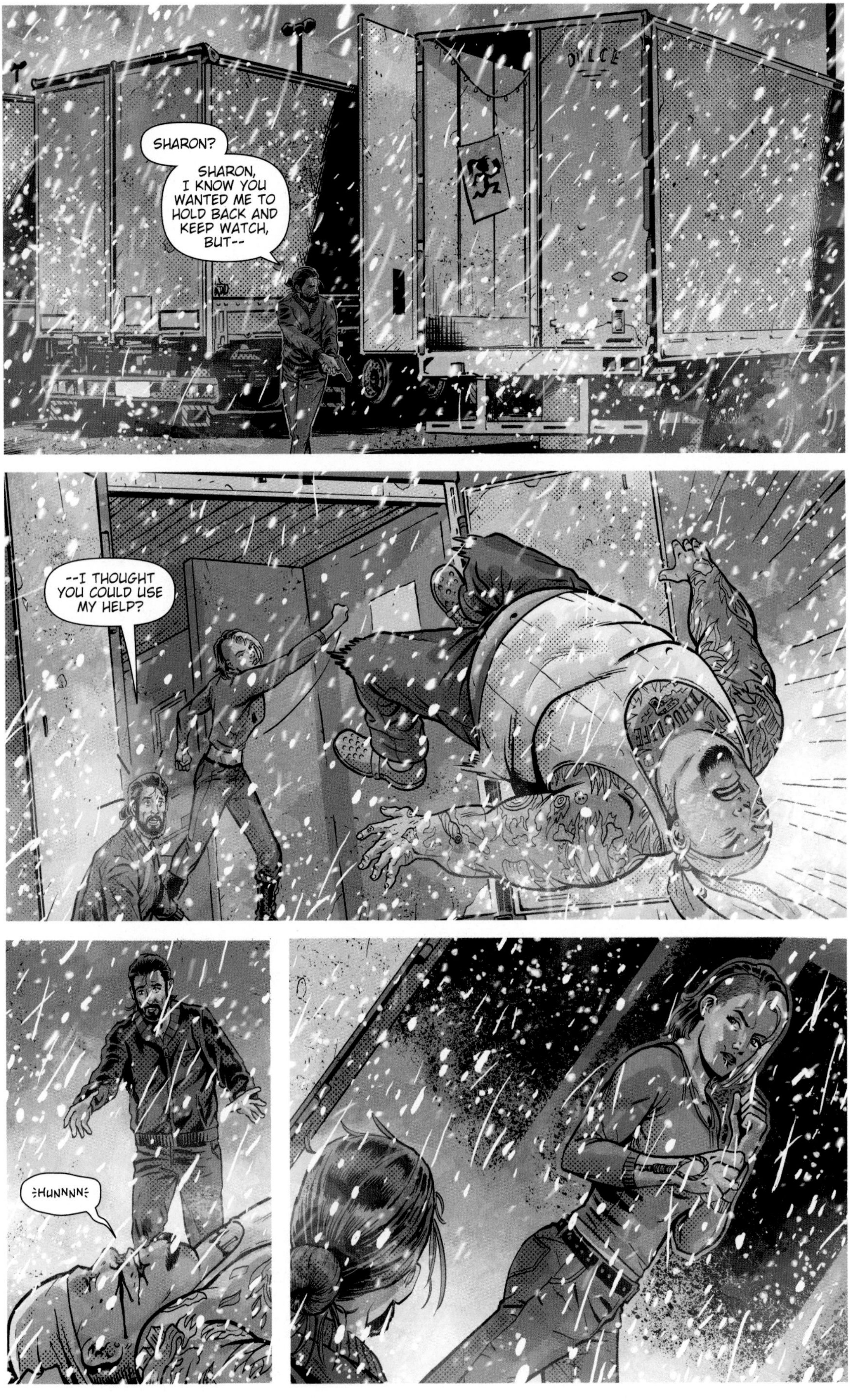
SHARON?
SHARON, I KNOW YOU WANTED ME TO HOLD BACK AND KEEP WATCH, BUT--
--I THOUGHT YOU COULD USE MY HELP?
HUNNNN

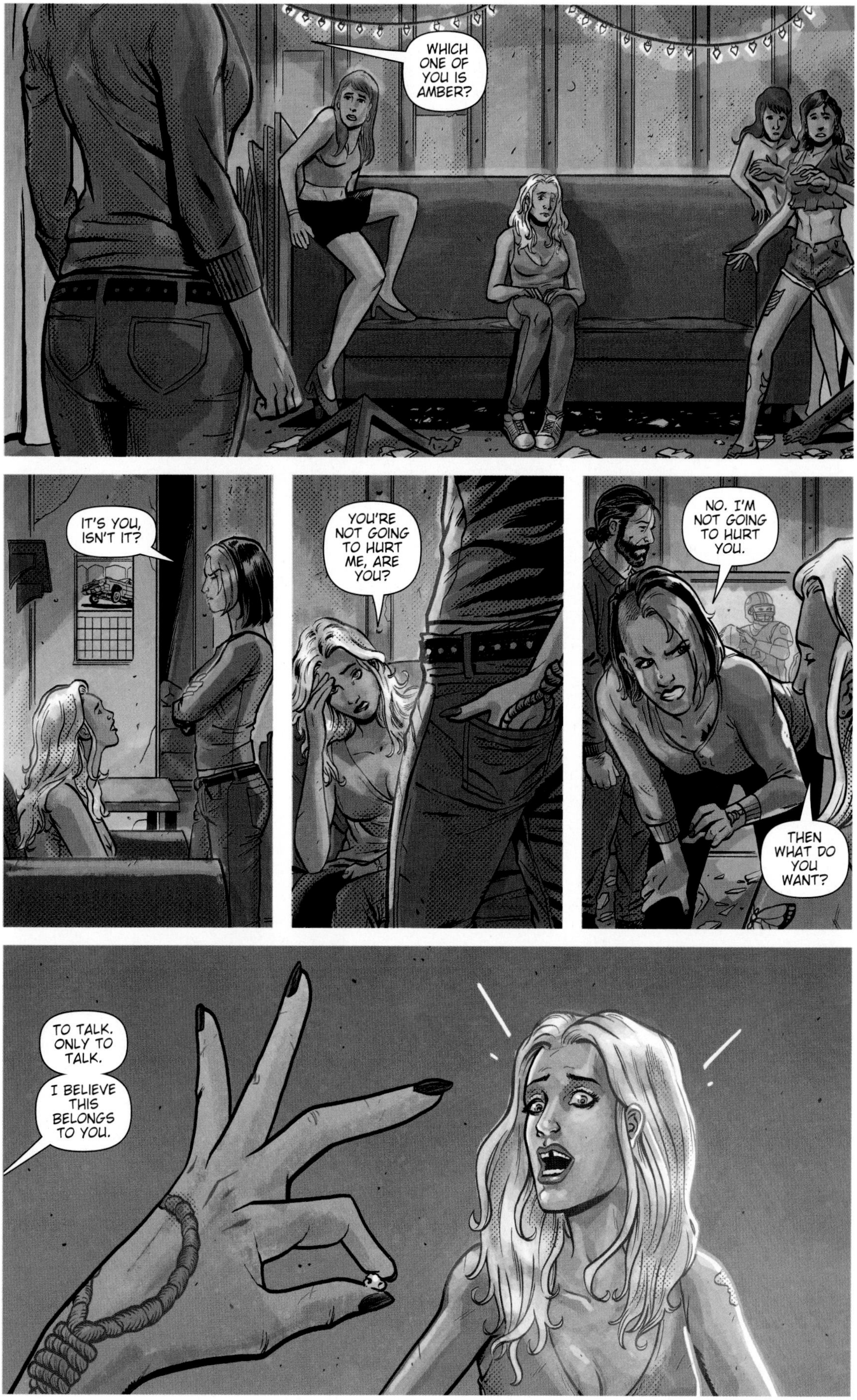
WHICH ONE OF YOU IS AMBER?
IT'S YOU, ISN'T IT?
YOU'RE NOT GOING TO HURT ME, ARE YOU?
NO. I'M NOT GOING TO HURT YOU.
THEN WHAT DO YOU WANT?
TO TALK. ONLY TO TALK.
I BELIEVE THIS BELONGS TO YOU.

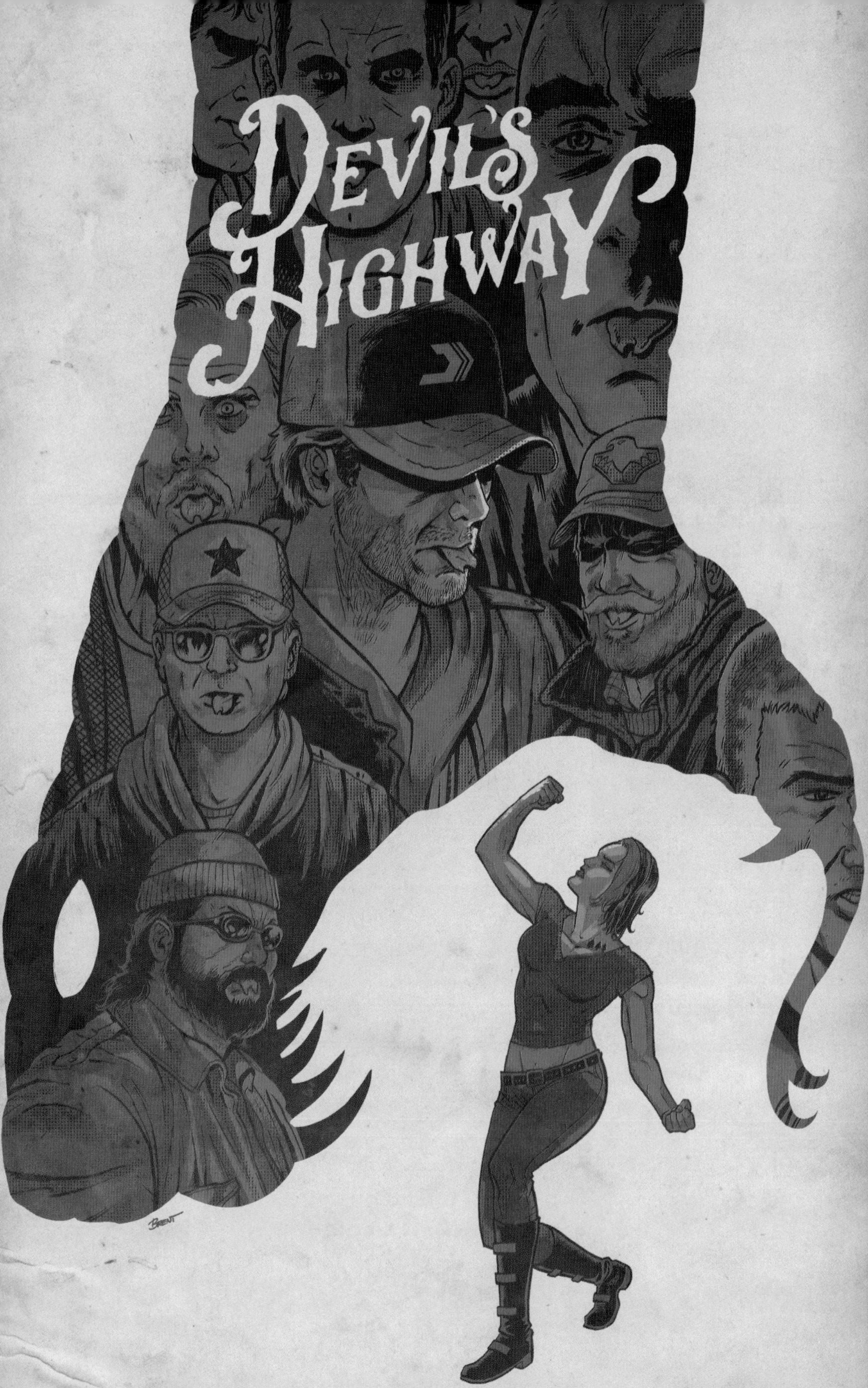
DEVIL'S HIGHWAY
BRENT

Benjamin **PERCY** Brent **SCHOONOVER** Nick **FILARDI**

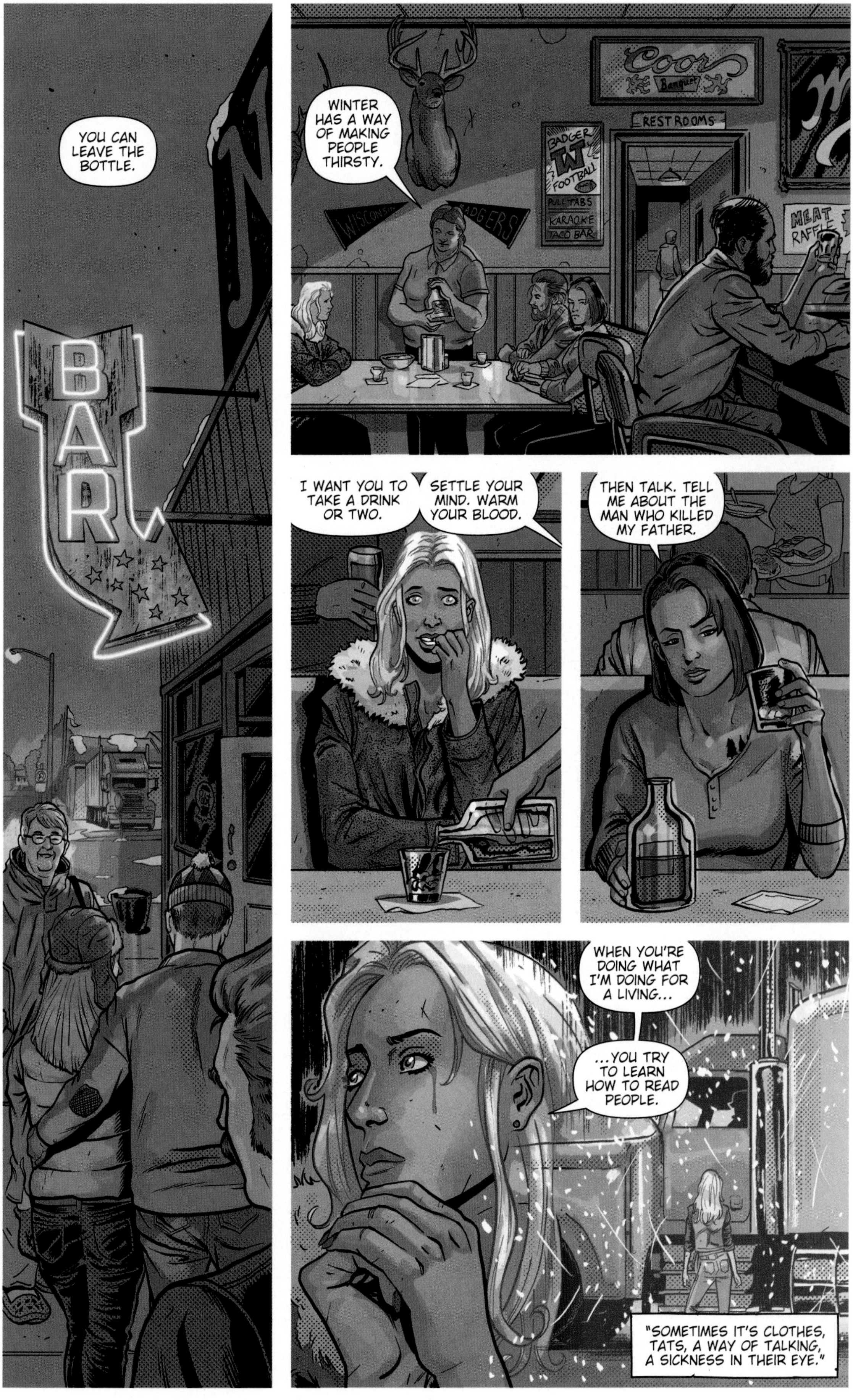
YOU CAN LEAVE THE BOTTLE.
WINTER HAS A WAY OF MAKING PEOPLE THIRSTY.
I WANT YOU TO TAKE A DRINK OR TWO.
SETTLE YOUR MIND. WARM YOUR BLOOD.
THEN TALK. TELL ME ABOUT THE MAN WHO KILLED MY FATHER.
WHEN YOU'RE DOING WHAT I'M DOING FOR A LIVING...
...YOU TRY TO LEARN HOW TO READ PEOPLE.
"SOMETIMES IT'S CLOTHES, TATS, A WAY OF TALKING, A SICKNESS IN THEIR EYE."

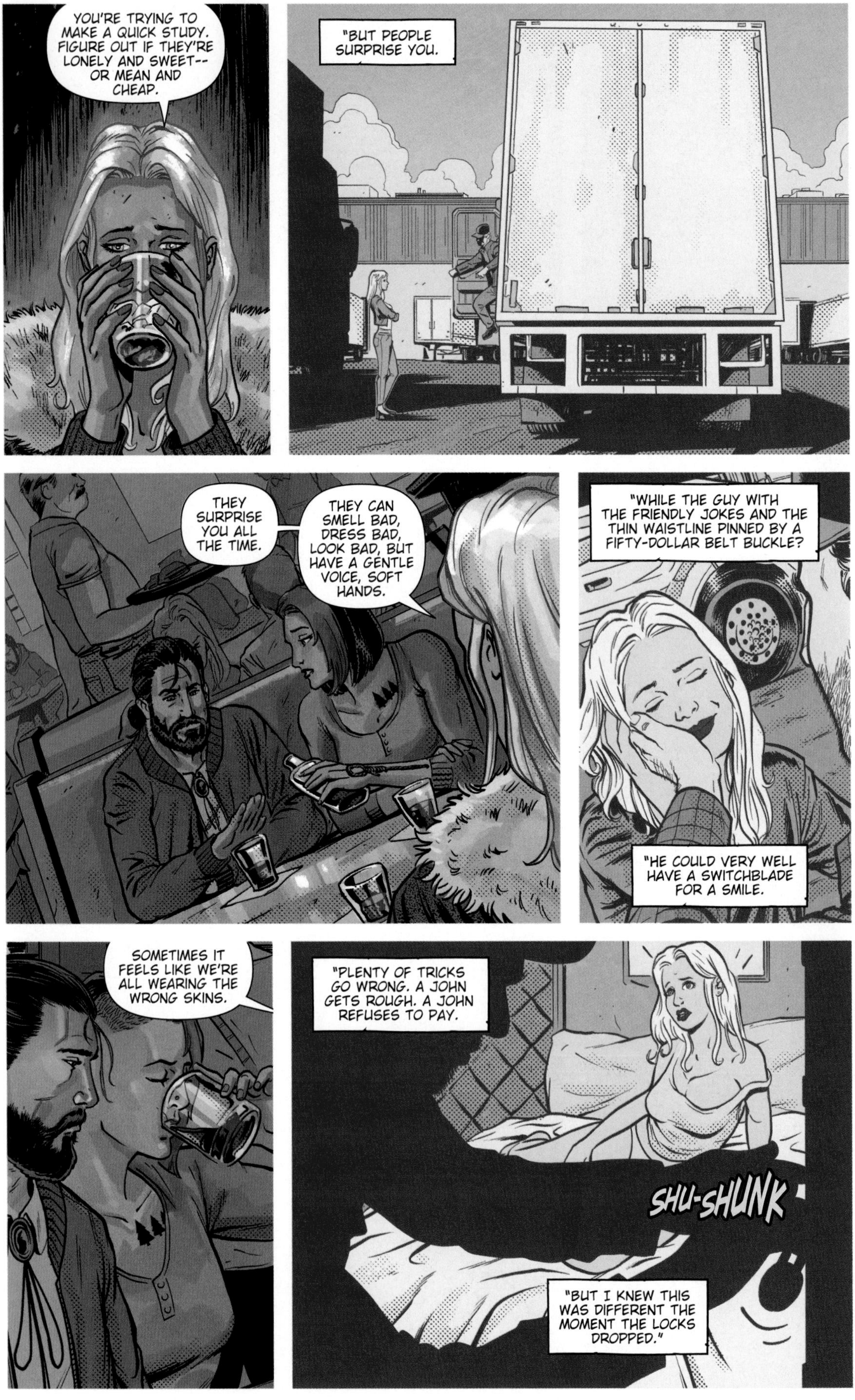
YOU'RE TRYING TO MAKE A QUICK STUDY. FIGURE OUT IF THEY'RE LONELY AND SWEET-- OR MEAN AND CHEAP.
"BUT PEOPLE SURPRISE YOU.
THEY SURPRISE YOU ALL THE TIME.
THEY CAN SMELL BAD, DRESS BAD, LOOK BAD, BUT HAVE A GENTLE VOICE, SOFT HANDS.
"WHILE THE GUY WITH THE FRIENDLY JOKES AND THE THIN WAISTLINE PINNED BY A FIFTY-DOLLAR BELT BUCKLE?
"HE COULD VERY WELL HAVE A SWITCHBLADE FOR A SMILE.
SOMETIMES IT FEELS LIKE WE'RE ALL WEARING THE WRONG SKINS.
"PLENTY OF TRICKS GO WRONG. A JOHN GETS ROUGH. A JOHN REFUSES TO PAY.
SHU-SHUNK
"BUT I KNEW THIS WAS DIFFERENT THE MOMENT THE LOCKS DROPPED."

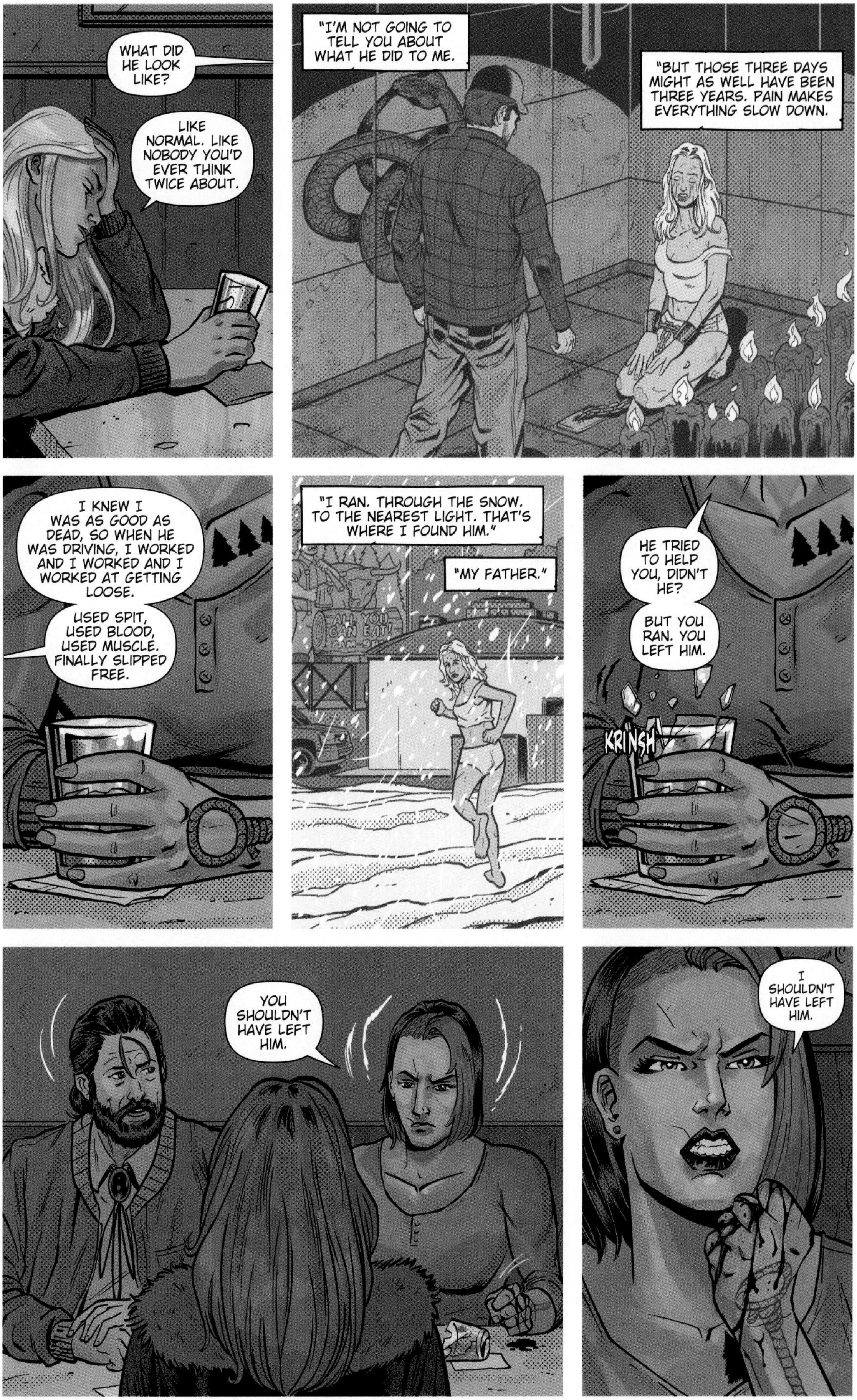
WHAT DID HE LOOK LIKE?
LIKE NORMAL. LIKE NOBODY YOU'D EVER THINK TWICE ABOUT.
"I'M NOT GOING TO TELL YOU ABOUT WHAT HE DID TO ME.
"BUT THOSE THREE DAYS MIGHT AS WELL HAVE BEEN THREE YEARS. PAIN MAKES EVERYTHING SLOW DOWN.
I KNEW I WAS AS GOOD AS DEAD, SO WHEN HE WAS DRIVING, I WORKED AND I WORKED AND I WORKED AT GETTING LOOSE.
USED SPIT, USED BLOOD, USED MUSCLE. FINALLY SLIPPED FREE.
"I RAN. THROUGH THE SNOW. TO THE NEAREST LIGHT. THAT'S WHERE I FOUND HIM."
"MY FATHER."
ALL YOU CAN EAT!
HE TRIED TO HELP YOU, DIDN'T HE?
BUT YOU RAN. YOU LEFT HIM.
KRINSH
YOU SHOULDN'T HAVE LEFT HIM.
I SHOULDN'T HAVE LEFT HIM.

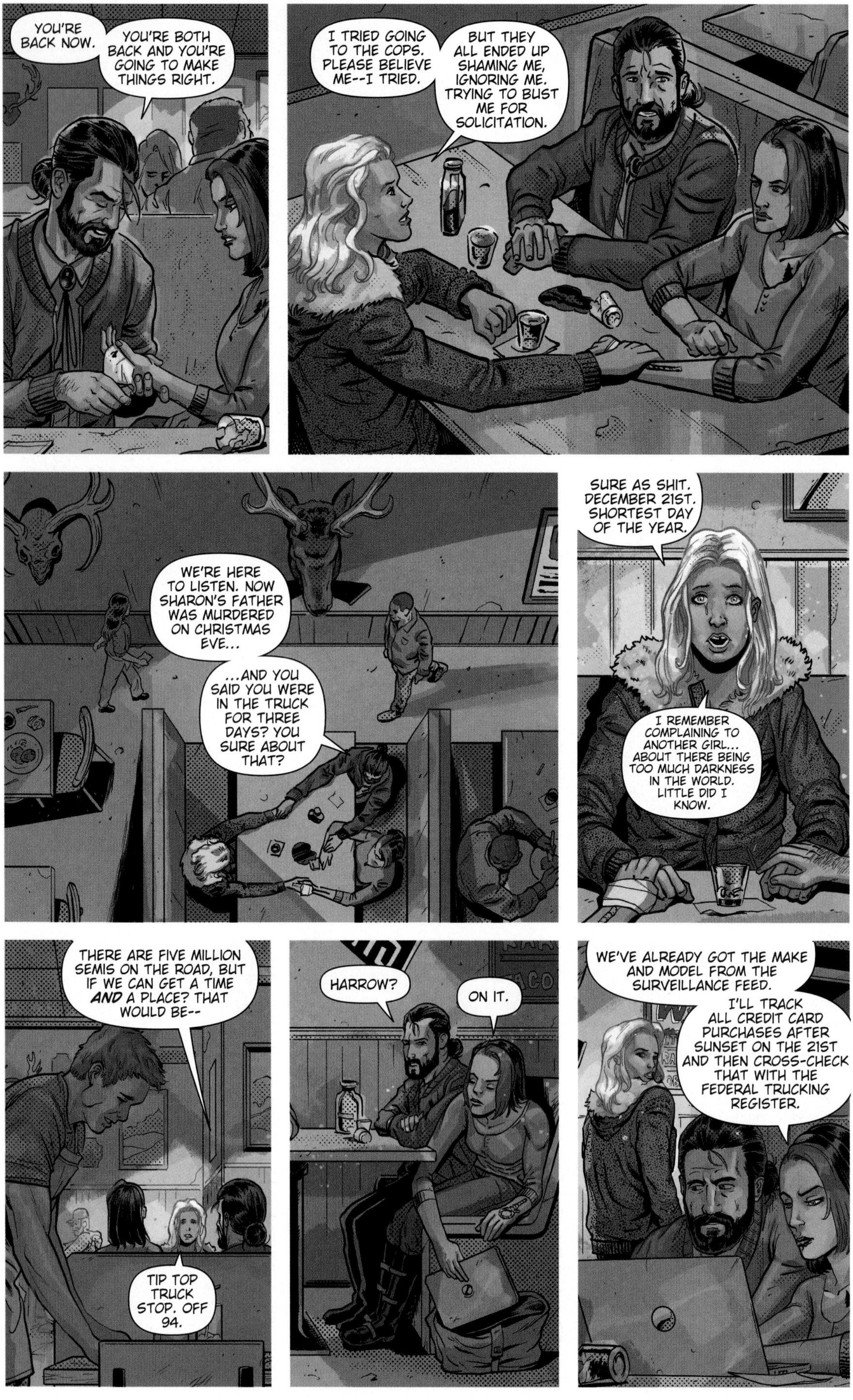
YOU'RE BACK NOW.
YOU'RE BOTH BACK AND YOU'RE GOING TO MAKE THINGS RIGHT.
I TRIED GOING TO THE COPS. PLEASE BELIEVE ME--I TRIED.
BUT THEY ALL ENDED UP SHAMING ME, IGNORING ME. TRYING TO BUST ME FOR SOLICITATION.
WE'RE HERE TO LISTEN. NOW SHARON'S FATHER WAS MURDERED ON CHRISTMAS EVE...
...AND YOU SAID YOU WERE IN THE TRUCK FOR THREE DAYS? YOU SURE ABOUT THAT?
SURE AS SHIT. DECEMBER 21ST. SHORTEST DAY OF THE YEAR.
I REMEMBER COMPLAINING TO ANOTHER GIRL... ABOUT THERE BEING TOO MUCH DARKNESS IN THE WORLD. LITTLE DID I KNOW.
THERE ARE FIVE MILLION SEMIS ON THE ROAD, BUT IF WE CAN GET A TIME ***AND*** A PLACE? THAT WOULD BE--
TIP TOP TRUCK STOP. OFF 94.
HARROW?
ON IT.
WE'VE ALREADY GOT THE MAKE AND MODEL FROM THE SURVEILLANCE FEED.
I'LL TRACK ALL CREDIT CARD PURCHASES AFTER SUNSET ON THE 21ST AND THEN CROSS-CHECK THAT WITH THE FEDERAL TRUCKING REGISTER.

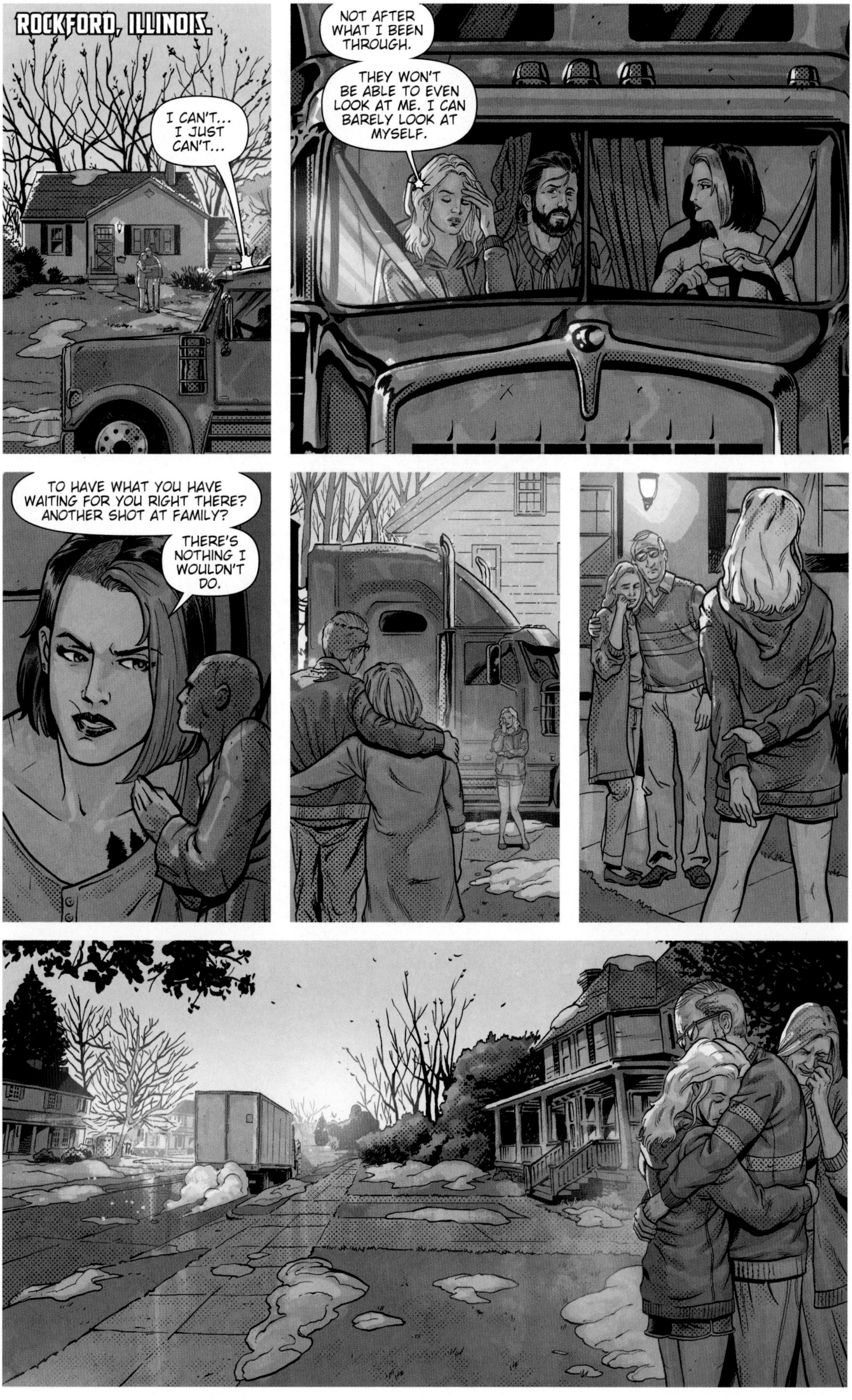
ROCKFORD, ILLINOIS.
I CAN'T... I JUST CAN'T...
NOT AFTER WHAT I BEEN THROUGH.
THEY WON'T BE ABLE TO EVEN LOOK AT ME. I CAN BARELY LOOK AT MYSELF.
TO HAVE WHAT YOU HAVE WAITING FOR YOU RIGHT THERE? ANOTHER SHOT AT FAMILY?
THERE'S NOTHING I WOULDN'T DO.

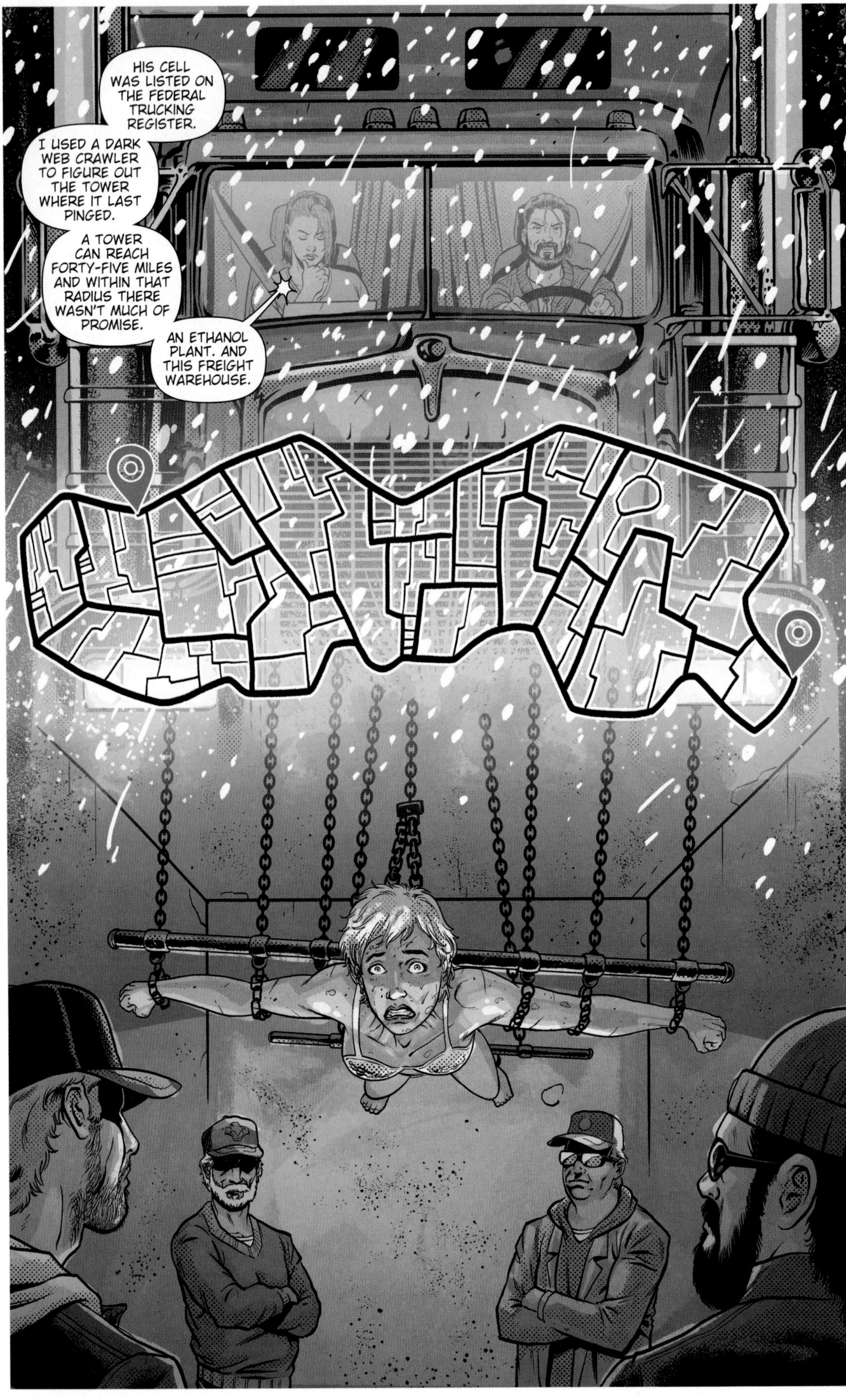

HIS CELL WAS LISTED ON THE FEDERAL TRUCKING REGISTER.
I USED A DARK WEB CRAWLER TO FIGURE OUT THE TOWER WHERE IT LAST PINGED.
A TOWER CAN REACH FORTY-FIVE MILES AND WITHIN THAT RADIUS THERE WASN'T MUCH OF PROMISE.
AN ETHANOL PLANT. AND THIS FREIGHT WAREHOUSE.

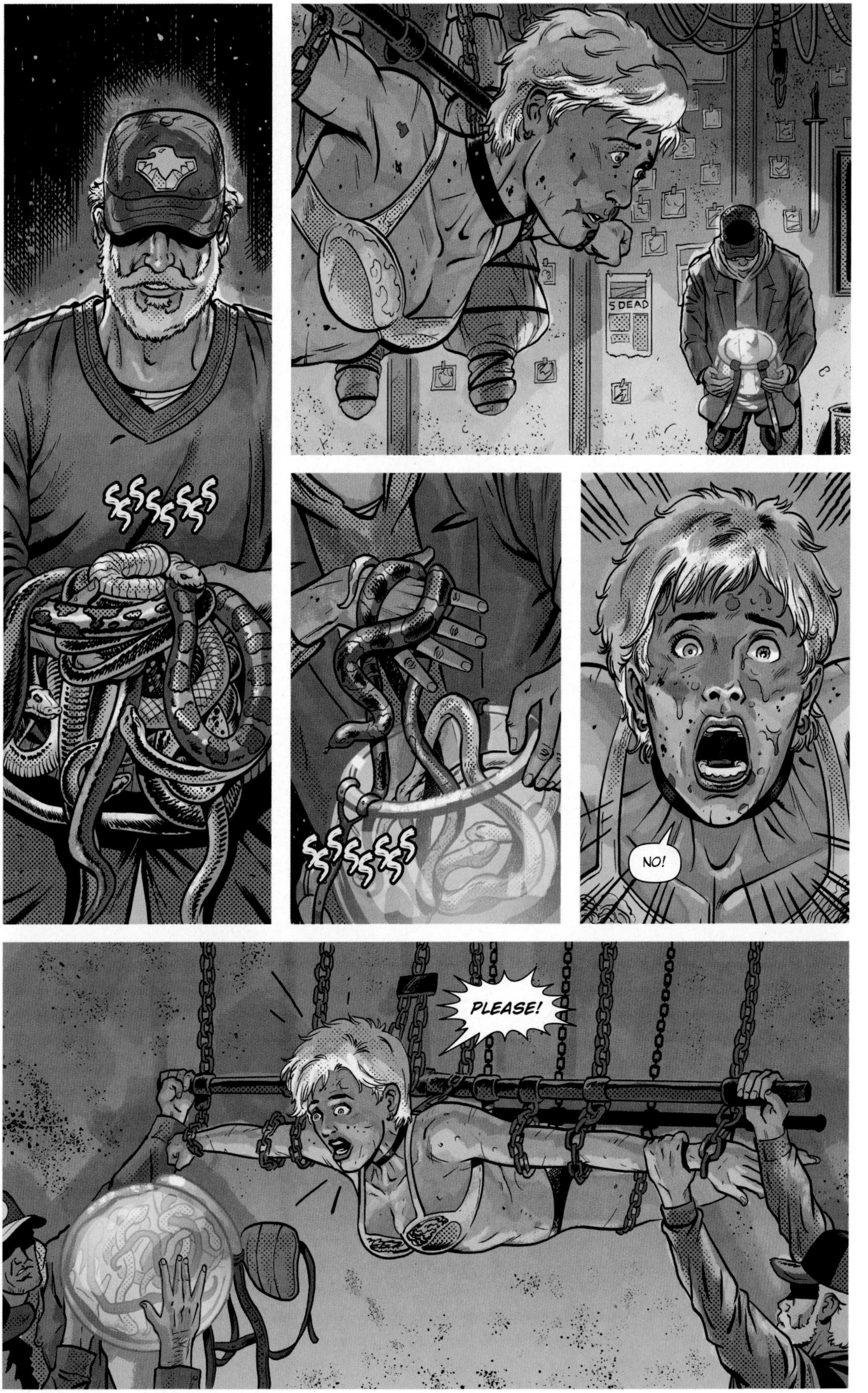
5 DEAD
NO!
PLEASE!

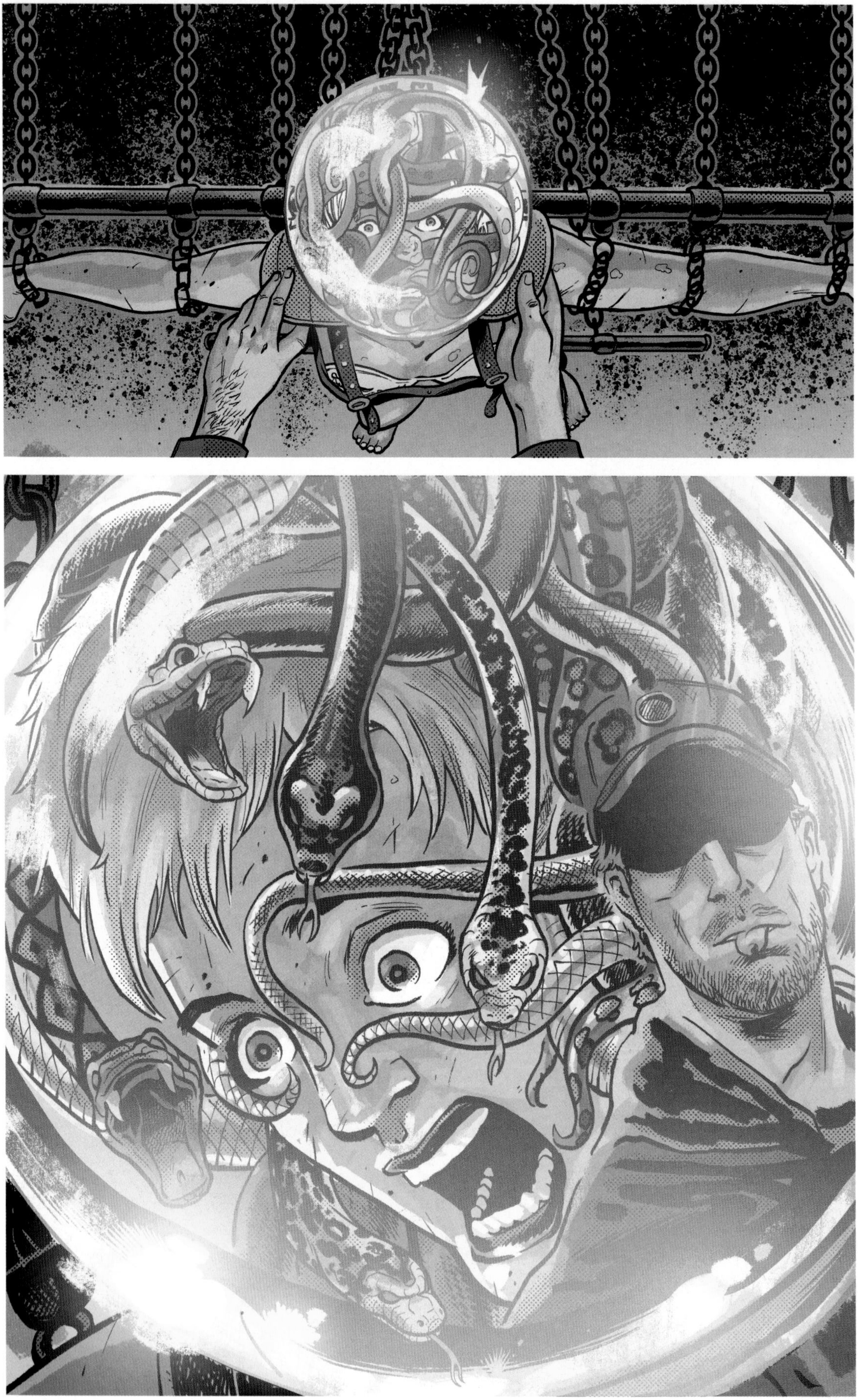

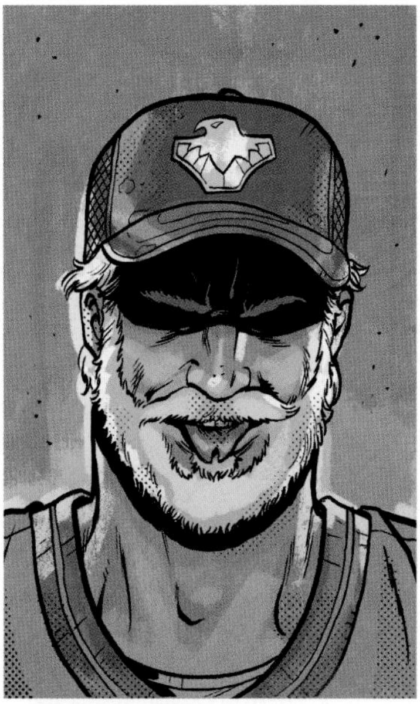
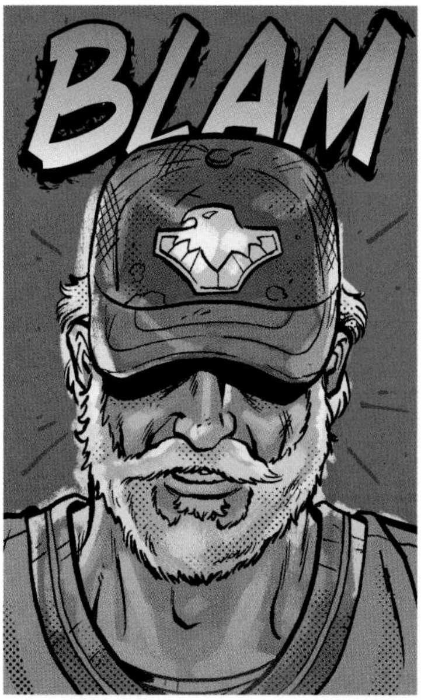
BLAM
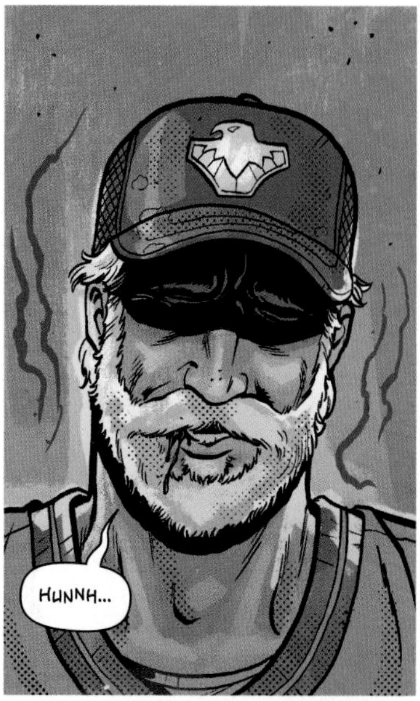
HUNNH...
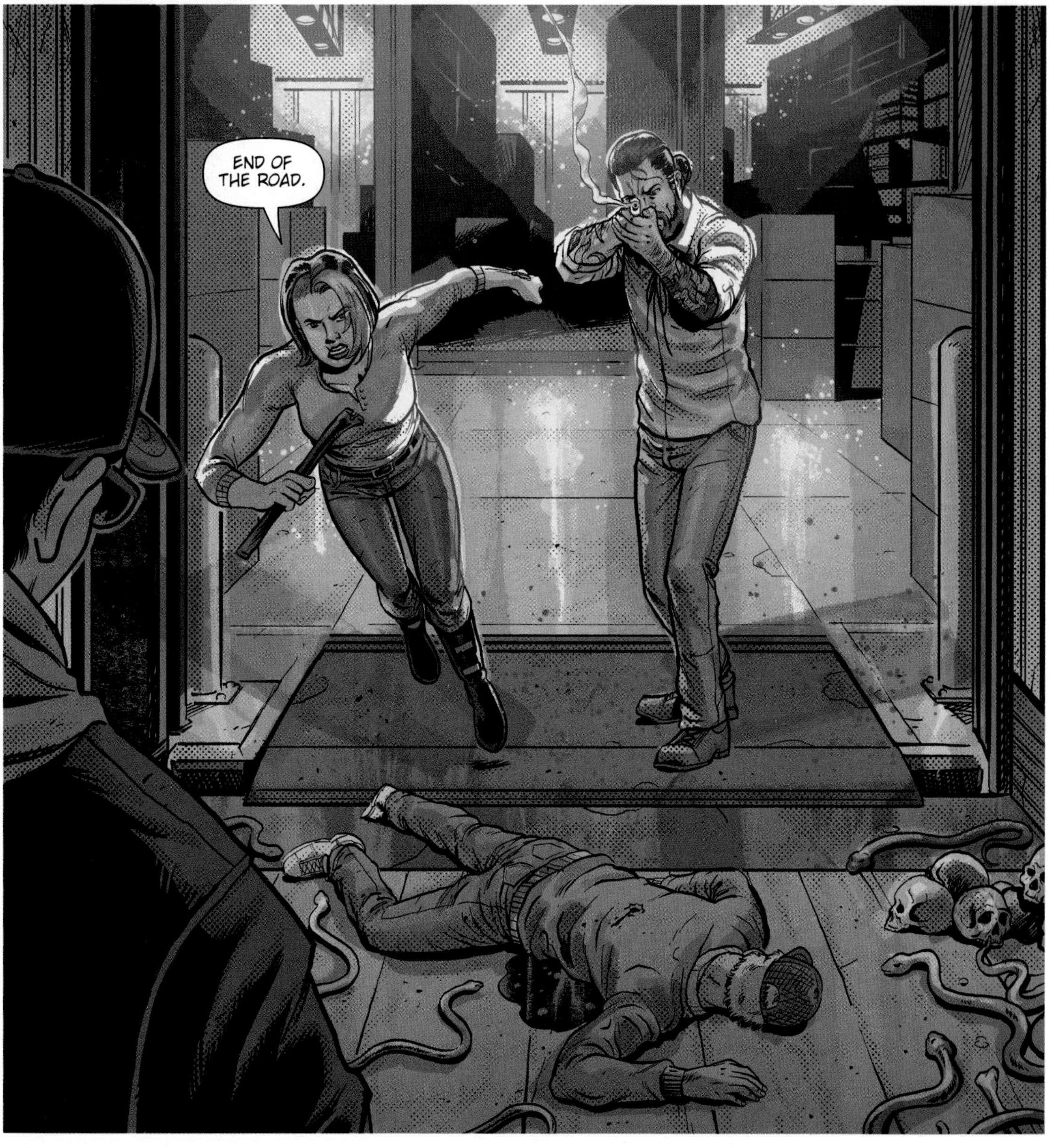
END OF THE ROAD.

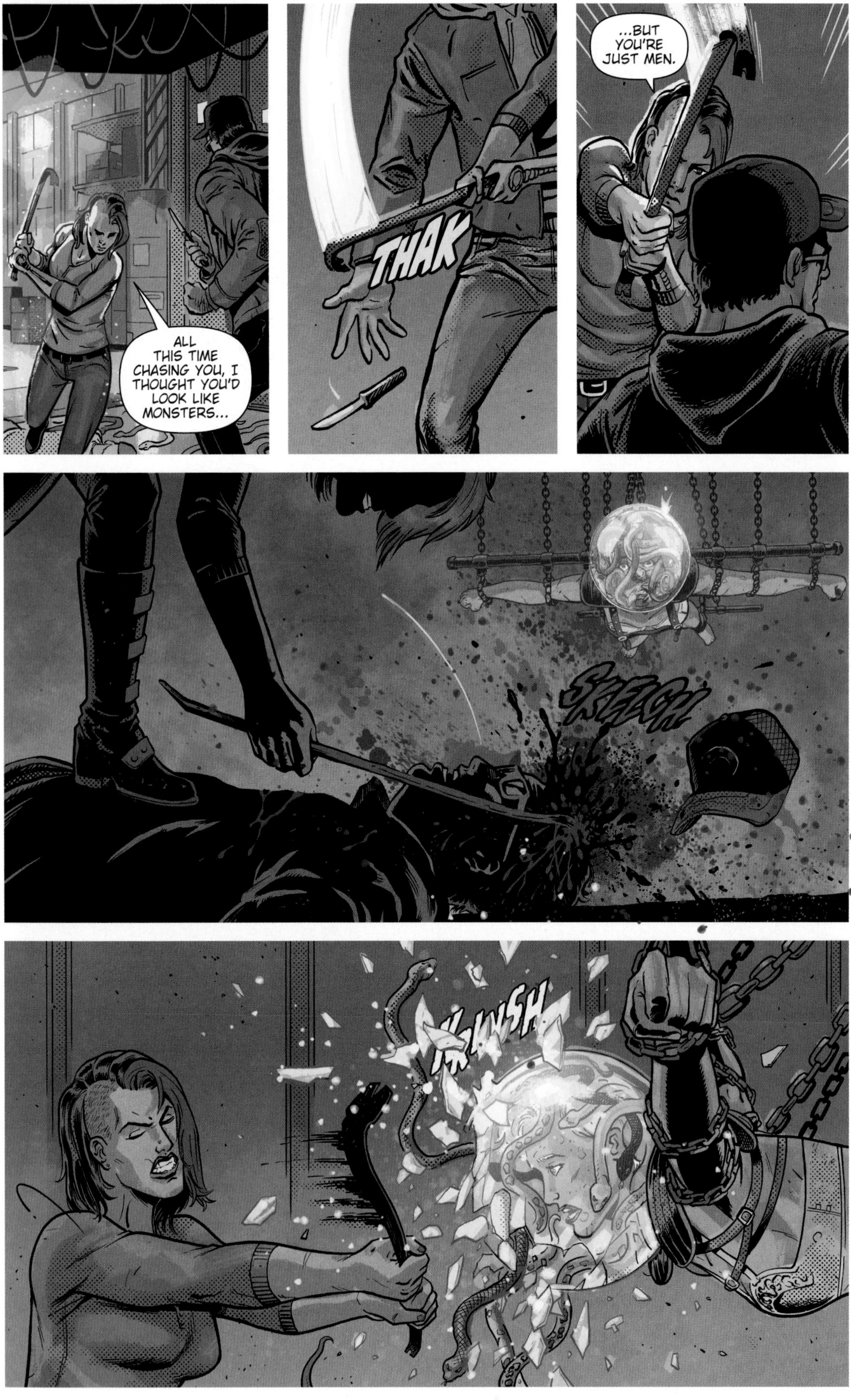
ALL THIS TIME CHASING YOU, I THOUGHT YOU'D LOOK LIKE MONSTERS...
THAK
...BUT YOU'RE JUST MEN.

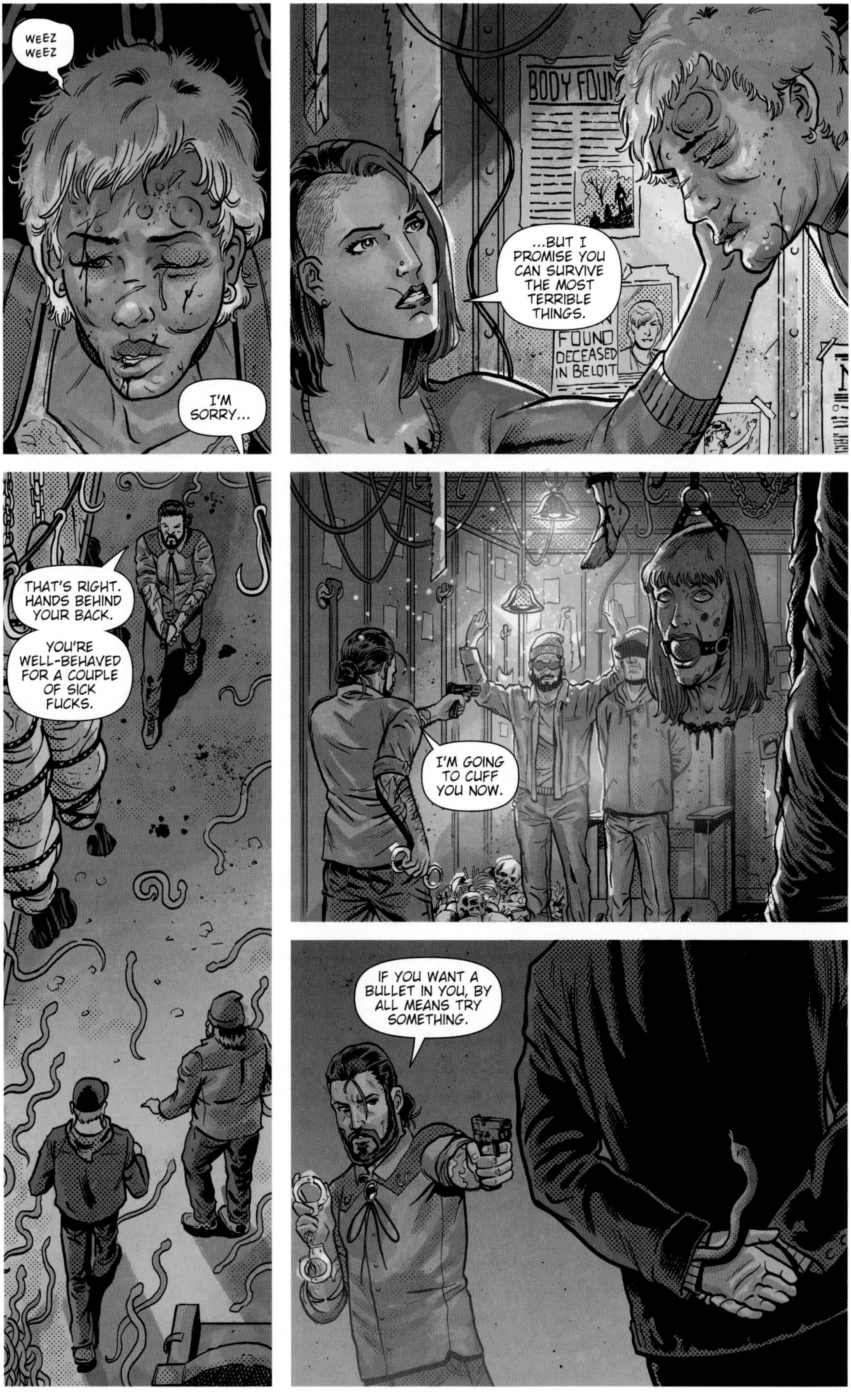

WEEZ WEEZ
I'M SORRY...
BODY FOUN
...BUT I PROMISE YOU CAN SURVIVE THE MOST TERRIBLE THINGS.
FOUND DECEASED IN BELOIT
THAT'S RIGHT. HANDS BEHIND YOUR BACK.
YOU'RE WELL-BEHAVED FOR A COUPLE OF SICK FUCKS.
I'M GOING TO CUFF YOU NOW.
IF YOU WANT A BULLET IN YOU, BY ALL MEANS TRY SOMETHING.

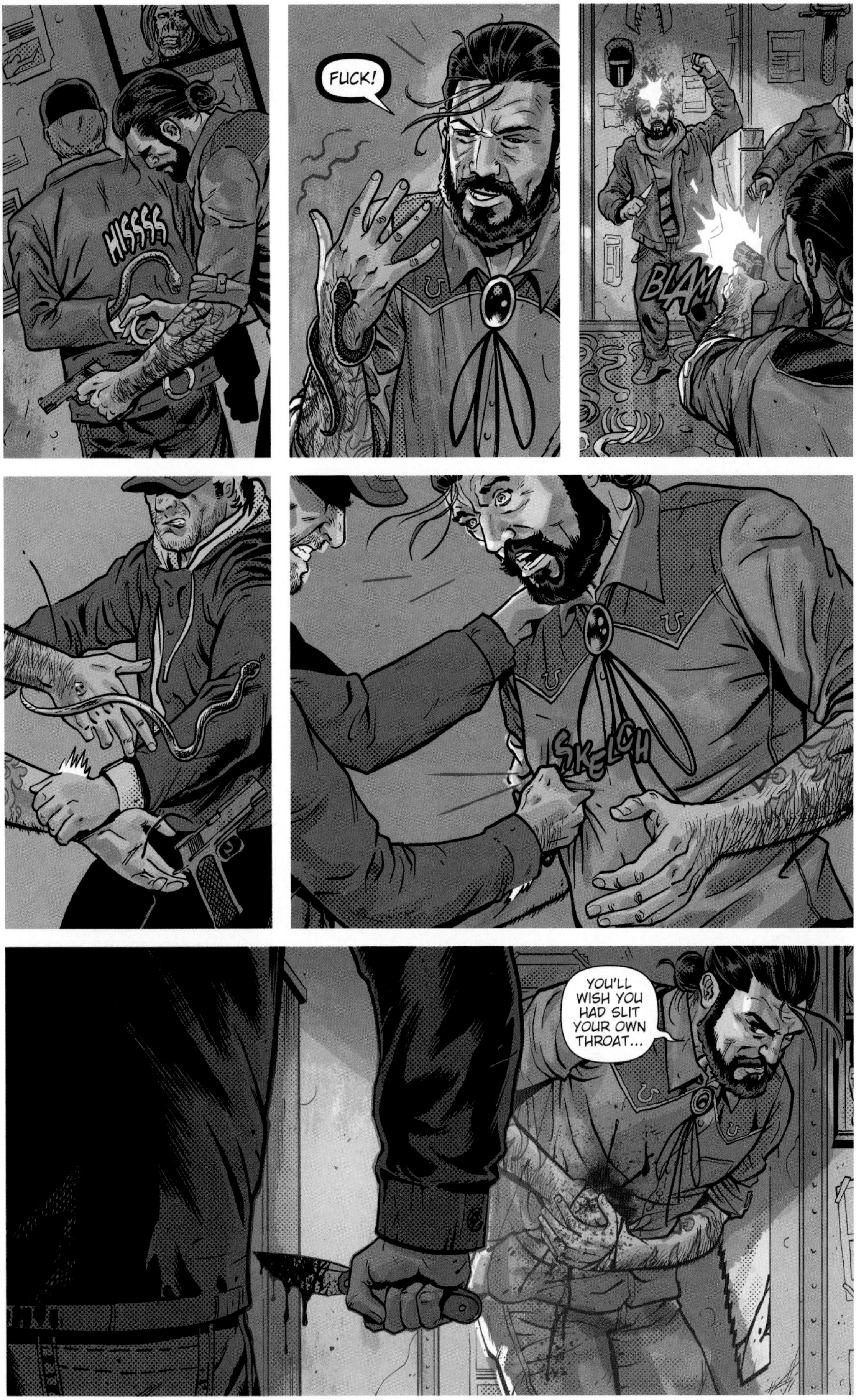
HISSSS
FUCK!
BLAM
SKELCH
YOU'LL WISH YOU HAD SLIT YOUR OWN THROAT...

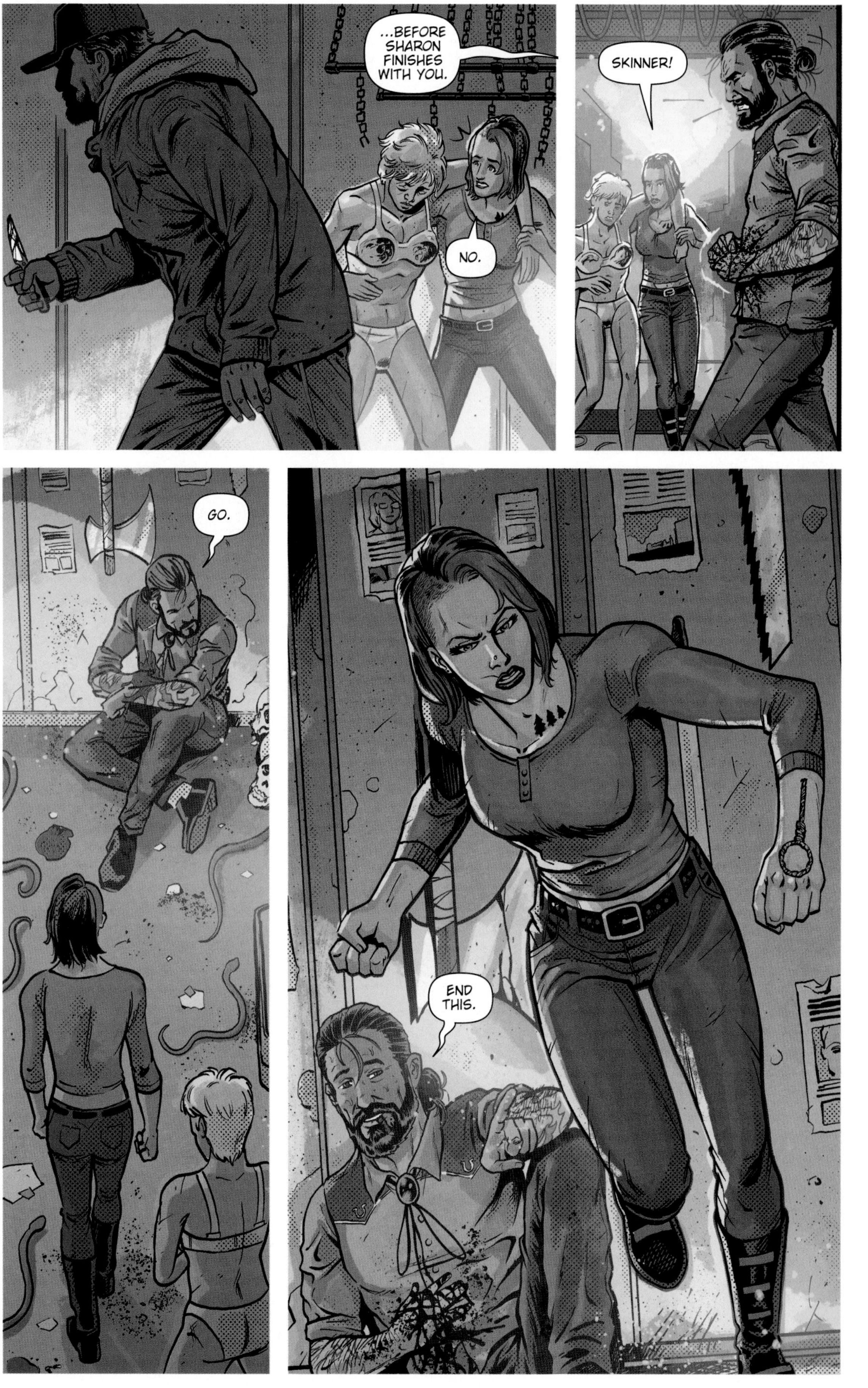
...BEFORE SHARON FINISHES WITH YOU.
NO.
SKINNER!
GO.
END THIS.

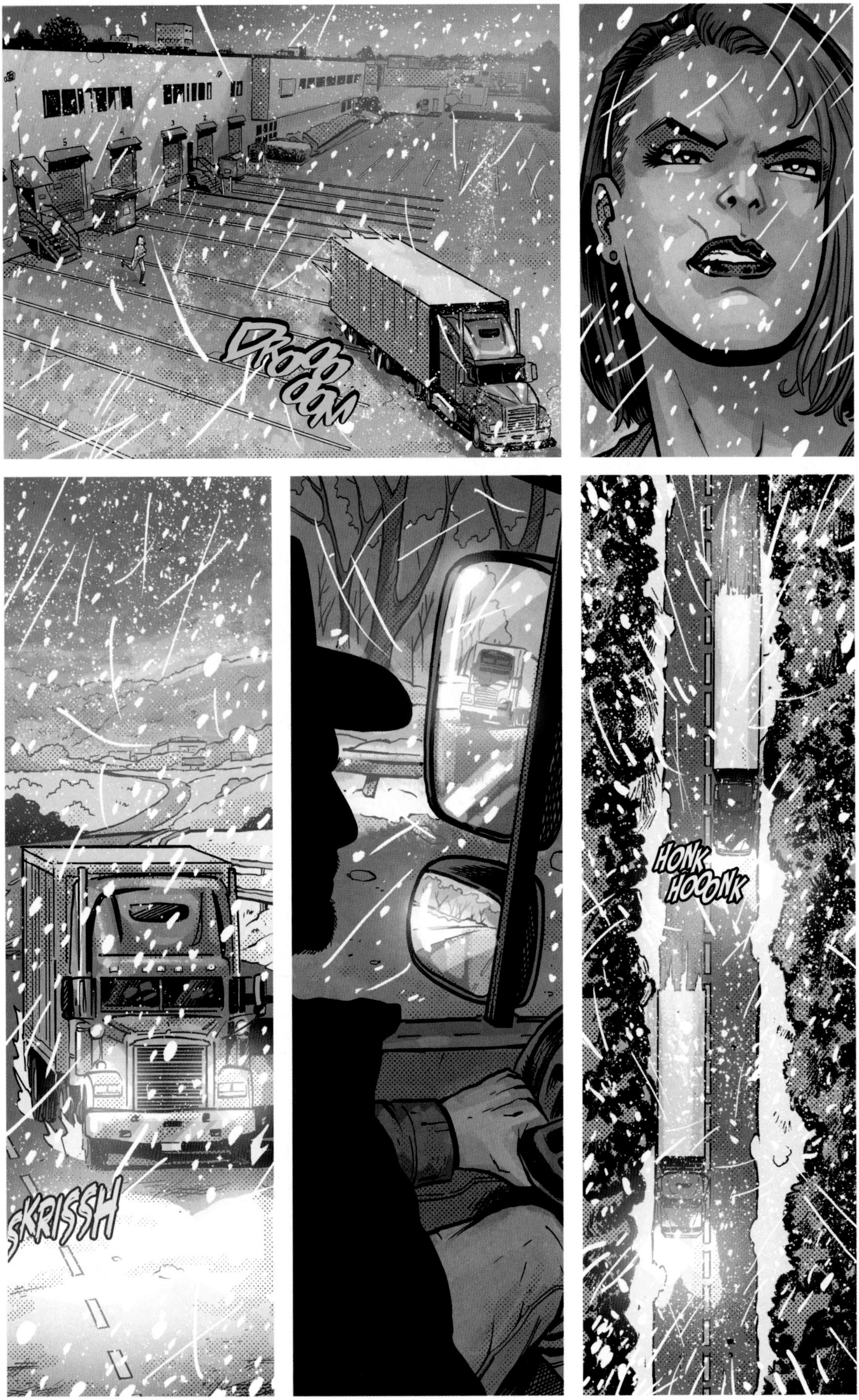
DROOOOM
SKRISSH
HONK
HOOONK

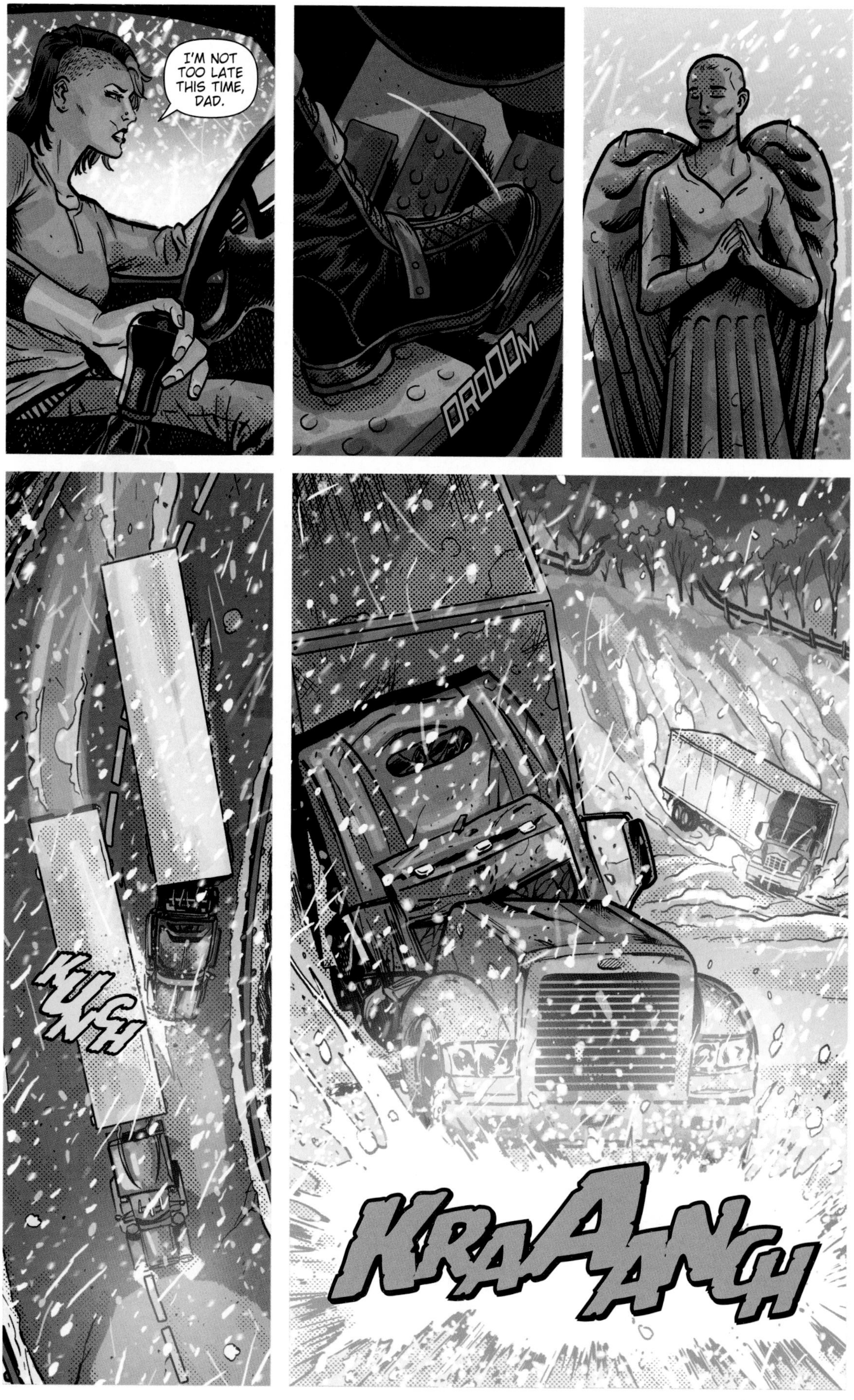
I'M NOT TOO LATE THIS TIME, DAD.
DROOOM
KLUNCH
KRAAAANCH

WE BOTH SHED OUR SKINS.

WE BOTH BECAME SOMETHING NEW.

AND NOW I AM UNHINGING MY JAW.

AND SWALLOWING YOU WHOLE.

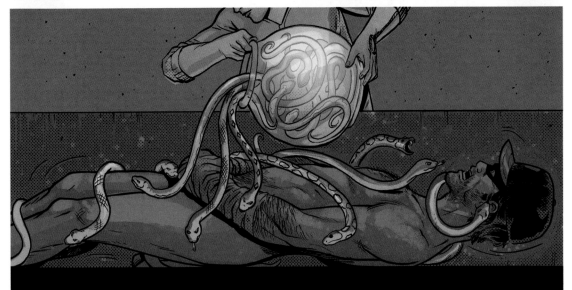

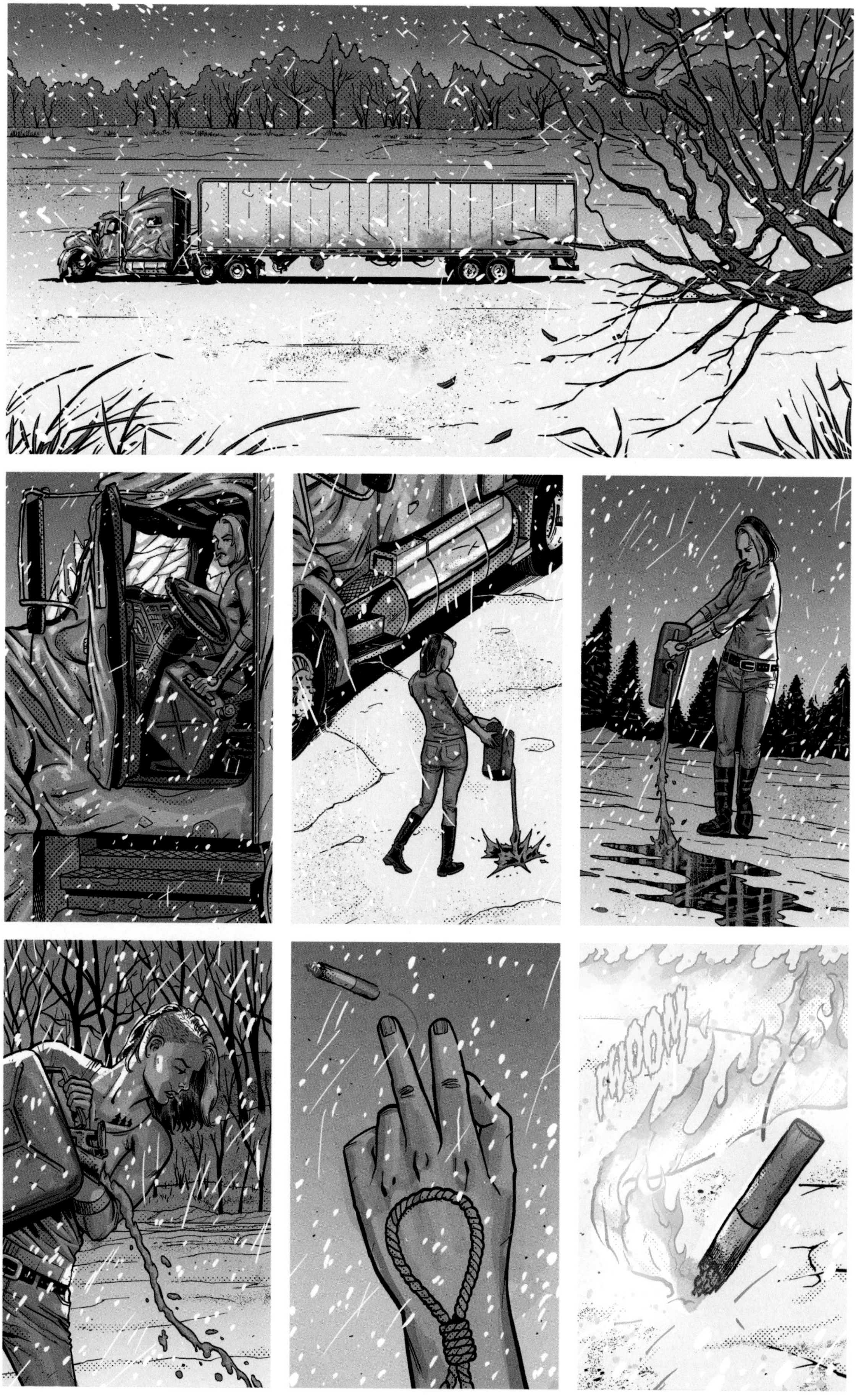
FWOOM

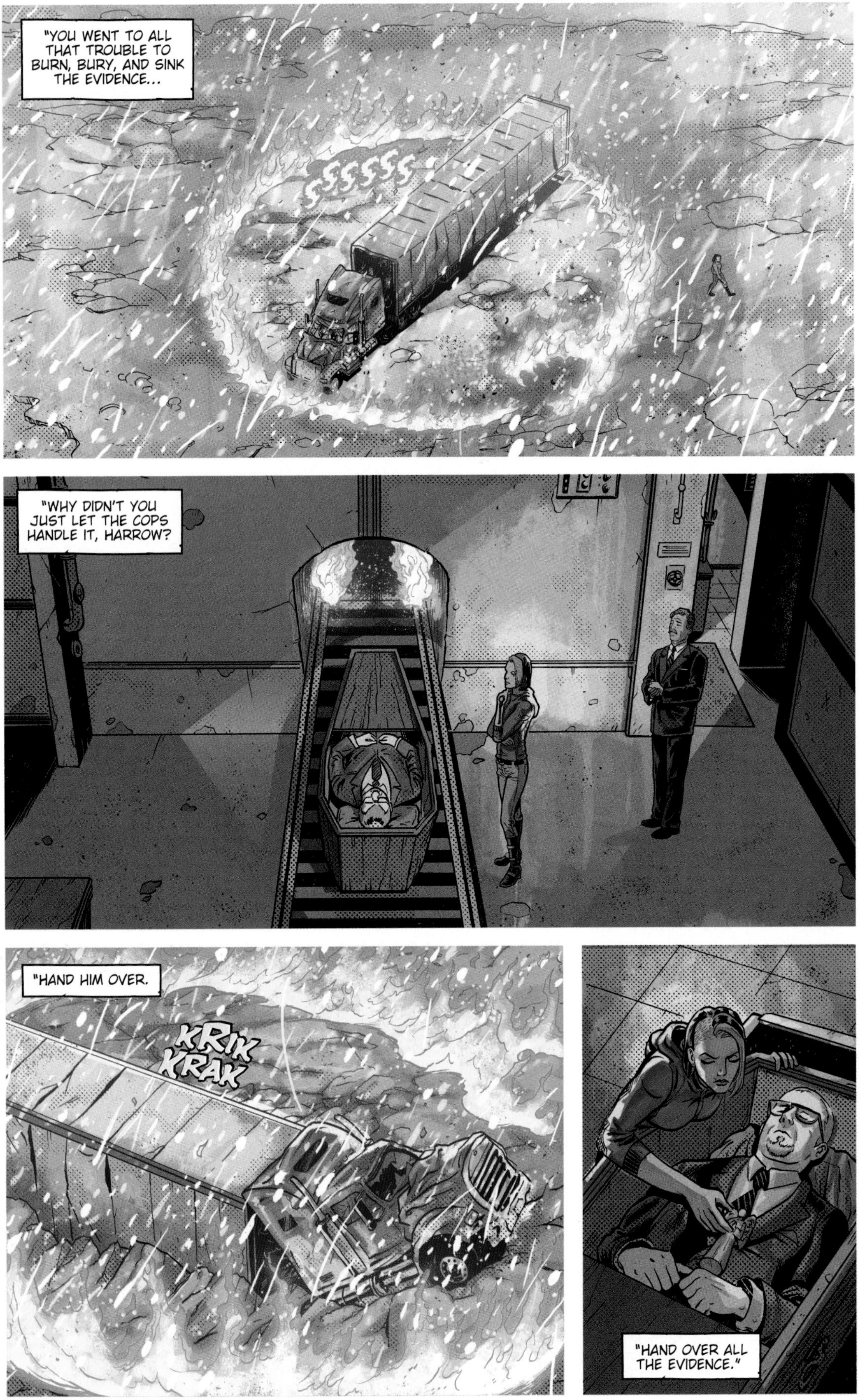
"YOU WENT TO ALL THAT TROUBLE TO BURN, BURY, AND SINK THE EVIDENCE...
"WHY DIDN'T YOU JUST LET THE COPS HANDLE IT, HARROW?
"HAND HIM OVER.
KRIK KRAK
"HAND OVER ALL THE EVIDENCE."

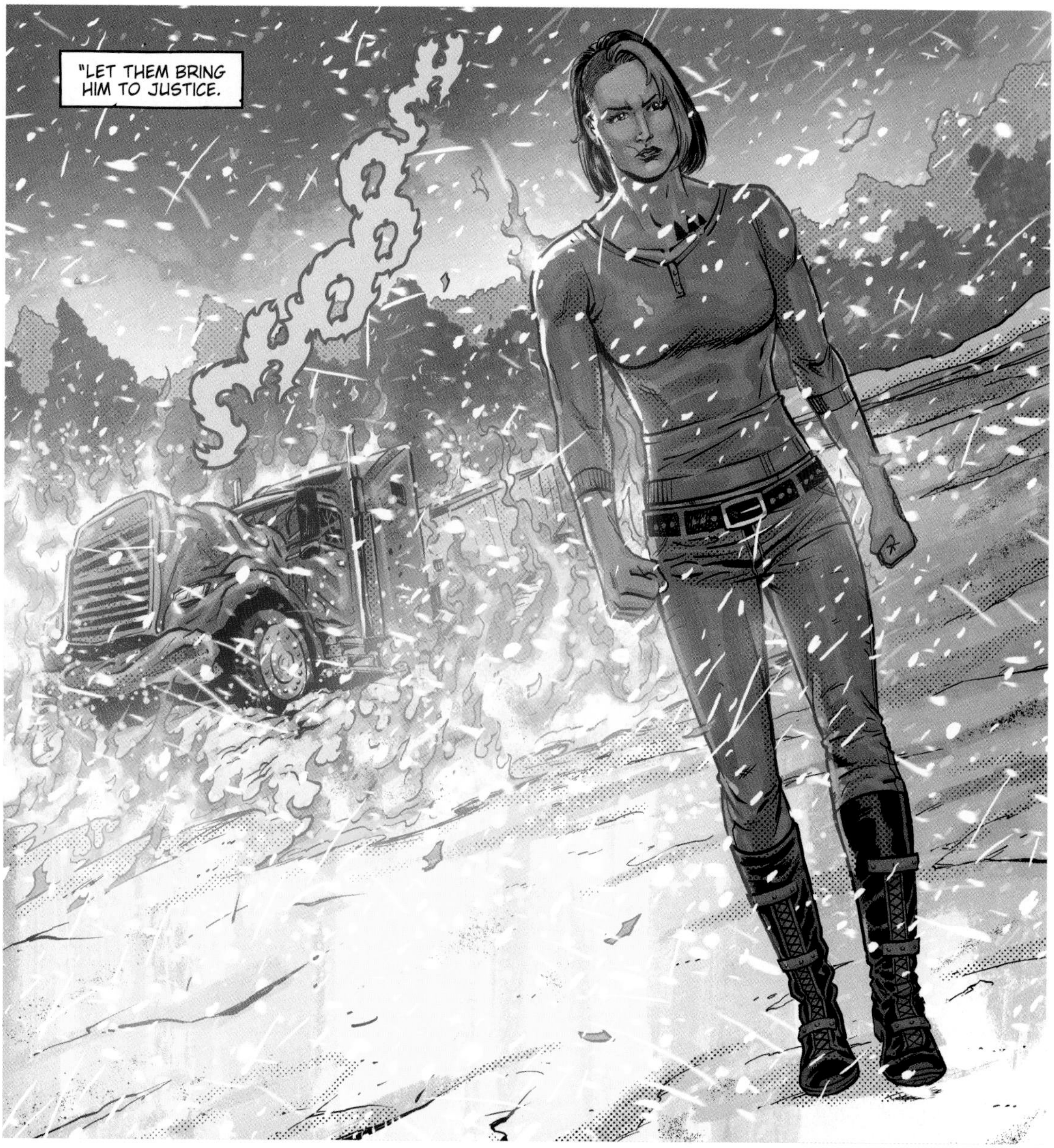
"LET THEM BRING
HIM TO JUSTICE.

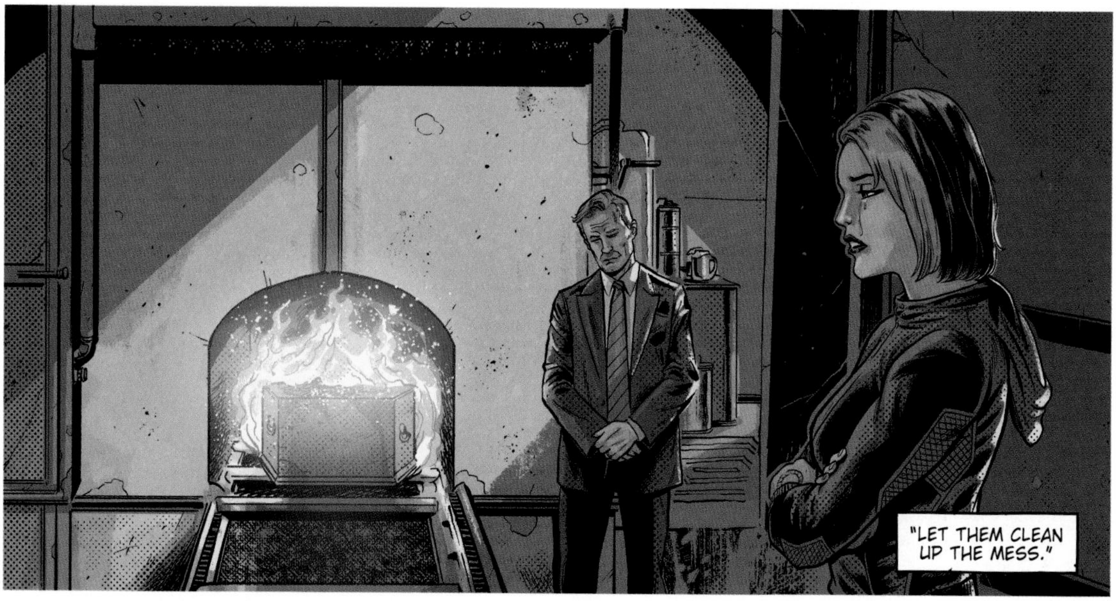
"LET THEM CLEAN
UP THE MESS."

ALSO...I'D TELL YOU YOU'RE NOT SUPPOSED TO SMOKE IN HERE, BUT YOU'D PROBABLY TELL ME TO FUCK MYSELF?

GO FUCK YOURSELF.

AND NOBODY CAN KNOW ABOUT WHAT WE'VE DONE, BECAUSE THEY'LL GET IN OUR WAY.

THERE'S STILL WORK TO DO.

WAIT. THAT ISN'T YOUR LAPTOP. DID YOU GET THAT FROM--

IT WAS STASHED IN A SECRET COMPARTMENT IN THE CAB OF HIS TRUCK.

YOU'RE THE ONE WHO SAID IT. THERE ARE MORE THAN A DOZEN SERIAL KILLERS OPERATING AS SEMI DRIVERS.

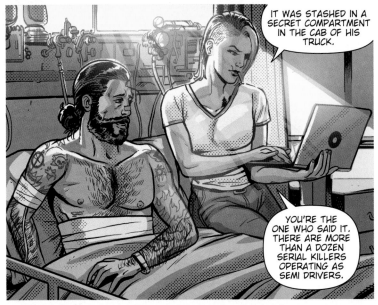

THAT DOESN'T JUST HAPPEN.

BELLY: So excited to try out some new toys in the playhouse.

COWBOY 02: It's been too long. I've got a craving.

BABYTEETH: Wish I could be there. You boys try not to have too much fun without me.

MONGREL: I got my boy this weekend. But I'll be thinking of you all while we are catching walleyes on Lake Delton,

VIKING: I just talked to Z a̶ ̶e̶'s looking forward to playing in the playhouse

SOMEONE HAS TO BE ORGANIZING THEM.

Z: Yessir. I'll be coming up from Dallas. Long haul but I didnt want to miss this.

KingCobra: Enjoy gentleman. You deserve it.

BABYTEETH: King...You home?

MONGREL: Hey King... need to chat when you get a minute.

BABYTEETH: Cobra I really need to talk when you have a moment.

MONGREL: Same here.

VIKING: What's going on fellas?

MONGREL: Could be some major shit going down.

BABYTEETH: Yeah. Not good man.

BABYTEETH: I'm getting a lot of chatter coming my way.
MONGREL: Same here. Was expecting a quiet holiday weekend.
VIKING: Really? I was offline last couple days. Mom's not well.

HONEY!

YES, DEAR?

DINNER!

I'LL BE RIGHT THERE.

BABYTEETH: Is it true?

MONGREL: Z's gone dark. Belly and Cowboy 2.

BABYTEETH: Do we need to be worried?

KINGCOBRA: Until we learn more, assume we've been compromised.

KINGCOBRA: Save your venom. Stay your appetite.

KINGCOBRA: And let the mice fatten.

DAD!? MOM SAYS--

COMING! I WAS JUST FINISHING UP SOME WORK.

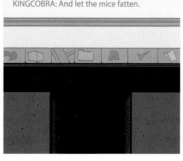

CONCLUSION OF VOLUME 1.

LETTERS FROM THE CREATORS OF

DEVIL'S HIGHWAY

Benjamin Percy

Night was falling as I drove the I-57 corridor through Illinois. The blacktop was empty except for a semi in the distance. As I approached, I could see that the truck had bullhorn pipes that spouted black clouds of exhaust. The trailer was coated thickly in dirt, and on the rear door a message had been scrawled. The big cartoonish letters spelled out, "SHOW ME UR BOOBS."

I wondered what kind of creep would do something like that. So I pulled into the left lane and cranked up my speed to pass him. When I rolled by the cab, the driver turned his head to study me. And I shit you not: he was wearing a clown mask.

So…I showed him my boobs. And crushed the accelerator. And got the hell out of there.

This was twenty years ago. And my flesh still creeps every time I think about it.

Since that time, I've learned things. About the Smiley Face Killer, for instance. I've lived in Illinois and Wisconsin and Iowa and Minnesota, and over the years I've read the headlines about the bodies that form a pattern along the freeways.

I knew there was a story to be found, and I've interviewed truckers and followed their blogs and haunted their social media groups and hashtags and listened to their chatter on CB radios. I've always been fascinated—since I saw both *Duel* and *Over*

the Top as a kid—by their habits and culture and insider language. They're doing good, hard, essential work, but they also occupy a realm that is somehow invisible in plain sight. And sometimes things get dangerous at the truck stops and rest stops. Because of drugs, prostitution, even murder.

The FBI believes a dozen or more serial killers are currently operating tractor-trailers. If you think about it, trucking is a perfect fit for that lifestyle. The anonymity of constant travel. The vulnerable populations they're exposed to. The mobile storage unit they're dragging behind them.

The more I learned about trucking, the more I wondered if I had brushed close to something evil that evening in Illinois.

> *I wondered if I had brushed close to something evil that evening in Illinois.*

A few years ago, I got beers with my buddy and fellow Minnesotan—Brent Schoonover—and we started brainstorming a story. The story of a troubled woman named Sharon Harrow who infiltrates the trucking underworld in an effort to hunt down her father's killer.

It's been so much fun to bring this story to life with my friend, and he's done a brilliant job (along with colorist Nick Filardi) creating a "northern gothic" aesthetic. The storytelling unspools as a gritty, horrifying mystery that reads like a David Fincher film.

Buckle up and beware. The highway ahead is dark and full of sharp turns.

-Benjamin Percy

Brent Schoonover

When I was a kid growing up in a small midwestern town, my family would often take us to a little greasy spoon diner named Cliff's. Cliff's was a family-friendly hole-in-the-wall that was mostly frequented by townies and truckers stopping off I-90 for a quick meal. Cliff's was nothing to marvel. Wood paneling. Mediocre food. A bad sound system that belted out old country tunes. But it was cheap and Cliff was a hell of a nice guy, greeting everyone who came in.

At the front of the place was a small gift shop. Nothing for kids to get excited about. Only things I remember coming home with are some Desert Storm trading cards and a bootleg Packers Super Bowl T-shirt. If you followed the long hallway to the bathrooms, though, you would realize there was more to Cliff's than what you saw at first glance. There was a backroom doorway that was covered with beads on strings. After a dozen visits I finally got the courage to just pop my head in back to see what was in the mysterious room. The first thing I saw was a giant velvet painting of a beautiful naked black woman on the wall. Below that was a glass case with assorted bongs and drug paraphernalia. The entire room was sex and drugs and assorted furniture and sound system equipment that had to have "fallen off the truck." I stood there taking it all in when out of nowhere a tall unkempt man in a wide-brim hat with a cigarette hanging out of his mouth yelled, "Get yer ass outta here!" And I quickly raced back to my pancakes and chocolate milk.

> *I want every issue to feel like you are taking a step deeper into a world you aren't totally sure you should be in.*

This moment always stuck out to me. Cliff's was more than just a diner. It was serving a part of society that was darker than anything I knew at that time. It fascinated and scared me all at once. I wanted to know more about what I had seen but didn't know how.

That is the feeling I hope readers of *Devil's Highway* take away. I want every issue to feel like you are taking a step deeper into a world you aren't totally sure you should be in, but you are too intrigued to leave.

-Brent Schoonover

Sketch from 2019 New York Comic Con by Brent Schoonover

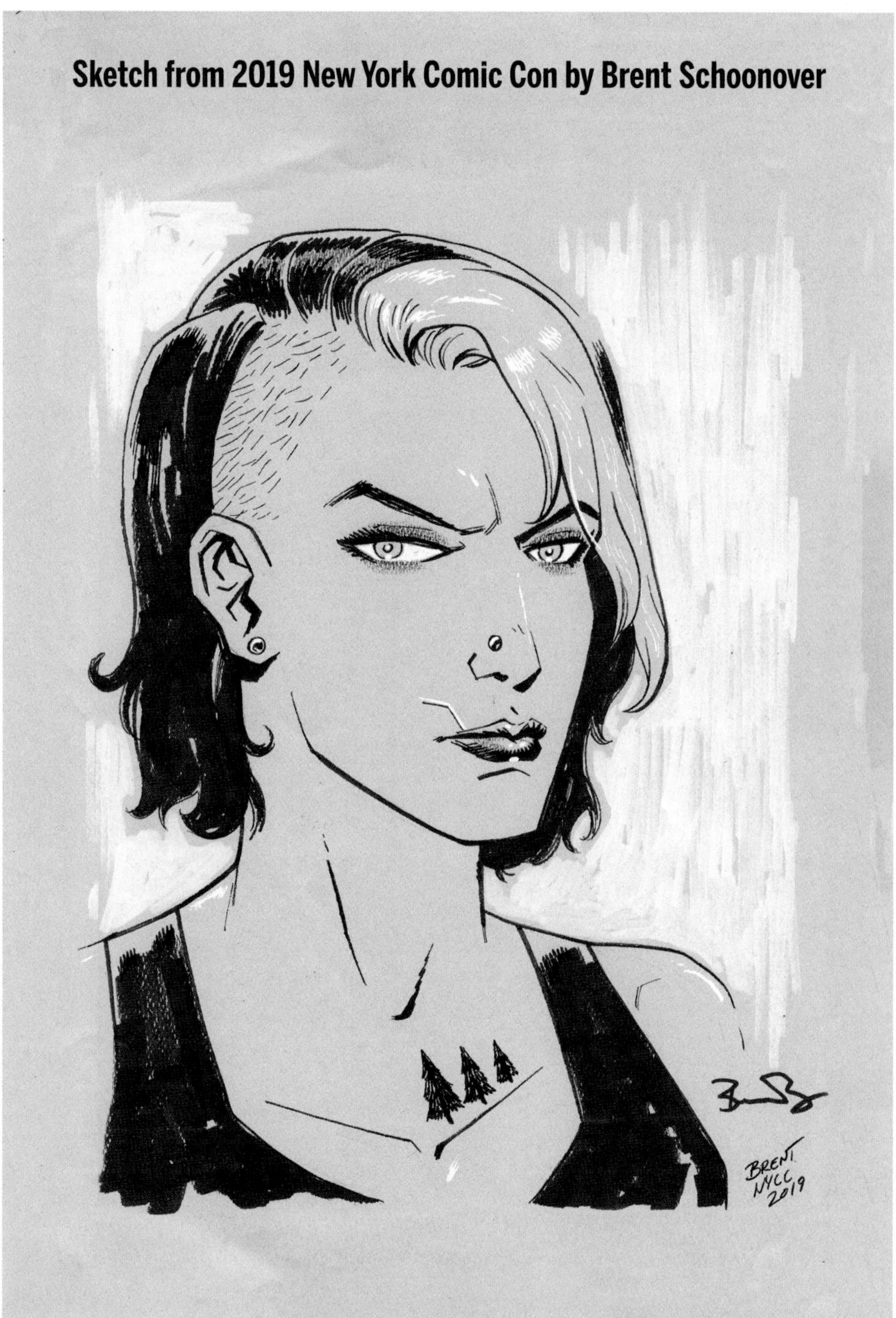
BRENT.
NYCC
2019

ORIGINAL PITCH PAGES AND CONCEPT DRAWINGS

Originally Sharon was not a super confident badass. She was more of a fish out of water, letting her emotions and quest for revenge be her guide. Sharon was going to struggle at first, but her confidence and determination and capability would gradually increase. And her semi-truck would match her emotional development. At first, she'd strip the gears and run out of oil and shred the tires...and think she's made a terrible mistake, chasing this impossible mission...but eventually the road would mold her into a tough, hardass blacktop fighter. From art school to underground fight pits.

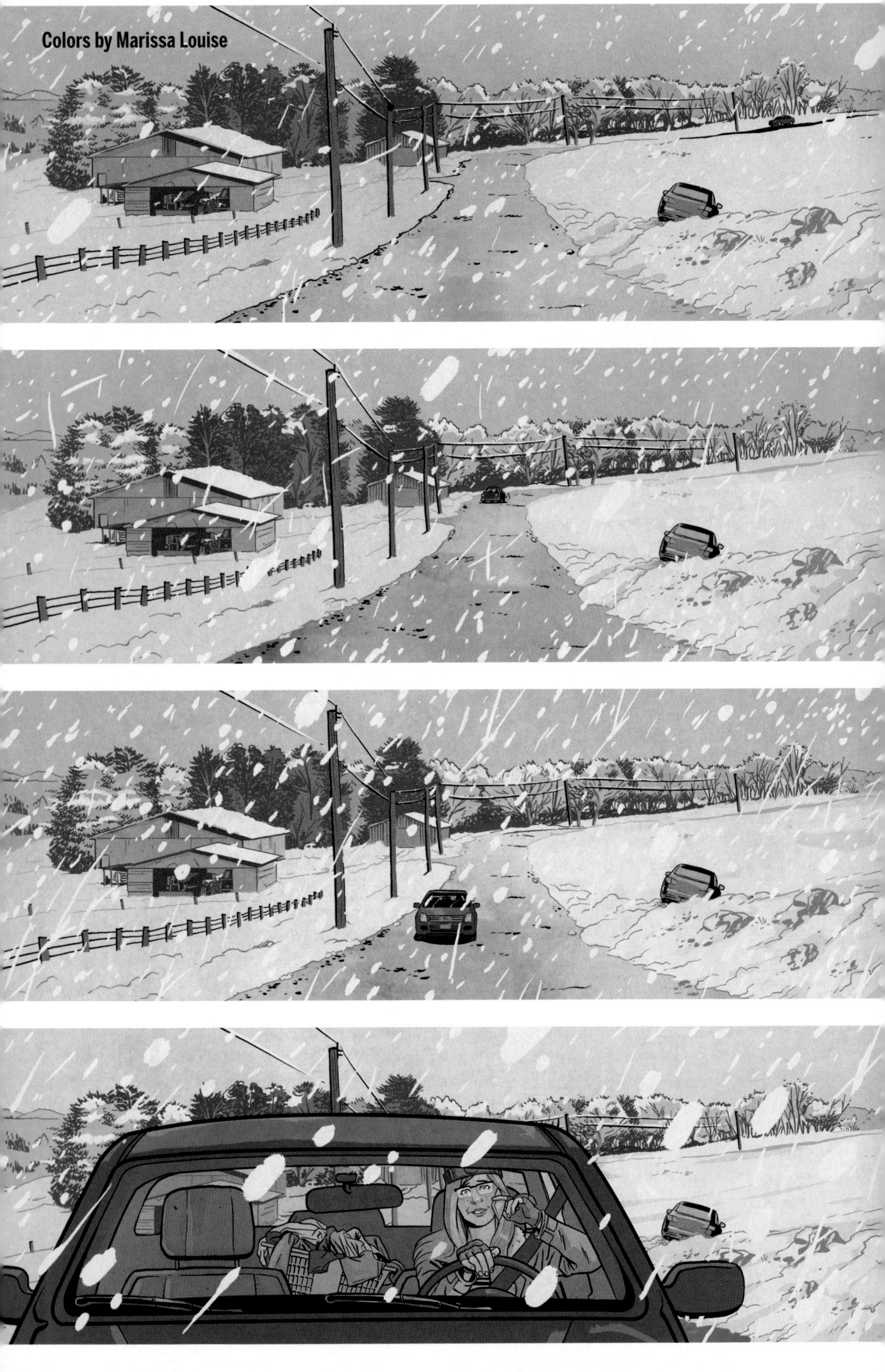
Colors by Marissa Louise

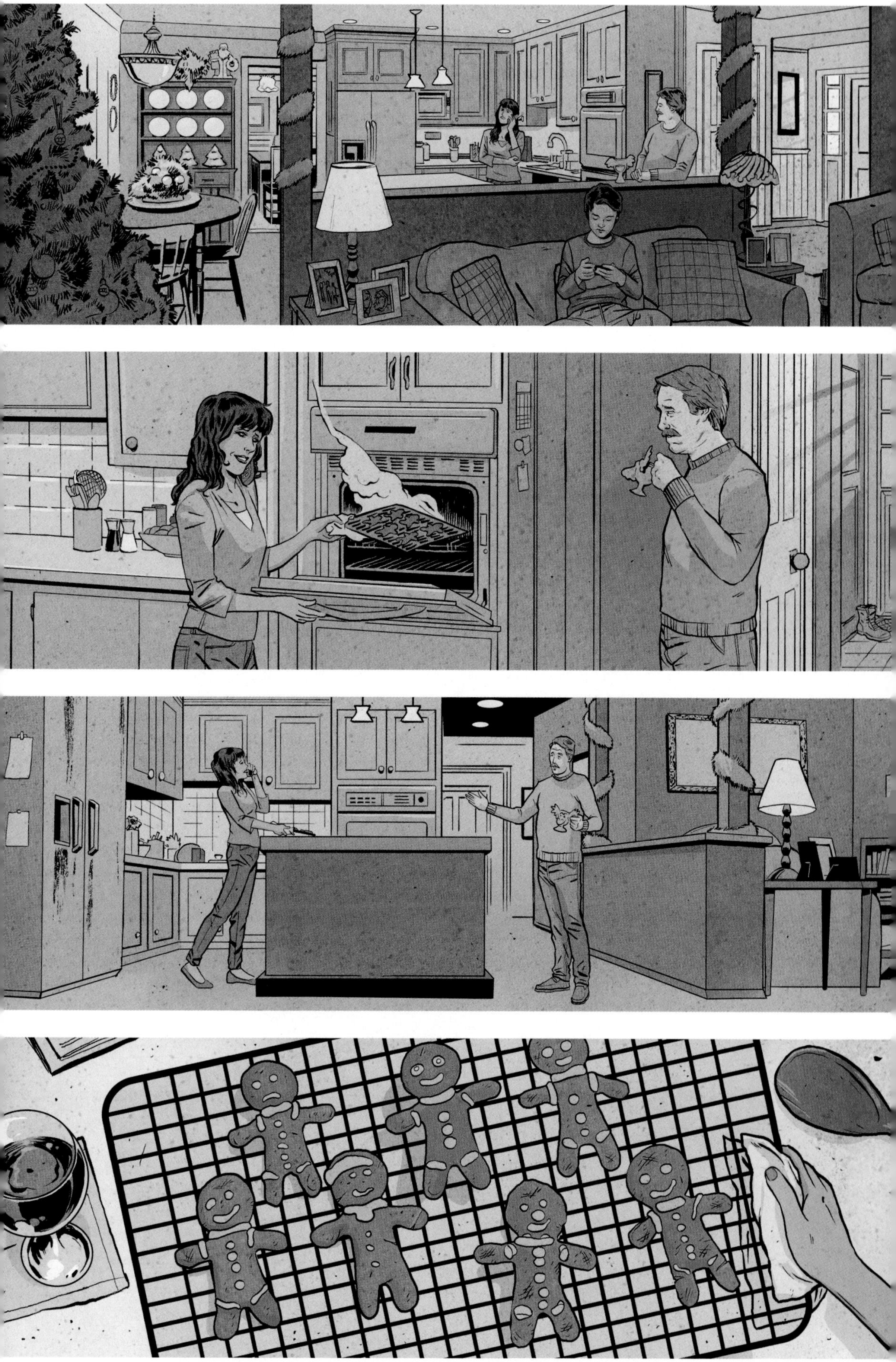

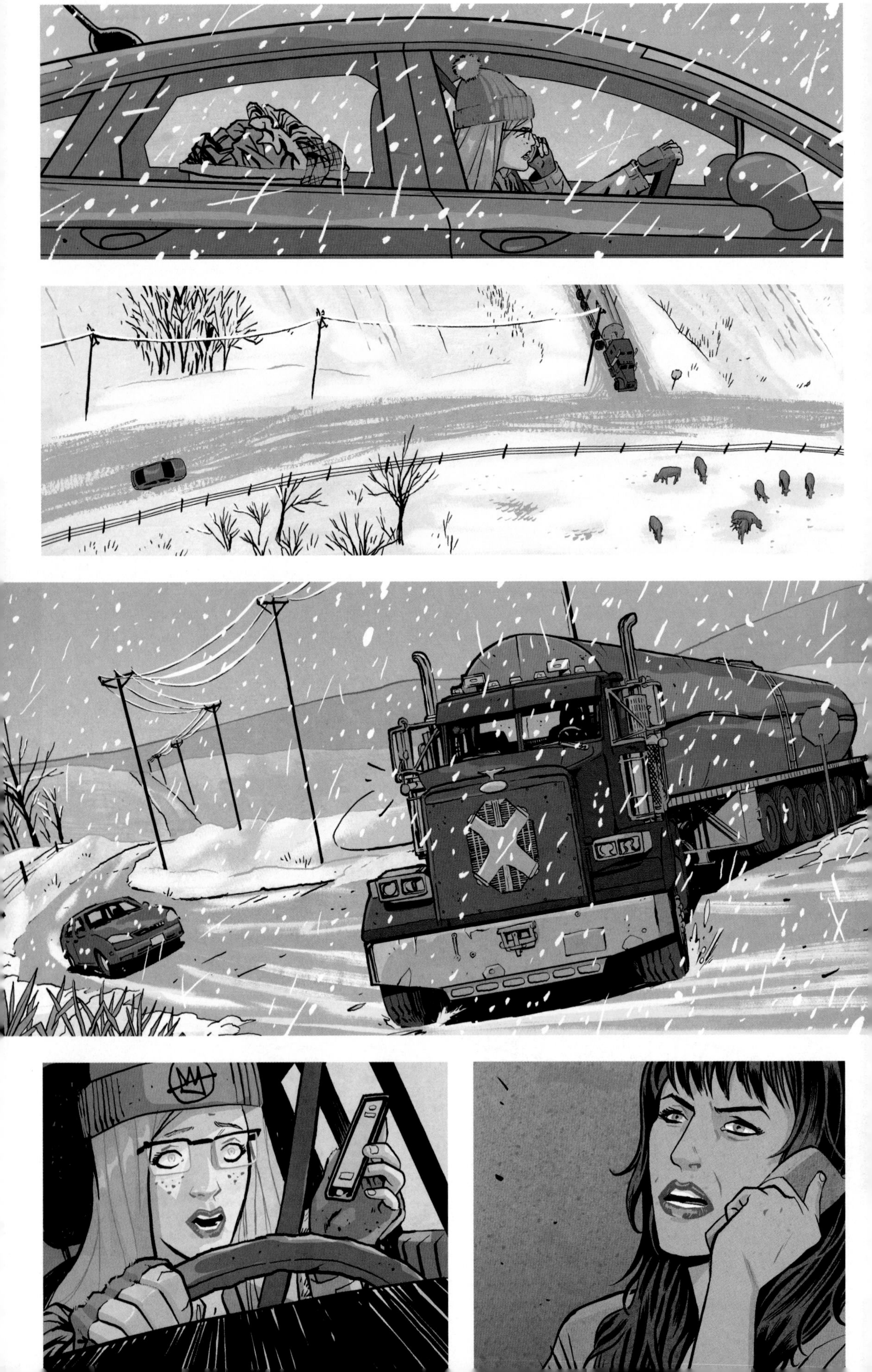

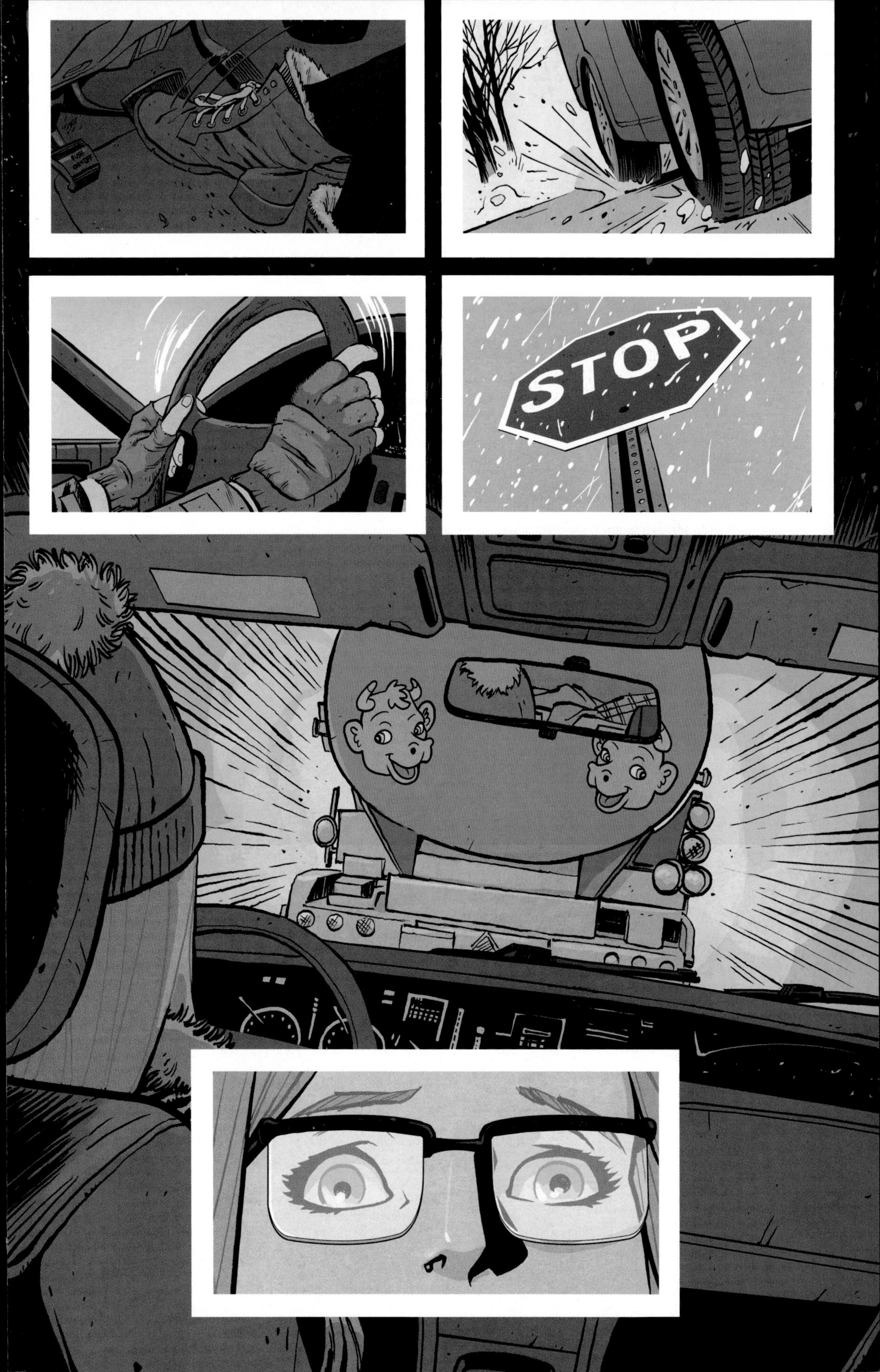
STOP

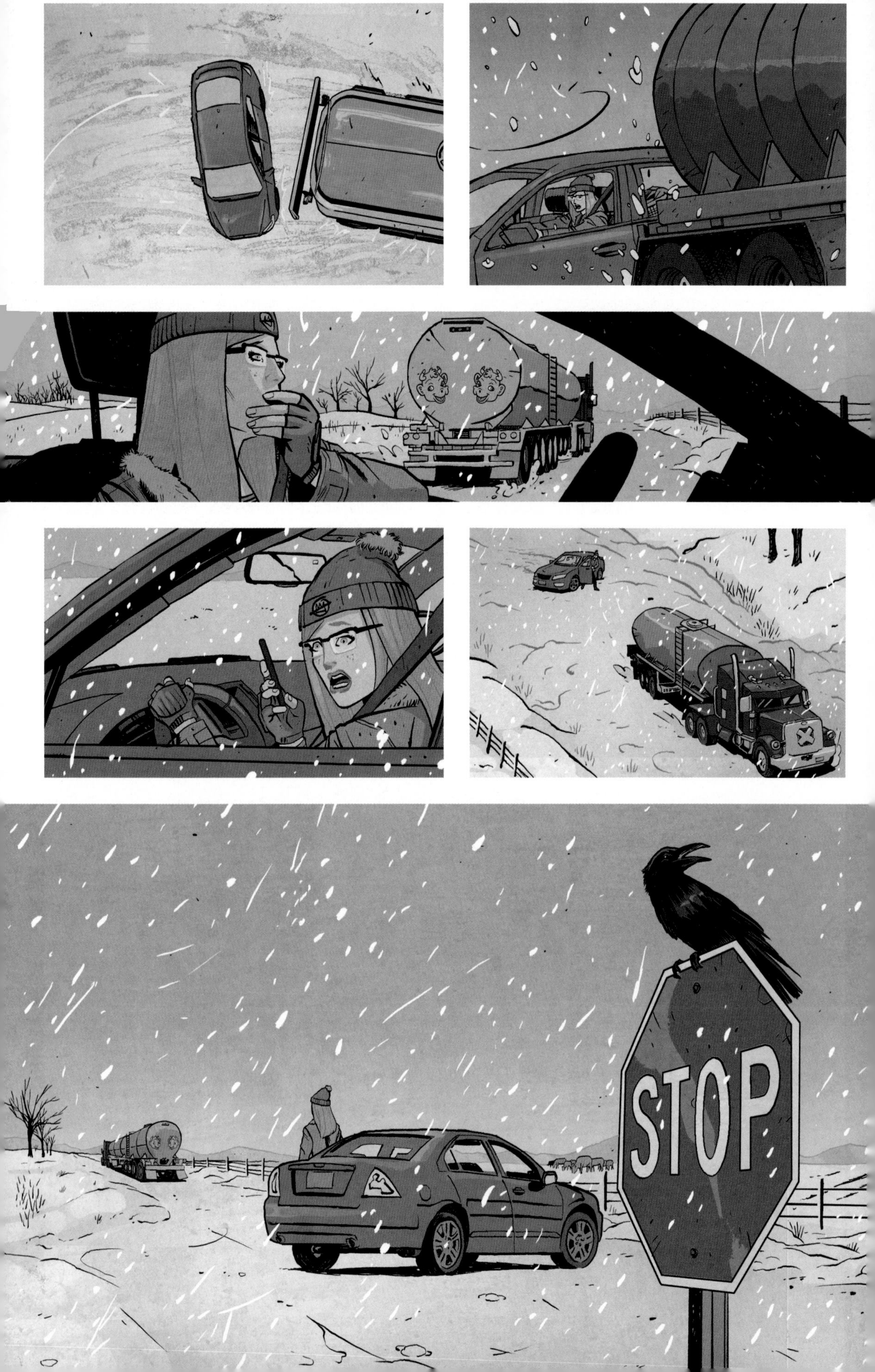
STOP

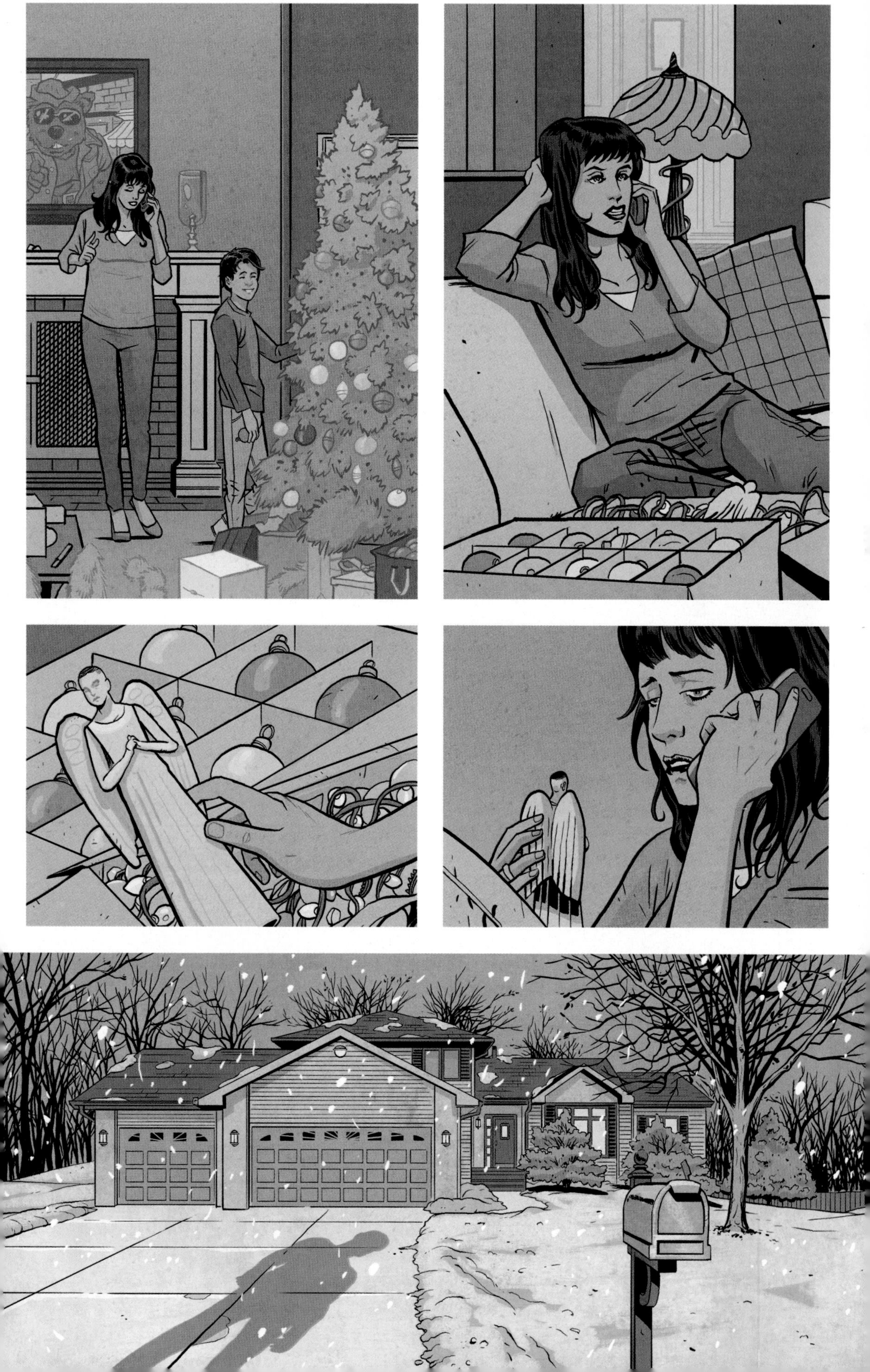

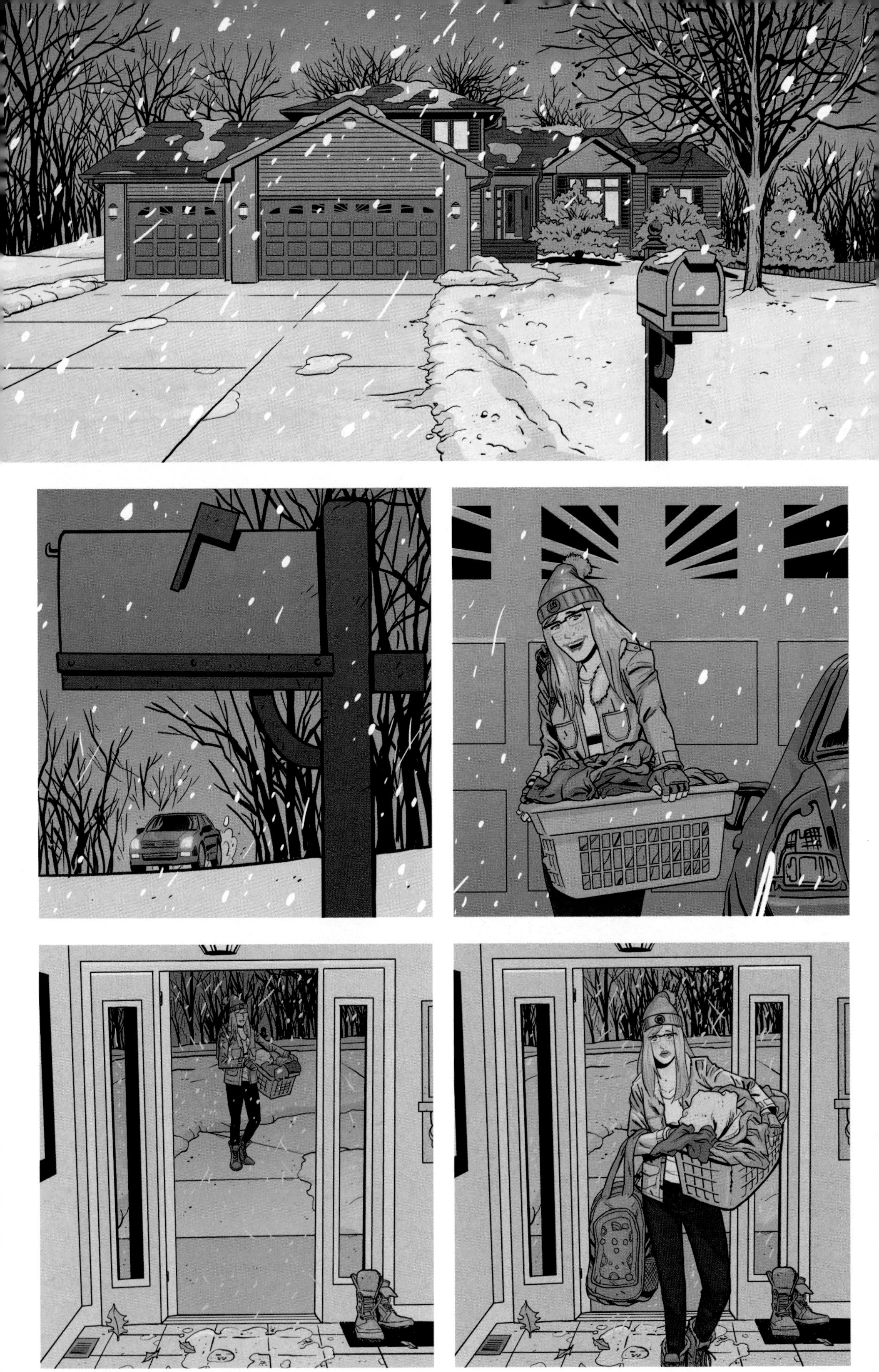

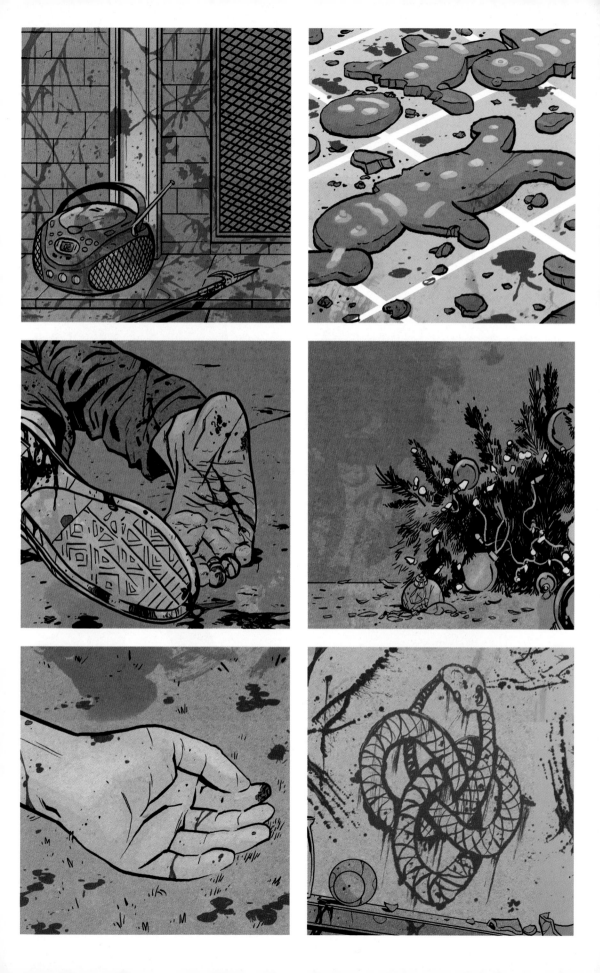

EARLY DESIGN CONCEPTS FOR SHARON

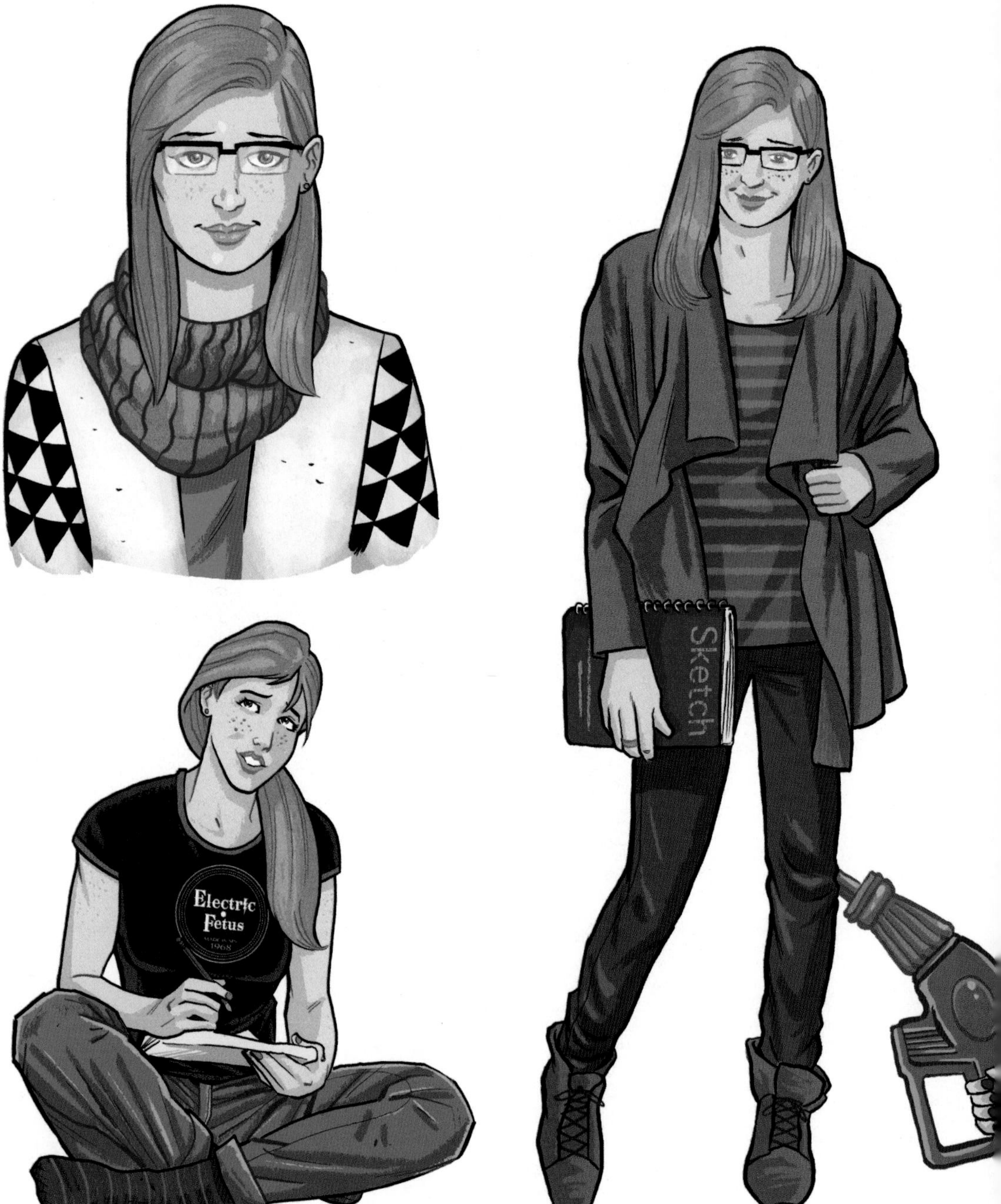
Electric
Fetus
1968
Sketch

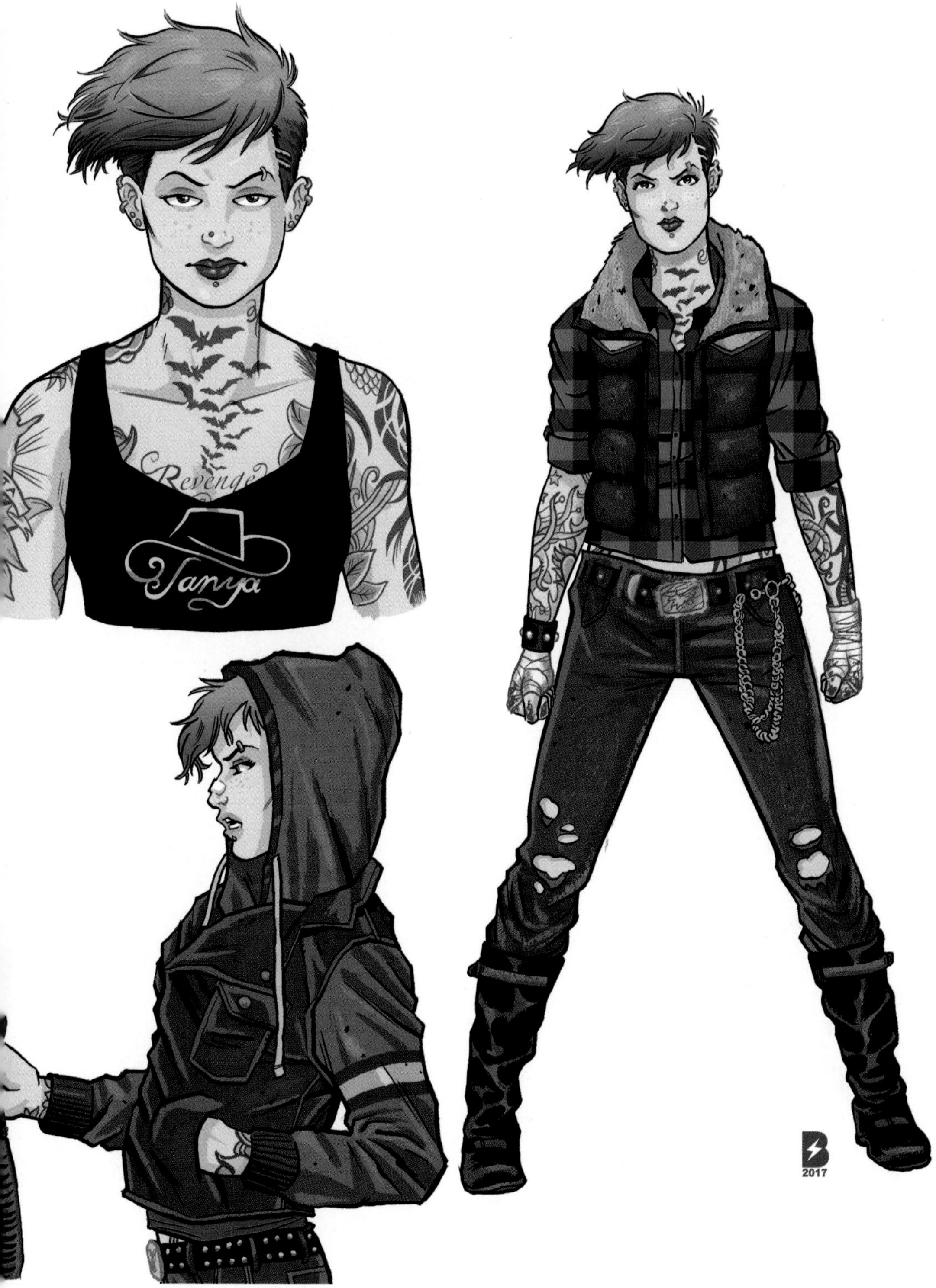
Revenge
Tanya
2017

EARLY CHARACTER DESIGN CONCEPTS

Devil's Highway

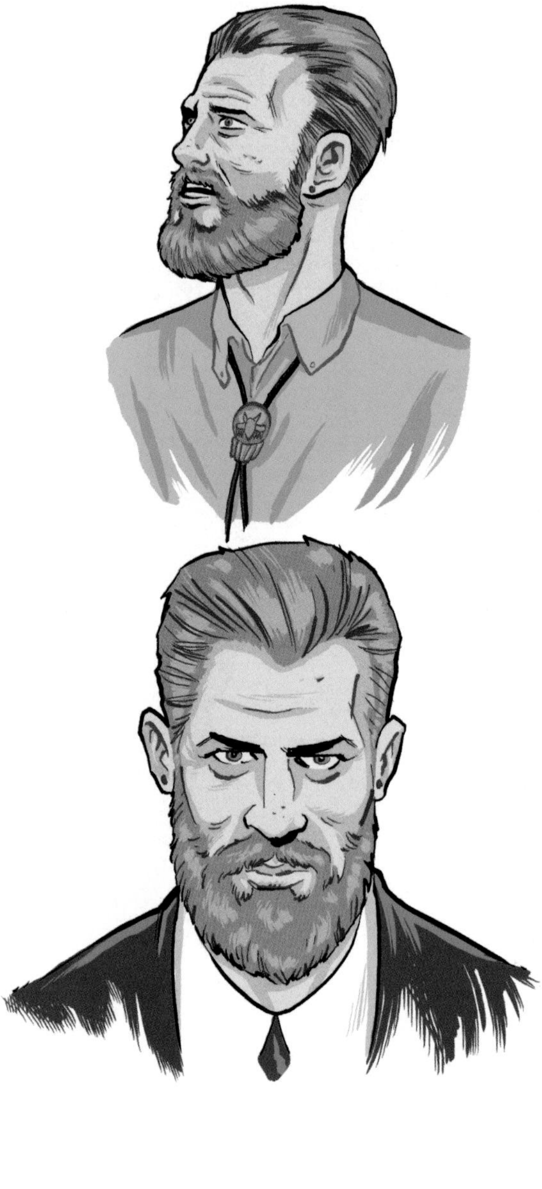

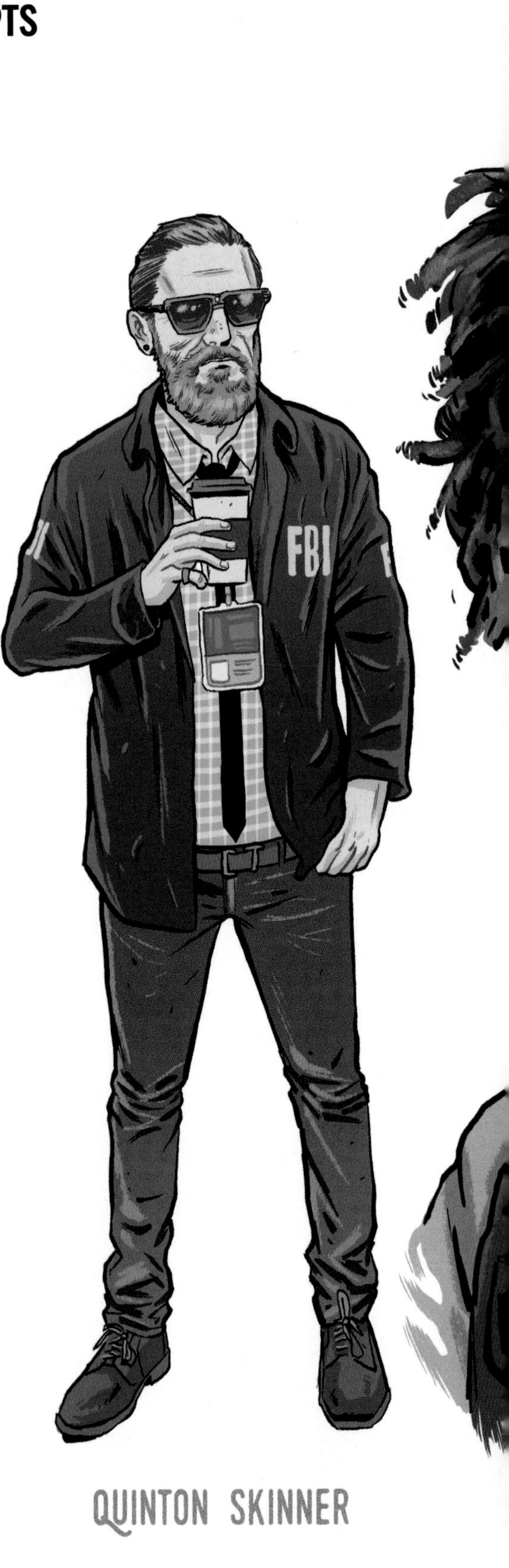
FBI

QUINTON SKINNER

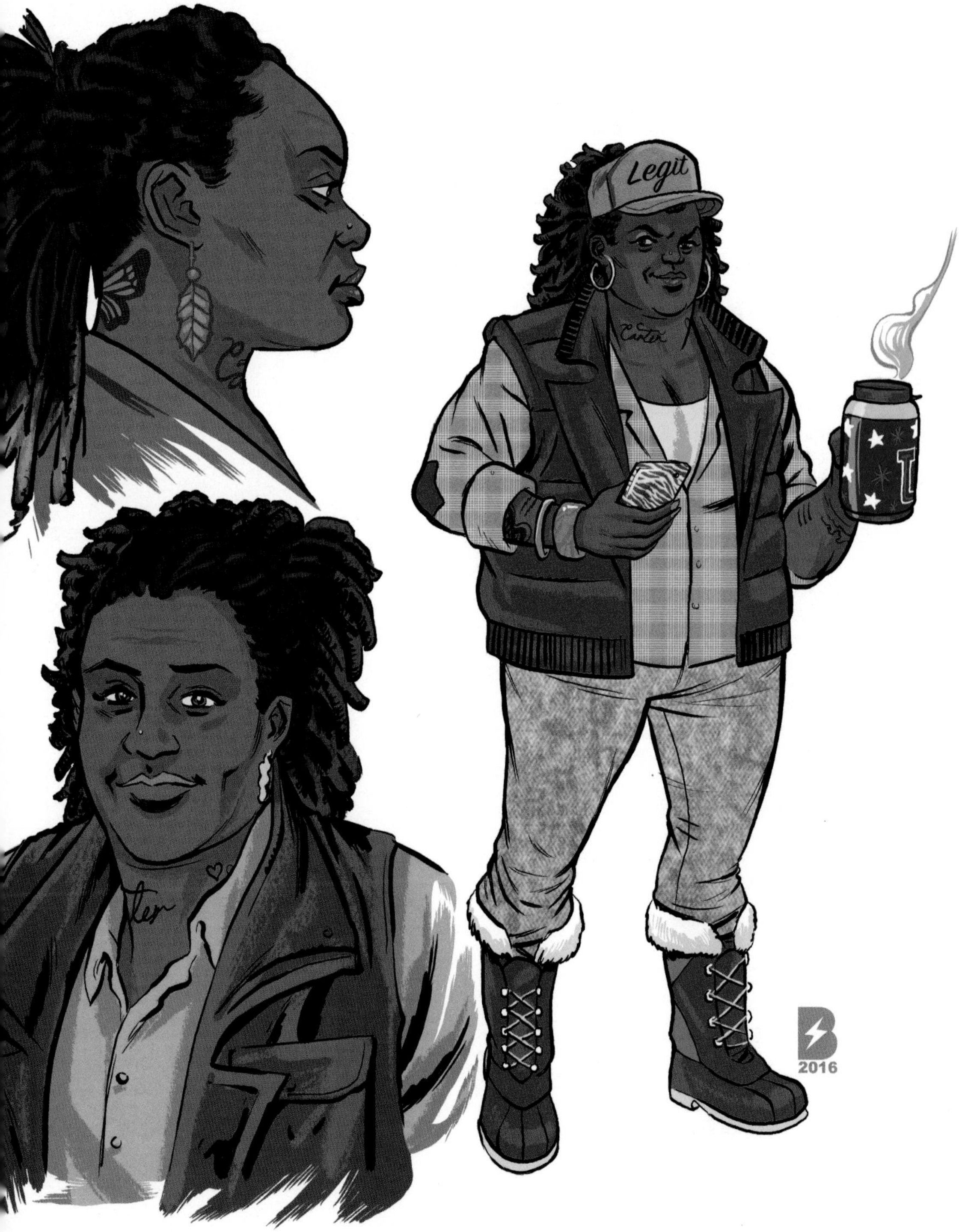
Legit
2016

REESE PANCAKE

PAGE 9 (seven panels)

Panel 1
Exterior. Day. Gray skies. Back at the diner. Snow has fallen, but it's been blown around enough that there is the occasional bare patch on the ground. That's just background detail though. Our focus here is the entrance. It's been cordoned off with crime tape. Sharon stands before it. Maybe in a posture that mimics her father's. That moment in the first scene—when he was on the other side of the door when he closed for the night.

SHARON (NARRATION):   The register was emptied.

Panel 2
Close as she tears down the crime tape.

SHARON (NARRATION):   But the bloody footprints
                        of the man—size 13—
                        didn't go there first.

Panel 3
Interior. She stares at the section of floor where her father lay dead in the photo.

SHARON (NARRATION):   They instead went
                        directly to the back door,
                        which was left open.

Panel 4
Then holds up her phone—which carries the murder scene photo—in such a way that it overlays the present, making it seem as though he is there with us. A doubling image.

SHARON (NARRATION):   And then to the closets.
                        And even the freezer.

Panel 5
She gets down on the floor, moving from a crouch to a fallen position.

SHARON (NARRATION):   Robbing the place was
                        an afterthought. Or a
                        diversion.

Panel 6
Now she lies fully on the floor. Mimicking the posture of his death.

SHARON (NARRATION):   Whoever did this was
                        looking for something…

Panel 7
We change the point of view, taking on her vision from the floor. She's looking at the front window, where the woman left behind a bloody print.

SHARON (NARRATION):   …or someone.

PAGE 10 (seven panels)

Panel 1
Interior point of view. We're looking out at the bloody fingerprint. And Sharon. Who stands in the cold, studying it, her breath fogging.

Panel 2
She puts up her hand and puts it in the same place as the woman's.

Panel 3
Then she snaps a photo.

Panel 4
And turns around....taking in the truck stop in the near distance.

Panel 5
She walks toward the truck stop—and along the way studies the patches of snow mixed in with browned grass.

Panel 6
She pauses. And reaches down.

Panel 7
Here she finds, in the browned grass, a tooth. A human tooth.

PAGE 11 (anels)

Panel 1
Now she is at the truck stop. She stands near the pumps and looks up. A pop up (or a tracery) indicates the security camera she's looking at.

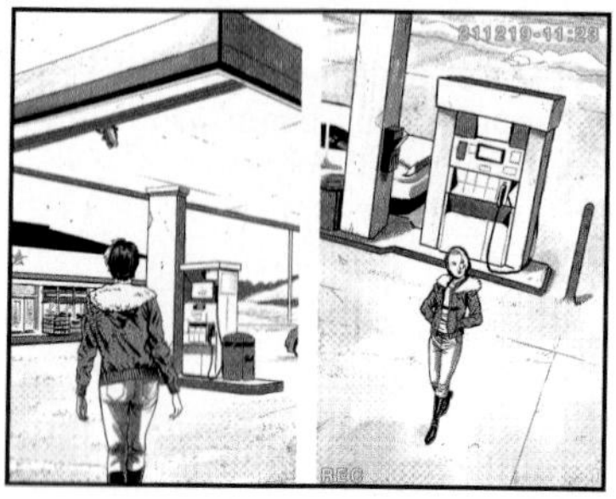
211219-11:23
REC

Panel 2
She stands near the entrance to the convenience store…studying another security camera (with the same guiding principle of the previous panel—either a pop-up or a tracery).

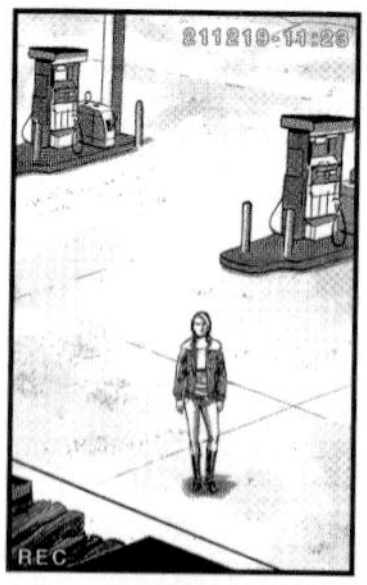
211219-11:23
REC

Panel 3
Interior. This is the sort of rural convenience store that sells plenty of crap—like country music CDs and American flag T-shirts and bald eagle ceramic figurines—along with its slim jims and corn nuts. She's looking up at yet another security camera—this one near the register.

FAST EDDIE (just behind her): Can I help you?

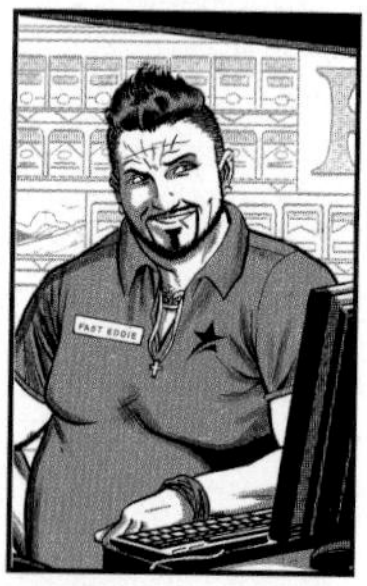
FAST EDDIE

Panel 4
Fast Eddie is the obese store manager. He has a failure of a mustache clinging to his upper lip. He's obsessed with what little power he has over his neon-lit domain. His nametag reads "Fast Eddie, Manager."

SHARON: I need to access your surveillance video records.

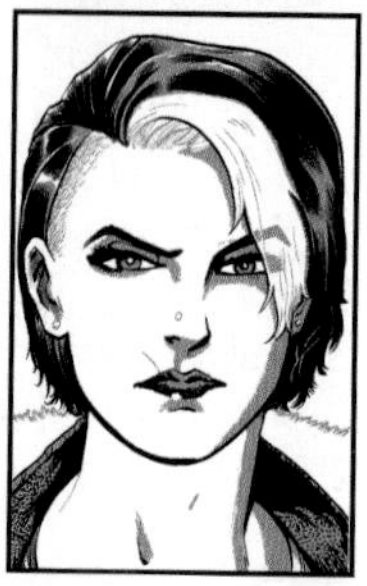

FAST EDDIE: Maybe you could try smiling when you ask somebody to do something? Or saying please?

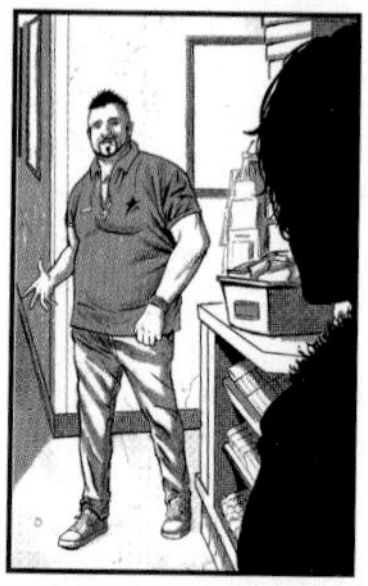

Panel 5
He puts one of his fat hands on her shoulder and she looks at it with distaste.

SHARON: I'm not asking you anything. I'm telling you.

FAST EDDIE: Yeah? What's in this for me?

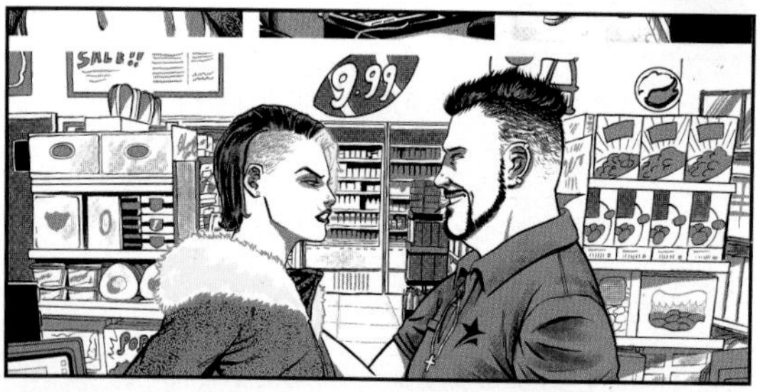
SALE!!
9.99